PRAISE FOR DANIEL PYNE

Water Memory

"It is refreshing to see, in a genre prone to impossible superheroic feats . . . a protagonist whose injuries leave real scars . . . *Water Memory* is elevated from its genre moorings by the parallels it draws to classic seafaring literature, including *Lord Jim* (whose title character's journey is echoed here) and even Coleridge's 'The Rime of the Ancient Mariner,' excerpted for the novel's epigraph. But neither that nor the well-placed and succinct flashbacks, illuminating the flash points in Sentro's past that led her to this fateful moment, can distract a reader from the ripping good yarn Pyne has spun—or the prickly, endearing Aubrey Sentro, ugly scars and all."

—*Los Angeles Times*

"A mysterious woman on a mysterious path, danger in the future and from the past—*Water Memory* holds a hypnotic grip on you from the very first page. This is Daniel Pyne at his very best."

—Michael Connelly, #1 *New York Times* bestselling author

"Deceptively explosive, *Water Memory* pairs the cleverness and precision timing of Daniel Pyne's riveting storytelling with his addictive, action-packed plotting and unforgettably vivid cast of characters."

—Karin Slaughter, *New York Times* and international bestselling author

"Pyne keeps expertly mixing up his pitches long after you've stopped expecting anything but blazing fastballs."

—*Kirkus Reviews*

"Fans of action flicks will enjoy."

—*Publishers Weekly*

"A flash-bang actioner, limned in rich, organic prose . . . a classy read."

—*Booklist*

"A must-read for any thriller fan looking for a different angle into the black-ops world."

—*Mystery and Suspense Magazine*

"A deftly crafted and simply riveting read, *Water Memory* effectively showcases author Daniel Pyne's impressively entertaining narrative storytelling style as a novelist."

—*Midwest Book Review*

"A refreshing, pulse-pounding structure . . . Think *Die Hard* on a cargo ship as shell-shocked special operator Aubrey Sentro finds safe passage that turns out not to be so safe at all when pirates seize the vessel . . . *Water Memory* is original, wondrously paced, and, well, memorable."

—*Providence Journal*

"*Water Memory* is a speedboat on steroids, and Pyne's use of the present tense and blind narrative turns fuels the propulsion. Tackle this one while you're wide awake, hang tight until the end, and wait for *Vital Lies*, book two in the Sentro series, due out a year from now."

—*Mountain Times*

"Since screenwriter and author Daniel Pyne has been involved in the writing of some of my favorite movies and TV shows, from *Miami Vice* to *Bosch*, it should have come as no surprise that I would thoroughly enjoy *Water Memory*. I did not realize, however, just how intense and exciting it would be, from start to finish. It is without a doubt one of those the-world-goes-away-while-I-am-reading-this types of books."

—*The Nerd Daily*

Catalina Eddy

"Daniel Pyne flips all the standards upside down with *Catalina Eddy* and in the process delivers a classic California noir—times three. This is Pyne's masterpiece. I guarantee no reader will go wanting."

—Michael Connelly

"Pyne delivers his noir in vivid, often gorgeous prose . . . although television may be where the action is, it's a big, all-out novel like this that lets Pyne display the full range of his talents."

—Patrick Anderson, *Washington Post*

"While these three stories are connected through loosely related characters, they are, more importantly, linked by compelling storytelling, and by laughter, love, and honor."

—*Huffington Post*

"The three novellas, taken separately, are each well-crafted noirs. They've got the mood, the characters, the settings, and the stories that keep noir fiction alive. But taken together, *Catalina Eddy* is much greater than the sum of its parts. Daniel Pyne really gets it—his language is deft, his storytelling skills spectacular."

—*LitReactor*

"Engaging and satisfying . . . a worthy addition to the shelf, between "noir" and now."

—*Kirkus Reviews*

"Pyne's wounded characters walk their mean streets honorably in this compelling account of attempts to find sense in a senseless world."

—*Publishers Weekly* (starred review)

"Pyne, who has also written successfully for television and film, turns in a quick-paced trio of gritty yarns with staccato dialogue and grim survivors, all seeking redemption in whatever form is allowed."

—*Library Journal*

"*Catalina Eddy* is . . . very visually written—[Pyne] puts the reader firmly into each scene as the story unfolds."

—Ruth Kinane, *Entertainment Weekly*

Fifty Mice

"[A] wonderfully paranoid jaunt through competing realities . . . Pyne's confident hand guides readers to a surprising, popcorn-dropping final twist."

—*Publishers Weekly*

"Drawing on the noir tradition . . . a serious consideration of memory and how it functions, or doesn't."

—*Booklist*

"Exceedingly clever, expertly timed, and dripping with paranoia, the nightmarish scenario at the center of this thrilling story turns on a kick-ass dime."

—Karin Slaughter

"Screenwriter and author Pyne (*Twentynine Palms*) weaves a smart, exceedingly clever, and unusual tale with a horrible secret at its center, which is as much a late coming-of-age story as it is a thriller. Fans of brainy noir will find much to love in this highly satisfying, big-screen-ready book."

—Kristin Centorcelli, *Library Journal*

"A unique thrill ride . . . a real cat-and-mouse story . . . This plot is both gripping and suspenseful, as the author offers up a secret that will make all us 'normal' people out there think long and hard about the people powerful enough to change lives in an instant. Pyne is an extremely clever writer."

—*Suspense Magazine*

"[Pyne] knows how to control a thriller, but in *Fifty Mice* he intentionally removes any notion of control. There is no telling what will happen from one page to the next because he creates a flawed, vulnerable character with no sway over his own memory. *Fifty Mice* illustrates the obscurity of life, how easy it is to erase a life not lived, and how difficult it can be to tell the difference between a mouse and a man."

—*Boston Herald*

"It's an exciting, disturbing read. The words fly. The story twists and turns inward, then outward, then in on itself again, and everything that happens might be a ruse—social, mental, or both."

—*LitReactor*

"*Fifty Mice* is loaded with surprises, twists, and turns that kept this reader guessing until the very end."

—BookReporter.com

Twentynine Palms

"Character is key in this deliciously edgy thriller, screenwriter Pyne's (*The Manchurian Candidate*) first novel. With dialogue that sings and action that sizzles, this is a prime candidate for the big screen."

—*Kirkus Reviews* (starred)

"Pyne, who is a successful screenwriter, limns a wonderfully plausible look at a showbiz-soundstage moment: a clash between a loony director who speaks only quasi-mystical gibberish and an idiot box-office titan channeling De Niro. *Twentynine Palms* is great fun."

—*Booklist*

"Loss and redemption in the high desert, with enough colorful characters and twists of plot to keep the reader turning pages. *Twentynine Palms* is classic Californian noir."

—Kem Nunn, author of *Tapping the Source* and *Tijuana Straits*

"Daniel Pyne's *Twentynine Palms* is a terrific novel, both a first-rate thriller with sweet and comic twists and a moving love story. It's also got some of the best poetic and moody writing about LA and the desert community I've read in a long time. A one-sit read, which will leave you smiling."

—Robert Ward, author of *Four Kinds of Rain* and *Total Immunity*

"Pyne sure-footedly blazes a fresh trail through Chandler country in this taut, expertly wrought desert noir. *Twentynine Palms* will leave you buzzing like a heat-dazed cricket."

—Jonathan Evison, author of *All About Lulu*

VITAL
LIES

VITAL LIES

A THRILLER

DANIEL PYNE

THOMAS & MERCER

Text copyright © 2022 by Daniel Pyne
All rights reserved.

Published by Thomas & Mercer, Seattle

www.apub.com

Amazon, the Amazon logo, and Thomas & Mercer are trademarks of Amazon.com, Inc., or its affiliates.

ISBN-13: 9781542031042 (hardcover)
ISBN-11:1542031044 (hardcover)

ISBN-13: 9781542029995 (paperback)
ISBN-10: 1542029996 (paperback)

Cover design by Rex Bonomelli

Printed in the United States of America

In memory of Guyla, whose strength and grace were epic

Memory believes before knowing remembers.
Believes longer than recollects, longer than knowing
even wonders.
—William Faulkner
Light in August

Dead men don't bite.
—R. L. Stevenson
Treasure Island

December 3, 1990, 15:07 (Utc+01)

A shrouded winter sun bore down on her with the cruel promise of a warmth it couldn't provide. Her legs ached from so much walking after months spent in two-by-three-meter isolation cells; her eyes ached, unaccustomed to the bright day's light. The wind gusting up the *Allee* lifted the blanket wrapped around her narrow shoulders and knifed through her thin smock. Still convinced that they'd come after her, she'd been pushing herself for a couple of hours, feet blistered by the pair of ill-fitting shoes she'd found in the abandoned staff changing room, where the lockers were flung open, showing telltale signs of a swift emptying as the prison guards got the hell out before the full fury of the newly liberated East German citizenry came crashing in on them.

On first glance, anyone looking out at her from the steady stream of traffic heading west to the wall would have thought she was a broken-down, middle-aged hausfrau shuffling, scared, glancing back over her shoulder, eyes dark, sunken, her skin pale and raw. In fact, she was not even twenty, a girl who'd grown up too quickly; shivering, disoriented, nauseated, racked by the beginnings of withdrawal from whatever cocktail of Stasi drugs she'd been given steadily over the past eleven months.

So much of what had happened was a jumbled blur. Or white noise.

Long, stark indigo shadows fell across the cobbled street, a smear of sun already low in the west; her loose shoes stumbled on a displaced sidewalk slab, but she caught herself and stopped to rest. From a passing rattletrap Trabant, a student shouted out to offer her a ride, and because she wasn't sure how much longer she could keep walking, she accepted.

There were already too many people in the car, so she had to sit in the back seat on the lap of the boy who invited her. His name, he said, was Markus. He smelled like unwashed laundry and marijuana and bootleg vodka, and the facial hair he was trying to grow reminded her of failed crops in West Texas. His breath was sour with coffee, and his fleshy, warm hand found a way under her smock to her knee, where his touch made her feel sick, but she let him leave his hand there because asking him not to would take more energy than she had left in her.

"What's your name?" they asked.

"Trudi," she lied.

"You're American," the girl in the front seat decided, looking back at her with serious blue eyes, pale and innocent and beautiful. The Aryan ideal.

"No," she lied again, for no reason except that it had become habit.

"Where are you coming from?"

"Jail," she told them. "Hohenschönhausen," she added, and the car fell deathly silent except for the steady keening of the two-banger motor.

Smoke had sifted and settled over the city, thick from all the burning documents—incinerator stacks were still pumping ash into the sky—and she thought she could hear a dull roar of people massed up ahead. The Trabant shuddered to a crawl. Traffic was gridlocked on the street, the cars honking, people leaning out of the windows waving West German flags and shouting things that a week before would have been cause for their arrest and torture.

The boy's hand moved higher up her thigh; she looked at him sadly, wondering feverishly for a moment what it would be like to be nineteen and tasting freedom for the first time. New girl on your lap, all your best friends in the car, a glorious future stretching ahead of you, a movement, a revolution, the possibilities endless and surely bright.

She imagined going with them, reinventing herself. Finding a romantic little cold-water attic squat in Friedrichshain, getting a job in a bookstore, sleeping with as many boys as she wanted, or none at all. She'd take classes at the free university, stay up all night in cafés arguing about pop music and politics and religion; she'd become someone else, pretend that the past year hadn't happened—or that her past nineteen years hadn't happened—but the boy's hand moved higher again, and she thought about her husband and her baby and how her determination to see them again had sustained her through the worst of whatever she'd endured.

"*Wiedersehen*," she whispered in the scruffy boy's ear, lifting the handle to wing the back door wide; then she slid from his lap and tumbled out into the roiling river of East Berliners flowing inexorably toward the West and the illusion of freedom.

PART ONE:

IN WHICH SHE GETS PULLED BACK INTO THE MAELSTROM

CHAPTER ONE

His first mistake was taking back roads from the beach to avoid the inevitable Sunday traffic jams on the highway. His fatal mistake, the one he would rue so much later, was stopping to help the couple with the BMW on a switchback turnout near the village of Aulesti.

The heat of the lazy day lingered inland even as the sun tucked behind the coastal hills. A blued humid air lay deep and heavy in the narrow valleys, smelling of beech and fir and the sea. Xavi Beya had a carload of sleepy kids, wife Paola zonked in the passenger seat, surfboards strapped to the roof of the Peugeot, and every intention of getting home and putting them all to bed and then soaking in the tub and watching on his tablet the replay of Valladolid's Camp Nou contest with Barca. He'd made a point of avoiding the radio news all day so he wouldn't hear the score.

But the pretty woman caught his eye. What was he thinking? Well—he wasn't, was he? At least not with his head.

She seemed to shimmer in the headlights when they found her, even though the dusk's glow hadn't quite died yet; she stood back from the Beemer's steaming engine compartment while her boyfriend artlessly flailed at wires and hoses, obscured by the hood. Long legs in high-rise jeggings, long black hair pulled back, her loose shirt likely tied up under her breasts on account of the heat, and one of her little black kitten-heeled mules bent out coyly as she scrolled on her phone.

The face of an angel. Beya glanced at his sleeping wife, mother of his three children and, it had to be said, blameless victim of the wear and tear. But he braked, pulled over, and reversed the car back into the turnout.

"What are you doing?" Paola said, startled, waking up.

"Someone with car trouble."

"Let them call for service."

"I'll just be a minute."

"Why get involved?"

He was already out of the car, walking to where the beautiful woman stood like a vision, staring. Those emerald-green eyes bored into him.

"You need any help?"

She made a graceful, helpless gesture. Her lipstick was a perfect shade of brown, like a model in a magazine. She shifted her hips. *Here's trouble,* Beya told himself happily. But no harm in just looking, was there?

The boyfriend came up from under the hood, wiping greasy hands on his chinos. A hedge of white hair, thickened brow over colorless eyes, chalky skin with lurid red highlights: *Albino,* Beya thought and couldn't help wondering what this beautiful woman was doing with someone like that.

"Do you know anything about cars?" the boyfriend asked. His Spanish came with a heavy accent, possibly Russian. Slavic, for sure.

Beya acknowledged humbly he had a repair shop in Basauri.

"You are a gift from God," the woman said, with a Spanish accent not from Spain: thick, sharp. South American, maybe.

Beya turned to her, smiling, and saw his Paola behind her, coming stiffly from the car with a scowl and her jealous eyes pinned on the young woman's painted-on pants.

"Xavi?"

Uh-oh.

8

"We'll see," Beya said quickly, intending to join the boyfriend at the car before his wife could stop him, but a sudden change in Paola's expression caused him to hesitate, and then something crashed against the back of his head, and he saw stars and heard his wife yelling.

It had been a long time since Beya had been in a scuffle, but he hadn't forgotten how to roll with a sucker punch. During his days in ETA, he'd done regular battle with the truncheons of the Ertzaintza riot police—known as the *beltzak* because of the color of their uniform—who, despite their body armor and helmets and superior numbers, usually proved no match for the feral determination of the Basque separatists.

This was one pale man and his pretty girl bait.

Muscle memory kicked in; in a practiced motion Beya gathered, rebounded, and cocked his shoulder as if to take a swing, but when the pale man made as if to slip the blow and counter, Beya kicked him in the balls and ran.

There are no rules.

His wife still stood stunned and confused at the back of their wagon. Beya yelled, "Drive away!" and scrambled up the steep shoulder of the turnout to plunge into the dense cover of the blackthorn and broom. He wanted to circle back, flag down his wife farther up the road, but he didn't hear the car's engine and was suddenly aware of two more men coming after him.

Carjackers, Beya thought in a panic. He needed to get back to his family. With one of the men hard on his heels, Beya climbed a hundred feet through the thick brush, branches tearing at his clothes, then started a controlled slide back down, under the thicket, past the heavy breathing of one of his pursuers. His wife's voice, high and plaintive, rose below and behind him. He'd overshot the turnout. His hand found a heavy broken limb that could serve as a weapon, and he continued his controlled slide downslope, then emerged with serendipity right where the fourth carjacker stood, waiting, but facing the wrong way.

Before the man was able to react and turn, Beya clobbered him with the birch branch. He groaned and fell. The albino was still down, in front of the Beemer, grimacing, sweating, holding his groin. The carjacker upslope was shouting that he'd "lost the target." *Target?*

No sign of the pretty woman. Beya sprinted for the Peugeot. His wife was back in the passenger seat, the kids staring from behind Paola wide eyed as he fumbled for the keys in his pocket, ready to get in and go.

But as his hand touched the door handle, he felt steel kiss the side of his head. He recognized the make and model of the gun in the girl's steady hand.

"Get to your knees." Somehow he placed her accent then: Cuba. So far from home. *Those lovely green eyes,* he thought, gazing into them, *are empty of malice.* She wouldn't shoot him. Not this beautiful girl.

"You can have everything in my wallet," he said. "The credit cards have high limits. I won't report them until tomorrow."

She said nothing, but a spooky smile creased her face.

"Let me just . . ." He moved slowly. Telegraphing his every move. *She won't do it. It's not in her.* The door latch clicked; he started to swing it open.

"Don't," she said.

"You won't shoot me," he assured her.

The muzzle flash blinded him, and there was a subsequent roar that became a single nervy high-pitched tone. His legs buckled before he felt the lightning bolt course across the side of his head.

She shot me, he realized and assumed he was dying.

The last thing he heard was the screaming of his children and the pitiful scrape of his beach clogs across the turnout as someone dragged him away from the car.

CHAPTER TWO

It's just another dream she has. Or that's what she's always told herself.

Not exactly a nightmare, but disturbing enough.

Ever the same, never resolved.

Over the years working in the shadows, she's had countless others, stress dreams and false memories. It comes with the territory—the subconscious working off the pressure, the uncertainty, the anxiety; a way for her mind to work its way through its frustrations and fears.

But none as persistent as this one.

Forest, northern Europe by what she can make of it in the darkness, chilly, but it's a dream, so she never feels it. A generator kicks in and three portable lights surge on, hellishly illuminating an abandoned work camp. Rusted Quonset huts and a big old auger drill on a Soviet-made front loader that's been hard at work: there are seven freshly dug cylinders, cored ten feet deep in the hard-packed dirt of the yard.

Six prisoners—four frightened older men and two numb young women—are being lowered into the holes by uniformed soldiers. One by one. Duct tape ripped off their hands, hoods removed. A bearded man in a tattered suit can't stop shaking. But their faces are indistinct, unmemorable. No one she knows or has ever known.

A sampling speak low Prussian:

—Please don't do this. I have money. I have connections in the central committee.

—You're putting us in graves?

—Hey. Listen to me. I'm not like these others. I'm not.

Aubrey Sentro is last in line. Naked, sometimes shivering, hooded—but because it's a dream, she can see, through a threadbare patch like a confessional screen, as much as she will.

Waiting. Listening.

—I will need the name and number of someone I should call to arrange for your freedom.

The officer in charge has a purple collar on his uniform and white-blond hair. She thinks she should recognize him but never can; she finds him attractive and feels ashamed of it because in her dream she's still married to Dennis.

She hopes the handsome soldier doesn't notice how she stares.

Repurposed heavy iron sewer grates are staked securely over the holes after each prisoner goes in, to create a kind of subterranean cellblock.

—Don't put me down there. Don't do it. I'm not going.

The other young woman has a face Sentro has always been afraid to look at, in her dream state. Why? Disfigured? This woman struggles violently with her captors, screaming, legs scissoring, arms flailing, but they always subdue her and lift her and drop her down into the darkness, where Sentro hears the woman begin softly whimpering, like a child.

—Be calm, one of the captors will call down to this woman politely. *Soil is soft. If you try to climb out, the walls of the hole could collapse.*

Sentro never feels like she needs to know who these other prisoners are. Or maybe she does and has forgotten. She never feels panic. Only resignation. And shame.

—Now tell me who I should call to arrange for your freedom.

His manner is cordial, almost apologetic; his face is cruel and pretty, his eyes shining malevolent black. She knows she should hate him. His statement is meant for all of them, but his gaze always seems to find Sentro last and always lingers like a lover's caress.

And when she replies, "I'm pregnant," and wakes up, her heart is pounding.

Just a dream.

Until now.

CHAPTER THREE

"I'm remembering things I don't want to."

Whenever she told her daughter, Jenny, this, she got the predictable eye roll. "I guess cholinesterase inhibitors could do that," was what the psychologist now said. "I've never had anyone complain."

This new doctor, Jenny's ooga-booga Santa Fe headshrinker ("Checkup from the neck up" was her daughter's mantra) with her jangly turquoise-and-silver bangles, no makeup, and suspiciously perfect I've-gone-natural gray hair, seemed nice enough—but Aubrey Sentro missed her gawky Baltimore brain doctor more and more, the further she moseyed down the TBI road less traveled.

"She says 'super' a lot," Jenny warned, when pressed. "Not sure where that comes from. But hey, if she can help you . . . right?" Jenny let the implication hang.

Help me what? Sentro wondered. She thought she'd been doing pretty well since she left her old life behind. But she made the call, scheduled sessions, and gave it the old college try (though she hadn't exactly ever been to college) for her daughter.

"How are we doing otherwise?" the doctor asked.

We? "Honestly, I don't feel much of a change." This wasn't really a lie; after half a dozen sessions at the Almayo Memory Clinic—puzzles, mental exercises, mind games, mild hypnosis (that didn't work), meditation, yoga, vitamin supplements, Thai massage—Sentro didn't feel any different, although she had to admit her memory had stabilized. No headaches for a while. Fewer worrisome gaps. But the eccentric recall of random operations and personal history she had long assumed was lost to her . . . well, that was getting uncomfortable. And confusing.

"Remember, with head injuries, serial concussions—you're not always the same person after as before."

"You've made that very clear, yes." *And I'm not at all sure how I feel about it,* was what she chose not to add.

"Happy birthday, by the way."

The strategic non sequitur. Well, crowding fifty was not something Sentro wanted to discuss, so she stayed on point. "Can I trust these relics I seem to keep digging up?"

"Hard to say. Our perception of the past is fluid. Corrupted by the present. The wall that separates imagination and memory? Pretty flimsy." The Santa Fe shrink talked like she was on NPR. The air of erudition, the crisp enunciation, the amiable but pointed questions. "How do they manifest, these relics?"

"I dunno. Strange dreams. Disturbing dreams. Partial recall. Flashes of things: people, places, objects. Always visceral. Like, reflections off a glass of water will suddenly bring back to me a vivid image of a remote lake I could swear I've never been to. Some of the recall I can't hang on to for very long, and most of the time I don't even understand where they're coming from—the context."

"Everything with the subconscious is rooted in an experiential truth."

Which was what Sentro was afraid of. Although, yeah, not in that specific salad of academic words. She shifted in her chair, glanced out the window at the towering thunderclouds gathering over the Sangre de Cristos, and wondered if there would be rain on her trip back to the ranch.

The psychologist waited. She always waited. It was a ploy Sentro understood well from what Jenny liked to call the spook life: silence creates a vacuum, which, of course, nature abhors, and demands that it be filled. The tactic almost always works in interviews and interrogations, to keep someone who needs to unburden themself talking.

Sentro was good at waiting too. Better than any shrink.

"Aubrey?"

"Dr. Mathers."

"Kimiko. Please."

Sentro didn't want intimacy; she wanted reassurance. "All right. You look troubled by something."

"I'm feeling like there's a piece of this puzzle you're leaving out," the doctor said, then folded her hands in her lap. And waited.

"A truth, you mean."

"Maybe. It's super important that you be candid with us, Aubrey."

They stared at each other for a while. *Busted,* Sentro thought. But maybe that wasn't such a bad thing.

"I joined the army at eighteen," Sentro began, then hesitated. She was unsure how much of this she would or could tell. It wasn't classified anymore. But it wasn't known by many, and she felt a palpable unease in talking about things that for years she had reflexively suppressed. "I'd had a baby. I had to support myself, my family. My husband was in college." A white lie, but she felt no need to throw Dennis under the bus.

"After basic they gave us a battery of tests. I did something right or wrong—depending, I guess, on how you want to look at the life that resulted—and got assigned to intelligence. Crash course in languages, which, to my surprise, I was good at. German. Six months in I got posted to Berlin, where I was given an assignment to infiltrate the East German secret service—the Stasi—as a translator. Our side was hoping to identify their top brass so that after reunification, they couldn't disappear into the woodwork with their secrets and ill-gotten gains and avoid criminal charges."

"This was when?"

"Eighty-eight, eighty-nine," Sentro hedged, keeping it vague.

16

"You were eighteen."

"Yeah."

"Sweet Jesus. Just a girl."

"I guess. Yes." Sentro noted the shrink leaning forward, hooked now. Everybody loves a spy story.

"How were you supposed to infiltrate the Stasi? There was that movie; I can't remember the name. I thought they were considered—"

"They were. The best," Sentro said, cutting her off gently, "and most ruthless. It was tricky and complicated." Once she got started, she found the words flowed more easily. It was how normal people shared their lives, right? "But remember, everything was coming apart at the seams in Eastern Europe. Gorbachev was cutting the satellite states loose. It was the Wild West, dog eat dog, lots of double-crossing and confusion and so many mistakes being made by greedy, corrupt apparatchiks grasping at the spoils of a failed regime. My CO was a good guy; my handlers had a smart plan. I trusted them. At first, it all went smoothly. I quickly got close to this young, brash Stasi hotshot, which gave me access to pretty much all of the major players."

The doctor's eyes narrowed. "Got close."

Sentro did love messing around with this part—with where someone's mind always went when she mentioned the honey trap—and she didn't get to tell the story very often, so . . . "Their head of intelligence, Markus Wolf, invented something he called the Romeo method. East German agents would cross to the West to romance secretaries and clerks who worked in key Bundesrepublik ministries, with the goal of getting them to pass on secrets to the Stasi. Sometimes, so lovestruck, the targets didn't even realize they'd done it. It was extremely successful. But created a blind spot."

"How so?"

"Lotta times the tactic you don't ever see coming is the one you yourself have perfected."

Kimiko furrowed her brow. "You were married, though. With a baby." Not judgmental, the shrink just seemed to be trying to fill in where Sentro had purposefully left blanks.

"I was." She felt a familiar twinge of guilt about how her family had been impacted by her choices; she became needlessly defensive. "I was also young and ambitious and considered kinda pretty and had, in retrospect, a dangerous overabundance of confidence from all the props I'd been getting from command. It was heady. I felt invincible. But I didn't break my vows," Sentro added, as if to reassure herself it was true. "To God or country or Dennis. I just walked the razor's edge." *And live with the consequences,* she thought.

"Do you miss it? The job you did. All the endorphins, the adrenaline rush—it can be addictive, I know."

"No," Sentro lied after a moment.

She took a deep breath. "I'd been operational for about six weeks when I discovered that the Stasi had a mole inside the American embassy, and based on his intel the East Germans were about to come crashing down on a covert CIA cell and its sources."

Again, the shrink said nothing. But she was clearly dying now to know what happened. Sentro took a drink of water. *Stick to the facts,* she reminded herself but started to question what she was hoping to accomplish here. There was such scant profit in looking backward.

"I didn't have time to weigh options. I took the bullet for my countrymen."

"The Stasi shot you?"

"No. No, I blew my own cover to buy time for the others. The agents went to ground, avoided capture, and found their way back to safety. The sources were exfiltrated and given new identities."

"And you?"

"I was a hero. You know. Eleven months later the wall came down, the GDR government collapsed, every man for himself. And I walked out of a cell and back to freedom, commendations, promotion. The

18

start of my brilliant career." *And the end of any hope for a normal family life.* Had she been selfish? Who was to say that taking the safer path wouldn't have led her to a darker place? Like her mother.

"But those eleven months—"

"Yeah." Sentro shook her head, shrugged. "I got arrested for espionage. Sent to jail. Interrogated."

"Tortured?" the shrink asked. Sentro couldn't confirm or deny it. "That's what you're having nightmares about."

"I don't remember, is the point," Sentro said, leaving out that she'd decided right away that not knowing was better for her and everyone she loved. "I was sedated—well, drugged—morphine, mescaline, cocaine, scopolamine, psychotropics. That I know of. Maybe some LSD?" She thought about it for a moment. "Something the Russians call SP-117. I don't know what that was. I don't remember what it did to me."

"Drugged the whole time?"

"Part of their strategy was winding me up and then winding me down. Using the withdrawal to try to break me. Wear me out."

"Why?"

Why? *Because that was the game,* Sentro thought, but she didn't say it.

There was no other logical reason why. At nineteen, six months into her deployment, barely an E-4 specialist, it wasn't like she had any useful information to give up beyond her own narrow assignment. And anyway, the Soviets had Aldrich Ames and Robert Hanssen feeding them US intelligence gold direct from Washington. The Stasi had at least a couple thousand West German citizen collaborators, not to mention high-level double agents in every ministry.

"I don't know why," Sentro said. She wondered if she'd shared too much and wasn't going to tell the shrink the rest of it. The part she wasn't even sure was real.

"Why do I still feel like you're holding something back?"

"I'm not, I promise," Sentro lied. "It was an unfortunate experience. And that's about the size of it." Her father used that phrase a lot.

"Aubrey, why didn't you tell us all this during your intake evaluation? It's a super significant, traumatic episode that most assuredly has a bearing on your condition. In addition to the serial concussions you've suffered, you probably have posttraumatic factors that are contributing to your TBI."

Not the same person. No shit. But in the spirit of their new first-name intimacy: "Oh, Kimiko, believe me, I dealt with fallout from all of this a long time ago. The VA actually stepped up, helped a lot. I was given time to recover, extensive therapy, plenty of follow-ups. They were worried about me. But I went through my captivity in such a deep fog; they said it may have actually helped."

The doctor began to shake her head. "I can't agree."

"It doesn't haunt me."

"It does now."

Sentro couldn't really argue with that but continued, "Well, I guess that gets us back to my original question. The new memory drugs you're giving me. Could I be constructing false narratives? Connecting the wrong dots? I mean—because I have forgotten some of what I did remember back then, could I be filling in those gaps as well as the gaps in my remaining memory of what happened with . . . ?" She lost her train of thought. Fuck.

"Everything with the subconscious is rooted in an experiential truth," the shrink said again.

Sentro was suddenly aware of the faint aromatic smell of sage. "Smudging" was the Anglo appropriation of an indigenous New Mexican folk remedy Jenny had told her about, involving much waving around of a smoldering bundle of dried sage and other aromatic weeds to chase away bad spirits, which, in a headshrinker's clinic, Sentro figured, probably ran amok.

"I think that's enough for today," Dr. Kimiko Mathers said brightly, setting aside her pad and pen.

"I think that's an understatement," Sentro agreed with relief.

Ushering her out, the shrink added, "For the next time, I want you to write down your dreams, as much as you can remember of them."

Next time, Sentro mused. After every session she thought it might be her last.

Jenny was in the waiting area, putting down a *Cosmo*, watching her mother emerge. "How'd it go?"

"Super." Sentro smiled.

Her daughter gifted her another epic eye roll.

Chapter Four

They'd dressed him close to type: a grim-looking tradesman with a shabby rucksack and tool kit between his feet, sitting alone on the stone steps of the monument to the Dos de Mayo fallen, waiting for the Bolsa de Madrid to open. Light softened by high clouds dulled the city's sharp edges. The Plaza de la Lealtad was empty and peaceful, and this morning he felt a strange, sad kinship with the Spanish rebels who had died rising up against French occupation two hundred years ago, even though his loyalties remained with the Basque Country, and his enemies had always been the very Spanish nationalists who had made their doomed stand that day. A gentle breeze surged and rattled the trees' canopy of leaves.

Exhausted, hollow eyed, trembling, Xavi Beya hadn't really slept since his family was ripped away from him. He was living a nightmare from which there was no waking up. Before embarking on this morning's errand, they'd shown him live muted video of his wife and children huddled, scared, in an empty room somewhere, to remind him of the stakes. As if that were necessary.

Stock traders and staff hurried up and in among the half dozen towering Corinthian columns that supported the palace building's grand portico. There were security stations just inside the polished brass doors: metal detectors, bag check, and Guardia with wands.

Beya had tried to convince his captors that the bandage on the side of his neck was like a big flashing light that would alert security that he was someone to be stopped and searched. The Cuban woman assured him that the search at the service entrance would be less rigorous, and the bandage would draw their eyes off his face. It would be all they'd remember; he'd be reunited with his family after the deed was done.

Amateurs. I am dealing with amateurs, he decided, and it scared him all the more.

Ten years ago (another life!) he'd been active with ETA in the struggle for Basque Country autonomy but had rarely ventured this far south. He'd stepped back after the birth of his first child and the fuckup at the bank in Ondarroa, when a bystander had stupidly died—how had these monsters known he was involved? Beya was a *legala*—a "legal one," never arrested, unknown to the police.

Who had betrayed him?

City-center church bells began to sound the hour. The stock market was in session. *Do this and get your family back,* he told himself. He rose stiffly, shouldered the rucksack and lifted the tool kit, and walked down the steps toward the Palacio de la Bolsa de Madrid.

———

From where she stood near the Apollo Fountain, nervously chewing the last stick from her pack of Splot, she was able to watch the Basque mechanic work up his courage beneath the memorial column, then follow his progress across the road that circled the plaza. He angled along Paseo del Prado, looking less committed than she would have liked, and then accessed the rear service entrance of the stock exchange from Calle de Juan de Mena.

She checked the time on her phone and started the stopwatch app. She'd allow him ten minutes to get in and out, though she had no reason to doubt he'd do what they'd asked of him. The Basque wanted to have his family safe, released. He seemed to believe it when she told him he'd be back with them soon.

Yusupov was in the van, waiting for pickup. She didn't much trust the Chechen, with his leering attention and questionable agenda—but she trusted that self-preservation was his guiding principle, and as long as she stayed in front of that, they could work together well. Not that she'd been given a choice. Technically this was the albino's play; there was no operational reason for her to be here except that Fischer had sent a frantic flurry of text messages worrying the smallest details over which, from Havana, he had no control, and anyway she had it handled. *He's getting like an old woman,* she thought, wrapping what remained of her Colombian chewing gum in its foil to drop and nudge it into the gutter with her Jimmy Choo.

She opened TikTok, watched distractedly a couple of mildly amusing cats, then closed it again and put her phone away.

She felt antsy, discontented—unhappy, fundamentally—and it wasn't her period coming on or the aggravating text queries that kept pestering her from Cuba; it was as if something were swirling in the air all around her, a vague foreboding that her world was about to tilt.

Like a rocking chair that moves by itself.

She'd light a candle, in the church she'd passed earlier, walking to the fountain.

Not that she believed in God or anything. You know.

But darkness? Evil?

That shit was real.

———

Beya worried over the teal tubes as he drew them from the false bottom of the tool kit. They didn't look anything like the Semtex or Titadyn he was familiar with from back in the day. For one thing, Titadyn had salmon-colored casings. And was chubbier, he seemed to recall.

As the Chechen had predicted, security at the service entrance was a formality. There was a backup of vendors impatient to get to work. Once he'd showed his papers, the job order, one guard had opened the kit to glance inside, while another ran a hand through the backpack, and then they'd sent him on his way.

In and out in ten minutes. He didn't have a watch. His hands shook as he fumbled with the detonator wires, but he managed to get them attached and nestled the device in a gap between CPUs along one wall of the tiny server room. Flip of a switch, a blue diode flickered, and the timer began a countdown.

The AC kicked on, and a cool breeze chilled the sweat on Beya's neck.

Tool kit, rucksack, quick look around; his hand was on the door handle when it swung open and an in-house IT man blocked his way out.

"Oh, sorry."

"Who are you?"

Shit. Beya pulled his papers out and showed them.

The technician wore a skinny tie and had eyeglasses so thick his eyes were distorted and alien, blinking repeatedly as the man pondered what Beya assumed was a counterfeit work request.

"Who called this in?" The signature on the form was a scribble, probably on purpose.

"Man, I just get a text and an address," Beya vamped, trying to hide his north-coast accent, just in case. "They don't tell me who or why."

They drifted out into the corridor. The server room door clicked shut. Tick tick tick.

"What were you doing?"

"I had to swap out a motherboard. Like it says there," Beya added, hoping it did.

It didn't. "No, no, no—there's something, there's something . . ." The IT guy's eyes were blinking like crazy, and he pulled out his phone. "I gotta make a call. Stay put."

Beya edged away.

"Stay."

"*Tipo*, I gotta pee. I'll be . . ." The call connected, the blinker was distracted, so Beya fled. "I'll be right back."

He took a stairwell, the sharp questions of the IT guy on his phone call chasing him up to the street level.

At the service doors they needed to check his bag and kit again on the way out. In case he was stealing something? Tick tick tick; Beya expected the IT guy to come running down the corridor at any moment.

Or no—he'd go into the room first. Wondering what the fuck had happened. The blue LED glow drawing his eye to the device. There wouldn't be time for much more.

It was Ondarroa all over again.

Tick. Tick. Beya dropped the tool kit and started to run when he got to the street, down Calle de Juan de Mena as fast as he could go. The albino had warned him not to rush, not to call attention to himself.

The bomb in the basement of the Palacio de la Bolsa exploded before he reached the corner, the concussion blowing Beya off his feet and into the road. Glass shattered in all the adjacent building windows, fell like hard rain to the street.

His limbs tingling, his ears ringing, he cut his hands getting back up. He felt a weight on him he wasn't sure he could carry. The bandage flapped free of the wound on the side of his neck, so he pulled it off. The wound was weeping. He couldn't hear anything except his own pulse pounding.

Trees had been stripped of leaves. Parked cars had been pushed up onto the sidewalk, their warning lights flashing like raw panic. A wall of smoke overtook him, smoke and swirling tatters of paper; for a moment he thought the bomb had brought down the entire palace building, but then he could just make out its edges as the debris began to settle.

High beams flashing, a van came barreling toward him out of the brume. He braced himself, but it swerved around and a door swung open and there was the albino behind the wheel, shouting at him, gesturing: *Get in.*

Later he would learn that the explosion had caused half the trading floor to collapse. Dozens were injured, many seriously, but only a single employee of the Bolsa remained missing from the basement server area where the bomb was believed to have been located.

Data wiped. Fortunes crushed. Millions of transactions lost in a millisecond, midtrade; the entire world financial market would suffer the aftershocks for weeks.

But from surveillance cameras and witness testimony, a picture quickly emerged of the terrorist alleged responsible: a former ETA foot soldier named Xavi Beya.

Chapter Five

The wedge of light that leaked out, along with a hushed argument from under the apartment door, ran across the shabby carpet to a graveyard of desiccated roaches collecting along the seam abutting the baseboard. Welcome to Clichy-sous-Bois. CSIS special operative Ryan Banks listened in on a courtesy wireless feed from a directional microphone aimed in via the next building, but he didn't understand much Spanish, and most of the argument could be heard live through the apartment doorway, just down the hall from where he could only watch and wait.

It was a GIGN operation because the tetchy Parisian counterterror assault unit wasn't about to let a bunch of sharp-elbowed, English-speaking black-op interlopers butt in and harsh their mellow; French intelligence had thrown a minor shit fit about letting Banks even tag along as the Five Eyes liaison. They didn't need any outside help. *Look but don't touch* was Banks's marching order.

Septien, the dashingly roguish GIGN team leader, tugged his balaclava eye slot under his chin so that Banks could appreciate his new white dental laminates and he could breathe fresh air.

"We detect a heat signature for five individuals," he murmured, holding up five fingers as if Banks would need the visual aid. "Your target is confirmed."

"We gonna wait for him to come out?"

Septien shrugged. The smell of cooked sausage came down the corridor from the other direction. A dim trill of laughter. Banks felt his stomach rumble. "Merguez," the Frenchman guessed. "With peppers and tomatoes and yogurt, plenty of pita. These banlieue are very popular with the Algerians."

Because it's the only place you let them live, Banks thought but said, instead, "You should move the other residents somewhere safe."

An empty stare was Septien's answer, followed by the snap of the black face mask going back into its proper position. Banks didn't like the French. Always making you aware you were not in their club. Even in Quebec, where the weird fucking French-adjacent language they spoke made the real French cringe, Banks too often felt like a foreigner.

Septien had twice made Banks assure him he wasn't Quebecois. As if it wasn't obvious. Septien was a smug little man.

The argument in the apartment continued, something about promises broken, mistakes made, the job not yet finished. Were they talking about the stock exchange bang and burn? Banks could easily tell which one must be the target: Xavi Beya. The other, even speaking Spanish, sounded Russian.

It was ECHELON in Gibraltar that had somehow located the fugitive, but they had held this intel back from Spain. Banks got the middle-of-the-night text and hopped a cheap flight from Leipzig to Orly, where he was met by a couple of government antiterror spooks who helped him put the tac team together.

The Spanish government was convinced the stock exchange attack had been Basque separatists. AUSCANNZUKUS, the five signatory states to the UKUSA Agreement—Australia, Canada, New Zealand, the United Kingdom, and the United States—were less confident. It'd been over two years since ETA had announced a complete disarmament. Tensions between the north and Madrid were low; Catalonia was the bigger headache now.

No, some of the Five Eyes thought this was a rogue actor throwing up a smoke screen. But why?

Banks had been tasked with bringing Beya in alive. Off book.

The corridor's quiet was shattered by a gunshot. Flurry of hand signals, and the French assaulters swarmed and broke down the target apartment door.

More gunfire met them. A body sprawled backward, and two of his GIGN teammates pulled him to cover. Muzzle flashes lit the corridor in quick bursts. The fuse box blew; lights went out. A panicked shouting ensued, Spanish, French, Russian. More gunfire popped holes in the hallway plaster. Despite having promised to hang back, Banks followed Septien in.

It was a cluttered apartment, a warren of narrow passageways and tiny rooms with bare mattresses and clothes hanging; too many places to hide. Banks smelled sulfur and sweat, saw two lumped figures prone on the floor near a big window with broken panes. Silver moonlight cast a cold edge into the darkness.

Members of the assault team were calling to each other from back rooms. The pop of another gun, and a burst from an automatic responded.

Banks and Septien heard the noise down the hallway at the same time. Septien gestured for Banks to stay put and darted forward with the laser sight of his assault rifle sweeping ahead of him. Banks, unarmed, followed him anyway.

At the end of the corridor was a big space filled with cardboard boxes—wide-screen televisions, if the markings were to be believed. Septien hesitated at the doorway, looked back with eyes wide in the frame of his balaclava, said nothing, crouched, and stepped through.

The bullet that hit him went right through his head, and the pink mist resulting momentarily blinded Banks, right behind him. The Frenchman flopped and folded. Glass breaking, a clumsy clatter, Banks recovered in time to see two shadows going out a window onto the roof. One of them had to be Beya; the other had skin so pale it glowed in the moonlight as he fired wildly back into the apartment, stitching the wall above where Banks flattened himself. The shooter was buying time to get away.

Banks went after them, of course. Neglected to take Septien's weapon, ran across the rooftop to the other edge, hoping to get a glimpse of their descent, but saw only the flashing top lights of emergency vehicles arriving in the building's driveway.

He spent a while searching for their escape route. The fugitives had vanished. There were several residential towers in the complex, bleached silver by a half moon, multiple rooflines, access stairs on each. Denizens of the Clichy projects leaned out windows and heckled Banks as he headed back. Coming into the apartment through the broken window, he was nearly shot by friendly fire.

Paramedics hurried in and went to work on the GIGN captain, but Septien was dead. A couple of his team members slumped in the hallway outside the flat, wiping tears away. Staging lights supplied by forensics gave the apartment a new, special, hellish feel. Banks moved through the crime scene like a ghost, nobody meeting his gaze, nobody engaging.

Two men dead in the main room, a good guy wounded, another dead suspect farther in, where he'd managed to cause havoc—a total of three GIGN assaulters were on their way to hospital.

And Septien. Banks felt guilty for having ragged on the Frenchman, even if he'd kept it to himself.

In the tiny grubby kitchen, where the directional mic technician insisted the main part of the argument had taken place, Banks found the breeding ground of the roaches along with a handgun on a chipped Formica table, some loose ammunition, burner phones, a Kevlar vest draped over the back of a chair, and a splintered hole blown in the floor by a gunshot, through which two little kids in the apartment below were looking up at Banks and giggling.

31

"Banks." The GIGN second-in-command held up one of the burner phones from the kitchen table and wiggled her eyebrows. "No pass code."

As she brought up some pictures, Banks said, "The first gunshot was an accidental discharge." He pointed to the hole in the floor. "Beya, maybe. Unfamiliar with the weapon?"

Septien's second either didn't understand him or didn't care; she showed Banks what she'd found on the phone. Pictures of an older man, stocky, northern European, with a shaggy Beatles cut of salt-and-pepper hair and matching soul patch. More lines on his face than a city road map. Banks didn't recognize the man, but it wouldn't take long for facial recognition to get his name. The Frenchwoman's smartphone hummed. She handed the burner to Banks and walked into the corridor to take her call.

Alone for a moment, idly scrolling past the photographs, Banks found a single screen grab of a Google Maps search.

Pinned was a restaurant in the Marais.

He stared at the picture, thinking, then deleted it. Put the burner phone back on the table and walked out.

CHAPTER SIX

There was the usual family fracas the night before Sentro left for Paris. As if sensing trouble when Jenny threw another failed flourless-chocolate-cake attempt in the trash, Clete, the current wrangler with benefits, wisely finished mucking out the stalls and hightailed it to his RV. Jeremy made a guest appearance on Zoom, invited by his sister; it was a two-hander, tag team, the topic of discussion: Should Mom Stop Moonlighting in the Spook Life?

The answer was yes; it was always yes. And Sentro secretly hoped that they wouldn't ever give up trying to convince her. Having retired from her job as a contract security-solutions specialist, she had intended to avoid any mission creep and keep her promise to her children (in the initial months after her leaving them, Solomon Systems had kept offering "a little contract work," which she'd respectfully but firmly declined). But other calls came in, a handful of old assets and shadow warriors who, like Arshavin, had made their fortunes in the geopolitical wreckage of the Cold War and wanted her to give them insight (*strategic consulting* was how she billed it) into this brave new world of crony capital carpetbaggers and stateless grifters, for whom the old rules of engagement no longer seemed to matter.

It paid some bills. It kept her mind busy.

"You said you wanted a clean break," Jeremy pointed out.

"It's not intelligence work, and not even remotely what I used to do. It's consulting," Sentro reminded them, not for the first or, probably, last time.

"With sketchy characters from your sketchy past," Jenny said.

"Really rich ones," was Sentro's go-to trump card. But the truth was, after six months away from it, set adrift in the vaulted skies and vast expanses of first West Texas and then New Mexico, she'd begun to ache for her old job enough that an infrequent red-eye to Europe or Asia was useful in easing the withdrawal she was feeling, while at the same time affording a sharp reminder of why she'd gotten the hell out of the game.

Win-win.

"You're an addict." Jenny had given up weed when she moved in with Sentro and knew a thing or two about cravings.

"You nearly got me killed just taking a cruise," Jeremy added.

"You're right," Sentro admitted. "You're both right."

Jenny drove her to the airport. Jeremy's girlfriend—or was she a fiancée? Sentro found herself strangely reluctant to ask—made all the travel arrangements.

It was, even in disagreement, a family affair. But that was real progress, wasn't it?

No more secrets, she would congratulate herself, knowing full well it wasn't true.

———

"Five hundred million dollars gone, poof. In an eyeblink. Everything is fucked to shit, for sure."

"Didn't I advise you not to fool around with Spanish futures?"

Ignoring her: "I had to leverage my position in the Odessa pipeline to cover the debt."

"The world markets are in a tailspin."

"Do I look like I care about anyone else?"

It was always best to let Ilya Arshavin choose the venue for their meetings, to avoid the inevitable whining ("Too expensive, too cheap, too chic, too shabby, too far, bad service"), but his picking the pop-up shawarma place surprised Sentro until she realized it was close to all the boy bars the Russian expatriate loved to frequent when he was in France.

"It was not terrorists. It was not *euskaldunak*."

"You lost me. Does that mean Basque?"

"In Basque. Yes." He ran his hand through his hair and scratched the unfortunate chin crawler he no doubt thought was hip. "But you, Aubrey Sentro, know this already." Arshavin's hooded eyes bored into her. They were at a table on the sidewalk. Sunshine poking through a threatening cloud cover couldn't make it down to the bottom of this narrow street, so they sat in a kind of eternal twilight, which matched Sentro's mood; the neon sign overhead fizzed and threw its rainbow colors over them.

"I don't know anything," Sentro protested, which was only half-true; she knew that ETA had disarmed over two years ago, though she blanked on the name of the leader who did it. Spain's Basque problem had cooled to a simmer.

"No. Of course not. You are just my useful idiot, thin slicing your sources, but with no opinion of your own." The Russian was mocking her, but she didn't mind.

She had a long history with Arshavin, some of which she no longer remembered, stretching back to Berlin days, when he'd been a low-level Soviet KGB-adjacent apparatchik selling secrets to the West not so much for ideological reasons as because he felt the winds of change blowing and sensed all the opportunities that might present for a man, properly positioned, with connections on both sides of the wall. Taking a shrewd, minor stake in a Ukrainian sand-and-gravel collective that got privatized after the dissolution of the Soviet Union, Arshavin had grifted and cronied his way to a billion-dollar Russian Republic hedge fund by the turn of the century. Predictably, then he ran afoul of Russia's president, managing to just get himself and the bulk of his assets out of Moscow before FSB agents could level bribery, corruption, and tax evasion charges against him. Now he lived in exile somewhere, probably England, but again Sentro got the equivalent of a *404: page not found* message when she dug in her memory for the answer.

Just the jet lag, right? She drank some fizzy water.

"I love you, though. Do not ever doubt this," Arshavin mumbled, his mouth full of laffa and chicken.

"So who do you think it was?" she asked him.

Arshavin gestured dismissively and glanced over a shoulder to where his bodyguard, Charlotte Madsen, sat at her own table, dark glasses shading restless eyes, pretending to read a book. "Now she mocks me."

Madsen stayed poker faced.

"I don't have access anymore to the kind of intel you think I do," Sentro said.

"Why didn't you sleep with me when I asked, when you were young and reasonably hot and my dick worked without a goddamn pump?"

Reasonably?

"You should consider this great compliment," he clarified.

"I dunno why, Ilya," Sentro deadpanned. "I was married, and you were gay?"

"Everything is negotiable," Arshavin grumbled, and Sentro knew he believed it was true. "You could have been my second wife," he added. "She lives in Monaco, got about a hundred million in settlement. The kids aren't even mine."

Sentro looked to Charlotte, who buried a smile. She was forty, thick waisted, biracial—a formidable former Kommando Spezialkräfte who had more or less followed in the footsteps of her German Nigerian father. But her hair was smartly styled, her nails perfect. Skirt, blouse, blazer: a spinster on vacation. Madsen had been with Arshavin since his Moscow days.

And when was that? Midnineties? Midaughts? Sentro knew it didn't matter, but it bothered her that it was one more thing she couldn't recall. Like all the expat oligarchs, the Russian was paranoid about getting rubbed out like Berezovsky or—like Litvinenko and Navalny—poisoned. Or worse.

"Not ETA terrorists, not Basque terrorism," he reiterated. "Something new. Funded by private sector. There have been other incidents we don't hear about."

"You're sounding like a Reddit conspiracy kook."

"Truth comes from strange places."

"No. It doesn't."

"Well, forget geopolitics; now is geo-economics."

"But why, Ilya? What's the endgame?"

The Russian shrugged, his shoulders round, his expression grim. "I am scared," he admitted, and Sentro didn't know what to say to him; on her flight over from the States she'd watched news coverage of the Madrid bombing, but the rest of Arshavin's insider intel was all news to her, and she truly was no longer in a position to find out more, even if she wished to do so.

He polished off his shawarma and sat back, clearly sated. Studied Sentro, scowling. "I don't care for this wig and disguise you like wearing," he said.

"I don't want it widely known that I'm still dabbling."

"Afraid of your old enemies," he teased.

"No. Afraid of yours."

Arshavin looked only a little chastened. "I see. Well. How is your head?"

"It's better," Sentro said and hoped she wasn't lying.

"Your mind was what we all fell for," the Russian said then, getting serious. "On a scale of ten you were, hey, honestly? Seven. Maybe six. But once the words came out?" He seemed satisfied to let the thought hang.

"I was just a girl," she said.

"Never just a girl," Arshavin assured her.

CHAPTER SEVEN

Banks had his own rent-a-goons, this time clandestine, compliments of the "cousins" (as MI6 liked to call them): two reliable Algerian private contractors Banks knew the CIA had on speed dial, and a friend-of-a-friend ex–Green Beret hard man just back from the Syrian border, where, he'd sworn, "things were pretty damn dull."

It was a risk Banks was taking—a potential diplomatic horror show if things went south, a monumental waste of time if he had it all wrong—but he couldn't afford to let the French drive the bus this time. Clearances were being made at a higher level. Or so he hoped.

"Who's the unsub cougar blonde he's talking to?"

Banks didn't know. He recognized the old KGB dude from the photograph in the Clichy safe house burner phone; he was sitting outside the restaurant pinned on its Google Maps. A plus-size former German Army soldier aptly named Lotte Madsen watched from a table nearby and was evidently Ilya Arshavin's security detail; the Green Beret recognized her from various joint operations in Islamabad and Kabul, back in the day.

"You don't want to mess with Lotte," the Yank observed. "She's good, damn good, but also several McNuggets short of a Happy Meal."

Nobody really cared to know the specifics.

Third day of a chancy vigil that had fortunately paid off with Arshavin's appearance, Banks and his crew were cramped in the back of a rental van watching grainy mounted camera feeds of the sidewalk shawarma joint on wireless tablets. Fixed frame, limited zoom function. Espionage on a budget. Because Banks was ghosting this, there was no budget. They'd scraped him together some funding from petty cash.

The Russian oligarch appeared to be charmed by his companion. Their discussion was playful, animated; Banks had to wonder if she was a professional escort, even knowing, from the brief NATO bullet points, Arshavin's fondness for men.

Who the fuck was she? Something made Banks think he should know.

"That's not her real hair," one of the contractors said.

"No, no, it is," said the other. "It's how old chicks look in the Bible Belt."

No sign of the target. Banks wondered if the meeting—assuming that was the meaning of the cryptic message he'd seen on the burner phone—had been scuttled in the wake of the safe house raid. His thoughts drifted. The call from Gilly that had woken him up to a pink Paris dawn was still troubling him. She wanted a commitment. Banks had difficulty deciding what shoes to wear most days. Commitment meant attachment, and Banks didn't like to get too close to anyone. Easy come, easy go, right? Because if people are disposable, it doesn't hurt so much when you lose them.

Lunch was breaking up; Arshavin stood, still mansplaining something to his blonde guest, bellicose, ending with self-possessed laughter. Her smile lacked the Russian's commitment, but he didn't seem to care. The two women rose, following his lead. There was a brief hug between Arshavin and his lunch date, the ritual double kiss. A black Peugeot Banks assumed was the Russian's ride glided up in front of the restaurant, momentarily complicating the view of the sidewalk dining area.

The blonde hung back and exchanged pleasantries with Madsen, who was hemmed in by an occupied adjacent table, forced to wait while chairs got scooted around to provide her a path out.

And that was when Banks saw him.

"Oh shit."

Xavi Beya materialized as if out of nowhere. Hoodie and some baggy jeans, but his haggard face caught a shaft of sunlight reflected off a high window on the building across the street.

Banks's team tumbled from the van in a panic. Beya had said something that caused Arshavin, almost at his car's open door, to stop and look. Banks was running. He might have shouted; if he did, it was lost in the roar of a 9 mm Glock Beya raised and fired point-blank into the Russian.

———

She wasn't looking at Arshavin when the gun went off. Charlotte had asked something about life in New Mexico, and Sentro had turned to answer. Later, she wasn't able to remember what they'd said to each other, but her back had been turned to the street, and the harried shouting, in accented English, that had preceded the gunshot just made it all that much more confusing.

Nothing very useful had been accomplished during lunch, and Sentro had felt a little like a fraud, charging Arshavin a handsome fee to tolerate his bluster and offer observations and advice he probably could have gotten from a cursory reading of the *Economist*.

And now, turning, horrified, she watched him drop to the sidewalk and saw men with black balaclavas running toward the café from the street. A hunting pack—surveillance team—who must have been waiting for something like this to happen. It took her a moment to find the shooter among the emptied shawarma-café tables; he was so ordinary: a slight man in a hooded jacket who looked like he hadn't slept in days.

He let the gun fall to his side and made no attempt to run.

The bullet had gone through Arshavin and struck a passing pedestrian, who was down in the street, yelling for help. The sulfur smell of the gunshot stung her nostrils like an uninvited old friend. Patrons dove under their tables or scrambled into the building. Reflexively Charlotte Madsen had drawn a compact handgun from inside her jacket and pushed past Sentro to skid to her knees beside her employer first. Blood smeared her hands and blouse.

"We have met the enemy, and he is us," the shooter called out, in Spanish. And then repeated it, in English, louder.

Madsen turned with her weapon raised, searching for the assassin, but the hunting pack had already arrived and crashed down on him; they stripped the Glock from his unresisting lowered hand, pinned his arms back, threw a hood over his head, and muscled him out into the narrow street, where a van came skidding up, its side door already open. They trundled him inside, and the van was accelerating down the street with its human cargo before the door got pulled closed.

Motionless in the bedlam, Sentro felt like a player in a VR game: surprised, but watching, oddly detached. It didn't occur to her until much later that she could have been killed. As the van roared away, and before the door slid shut, a young white man who'd just pulled off his mask looked back at her with a puzzled expression she recognized because she'd been on the other side of it so many times: *Who the fuck are you, and why aren't you reacting the way a normal person would?*

Why indeed?

Madsen cradled her dying employer in her arms, murmuring softly to him as his eyes went cloudy. He was trying to tell her something. No words formed. Her tears fell to his face.

Sentro heard the van slow, then brake, and looked up in time to see it take a sharp left turn at the corner.

When she thought back on it later, she remembered a vague awareness of someone else at the scene who'd reacted the way she had; she felt eyes hard on her from the shadows inside the shawarma pop-up, eyes of someone unfazed by the senseless violence.

But watching the van disappear, she couldn't help it: old instincts kicked in.

And Sentro gave chase.

———

She didn't know the city all that well, but the Marais was an ancient neighborhood, which meant narrow, curving one-way streets, dead ends, double-parked vehicles—no efficient grid designed for the easy flow of modern traffic.

That the van would head south was a lucky guess. Paris police headquarters was on the Île de la Cité, but Sentro doubted the men who'd taken Arshavin's killer were cops, or even French. Somehow she recalled there was a helisurface on the Left Bank, at the Val-de-Grâce military hospital, but that would mean that the French had agreed to this exfiltration, and if that was the case, why the black masks and unmarked van?

It didn't bother her that she was unarmed. One of the less-discussed side effects of serial concussions, something she'd been warned about but hadn't shared with her children, is a diminishment of the ability to assess risk. You get more reckless. Even in retirement.

She darted out of the shawarma patio, crossed the street, cut down a sliver of an alley, and came out on another narrow Marais road in time to watch her target swerve around a double-parked produce truck and thread its way past the Pompidou Center.

Sentro cut the corner, past a Tin Man mime painted silver, and ran through the tourists milling around the Stravinsky Fountain. It felt good, running. She knew that wouldn't last. Down another narrow cobblestone street, where she struggled to keep her ankles from turning, she felt a tightness in her hamstring and saw the van flash in and out of view up ahead, avoiding the boulevard, where police cars, mournful sirens wailing, hurried back toward the shooting.

When the van went straight down a side street at the Tour Saint-Jacques, Sentro took the diagonal through the square, past the gaudy gothic tower. Once again she'd guessed correctly that they would take the Pont au Change onto the island in the Seine. Less traffic.

The skeletal scaffolding that cloaked Notre-Dame rose grimly to her left. The van swerved right onto the road along the river and would have outdistanced her but got jammed by street repair on the back side of the massive Palace of Justice complex.

Sentro veered down steep stone steps to the south quay of the Seine itself, hoping to get beyond the road crew from below them and overtake her target there.

But then what? She didn't intend to intervene. She just wanted to know who the hell had been watching and waiting for the shooter to make his move on her old friend. And where they were going with him.

CIA was the easy answer to the first question. The clean young white man seemed a pretty clear giveaway. But something about the balaclava rendition team felt off.

Was Ilya Arshavin even a friend? She felt his death not so much with sadness as with a sense of loss. Another piece of her past falling away. Jenny was always accusing her of being cold. Jeremy gave it more nuance: "It's not like you don't care, Mom," he'd say. "It's more like you can't."

A bicyclist shouted and veered out of her way. Sentro slowed. Her lungs burned; her legs were cramping. Now her hip hurt. The wig was making her head sweat. What the fuck *was* she doing? Her children's fretful judgment flared. She pushed it away, kicked off her flats, and ran barefoot on the sandy jogging path to another set of stairs that led back up to the street.

She was too late. Freed from the roadwork jam, the van shot past her, veering off onto a service road that slipped under the grand old Pont Neuf and ended at the little park on the point.

A big old unmarked Mi-14 amphibious helicopter thundered over the Latin Quarter and made a wide turn over the river to hover and then slowly settle along one side of the little park, just past the Captain's Bar.

Sentro stayed up on the bridge; she jogged across the road, around the statue of Henri IV, to the railings heavy with tourist lovers' locks, where she could look down at the men from the van, wrangling their asset into the chopper's waiting cargo bay. The van was already driving away. The copter's rotor tossed the park's trees like a violent storm, and it rose quickly, gone before anyone casually watching could even register what was going on.

The impeccable timing of the acquisition and extraction was impressive, if chilling. Had they known Arshavin was a target? She watched the helicopter follow the river, rising, rising, until it disappeared behind the pillows of heavy clouds rolling in low over Paris.

"Who the fuck are you?" he said, low, almost conversational, from close behind her. "And what do you want?"

The white man from the tactical team. She smelled all the coffee he'd been drinking. She made a slow turn so as not to give him any reason to kill her, in case that was on his mind. A little older up close than she would have guessed, he was sweating from the run back to find her but not winded. Well trained, great shape, not unattractive, desperate to seem reasonable. So definitely not an American friend. She felt the cheap thrill of engagement. Game on.

Canadian?

"I know who you are; you're CIA," she said anyway, just to mess with him.

His nervous blink told her she was right that he wasn't.

"I know the type," she added, thinking: *And you are not it.*

"Who are you?" he asked again, not as nicely.

"I'm a curious person, wondering why some ninja boys just trundled a killer away before the French police could deal with him."

"You kept pace on foot with a moving vehicle for about half a mile. That's not normal."

There. There was the tell, albeit very faint: "aboot." Canadian Security Intelligence Service. But what the fuck was he doing in Paris, exfiltrating assassins? The northern neighbors didn't engage in that sort of fuckery.

"Running is a hobby," she offered as an explanation.

"So is snooping, I guess."

"Big sense of wonder," Sentro agreed.

"What's your relationship with Ilya Arshavin?"

"You don't have any jurisdiction here," Sentro reminded him. "FYI." But then she wondered if maybe he did.

"Who *are* you?"

He really did seem to want to know. She didn't blame him. She took a long pause to see what he'd do. He waited for her. Smart. "Nobody," Sentro said finally and started to walk away.

The Canadian reached out and carelessly grabbed her arm, and for a brief moment she thought about breaking his wrist just to, you know, teach him to be a little more careful about people in the future.

"I'm gonna need you to come with me," he said grimly.

It occurred to her it might be worth it. Surely on the other end of this would be somebody she would remember—or more likely who'd remember her; she'd done some contract work for CSIS when she was working at Solomon—somebody who might give her some better answers.

And then what? Her client was dead. It was upsetting but had nothing to do with her. She thought, *No.*

"All right," she said.

It started to rain as they walked back over the plaza, around the monument, Henri IV glowering down at them from his horse as they jaywalked across the street. The Canadian must have called for backup. Or a prearranged ride.

"Where are you taking me?" The CSIS agent said nothing. "Is it far? 'Cause I've gotta . . ." Sentro hesitated for effect. "All that running. Lady business."

He just stared at her, as if uncomprehending.

"Time of the month."

Now he was blushing. Frowning and blushing and momentarily at a loss for words. She was starting to like this earnest young spook, in spite of everything. There was a café awning just down the sidewalk.

"Your bag is back at the shawarma joint," he said.

"They have tampons in all the restrooms, here."

Suitably rattled but refusing to show it, he walked her to the door and escorted her in. A lot of empty tables, a closed kitchen, and a back exit at the end of the hallway where the restrooms were, but the Canadian parked himself where he had a clear view of it. Smart. Two women squeezed past them, and Sentro followed them into the loo.

Her French was passable. She had her passport and credit cards in a hidden money belt around her waist. As she pulled off the blonde wig and glasses, shook her sweaty, drab brown hair out, and wiped off the lipstick and war paint she wore for clients because it seemed more professional, she explained to one of her new friends that the man waiting for her outside was trouble, and wondered if they could possibly help her get past him.

She didn't need to provide details. Just the right tone and a touch of nervous agitation.

The taller one even had a spare scrunchie.

The Canadian agent was on the phone when she came out with one of the women. Not business—his call was personal, his voice hushed and husky. *Possibly a woman on the other end*, Sentro thought. He glanced up and saw two brunettes, one with her hair up, plain face, no makeup.

No recognition. He even angled away from them and fell silent as they went past.

The old Sentro wanted him to look right into her eyes so she could thrill at how thoroughly he'd been fooled. The new Sentro, not even fifty but put to pasture, struggling sometimes to remember the simplest things, a middle-aged American widow with lots of lists and leisure time, just kept walking through the steady rain, still skilled in the game, to lose herself among the throngs of tourists taking selfies on Paris's oldest bridge.

CHAPTER EIGHT

Traffic-cam surveillance footage from Place Dauphine skittered forward on the screen; Banks had already been through it, but Henry Otter hadn't, and the former marine wasn't about to let Banks queue up the relevant time frame.

"You'll miss something," Otter rumbled at him, which was irritating but expected. Drummed out of ONCIX because of his fondness for advocating deep state purges, the old spook was legendary (to a fault) for not trusting anything but his own eyes. Plus, he trended toward batshit right-wing crazy. Not that that ever kept a good spy down for long.

Banks was the primary liaison between Otter's contract-intelligence group and the five signatory states to the UKUSA Agreement. Having made the mistake of getting good at handling loose cannons, he was frequently stuck in Kyiv, listening to this bullshit so no one else had to.

"All these liberal snowflakes bloviating, and meanwhile local militias are forming across the United States. Loyal Americans, who know their domestic enemies as well as their locations, in detail, and will be able to act swiftly to eliminate them and the threat they pose. If, you know, it all comes down to that, some day."

On the monitor, customers' images flickered in and out of the café. Banks watched and waited, impatient, for himself and the mystery blonde to make their appearance at 14:32:11.

"Personally, I'd go for immediate and lethal punishment of the disloyal by citizen firing squads chosen by lottery," Otter said. "Leading Democrats, Hollywood elitists, pretty much all the journalists, traitorous academics. So-called American Muslim jihadists . . . or, hell, just Mohammedans in general, fuck it. No constitutional protection for US citizens who wage war against their country."

"There," Banks said.

"There," Otter echoed, as if he had just found the place. He froze the image and studied it. "That's them?" He zoomed in on the blonde's face until it was nothing but an abstract of pixels. *This is where, in the movie,* Banks thought, *I would say,* Can we enhance that?

"What the fuck did I just do?" Otter said. He put the image back in the proper proportions and, studying it, made a cartoon frown face. "No, no idea who that woman is, sorry." He started the surveillance video running again; Banks and the woman walked inside.

"Later," Banks said, irritated. "Scroll to later. She never came out of the restroom, which implies she did but wore a disguise."

"Or took one off," the old CIA hack pointed out. "And you let her get past you." He made a wheezing noise, exposing a missing incisor in his feeble attempt at expressing amusement.

Banks pushed Otter's hand off the mouse and advanced the footage to where he wanted it.

"Here."

The awning, the café. Two women came out onto the sidewalk, walked in opposite directions: one toward the Pont Neuf, one under the camera and out of view. Banks goosed the frame rate, and another woman scampered out of sight under the camera. A man opened an umbrella and walked across the road to look down at the river.

More time passed, and a couple emerged and got in a waiting Uber that drove away.

Then, after a longer wait, Banks could be seen, exiting the café, standing on the sidewalk, looking in both directions. Lost.

"You musta been pissed."

Banks said nothing. The footage kept running. Cars scurried up and down the street.

"How long are we gonna keep watching?" Otter asked.

"I waited about thirty minutes. I checked the bathroom stalls, the alley."

Otter was just nodding. "Sure you did." He took the mouse back from Banks and reversed the feed. Back, back, back to when the two women emerged together.

"Gotta be one of these two, Bubba."

Stop. The static image of the street shimmered. Banks said nothing, waiting. Otter glanced at him, then back at the computer screen and the two women. "But you know that now." Leaned close, lips pursed, looking fascinated. HVAC kicked on, flooding the bleak little viewing room with cool, stale air; a faint nose of burning rubber suggested the unit needed servicing. Otter, no doubt, would wait until it caught fire.

The old brick agent zoomed in on the woman who walked to the bridge again, until her face was nothing but dots.

"This one."

"Yeah. How about we run some kind of facial recognition? She's gotta be in the system."

"She's not, no." Otter straightened up, yielding the mouse. "But I know her," he said. "From another life," he added. "Berlin."

———

Her mother's reaction had puzzled her. The owner of the only market in Drywater had mentioned to Jenny "a strange girl" asking around about Aubrey Sentro. Spoke Spanish, Cordero had said. But didn't look it.

Jenny's mom had shrugged it off. But there was a palpable tension underneath the gesture. Her eyes had been overcast since she'd returned from Paris.

Reading her mother's impenetrable expressions was a skill Jenny Troon had only recently begun to hazard. Growing up, she'd felt incapable of doing it; then after her father died, she'd gone through a defiant phase of refusing to even try. Usually the recent, infrequent work trips seemed to give her mom a lift; something unpleasant must have happened on this one. Jenny wondered if the strange girl with questions was related to it.

Moving to Texas had sort of made sense, but her mother's subsequent dumping all her savings into the broken-down horse ranch in East Bumfuck, New Mexico, after less than a year was totally a non sequitur, and Jenny had worried, at first, that it had been an early sign of a descent into dementia.

Rash judgment, faulty logic—wasn't that common in mental decline? Conversation with their mother was always a chess game she and Jeremy couldn't win, so one of her children had to go check it out in person.

"Which means you," her brother had decided, dryly, "since last time I went, and she shot me."

So Jenny took a break from her barista job, intending only a short reconnaissance, and borrowed frequent-flier miles from her brother Jeremy's flight attendant fiancée (whom he'd cute-met during his nearly disastrous attempt to rescue their mother from the so-called pirates almost a year and a half ago, now), and two planes and a bus ride later she was in the middle of nowhere on the edge of a one-street town of boarded-up brick and adobe buildings, save Cordero's Drywater Dry Goods (and a Starbucks, of course), watching her mother's new fire-engine-red F-150 rumble up, driven by a hunky, box-jawed cowboy not much older than herself—he came complete with a toothpick and a fathomless Clint Eastwood stare—who introduced himself as Clete.

She still didn't know his last name; he claimed he didn't have one. Like Bono, he said. *It must embarrass him*, Jenny thought.

They drove a faded two-lane blacktop for forever and a day through treeless, rolling prairie, then turned off and rambled awhile longer on a washboard gravel road to the very end, where some bleak barbed wire and a collection of weathered buildings and corrals were the sum total of her mother's investment.

No sign of horses then, but now there was Clete's spunky pinto quarter horse and two skittish Pryor Mountains mustangs he had adopted and was determined to tame. There was also a delicate but gratifying dance toward reconnection with her mother, who, not so much changed as evidently feeling liberated from the spook life, had begun slowly—often glacially, while they cooked, cleaned, idled, argued, gaped at the terrifying electrical storms, and made inexpert repairs on the adobe and outbuildings—drawing back the blackout curtains that for so long had made her Jenny and Jeremy's private riddle to be solved. Much to her surprise, Jenny had fallen in love with the place and stayed.

Mother-daughter time. Something they'd never had because her mother was so often away while Jenny and Jeremy were growing up. Was it awkward? You bet. And wonderful and weird, and fraught because for all her mother had confessed about her adventures in the shadows, Jenny was pretty sure she was hearing only the redacted highlights.

Still, it was better than nothing.

The sunsets never failed to thrill her.

Week five, she ran out of weed and didn't miss it much but would sometimes take an early morning walkabout looking for peyote cactus, even though Wikipedia said it grew mostly over in Texas, a couple of hundred miles away. She didn't worry much about where this all was going. The vast steppe, the stillness, and the emptiness did that to you: it seemed more than enough, here, to just be.

She nevertheless wore earplugs prophylactically when she slept, not wanting to know or think about what was going on in the master bedroom between her maybe-menopausal mother and the frisky cowpoke himbo.

"He's loyal and affectionate," her mother said.

"That's how people describe their labradoodles," Jenny pointed out.

But Clete ran the ranch and treated her mother like a fragile flower, and he taught Jenny to ride, and it turned out she was good at it; so very good, in fact, that now, six months later, Clete was helping her up onto one of the feral mares to see what Jenny could do with her.

"You're one with the horse," Clete reminded her, one of his many sagebrush-zen mantras.

"Until I'm not," Jenny noted.

"Clear mind."

"Yeah, yeah."

Her mother watched, legs hooked over the top rail of the corral fence. She didn't ride—seemed to have no burning interest in horses at all. *Except maybe as creatures of chaos,* Jenny mused. She'd told her brother her theory that the madcap Pryor Mountains refugees reminded their mom of her glory days. Generally intelligent, according to Clete, strong, sure footed, amazing stamina. Like all feral horses, he warned her, they were distrustful and easily spooked. But if you got past that, they'd bond tightly, tame, and "do pretty much any damn thing any other horse can do." Clearly, Clete—a man-boy who lived in a broken-down motor home parked at the end of a dusty box canyon where Jenny was pretty sure he was an uninvited guest—thought he'd tamed their mom. Good luck with that, Jenny wanted to tell him.

"Sounds like he makes her happy," was Jeremy's banal assessment.

"Let's not go there, okay?" Jenny would warn, feeling just a little queasy.

Her brother had promised he would come visit soon to give a second opinion but, so far, hadn't done either.

"Jenny, focus." Clete gripped the halter of the horse, and Jenny slowly stepped into the stirrup and swung her leg across the saddle to settle as lightly as she could.

The mustang tried to lunge away. Clete made one of his braying horse-whisperer sounds and stayed with her, boots scuffing up tiny dust devils. Jenny gathered the loose reins.

"Legs," Clete said.

"I know. I know."

He let go.

The horse seemed to levitate. Magic. Like a fairy tale, flying. Only at the last minute did Jenny remember to set her knees; she felt a shock course through her tailbone anyway when they landed.

Then it was a teacup ride. Spinning, spinning, reversing. A teacup on a jackhammer. She heard Clete whoop and holler. Dust rose around her. Her hips found a rolling rhythm, sort of like slow-motion twerking. She was one with the horse, all right.

And then she was not.

Flying, but without the horse.

Awkward landing, but she managed to tuck a shoulder and roll away.

Clete was helping her up, putting her hat back on her head. "That was awesome."

Jenny's legs and pelvis coursed with electric current. Her face flushed; her ears tingled. Not for the first time since she came west with her mom, she understood why teenage girls got obsessed with horses.

The wild horse cantered back and forth along the back edge of the corral, clocking them with crazy Bette Davis eyes. She didn't want anyone riding her; she didn't want to be broken. Jenny understood how she felt.

On the fence, her mother was clapping. Jenny recognized the expression from that brief time she'd played girls' softball: proud as hell, unapologetically loving, and thinking about something else, somewhere else, that she couldn't, wouldn't, ever talk about.

The chyron burned in at the bottom of the 4:3 frame said: *December 7, 1990. 10:31 a.m. Berlin, Germany.*

Pearl Harbor Day.

Bombs away.

It was a digital transfer of a VHS tape that had suffered a measure of degaussing. The interviewer and his subject frequently glitched and ghosted. Because the audio was so shitty, it took Banks more than a moment to recognize Hank Otter with all that hair; Aubrey Sentro didn't look old enough to drive a car. Ambient hum distorted their words. Sentro, in a tentlike hospital smock, her hair pulled back in a ponytail, sat across an empty table from Otter, but it didn't look like an interrogation room so much as an empty office they'd borrowed, and the footage had been shot from waist high, probably on a tripod, not some fixed room monitor in the corner. Part of a second man was just visible, closer to the camera, in a chair at the edge of the frame. Otter did all the talking. No surprise.

"Were you kept in solitary?"

"Sometimes." Sentro's voice was small, quiet. "Actually, I don't know." Forty-five minutes into this interview, Banks still couldn't believe how this young woman, who had been through so much, could hold herself together.

Otter, even then, was an arrogant dick. "The drugs."

"Yes, sir."

"Which you don't know what they were."

"No, sir."

"What did you tell the Stasi interrogators?"

Sentro hesitated. "Everything I knew."

"Everything."

"Pretty much. But then," Sentro added stubbornly, "I didn't know anything, really."

Otter made a note on the legal pad in front of him and sat back. "What if I told you we didn't find any trace of narcotics or other psychotropic substances in your blood samples?"

"You'd be testing me," Sentro said. "Because I can't believe you didn't. It was every day, for months and months. I'm still suffering withdrawal from the morphine."

"Heroin, in fact. Street grade. Consistent with East German underground product. Who's to say you didn't just go on an eleven-month high?"

Sentro stared at him and then shook her head. "Are you asking me questions or telling me how you want to spin this for your bosses at Langley?"

Watching her, Banks smiled. *Balls.*

Otter shrugged. "You want to know how many times the Stasi has sent a double agent back to us claiming they were tortured and drugged?"

"Sir, the Stasi is in disarray," Sentro told him. "They're hiding money, burning files. Every man and woman for themselves. And even if they weren't, they wouldn't need to turn and double somebody unimportant like me, because they've got thousands of agents already embedded in the West.

"They know everything we're doing," she added. "That's how your cell got blown."

"The one you fell on your sword for."

"I played the only card I had. Did your people in the East get out?"

Otter begrudged her the truth. "They did. Yeah. You're a big hero. And you can stop calling me 'sir.'"

Sentro didn't say anything in response. The second man coughed. Shuffling through some reports, Otter apparently found the one he wanted, because he smoothed it on the table and studied it for a moment.

Banks had read the abstract of the three-hundred-page case report: October of 1989, army wunderkind Aubrey Sentro infiltrates East German intelligence to put a face on a never-photographed Stasi spymaster known to the West only by his code name: Pogo. Several weeks in, Aubrey sacrifices herself to save a clandestine operation, then vanishes into the East German detention program. Eleven months later a traumatized Sentro, suffering withdrawal from the morphine she's been serially dosed with twice a day, wanders through Checkpoint Charlie to freedom. Little is known about what happened during her eleven months of captivity; young Sentro, peering back through the opioid haze, is not much help. She met Pogo but can't remember his real name or what he looks like.

Or doesn't want to? Thirty years later, the jury is still out.

"You ready to talk about the pregnancy?" Even on the shitty audio from the digitized tape, Otter's tone came across insincere and suggestive.

Banks watched young Sentro freeze on screen, her body language making *him* uncomfortable. She leaned away from Otter, not meeting the case supervisor's gaze. "No. Sir."

Otter wouldn't back off. "Was it aborted? The *Krankenakte* recovered from the annex doesn't say."

Sentro murmured something inaudible.

"What?"

Scrape of a chair leg, squeak of rubber soles on tile. She repeated the word again so softly the microphones barely picked it up, but Otter had heard it this time. *Stillborn.* He stared at her oddly. She cleared her throat and wiped what looked like tears from her cheeks.

CHAPTER NINE

From one of the Adirondack chairs on the front porch, she could sip her gin gimlet and watch her daughter help her cowboy shed the pintos of their saddles.

Gossamer curtains of rain slid across the western horizon, where the Sangre de Cristo Mountains rose modestly above the vast Eastern Plains of New Mexico. A setting sun set fire to the edges of the thunderheads that rose above them, and flicks of lightning sparked, here and there, like the random thoughts dancing in Sentro's head.

What the hell had happened in Paris? It still ate at her. Arshavin was buried, Charlotte Madsen hadn't returned Sentro's calls, and none of her back channels, including her old colleague Reno Elsayed at her old workplace, Solomon Systems, could offer any insight.

"Payback," had been Reno's best guess. "Arshavin left a lot of damage in his wake. Take your pick."

Early that morning, Sentro had done a round trip to Drywater in the truck, under the guise of needing more limes, but really to ask Cordero about his stranger sighting. Little Frank was as eager as he was unhelpful.

"Ho, no, ma'am, I didn't tell her nothing."

"Her?"

"Well, I suppose you never know. You know."

"But female trending."

"Yep. Wait, what?"

"You told Jenny she didn't look Spanish."

"Did I?"

"And she asked for me by name?"

"In Spanglish, mm-hmm. Luckily, I habla the lingo, having been one. I said, 'Don't ring a bell, no.' Your name, I mean," he explained unnecessarily. "I said, 'Nobody in this forgotten corner of hell answers to that description. Sorry.'"

"She described me."

"With these beautiful rolled *r*'s."

Nothing registered. Was it because she couldn't remember? Or didn't know? Sentro fought to shake off the rust of her willing disengagement from the game.

Fuck.

Clete, bless his heart, had thought she was "kinda maybe overacting a little" when she told him some former-life trouble might be chasing her. He donned his best don't-worry-little-darlin'-I'm-here-to-protect-you demeanor and assured her that whoever it was, "We'll see 'em coming before they see us seeing 'em." He had no idea of Sentro's past and didn't care to know that she was choosing not to tell him. "There are runners and chasers," he would say. "Runners? We never look back."

Twelve years younger and aggressively uncomplicated, Clete was lean and limber and smelled like campfires and aftershave. A help-wanted flyer she'd pinned on Cordero's community bulletin board had brought the peripatetic cowpoke and handyman to her porch not long after she moved in. He had references, in Walsenburg, Trinidad, and Raton; her old friend Reno Elsayed had run a deep-search background on him and found only a juvenile rap for joyriding, in Amarillo. Child of a single mom, last name Seward, he had washed out of Fort Lewis College, been rejected by the marines, and spent a good bit of time in Montana, framing houses. Sentro felt only a little bit guilty knowing so much more than he'd wanted to share with her.

Was she in love with him? No. But she loved having him. Sometimes, entangled with him in the dark of her bedroom, she could almost imagine he was Dennis when they were young and happy and looking out at life sprawling in front of them, bright and limitless, before the army had sent her to Germany for a simple eastward recon; before everything had changed.

The killing of Arshavin had rattled her, not because the oligarch hadn't earned an ugly splashing out over the course of his savage post-glasnost plundering, but because Sentro felt exposed in a way she never had before. She wasn't operational. She didn't have the support or resources of the government or of other private-sector professionals to fall back on. And her determination to get even further off the grid meant that the Old Spooks Desk in the basement of Langley had probably moved her file to a virtual morgue in the cloud and wouldn't be much of a last-resort safety net, if it came to that.

But who could be looking for her? The firewall between what happened and the new life she was trying to fashion remained, as far as she knew, intact. Her disguise had held, even for the Canadian, whom, anyway, she had already dismissed as a possibility; if he wanted to talk to her, he'd just guilelessly show up, the way they did. Charlotte Madsen had gone to ground, possibly worried that whoever had her employer killed wouldn't want to leave any loose ends. Nobody seemed to know where the German bodyguard was, but the unforgiving plains of eastern New Mexico were a pretty unlikely place for her to hide.

Could Arshavin's death be somehow connected to the Spanish stock market bombing? Sentro was wary of coincidence.

"You just got here," Clete had pointed out when she told him she and Jenny might be moving on and that she'd have to sell the horses and the land because all her savings were tied up in them.

"Nobody's gonna buy this place for what you spent," Clete assured her.

She wished she had a counterargument but suspected he was right. The ranch wasn't an investment; it was a refuge, and whether she'd overpaid or not, she really didn't want to lose it.

"I could probably get you some money for the mustangs," Clete said. "But there's a chance whoever buys them will send them to China or some damn place to be, you know, eaten."

Okay, well, that wasn't going to happen. Maybe she just needed to take her daughter and fade away for a little while. Last she checked, her father's old Airstream was still on his scrap of land outside Guaymas, Mexico. She was a bit player in the Paris drama, and it would eventually blow over. Drowned out by the next loud noise; that was the new reality. In this century, with its stateless shadow wars and corporate espionage, the ground just kept shifting; nothing lingered, nothing sustained.

"You tell Jenny about your plans yet?" Clete had asked her.

Sentro hadn't, no.

They were walking up from the stables, laughing, banging the dust out of their hats. Her daughter looked happier than Sentro had seen her in a long, long time. Clete had made her lose the piercings when he taught her to ride; the high-country tan took the edge off her tattoos. Sentro had loved and marveled at her daughter's resolute perfection since the day she was born. A twinge of jealousy: Jenny was young, free—and probably a better fit for Clete when it came right down to it. By her midtwenties, Sentro had been saddled with a mortgage, two toddlers, a well-meaning but unemployable husband at home taking care of them. She also had her honorable discharge and a fancy new job with the agency: black ops, sorting out the atrocities of the Croatian War of Independence, back when there was still some trace of the quaint Cold War conviction that they were crusaders for a better world.

Her children might not ever understand. Did it matter? The past was immutable, the future a puzzle. She was changing, like the Santa Fe shrink said.

Or was she?

Sentro took a long sip of her cocktail and considered her scrappy ranch. The gentle quiet overtook her. A crow made a rattling sound. Tension in her shoulders eased. Maybe she *was* overreacting. All the years when everything connected. Maybe this time she was just a bystander to the madness.

If she stepped back and looked at it objectively, the Paris shooter was likely a one-off. Either somebody Arshavin had fucked over or someone working for another oligarch who wanted something Arshavin had. A crime of opportunity committed in the wake of a terrorist bombing.

But why would the Canadian, Banks, and whomever *he* was working with be so interested? That implied an intersection with realpolitik.

Connections.

Ukrainian oil pipelines popped into her head for some reason. She'd write herself a Post-it note so she wouldn't forget to check what happened to Arshavin's heavily leveraged project.

She remembered the shooter's expression when he spoke after killing the Russian—but what was it he'd said?

Sentro drew a blank.

"Mom."

She looked up at her daughter now and wondered how long she'd been standing there. Clete was audible, already inside, banging pots and pans as if he knew how to cook.

"Mom, you all right?"

"Yes."

Jenny kept studying her. Trying to read her. Sentro felt a shiver; how many times had she seen that same curious face looking back at her in a mirror?

"I'm gonna make lentil soup and a cactus salad," Jenny was saying. "Okay?"

"Perfect. Sounds like the cowboy wants to help you," Sentro said.

Jenny's eye rolls were always worth it. "He can make some more horse noises while I chop cilantro."

"You rode that pinto today like you were born to it," Sentro told her as she started inside.

"I know, right?" Jenny beamed. It still touched deep when Jenny craved her approval—and that Sentro got such pleasure from giving it. "Clete's a good teacher. Who'da thought my secret superpower was saddle bronc riding."

"Your grandfather."

"Maybe you should try."

"I'll stick to riding cowboys."

"Ew," Jenny said. "Mom. Just . . . ew."

CHAPTER TEN

Shabby sex in the custodian's closet was the negotiated compromise, because a utility washbasin had once before proved the perfect height, plus it was still raining, a miserable drizzle that had begun leaking from the slate-gray sky before dawn, and anyway Gilly frowned on the very public nature of rooftop romance.

"Drones, for example," she explained to him, in a series of breathy gasps.

He was afraid this sink was going to break. The steel legs rattled. Typical American, Gillian had an assortment of unfortunate tattoos on a glorious surfeit of otherwise flawless skin; she liked to say she was plus size, but Banks saw all the right things in the right proportions, just extra helpings—he had no complaints. She reminded him of the generous girls from the Catholic school when he was growing up in Guelph.

"Slower. Oh my. There. There. Don't stop."

No thoughts of stopping, even if he could.

"Oh Lord, there." She raised her knees and squeezed him. "There there there there. Whoa." She went quiet. He felt her fly elsewhere and then sag against him, taking deep, sweet, shaky breaths that tickled his ear, her head angled against his, her unruly hair damp.

"Do you love me?" she whispered.

If he didn't, what was he doing there? "What do you think?" he said evasively, slipping his hands down to her hips and holding her against him. There were other girls who had asked him that, and he'd answered the way they wanted, and none of them had lasted.

Love confused him; on the one hand it seemed so simple, but then somehow it got complicated, weighed down by other emotions, conditions, circumstances, missteps, little things that came up when you least expected them. He didn't want to have to work on love; his assignments were tricky enough.

Commitment.

He hoped the subject wouldn't come up.

Sighing happily, Gilly gently lowered her knees, and he slipped out of her, and they began the always shy and awkward dance of decoupling.

Anyone watching them emerge from the closet together would know what they'd been doing. Fortunately, everybody in Otter's outpost—and there were only half a dozen contractors on the current case, including Gilly and Banks—was preoccupied with the interrogation of Xavi Beya.

There was pressure to deliver. They were all on a clock. Because the French government was screaming about the illegal rendition of a murder suspect, the Five Eyes had promised to turn him over in seventy-two hours. Hour fifty, Beya was still singing the same song.

Delia Hsi, another American, recently laid off from the NSA in a budget purge, was waiting for her partner, Gillian, as they came down the short hallway to the interview room; as if on cue, the door opened and the other team of interrogators emerged: a new hire, a former Polish prosecutor named Lewandowski (Banks couldn't remember his first name, much less pronounce it); and the diminutive nonbinary Czech who called themself Nula.

"We're not going to get anywhere without enhancement," the Czech grumbled. While Otter's employment of Nula seemed to violate his fast-held racist, sexist, narrow-minded bias, they were, he confided in Banks—end justifying the means, always—the most brilliant interrogator he'd ever seen.

"Why is it not possible that he doesn't know anything?" Lewandowski said. Everyone looked at him blankly. Nula made a face. The Pole stared back, obviously unfazed. "The neck wound is superficial, but it seems obvious he was forced to do what he did."

"What about the sutures in his side?" Delia asked.

"He won't talk about it. Perhaps, in addition to his family, they took one of his kidneys as collateral?"

"Whatever. He's scared," Banks offered. The others didn't disagree.

"Otter was looking for you," Delia said to Banks.

Nula yawned and handed Gillian a pad with notes and questions. "We're gonna order pho from that place across the river. You want in?"

They did not. Banks and Gillian traded smoldering looks that the others noted and filed, no doubt for future gossip, and then the two women went inside. For a moment Banks had a glimpse of Beya, slumped in a chair, no table, his shoes kicked off. He looked feverish, exhausted, and desperate. The door clicked shut. The genderqueer Czech and the clean-cut Polish prosecutor were already disappearing around the corner that Banks and Gilly had just turned.

A murmur of voices came through the interview room door, calm, conversational. Otter picked good people; he'd been running this NOC detention site in Kyiv for a little over three years, out of a former ornamental-glass factory on the right bank of the Dnieper. The old sandblasting equipment remained, untouched, on the ground floor, decades of fine dust shrouding it. The private prison was on the second floor: three reinforced steel-lined cells, assorted support rooms and offices, surprisingly low tech. Detainees weren't kept here for very long; they gave up what was needed—or didn't—and got shipped out.

Nobody ever talked about the ones who didn't.

Otter insisted that his success rate was extremely high, but because neither his work nor his clients officially existed, there was no record against which to check his claim.

Banks expected to find him in the viewing room down another dogleg in the narrow second-floor corridor. Two flat-screen monitors showed different views of the interview with Beya, and a long desk on the opposite wall held all of Otter's computers and monitoring equipment, but the big chair was empty.

A steaming takeaway Americano and a plate of warm khrustyky told Banks that Otter would soon be back. He sat in the chair and dialed up the volume on the interview.

"What time is it?" Beya was asking.

"Who made the bomb for you?"

The Basque shook his head. "No one."

The audio was perfect, surround sound and everything, from speakers Banks couldn't find. Gillian was taking the lead. "We were under the impression that your wife was the demolition expert. Do we have that right? Back when you guys hooked up?"

Beya's eyes danced back and forth between Gillian and Delia, his fingers drumming the table, his foot shaking. What pharmacological cocktail did Otter have him on?

"Where is she, your wife?"

"I did this alone," Beya insisted, in Spanish.

"Well, not entirely by yourself," Delia replied in perfect Spanish. "There's the albino dude you were barking at, couple nights before you did Arshavin, when the cops nearly caught you in Clichy-sous-Bois."

Banks watched Gilly lean forward and gently touch the Spaniard's leg. "We checked your house. Your wife's gone; your children are gone. What's going on, Xavi?" she asked him, like a mother trying to get her child to open up. "Who's pulling your strings?"

"No one," Beya insisted again. He wiped sweat from his face and hunched, staring at his trembling hands, grim. "Can you tell me the time?"

"See, that's just not believable," Gilly was saying softly, as she rose from the table to pace out of camera range, and Otter banged into the viewing room, startling Banks and carrying cream for his pastries along with some big-ass envelopes tucked under his arm.

"ETA made peace with the Spanish government years ago," Banks heard Gilly say from off screen. "Laid down their arms."

Beya said nothing. Folded his arms as if he were chilled.

"And why kill Ilya Arshavin?" Delia had a beautiful alto Alabama accent, melodic and refined. "What did he have to do with anything?"

Beya just stared at her. Defiant? Or scared shitless? Even on this great video feed, Banks couldn't tell. He needed to be in the room, but that wasn't allowed.

"Women should do all the interrogating," Otter said. He had wireless earbuds that were feeding him audio from Beya's questioning, even while he roamed. "The sheer torture of their unrelenting patience and kindness will break the strongest man."

"I thought you want women to get out of the workplace, make the happy home for their husbands," Banks said.

"I do. But. Meanwhile." It was always fun to see Otter try to thread the needle of his many dogmatic contradictions. He waved the envelopes, new subject. "Finally got back the MRIs from city clinic number five. What a fuckfest." Beya's festering stomach wound had been puzzling them for two days. Otter didn't have medical scanning equipment, and prying a mobile unit loose from the Ukrainian medical system without raising government interest proved a challenge.

Nula and Banks thought he'd been wounded by whoever was running him, and maybe they'd done a hasty patch-up that had gotten infected. Delia had thrown out the possibility of a tracking device, but there was no indication of metal inside the Basque. Organ theft was just a running joke.

"We have met the enemy, and he is us," Beya said to the two women questioning him, for what could have been the hundredth time. It was as if it were on autoplay—whenever he ran out of material, boom: say nonsense.

"Let's see what we have here," Otter muttered, spreading the film out, then holding each one up to a desk light turned outward. All Banks saw were swirls of color and shapes he didn't recognize. He wondered if Otter knew what he was looking at or was just vamping.

Frowning, Otter looked from the film to a couple of photos taped to the wall—Beya, shirtless, the ugly wound on his left side, below the ribs.

"Someone has put something in him," Otter said.

Banks got up to look.

"What time is it?" Beya was asking, on the double screens.

"What difference does it make? You got somewhere you gotta be?"

The film showed an odd shadow in Beya's side, translucent, inorganic, not normal. "They've put something in him," Otter said again, as if he couldn't wrap his mind around it. Then he added, "Plastic. What the fuck?"

Feeling horror rising, Banks glanced to the twin monitors, saw Beya sitting there in the folding chair, staring at nothing, pale, tears leaking out, his whole body trembling, losing his shit now and saying, over and over, "I'm sorry."

Delia asked him, "For what?"

How must it feel to know you're going to be vaporized by what's inside you? Banks couldn't see Gilly. There was no two-way communication with the interview room. His thoughts raced ahead of his movement, he couldn't form words, his feet felt glued to the floor, his heart was racing—

Otter said, "Banks?"

—he tore himself free and bolted for the door, throwing it open, not responding to Otter's question, whatever it was, just determined to get to the room that was just around the dogleg and—

—and—

—and his world came apart—

—the violent explosion from the interview room ripped through the walls of the second floor of the factory, more force than fire, splintering studs, shredding drywall, blowing out window glass, the force of its concussion punching through and lifting Banks and hurling him through one of the original plaster-lath walls into a storage room filled with beautifully etched mirrors that shattered when he hit them and, before he blacked out, refracted the hellacious light resulting from the rapid and violent oxidation of the bomb that burst from inside Xavi Beya into a beautiful chaos that, much later, Banks remembered thinking had been exactly and tragically right.

CHAPTER ELEVEN

She was walking back from the corral, on the phone with her son, when she saw the first plume of dust rise up from the road approaching the ranch.

A dry wind swirled out of the Pecos River valley and across the high plains; another lean year for mountain snowpack, the river was running shallow and warm, and the fishing, she'd been told by locals, was grim. But Sentro didn't fish.

Not for fish, anyway.

"No. Nobody strange has contacted me. I haven't seen anybody lurking and watching the house," Jeremy was telling her. "Mom, what's going on?"

As always, there was the internal debate she had with herself about how much to tell him. Ever since Sentro had come clean with her children about her career in the intelligence sector, she'd been walking a fine line between sparing them the ugly details and giving them the honest truth about where she'd been and what she'd done there.

"Some of my past sins may be coming back to haunt me," she said. "I just don't want you and Jenny to get pulled in."

"Again, you mean? Pulled in *again*."

"Okay."

"So what is it this time?"

Sun glinted off the windshield of the approaching car. Had to be a rental; whoever was driving showed no concern about blowing out the shocks.

"Mom?"

"Yes, dear."

"What the fuck?" His voice went up half an octave. Jeremy had nearly died the last time his world got tangled with Sentro's, on a cargo ship in a backwater South American port where would-be pirates had crossed paths with her. A series of unfortunate coincidences compounded by his naivete and her long legacy of lies. Their relationship still hadn't recovered.

"It's probably nothing."

"Your version of nothing is not the same as mine."

"Fair enough. Just . . ." She let the thought hang, and her mind wandered to a darker place: *If somebody who wants to get to me wants to get to them, they will,* she realized and felt useless for a moment. Parenting was a bitch, even when the kids grew up. "Just be aware," Sentro said. "Okay?"

"Like I could ever forget."

"Hawaii is nice this time of year. I'll pay for a week in an Airbnb; you could board Jenny's cat and take . . ." Sentro blanked on Jeremy's fiancée's name.

"Bryce-Ann," Jeremy said at the same time it came tumbling back to her. Too late. *Fuck.* It went downhill from there.

The Canadian special-ops man had parked by the time she got to the porch. He unfolded himself from his SUV and was stretching as her son rang off, nothing resolved. For a while he shaded his eyes to watch Clete and Jenny work with the horses; then he saw Sentro in the striped latilla shadows and walked in her direction.

Two blackened eyes, facial cuts, a hitch in his gait; Sentro had heard through her back channels about the suicide bomber at a black site in Kyiv. Arshavin's killer was dead, along with a couple of private contractors she knew in passing. There was a sadness to this young man she didn't remember seeing before—and she was positive that it wasn't something she'd just forgotten. He'd survived the bombing; she was sure of it.

"Aubrey Sentro," he announced, like he was pinning her to a bulletin board.

"Yeah. You don't need to tell me who I am or do that thing where you repeat everything you read in some file."

"A lot of redactions, actually."

Sentro just waited for him to say something else.

"Okay. Fair enough." He looked out at the corral again. Sentro followed his eyes to her daughter. A tremor of worry went through her. She would listen to his pitch, then send him away.

"Are you going to tell me your name, or is it classified?"

"Banks. Ryan."

Ryan. Toronto, she guessed. "I've been expecting you," she said. "Or someone like you."

Banks nodded. "I'm not CIA."

"No, you're not. You're too well adjusted to be with the agency. Is that, what, Ontario I hear in your vowels?"

"Guelph is where my family's from. Still there. I don't go back much, though."

"What do you want, Banks?"

"Glass of water would be nice. Cold beer would be friendly. That was a heck of a drive, getting here."

"Nobody asked you to make it."

"Well, yeah, in fact they did."

The Five Eyes was who Sentro was pretty sure had sent him. She studied Banks; his hollowed-out good looks, the sadness he wore like an overcoat sagging heavier than just from the death of some colleagues. She understood loss and recognized it in others, even if she was as clumsy and stubborn in managing it as this young spy seemed to be.

"Were you in love with her?" For some reason, she wanted to know. Sentro had decided, in retirement, to remove many of the filters she'd spent her career developing and refining. Guns into plowshares.

Banks took half a step back, as if sucker punched by the question. "What?"

"What was her name?"

He hesitated. "Gilly. Gillian."

"A fellow Canuck, eh?"

"Ha. No. One of you. A cousin."

"I'm so sorry. I mean, for your loss."

He shrugged, didn't say anything else. Disappointed with herself for scuffing a basic act of human decency, Sentro nodded and looked away, buying time to calculate how she might manage the big ask she guessed was coming next. A part of her wanted to say no and send Banks on his way; a part of her suspected that other part was fooling itself.

"Do you know who put the bomb in your unsuspecting Basque?"

"We think we do, yeah."

"And it's someone I know," Sentro said as it registered, turning away without bothering to let Banks answer. She opened the front door for him. "You'll stay for lunch, so you can tell your team you gave it your best shot.

"My daughter's a vegetarian," she added as he slipped past her into the indigo shadows of the low-slung adobe. "And she does all the cooking.

"Pretend it's delicious, okay?"

CHAPTER TWELVE

Leaping off his balcony was pretty much the last thing Ludor Lenkov might have been expected to do, but Madsen would blame herself for not stopping him if it came down to that, and she was so shaken by her failure with the man that she couldn't remember afterward if she'd taken enough time to erase herself from his apartment. She didn't want the Leipzig police asking around after her.

"Pogo," was all he'd said before he went over the edge. The whole thing had been a shit show, really. Arshavin's death was unraveling her.

Madsen had only worked for him since leaving military service. She'd chosen not to judge how he'd come to be a rich man. After ten years with the Bundespolizei's elite GSG 9 in the seventies, her father and mother had settled in Solms to spend their postmilitary lives grinding lenses for Leica, solidly middle-class jobs that nevertheless afforded few luxuries. Arshavin had introduced her to another world, and she loved him for it, even if some of his forays into the darker realms of gay Europe had made her job of protecting him a constant challenge.

Now he was gone, and she felt adrift. All she could cling to was an acute desire for payback and the knowledge that her boss had sold his soul to Lenkov—a junior-circuit wannabe compared to Ilya Arshavin—after the bombing in Madrid, and Lenkov, in her estimation, had been less than surprised by its happening.

A place to start.

Having followed the self-proclaimed copper czar from a breakfast with what looked to be a working girl in the Grandhotel Handelshof to the pointy City-Hochhouse skyscraper, where, she assumed, Lenkov would be doing business at the European Energy Exchange for a while, she had ducked into a department store to look at scarves. They were on sale. She craved a new Loro Piana. But the selection was disappointing, and the condescending treatment she received from the sales clerk—who, after a withering glance, took her for some farmer's wife instead of a professional who could easily have bought the entire stock, since she still had the platinum card Arshavin had issued her—guaranteed that her mood was foul when Lenkov emerged from the tower, bought his doner kebab takeout, and headed home to his Plagwitz-district penthouse. There was a driver and a security man, as well as a pop-up hipster bar on the ground floor that played annoying music. Madsen skirted the crowds of flanneled men and girls in leather, entered the parking structure through an emergency exit, left the driver (who had been conveniently idling in a loading zone, listening to hip-hop and checking his Tinder account) duct-taped in the trunk of Lenkov's A8, used the man's key card to access the private elevator, and found herself in the foyer of Lenkov's flat, staring at the pink chipmunk cheeks of the square-shouldered bodyguard (his name was Miller, or Müller—Charlotte had already forgotten) midway through his dinner.

There was a comical moment, the falafel wrap leaking greasily over his hands and causing him to hesitate before trying to reach under his expensive suit coat for the gun that he kept there. But it gave Madsen the advantage she needed. He was taller and massive, but in the time it took his brain to register what she represented and send a message to his limbs overriding any worry about dry-cleaning bills, she'd clicked across the parquet floor and planted the heel of her boot into his chest just so, fractured the sternum, and sent him backward, his head taking most of the weight of his fall and making a watermelony sound when it struck the floor.

Das war peinlich. She'd only wanted to neutralize him. If he wasn't dead, he would be fighting for his life in intensive care for days. *Scheiße.*

She stripped the gun from him anyway and listened for Lenkov. There was the distinct cacophony of a football match—fans singing songs, steady drumming, sharp patter of the play-by-play—but first her phone was humming.

Aubrey Sentro again. It had crossed Madsen's mind more than once, in her grieving, that Sentro's presence at Arshavin's shooting might not have been accidental.

She sent the call to voice mail with all the others.

The apartment had a beautiful view of the city, but Lenkov's decor left much to be desired. Twenty years younger than Arshavin, he'd been a struggling half-Georgian gypsy cab driver in Nizhny Novgorod until, as legend had it, one fateful night when he'd driven two drunken businessmen to the landfill south of the city and been told to wait. When only one man returned, hands bloody, face scratched, Lenkov drove him home and cleaned him up, read in the morning paper about a Yeltsin crony found strangled in the dump, and thus became personal assistant to one of the original Russian Republic oligarchs, who owned copper mines in Bashkortostan.

Three years of heavy drinking later, the oligarch's liver gave out, and Lenkov, using the secret he'd kept, contrived to take control of the entire operation. Like Arshavin, he'd more recently fallen out of favor with the current president and shuttled much of his fortune to Leipzig through intermediaries "just in case."

A nineteen-year-old Lithuanian fashion model had bewitched him to marry her, but she was in Vienna now, estranged, pregnant with twins, threatening an ugly, expensive divorce. So Lenkov was by himself in the study, a paneled room with barren bookshelves and a wall-size projection television on which RB Leipzig was having its way with Paderborn on an emerald-green pitch.

A small, soft man in a big, empty room, Lenkov looked lonely and lost until Madsen pressed the barrel of the bodyguard's gun to his temple. Then he looked terrified and furious, a useless combination. The last time she'd seen him, with Arshavin, Lenkov had been smug, almost giddy; quick to agree to loan Madsen's employer the money he needed, with the understanding that Arshavin would pay it back within thirty days or forfeit his shares.

Madsen's beloved Russian was dead less than a week later. And Lenkov controlled the Odessa pipeline. Twist of fate? Madsen didn't think so.

"Herr Lenkov," she said, in German.

His soft-boiled eyes were the only things that moved, a sidelong glance, with the soccer match shimmering reflected across them.

No recognition.

That was the nature of her job: invisibility.

"I worked for Ilya Arshavin."

"Where's Jurgen?"

"Is he your driver or the owner of this SIG Sauer?"

"What do you want? This room has cameras that go to my security people—"

"It doesn't, no, and Jurgen was the sum total of your security." Madsen had scouted the flat. "You're not rich or threatening enough to need more." *Die Roten Bullen* must have scored; Lenkov's surround sound boomed with a roaring ovation. She told him what she thought had happened in Paris: how Berlin intel had evidence that Lenkov's copper mine was tapping out and he needed an escape plan, how Arshavin's problem was the perfect solution to his problem, and how he'd decided not to let Arshavin cure his debt and instead had his hired assassin stalk Ilya to Paris, pull the trigger, and deliver the pipeline project.

"You're wrong," Lenkov told her, flop sweat starting to bead on his temple. The way he said it confirmed that she had some of the story right but didn't know everything—which was why she was there.

"Educate me," Madsen said.

"Shoot me and you'll never find out."

"Shoot you and I might. Kill you, probably not." It was an idle threat; Madsen had no stomach for torture.

The obstreperous Georgian in Lenkov came flashing out. "You have no idea. No idea what you're dealing with."

"Educate me," Madsen said again, unfazed.

"I'll need some guarantee you won't kill me after I do," he said, and she laughed. That was exactly what she was planning to do, but Lenkov took her momentary lapse of concentration as an opportunity to attack. He jammed her hand upward, away from his head, and the gun went off harmlessly. Caught off balance, Madsen fell clumsily onto her ass and watched the tricky little copper czar try to make a run for the balcony doors.

It got murky after that. She could easily have shot him but instead allowed him to go through the sliding doors and outside since, five floors up, there was nowhere for him to go.

She found her feet and followed him out. He threw something at her—a deck chair, a little table. All noise and no real menace. The city lights were beautiful, the breeze brisk.

"This was all Pogo," was what Lenkov said in total, or at least what she thought he'd said.

And then he was over the railing and onto the sidewalk below, and the alarm of the parked car his body had struck and bounced off was whooping crazily, its lights flashing.

He jumped. Or she might have thrown him.

Memory, in heightened circumstances, was a tricky thing.

Hurrying out, grabbing Lenkov's cell phone and leaving the elevator key card behind—intending to take the access stairs instead and, with luck, not be seen—she spotted them spread out on the marble kitchen counter: newspapers, several editions, in at least three languages. Front-page photos and coverage of a Spanish stock market bombing, the French accounts of the café shooting of Ilya Arshavin, Cyrillic headlines about a factory-district explosion in Kyiv.

Pogo?

Maybe she hadn't heard Lenkov right.

Chapter Thirteen

To Sentro's surprise, her daughter's meatless Hatch chili enchiladas were a big hit with Banks, who seemed not to notice they'd been (like most everything Jenny cooked) run through the deflavorizer. Banks even asked for a second helping, which proved useful because Clete, a bolt-and-run diner, had time to help Jenny clear plates and then amble, burping, out the front door before the Canadian circled back to the purpose of his visit.

Banks hesitated, though, when Jenny sat back down with them, and Sentro thought about kicking her out, too, but gestured for him to proceed. Whatever he had to say, Banks could say in front of Jenny. No new secrets. Just the old ones.

"She knows my shameful past," Sentro advised, trying to make a joke of it.

"Only the barest bones of it," Jenny pointed out.

"What does your cowboy think?" Banks asked.

"That she's some eccentric Texas oil baroness," Jenny said, amused.

"And anyway, if what you're going to tell me requires some kind of super security standing," Sentro continued, wanting to move off the subject of Clete and the alternate facts she'd told *him*, "I don't have the necessary clearance anymore to hear about it, either, so . . . give us HUMINT for Dummies, the unclassified version."

Banks said he was hoping Sentro would be the one to tell him things *he* didn't know.

As if she hadn't already guessed that was the case.

"Like what?" Jenny's eyes had a shine to them; from the moment Sentro introduced Banks, her daughter had been tongue tied and distracted. Sentro prayed this wasn't evidence of some latent genetic predilection of Troons for persons of intrigue (though she hadn't been one, hadn't even had a glimmer of becoming one, when her Troon met her) and their promise of chaos, heartbreak, and disappointment.

Unhelpfully, Sentro was flooded with fragmented memories of romancing her husband, more the feelings than the specifics; her love for Dennis Troon had been a powerful tonic, and it never wavered, even through the depths of their later troubles and the cancer that killed him.

"We've sourced the quote from Xavi Beya."

Sentro shook off the jumble of her random remembering. "Arshavin's killer?"

"His name was Beya. Yes."

Jenny frowned. "Your client in Paris *died?*"

Here we go, Sentro thought, and the next few minutes were spent trying to explain the shawarma shooting in the least sensational way. Banks proved useful in this endeavor, since Jenny seemed over the course of the lunch to have progressed from intrigued to smitten, despite what she was hearing. He kept it simple, matter of fact. She appeared more disappointed by Arshavin's death than shocked; Sentro had promised her children full transparency when it came to her former life in the game, and having heard some harrowing tales, both of them understood that there were sometimes tragic consequences of a life lived in the shadows. Not for her, she assured them. They took her at her word when she told them she was done with all that.

She was, wasn't she?

"It's a quote from a comic strip," Banks was saying when Sentro tuned back in, wondering what she'd missed.

"I don't remember what he said," she admitted.

"Mom has concussion syndrome," Jenny explained.

"I know. It's in the file," Banks noted.

"You keep files on people after they've retired?"

"Especially then."

"He's Canadian, Jen." Sentro couldn't resist teasing him. "*He* doesn't keep files on me. He *read* a heavily blue-penciled file that somebody in US intelligence shared with him, because spooks gotta snoop."

Jenny seemed to make a point of not reacting. Banks flashed her a tragic, grateful, wounded-warrior smile.

Sweet Jesus, they were *flirting*.

She got impatient. "Can you please remind me what it was that—" She drew a blank.

"Beya?"

"What it was that Beya said?"

"'We have met the enemy, and he is us,'" Banks recited.

Sentro was embarrassed the phrase had slipped away from her at the scene.

"Pogo," Banks said.

The name meant nothing to her.

"Comic strip from the last century," he continued. "Pogo was this unassuming, philosophical, everyman opossum in a swamp filled with colorful animal characters. Alligators, owls, hound dogs, turtles. Pretty political, for its time. Touched on McCarthyism, pollution, civil rights, Vietnam, Nixon. Walt Kelly was the artist. Strip ended in the midseventies."

Sitting back, shaking her head, Sentro shrugged. "You've lost me. Was the Basque a big comics fan?"

Banks took a moment, as if to organize his thoughts, but she could tell he was trying to gauge whether she was playing dumb. She wasn't. "It's also the code name your CIA station in Berlin gave to a wicked young East German Stasi spymaster in the late eighties."

A warning light flashed in Sentro's head. Her mouth got dry, her fingers tingled, her pulse thumped. Jenny's curious eyes darted to her mother. Sentro felt herself falling off a cliff, into a chasm of doubt. *Don't make me go back there, Banks.*

"His name was thought to be Günter Witt, but no one was ever able to put a face with the name or the code name." Banks stared at Sentro evenly. "Except you."

Jenny squeaked. "What?"

Sentro's head kept swinging back and forth, *no no no.* "I don't remember," she said, but she did, just not enough to make sense of any of it. This was the past that had begun creeping back up on her.

"Witt's dead."

"Or not." Banks shrugged. "Stasi magic trick."

"Wait. Is this about your secret fucking mission in Berlin before I was born?" Jenny asked, but Sentro and Banks ignored her for the moment.

Shifting the conversation sideways to get some distance, Sentro numbly guessed, "Beya blew up the stock exchange. It was three movements in one bloody opera."

"But not his show. Somebody had him by the balls. His wife and children are missing."

"Somebody." Sentro took a deep breath and then said, "Pogo." The code name felt odd on her lips. She was certain she'd never known it.

"Witt," Banks concurred. "And. You are, according to the CIA archives and case reports from Berlin Station, 1989 and 1990, the only Western espionage agent who has ever seen him or gotten close to him."

She felt both their eyes drill into her, for different reasons. Sentro had always been good at dissembling. She gathered herself, shoved back the terror and uncertainty that were buzzing through her head, and even managed a shadow of a smile, mostly for Banks. "I'm sure you're right, Ryan, if it's in the files. But I have these . . . well, blanks in my remembering. And that mission was so fraught, so traumatic for me—and messed up by the end.

"I remember going to Berlin. I was still a teenager. It was a lark. I get confused with the names and faces of my colleagues. But I do remember how the city had this incredible, electric energy, amped up by all the dark, disturbing romance of the Cold War, if you can call it that. I don't remember going to the Eastern sector, and I don't remember what I did there. Sure, I may have crossed paths with this man you talk about—"

"Günter Witt."

"—I may have even reported back to my handlers about having made contact before I got caught. I was young, I was ambitious, I wasn't exactly sure what I was doing—but believe me, Agent Banks, so much of what you've read in those records is a sanitized spook-life myth, conjured by armchair quarterbacks writing things afterward that they guessed were what had happened to me. The harder truth is that I was drugged; I was tortured. I lost my mind, a bit, to be honest, and only got it back because I had a husband who loved me and a baby who needed me, and I chose to let it go rather than dwell on it. Why would I want to relive it now, using the unreliable evidence of so many speculative hearsay accounts? All because the Five need to catch a ghost."

Jenny stared, as if riveted. Like she was holding her breath.

"You received commendations," Banks noted. "After that, they fast-tracked you right out of the army into CIA special ops."

"They did. But I don't remember what I did on the other side of the wall. I'm sorry. Most of what I do know, now? I was told about after. I'm glad, if it's all true, that I was able to do some good. I am. But these days, honestly, I find I've even forgotten a lot of what I was told." Sentro made a point not to look in the direction of her daughter, who she was pretty sure could see into her and would know which parts she was lying about.

She would have her reckoning with Jenny later. It was time the Canadian went away.

Banks bristled, stubborn. "Just give us a week. We have the resources to help you try to recover what you've lost."

"I'm sorry. No."

Clete came clomping back in, seemed to feel the tension in the room, and glared at the back of Banks's head as the Canadian pressed: "We need to know what we're dealing with. Who we're dealing with. As you say, the events appear linked; this has got to be part of something bigger. Something scary. We're running blind. Anything you can give us will be helpful."

Sentro remembered Arshavin talking about Madrid. *Something new,* he'd said. *Private sector. Other incidents. Truth comes from strange places.* He was frightened too.

"I'm sorry you drove all this way for nothing."

Banks stood up suddenly, his movement angry, his chair almost tipping. "So what do I tell the Five Eyes? That you don't give a shit about what happens in the world anymore?"

Petulance didn't look good on the Canadian spy. But how had Arshavin phrased it? *Not geopolitics, geo-economics?* Catching herself getting drawn in, Sentro tried to de-escalate. "One eye, two, five, fifty," she said evenly, "they'll have to do this one without me, Banks. Tell them whatever you want."

Jenny still hadn't moved. Banks let his eyes go across her as he turned and then found his way blocked by Clete.

"I'mma need to throw your sorry ass out the door, amigo?" Clete asked with his regrettable Bad Sheriff drawl.

"Go ahead and try," Banks chirped, almost as silly, looking road worn and frustrated, probably willing to get into it with Clete just for the release.

Sentro got up and between them, slipping her arm through Banks's to lead him out onto the porch and into the bright, hot, dusty day.

"I'm sorry."

"You keep saying that, but I don't think you are," Banks grumbled.

"I can tell you this about him," Sentro offered, wanting to give the younger agent something. She'd been in his shoes, and she couldn't help him; she *was* sorry, just not enough to overcome the sum of her misgivings. "It's not so much a memory as an afterimage. Like, the outline of something that was burned into me."

Something glimmered like a stray thought in the low rise north of her house and corrals. She felt a migraine coming on for the first time in months. New Mexico at high sun was a bleak, bleached otherworld, if you looked at it the wrong way.

They walked to his car. The day's ineluctable heat rippled off the hood.

"What happened in Kyiv? What you've already lost there? Barely scratches the surface of what could happen. If Witt is alive, you're dealing with the devil himself," Sentro warned Banks. "I want no part of it. And neither should you. Go home."

Chapter Fourteen

The Cuban girl centered her sight's crosshairs on the head of CSIS agent Ryan Banks and imagined the impact, the muted blur of blood and bone and brain when the NATO round went through it.

Reading lips was hardly her forte, but she could tell he was saying goodbye to the older American woman and that he didn't look pleased with whatever that woman had said to him inside the house, at lunch.

Aubrey Sentro.

What an unusual name.

They'd hiked in from the highway, she and Yusupov, after watching the Canadian agent's SUV turn onto the private road and disappear in a riot of dust. The albino had insisted they wear the annoying desert-camo jumpsuits he'd bought online "for the element of surprise," but for Mercedes Izquierdo, surprise was inconsequential. Whether she was seen or unseen, her endgame stayed the same, and there was only the one road in and out. They'd left Yusupov's creepy Cossack wingman, Burdovsky, to look after the car. He kept bitching about how sore he was from getting clubbed with the branch back in Basque Country. She was tired of his whining.

A burrowing owl made its rattlesnake noise, Yusupov squirmed, and when the Five Eyes liaison ducked behind the wheel of his rent-a-car, the gunsight found the American, allowing Mercedes to study her target's face for the first time.

Aubrey Sentro: bad haircut, no makeup, guarded expression. Eyes that felt uncomfortably familiar, as vivid green as Cuba's wet forests. This woman was younger than her own mother, by several years, and not so much pretty as comfort-food appealing; fit, smallish, and unassuming, which Mercedes had to remind herself could be evidence of a calculated deception. Carmen Izquierdo had always drilled into her youngest the importance of presentation, of glamour and mystery, for a woman; it was the first weapon Mercedes had learned to master. Long legged, lean, and fair skinned because, her mother told her, Mercedes's father had been a Russian diplomat who'd romanced her in a whirlwind affair and then abandoned them, Mercedes had been a beautiful raven-haired child who'd become, under Carmen's tutelage, a beautiful, raven-haired, heart-stopping young woman some men were afraid to even approach, while others mistakenly believed her perfection was their privilege. Many men had crashed and drowned on those rocks.

"Shoot her," the albino Chechen murmured.

Six hundred yards. Finger light on the sniper rifle's trigger, Mercedes wondered again why they'd been sent on this odd errand. America was a wondrous country; you could walk into a gun show and buy as many lethal weapons as you wished, then walk out with them in a festive canvas bag, no questions asked.

The target shaded her eyes, watching the Canadian agent drive away. Dust and the scope's magnification softened her features and exposed a melancholy Mercedes hadn't seen before.

What has she done? Mercedes thought. *Why would Fischer be afraid of her?* Mercedes knew he must be, given the tightness she'd heard in his voice after she sent him the picture from Paris.

"Hurry up. Shoot the bitch," the Chechen hissed. "And then we go."

No wind to account for. Aubrey Sentro cocked her head and seemed to look right at Mercedes—right into her—and she felt disoriented suddenly; her mouth went dry, her face hot. It rattled her. She struggled to keep her eye on the scope. Then the target turned away and offered the back of her head as she returned to her porch, where the younger woman had emerged. A daughter, Mercedes guessed, and felt a fleeting tickle of mourning for her own mother, and jealousy of this girl that was undeserved.

Her vertigo passed. Her breathing steadied. The burrowing owl rattled, then called; the rumble of the rental car on the road dopplered past and away. A smell of creosote was sharp in the heat.

Mercedes lowered the rifle, thinking.

"No." *Not yet.*

———

"Didn't I tell you?"

"You said she'd be a hard sell."

"No sale, as it happens." Otter sounded smug. "Now what?"

"I don't know. The committee will probably be pissed that I couldn't deliver. We go forward without her help."

Moths did their jittery dance of death around a ceiling light cupped in a cobwebbed grille.

The motel bar was a darkened alcove in the breakfast room, with an honor bar shelf of generic gin, whiskey, and tequila. No mixers, but you could buy juice or soft drinks in cans from the machine in the corridor that led to the lobby.

But there was ice. Plenty of ice in a huge, rattling stainless steel machine, with a big steel scoop and plastic buckets to carry it in. His parents' cottage on Georgian Bay had an old ice maker with a scoop and a bucket. It drew so much current it kept blowing the fuse box out and so was rarely turned on anymore.

"Ludor Lenkov did a header off his balcony in Leipzig last night," Otter said.

"I don't even know who that is," Banks told him. He was discouraged, and his Cuervo-and-tonic wasn't helping. It was a suggestion from a recipe card on the bar; a lightweight drinker, Banks never knew what to order or make.

"Lenkov? Nobody. Baby oligarch. But also the guy who held the paper on Arshavin's Odessa pipeline folly."

"Suicide for sure?"

Banks heard a vexed sigh on the other end of the call. "Did you tell her I was involved?"

"No."

"Okay, good. It isn't that, then."

"Isn't what?"

"Unrelated baggage between us. You know. Blood under the bridge. Not important," Otter assured him.

"I've seen some tape," Banks told him. "You grilling her in Berlin Station."

"Debriefing her," Otter corrected him. "We were all on edge."

"Maybe she really doesn't remember Witt. She didn't then."

Silence from Otter.

"I'm serious. Recent medicals from her stay at Johns Hopkins after the Porto Pequeno cargo ship dust-up are all up about possible memory loss—TBI and CTE. Persistent concussion syndrome."

"So I heard. Okay. Maybe." Otter didn't sound convinced.

"Tell me more about Lenkov."

"All I got."

"Another ex-Stasi knucklehead?"

"Too young for that. One of the pop-up kleptocrats that sprouted in Yeltsin's fertile garden of Russian Republic corruption. You coming back to Kyiv?"

"After I do the dog and pony with the Eyes. They're not going to be happy." Banks braced himself and drained his drink. "Anything to come back to?"

"I got new digs," Otter said. "An old Bandura shop, other side of the river." His tone dropped an octave. "We're gonna have a kind of a thing for Lewandowski, the girls, and Nula."

"A thing."

"Yeah. Tribute. You know. Be nice if you could be there."

"I don't know," Banks said, the weight of his grief over Gillian crashing down on him all over again.

"She'd appreciate the gesture," Otter said.

"She's real dead," Banks replied, cold, too hard, pouring a lot more tequila into his glass of Coke and ice this time.

———

The dream again.

Work camp, the augered holes in the ground; it's as if she can smell the soil.

Her skin itches, filthy; skim light slats down through the sewer grates, and she is suddenly aware of rain falling and water running over the sides. It eats away at the edges of the belowground cell in which she finds herself, undermining the slotted iron grating that locked her in.

She's soaked. If her hole fills, she'll drown. But somehow it occurs to her that by carefully clawing at one side, she might be able to create an escape route.

She grabs the bars of the grate and chins herself to try to see out into the yard. Her heart races; her breath comes short. Gray mist, rain falling harder; the rusted half-pipe huts are limned with light, and a well-fed, crimson-cheeked kid soldier standing in the shelter of an over-hang puts his gun down, walks out into the deluge, unzips his jeans, and starts to pee down onto the prisoner in the next hole.

She can hear the shout of outrage—Polish?—sees bruised fingers flutter up like trapped birds from below, rattling the bars, the soldier laughing but suddenly, half-emptied, making as if to take a step back, because the ground beneath his feet is giving way. He loses balance, and his golden pee goes everywhere, and the hole collapses in on the screaming prisoner and sucks the soldier down with it.

—*Hilf mir!*

Her husband's voice. Dennis. Speaking German. A language he doesn't know.

Soldiers sprint from cover, crowd the cave-in, so fearful about joining him that they're unable to pull their colleague out of the sinkhole that has swallowed him. They flail uselessly with the mud.

As quickly as they remove it, more floods back in.

Rain thunders down.

She has the feeling she's going to die.

From all her clawing and the water's erosion, a crawl space opens up around one side of the rack of bars holding her in. The rising water floats her up. She grasps the iron slats, and the grate slips to one side, leaving an opening that she tries to pull herself up through toward freedom, and she's successful in getting her head and shoulders out through the gap but is unable to squeeze any farther because her pregnant body won't go.

Which baby? Jeremy? Jenny?

High-beam headlights stab through the downpour.

Somehow Sentro has slipped free. She's splashing across the muddy yard to one of the Quonset buildings, ducking behind it as light sweeps past her. Into the shelter of an empty cinder block machine room, with huge rusting bolts jutting from the concrete pad where generators once were secured.

She can peer out through a cracked seam in the wall's corner, where she crouches, scared, shivering.

Out of the cab of an old hardtop four-wheel drive splashes the officer with the purple collar on his uniform and the angelic white-blond hair. In the stark storm light his eyes are flat shadows and his handsome face distorted, as if laid bare, all cruel angles and planes.

She knows him.

Death's apostle, fracking a mirthless smile.

Basted by the panic and commotion, Sentro's body jerks at sudden popping sounds—sharp, irregular exclamation points—and the knowing muzzle flashes in the falling twilight give way to a chilling hush—

—the yard has gone quiet. She strains to hear some sound of the soldiers, who can't have simply disappeared—

—or can they?

She presses herself into the cold block wall and waits for them to find her and—

———

—and was awakened, naked, sweaty, tangled in bedsheets on the wrong side, and Clete's hard body hot beside her where she normally slept. For a moment she didn't move, disoriented, still half-submerged in the swamp of her dream, feeling that cold dread of evil approaching, waiting for her pulse to slow, taking long, deep breaths to slacken the afterburn of imagined panic.

But something else made her body tighten again, something present in the house, moving, causing the air itself to stir almost imperceptibly.

She turned her head to listen better.

An unnatural deadness. A purposeful silence.

No, not something.

Someone.

Chapter Fifteen

She waited, hoping she was wrong.

Still nothing.

But Sentro could feel them—more than one, she guessed, hunters, in the main room, but already turning eyes to the hallway and calculating who might be in the rest of the house and where. The adobe rambled silent, long, and slender, a series of not-quite-square thick-walled additions over the years under crude, low, rough-hewn vigas that spanned wall to wall. Jenny's room was closer than where Sentro slept; they would find that doorway first.

Her pulse quickened. *What if I'm wrong?*

Her gun was in the drawer on Clete's side. A hot-pink "Freedom Barbie" NRA Second Amendment commemorative Smith & Wesson six-shooter with little hearts embossed on the custom grip, which Reno Elsayed had given her as a joke retirement present, because he knew she hadn't ever owned (or had any interest in owning) a personal sidearm. It was at least three things she hated in one absurdly glorious package, Reno had pointed out.

Go.

Silent, not quite wide awake yet, she shifted, turned, and stretched across Clete, her body waking his to what it assumed was more sex. She felt his big hands on her hips and his breath cool across the back of her neck.

"Hey now."

"There's someone in the house," she whispered. Saying it out loud made it sound so overwrought. They were in the middle of nowhere, and she would have heard it if someone had driven up. The drawer her fingers drew open was empty.

"Oh, I moved it," Clete explained, rolling onto his back so she could ride him cowgirl. "I was worried about rattlers in the stable; I took it out there and forgot to bring it back." *Like a normal person,* Sentro thought. His fingers gently traced the arc of her waist. "I might need a little fluffing after all that wine tonight."

"Clete, there's someone in the house." It didn't come out any better the second time.

He cocked his head and listened to hear what she had heard: nothing. "Prolly a coyote or a bobcat. Or . . . my little cougar getting spooked by the wind," he murmured calmly. "Did you leave that window in the big room open?" She liked him better when he *didn't* say so much, but he was already lifting her off him and starting to get up.

"What are you doing?"

"I'mma check it out."

"No, let me go." She tried to remember where she'd thrown her nightshirt.

He swung his legs off the bed. "Stay, darlin'. Stay. I'm bigger. Stronger. Younger." He said it all with his cocksure smile. Clete didn't know her history—what she'd been, what she'd done. *This is what he's been taught men do,* she thought, *protect their women.* Still shaking off sleep, she was trying to figure out a way to stall him without opening herself to what might be a long night of questions when he stood and stretched his glorious body in the darkness. His side silhouette, limned by faint moonlight, made her shiver, and Sentro felt foolish, suddenly, panicked for no reason except the dull aftershocks from Banks's visit and that troublesome dream she had now and then.

It was nothing; Clete was right. *Let him feel necessary.* Wasn't that what Dennis once admitted she'd unwittingly denied him?

Clete began to walk out.

"Whoa, cowboy. Put some pants on."

"I doubt critters give a goddamn what I'm wearing."

"What if Jenny wakes up?"

He winked at her—actually *winked* like the saucy American lothario in some cheesy old French film's sex romp—and stepped out lightly into the long hallway, his weight nevertheless causing the loose flagstone to shift under his footfall here and there.

She forced herself to wait. Fully awake, still on edge. Sat up and felt the air begin to stir again in a normal way, and the pressure eased and she released a big ragged breath when he called back from the main room, "Yep. Open."

Wait.

The room tilted then. She smelled it: perfume. She froze. So subtle she had almost missed it, the lightest whiff of the unfamiliar carried from the front of the house on a thermal. A scent not hers. Not Jenny's. Made light headed by a spike of adrenaline, she felt the violent rushing of that movement in her house she'd been so sure was coming when she awoke—strained for a proper sound to go with it, a struggle with an animal, or the skitter of escape and Clete's laughter, though she knew somehow it would be neither—heard instead to her horror a susurration that got cut off so savagely it could not have been anything good.

Jenny.

Her daughter was between her and whatever trouble Clete had found. And Reno's hot-pink fucking gun joke was in the stables.

———

The cowboy came into the room naked, full frontal, and Mercedes almost screamed when she saw him. He was beautiful. Broad shouldered and slim waisted, uncircumcised, with thick, ropy muscles and little blue eyes, so confident in his presence, in his power, unafraid—"Yep, open"—even when he finally sensed the shadow about to ambush him and turned directly into the path of the length of rusted rebar in the albino's hand, which plunged into his eye socket, through his skull, and punched out the back like a chisel through a coconut.

A hiss of air escaped his lips as they both caught him, she and Yusupov, so that his rubbery collapse wouldn't cause concern for anyone who might have been awakened by the whisper-chill of a cowboy's soul departing.

Vaya con dios, vaquero.

They lowered him to the flagstone, and the rebar clinked because they'd forgotten it would; for a moment they didn't move, listening, waiting for the house to tell them if they needed to worry about what came next.

Her eyes were still adjusting to the darkness. She'd put her long rifle back in the bag and had in her hand the silenced Makarov she'd purchased at the Phoenix gun show. The glow of various digital clocks in the kitchen plus the slanted light of the waning moon showed the full sprawl of the house in dim relief.

"Let's go get her." The albino openly itched for shock and awe. Mercedes knew just enough about this Aubrey Sentro to favor a more deliberate, measured approach. They had to assume she was armed and well trained, or why would they have been sent to deal with her? Plus, there was the daughter to consider, or whoever that young woman was. Also armed? Also skilled in the darker arts?

So many variables.

She took the lead down the corridor to the bedrooms. Small framed black-and-white photographs of empty, foreign streets composed a dotted line along one windowless wall, interrupted by doorways—to a bathroom, to a storage closet—and then another closed door. Bedroom?

The plaintive refrain of an old Cuban folk song kept cycling through her head for some reason:

Listen, friend,
don't stray from the path.
Listen, friend,
don't stray from the path.

Motioning Yusupov past her, she watched while he cleared the first two doors, then twisted the handle and unlatched the bedroom door. No squeak, it yawned wide. Mercedes slid to the opening, where a spoiled child's mess greeted her: clothes strewed all over the floor and chairs, brass double bed that looked like a large lazy animal had made a nest in it. The room smelled of savory and soap—*a young female*, Mercedes thought—but no animal or daughter was present. An open window was a clue they missed in the moment and discovered only later; it was a balmy night, letting a breeze in seemed natural . . . and anyway, if the daughter was taking a runner, how far could she get?

¡Óigame compay! No deje el camino por
coger la verada.

Holding the Makarov out in front of her with two hands the way she'd been taught, because she herself was a disciplined, tidy, obedient child, Mercedes crept down the rest of the hallway to the carved double doors at the end and used the silencer to part them.

A different scent escaped here: heavy, both male and female—sex and sweat overpowering the earthy adobe tones, as well as a gentle perfume Mercedes loved but couldn't ever find in Duty Free, much less Havana.

She was sure the room would be empty but swung in low and ready to shoot anyway. The albino, coming up uncomfortably close behind her, said, "Horses," and yes, now she heard the thrum of hooves on the prairie clay and siltstone, galloping away from the house, and by the time they got outside, there was not even a moving shadow on the plain to let her know which way they'd gone.

But she knew.

So did the chalky Chechen, who was already on his cell phone with Burdovsky, asking him to bring the car.

Listen, friend,

don't stray from the path.

Rolling her shoulders, she made her body relax. She'd let the two Russians take care of the hunting. She needed some time alone.

———

Sentro had barely enough time to pull on jeans and a hoodie and get to her daughter's room before she heard the intruders start to come down the corridor. Closing the door after slipping through it, she was surprised to see Jenny already awake, uneasy, eyes wide; evidently she'd felt the same weird breeze of someone in the house that Sentro had worried over. Without needing to say anything, Sentro had her daughter dressed and out the window into the yard in less than thirty seconds. It was a miracle Jenny could find anything in the scramble of her clothing, but miracles were what they would require now to survive.

They ran to the stables, where Sentro set the mustangs free while Jenny led Clete's pinto from its stall with resolute calm that Sentro recognized from her own odd talent for cool in the face of chaos. Clete's was the only horse tame enough to reliably carry two people. Old Sentro would have sent her daughter for help and stayed; new Sentro knew better than to press her luck, after all the years of pressing it. Jenny claimed she didn't really know how to ride bareback very well, but Sentro had seen her do it, and anyway, there was no time to find and rig a saddle; plus, her Freedom Barbie revolver, when she'd found it on the workbench, had only three bullets in the cylinder.

"Clete was trying to show me how to shoot it," Jenny admitted. Chasing off rattlesnakes was a lie. Poor Clete.

All her experience told Sentro that her cowboy had become collateral damage. The sudden sensation of void in the house as they left it had told her he was dead. She could still smell him on her, feel his calloused hands around her waist. But no tears spilled.

They had to go.

Having slipped the hackamore over its head and pulled the bosal snug, Jenny seemed to roll up onto the pinto like she belonged there, then offered a hand to help her mother climb up behind her.

"Where's Clete?"

"I don't know," Sentro hedged. "He can take care of himself, though."

Jenny didn't look convinced. "You're one with the horse," she said. She sounded so sure of herself. "Hold on to me tight as you can and lean wherever I lean."

Sentro wrapped her arms around her daughter and pressed her face against Jenny's straight, strong back and flashed on other times she had held her, promised to always protect her, smelled the same sweet familiar baby she'd given birth to, a scent she would never get tired of, and she braced for a ride she assumed could be brutal on her aging hips but would prove worse than she could imagine. With a nudge from Jenny's heel, the pinto leaped through the stables' back doorway and galloped into the inky expanse of Sentro's property and the BLM land beyond it.

For the first eight hundred yards she waited for the silent strike, the stray unlucky bullet outracing its own sound to find one of them—no, Jenny—in the darkness. She'd known it to happen. A sniper rifle with a night scope in the hands of a halfway-competent shooter they'd have no chance of outrunning once the interlopers realized she and Jenny had escaped. But sometimes even a hopeful bullet from a handgun could defy the odds.

Stop. She shoved her fear for her daughter away. It wasn't helpful.

Clete's horse raced across the prairie, and Sentro's bones screamed every time the hooves hit rocky patches, but no mayhem found them, and Jenny rode beautifully, and the crescent moon, sharp as a scimitar, leered down on them as they fled like normal people should.

Nothing useful or illuminating turned up on her first pass through the empty adobe. It was an old house, flawed and musty, which surprised her; Mercedes had always believed that everything in America was new and transient, that things were constantly being replaced by better things, more expensive things, the latest popular thing. That the past was forgotten.

She didn't like mysteries. Or surprises. The one time her mama had given her a surprise party, she'd burst into tears and run from the room. Hours later, found hiding in a cupboard in the neighbor's kitchen, Mercedes made Carmen promise never to surprise her like that again.

"Tell me what I need to know," she said aloud to the house, even though she wasn't sure what that would be. Everything about this detour into the American Southwest was a mystery. The target, the rationale.

What makes him care so much about you, Aubrey Sentro?

In the master bathroom she found prescription bottles for pills she didn't recognize. Vitamins, aspirin. A store sample vial of Aubrey Sentro's perfume, which she slipped into her pocket. No weapons of any kind here, or in the master bedroom. A collection of nice pantsuits and work clothes in dusty bags that hadn't been touched in a while. Sensible shoes. A man's leather jacket. Books about plants of the Southwest in a weathered, primitive breakfront. A box of junk jewelry. Two gold wedding bands, his and hers. A scuffed-up baseball-player bobblehead doll—*Pedro Martínez?* A perplexing absence of personal photographs or other kept memories of any kind.

The messy bedroom smelled faintly of lavender. The daughter, if that was what she was, was about Mercedes's size, if a little skinnier. Running shoes that didn't quite fit Mercedes. Sexy underwear hiding a plastic container with only some residue seeds and shake of marijuana. T-shirts with defiant slogans. A spare handbag had some old mascara and lip gloss that Mercedes kept, and two expired credit cards in the name of Jenny Troon. She took a stab at hacking into the girl's laptop, couldn't, and put it in her rifle bag for later.

Jenny. Jennifer.

Too many vegetables in the refrigerator, no meat at all. Diet Pepsi. Bunches of yellowing kale. A mango. Coconut milk, leftover blue corn enchiladas, and homemade yogurt that looked to have spoiled.

Her private cell hummed, and the screen glowed with the only name that ever called that number, and she answered in Spanish as she sorted through the scatter of papers on a messy old rolltop desk.

"*Hola?*"

"Is it done?" a whiny voice asked in Spanish, heavy German accent, passable grammar.

"I don't talk to you. Put him on."

"He's sleeping."

"Do I sound like I care, Wolfie?"

"You were instructed to report in."

"Wake him up. He can call me back." She swiped off, irritated.

Bills, junk mail, a stock-portfolio review, some pension documents. Another laptop that she'd have to hack later. In a bottom drawer, shoved to the back behind a tangle of chargers and computer cords nobody used anymore, where it must easily have been forgotten, she found a Lucite cube with snapshots on every side, one of those keepsakes that children gave to their *abuelas* for Christmas or just to remember them, far away. This one had faded pictures of a family from some indefinite past. Aubrey Sentro was easy to recognize, the frumpy hair and the fiery eyes; the two children, a boy and a girl, looking happy but suspicious that such happiness wouldn't last. The boy seemed fragile; the girl had a catcher's mitt tucked under her arm. There was a father (and husband?)

in one of them—or what Mercedes assumed was a father, since the girl favored his athletic good looks, and the boy had his eyes, not Sentro's.

Her cell hummed again. The screen lit up: Fischer. She answered and waited, slipping the photo of the two children out of its slot. Because of the connection and static, the thin tenor voice on the other end of the call sounded far away, which, since it was, felt romantic, old school.

"Why are you always so difficult?"

"I don't know. You molded me."

"Wolfgang thinks you despise him."

"He's an idiot, but he's right. I've told you I won't talk to him."

The sigh on the other end was of resignation, which worried her. She wanted more pushback; she expected it, didn't know what to make of this new development in their relationship. "So is it done?" he asked her.

"Why did you send me to do this?" she wondered absently, as if half asking herself.

"Who else could I trust?" he answered, elusive. Then he pressed, the way he used to, hard, cruel. "Is it done?"

She was waiting for it. She smiled. "No." Even over the white noise of the shitty connection, she could hear the intake of breath, feel the tension that was winding him up the way only she could do it.

"Who is she, *tío*?" she asked him, petulantly, pointedly, slipping the faded picture of the boy and girl into her pocket with the perfume. "And why do you want her dead?"

Chapter Sixteen

Like Sentro, Banks woke up naked, sweaty, disoriented, tangled in his sheets, but also clearly bewildered to find someone straddling his chest holding a pink pistol at arm's length, pointed down between his eyes. In the darkness it took him another evidently harrowing moment to place Jenny from his day at the ranch—Sentro could hear his shallow, anxious breaths—and while it seemed he could tell right away that she didn't know what she was doing, that made it scarier, Sentro knew.

"This is where it gets real tricky," she said and waited for Banks's eyes to find her in front of the window when the motel's twitchy neon vacancy light flared and made the curtain glow behind her. "You might be able to strip that gun out of her hand, or she might shoot you without even meaning to before you did anything."

"I'm not going to shoot you," Jenny announced, taking some of the raw edge off things, but the odd, amateur way she held the gun clearly didn't reassure Banks.

Sentro limped away from the window, favoring her hip. All the bones in her body ached from the frantic ride getting here, and it was why she'd had Jenny hop onto him instead of doing it herself. She wasn't sure she could have even made it up onto the bed. "Who's in my house?"

"What are you talking about?"

"In. My. House." She drew it out, letting her anger flare. "Somebody who wants to do harm to me and my daughter. And as there aren't really any other candidates, you either sent them or led them to us."

Banks reached out slowly and pushed the pink Glock away from his face. His hand curled gently over Jenny's, and she let him have the gun. Sentro thought her daughter might be starting to surrender to shock. Her face remained impassive, but her eyes had a manic spark. They hadn't talked about Clete since the stables, and his absence hung like a shroud over both of them.

"Where's the cowboy?" Banks wondered, on cue.

Sentro didn't respond, which gave him his answer. She appreciated that he didn't press for more. He put the gun to one side. She limped back to the window and cracked the curtain to scan the parking lot, empty except for the Canadian's rental SUV.

"Did they follow you here?"

"Not unless they had horses," Sentro said. "But I imagine they'll be coming soon."

"How many?"

She could see that Banks felt an urgency to get up, but (a) Jenny was still riding his chest, and (b) he probably wasn't wearing anything under the sheet. "Two that I know of. Their approach to the house must have been on foot, because I can always hear a car coming and it would have woken me up, so there might be another interloper—or two—back with their vehicle, because they sure as hell didn't hike in all the way from town."

Banks frowned. "You didn't get eyes on them?"

"We were pretty busy getting the hell out of there. What the fuck is going on, Banks?"

"I smelled a woman," Jenny said suddenly and, as if just surfacing to where she was, dismounted Banks and stepped off the bed to stand, looking awkward, across the room from her mother. Sentro stared at her, wondering how she could get Jenny safe and deal with this at the same time.

"I don't know who it could be," Banks said and pulled the sheet with him as he got up. Yes, naked, moving with an athlete's easy grace. "You sure it wasn't burglars or a home invasion?"

Sentro was getting impatient with Banks. "After what you told me today? And what I told you? That would be a pretty fucking unlikely coincidence." Angry with him or herself?

"Right. Shit. Look. If I brought them here, I'm sorry." His Canadian candor caught Sentro by surprise again; she studied him and worried about underestimating him, wondering what his true agenda could be. "I just wanted your help," he said, as if reading her mind. He flipped her the gun. "Pink."

"It is. Yes. Very."

Sentro checked outside again. There was only one dim pole light pooling in the parking area, and the washed-out colors cast by the motel's decorative neon trim and signage didn't add much illumination. The VACANCY light stuttered with a manic doom, but the darkness beyond the motel was absolute; the moon had set, and scattered clouds blacked out even the starlight. Perfect cover.

A fluttering half memory tangled through her thoughts: Three NLA rebels with a shoulder rocket scrambling across a parking lot in Skopje. Their ivory eyes sunk back, defiant, in the camo-greased hollows of their faces when they were finally strung out, shackled, on their backs.

They'd splashed their target before they got caught.

"Spook life," Sentro said to Jenny. "I thought I was done with it."

"Spook life," Jenny echoed softly. She finally looked scared.

"Lemme just get dressed," Banks said unnecessarily, and the women watched him gather some clothes and bang into the bathroom, catching the sheet in the door.

Sentro was trying to remember something else. From the blown op in Macedonia? No, something else. Her mind stumbled into its first real blank in months. Time slipped. Banks clattered around in the bathroom, faucet on, faucet off.

"Mom?"

The dark parking lot seemed to stretch and expand.

How many more times would she have to do this drill?

"Earth to Aubrey."

Sentro glanced back into the room at Jenny.

"Did you just drift?"

"No."

"You did, you drifted," Jenny said.

Stress will always be a trigger, was what the Baltimore brain doctor had warned her. She'd never thought about stress as anything but a minor inconvenience. It felt awkward and rote, but she was about to reassure Jenny that she wouldn't let anything happen to her when Banks came out of the bathroom, hair damp, in a T-shirt and jeans. He dug some clean socks from a backpack and sat to put on his shoes.

"There are only three rounds in this." Sentro held up the revolver.

"How did that happen?"

Sentro looked at Jenny. "I don't know."

"I have a SIG Sauer. Full clip." He dug in his bag for it.

Sentro shook her head. "You keep that one. Take my daughter somewhere safe. I'll draw them away from you."

Jenny yelped, "Mom!"

Banks stood up holding his gun, thumbing the safety, priming the chamber. He tossed Sentro the keys to his rental car. "No, you go. You know the territory. I might drive around in circles."

Headlights suddenly winked into view on the frontage road and grew quickly bigger, brighter. "Too late," Sentro said, weary of pointless chivalry and all the time and energy it wasted, and as she started to slip out the door into the breezeway, a burst of automatic gunfire tore into the frame and walls around it, shattering the big window but somehow managing to miss her.

Yusupov had decided not to make a meal of their approach; the older woman had to know they'd be coming, so it was more a matter of out-flanking her than taking her by surprise. Still slightly irritated that the Cuban girl had sent him to do her wet work (even though he knew that was why Fischer had sent him with her), he told Burdovsky to drop him off just beyond the perimeter of light, and then roll into the parking area at an angle, using the Canadian agent's rental car for a kind of cover but also ensuring that nobody would use it for a getaway.

The albino had taken the vintage "collector" Kalashnikovs out of the boot (there were so many different models at the fucking gun show it was comical—perfectly oiled and maintained, plus spare magazines, ammunition, and accessories, all in the original Soviet boxes); he gave one to his wingman and warned him to wait with the car.

Staying in shadow, Yusupov moved counterclockwise, keeping low, looking for the right place to set up. Proud Kumyk from North Ossetia, the albino was a bastard son of an arrogant minor warlord whom he'd betrayed to the Russian FSB during the Second Chechen War for safe passage to South America because, well, why not? His so-called father was an asshole; the Chechen cause was a shambles; Yusupov's principal interest was in survival. After wasting too much time with some impotent Al-Qaeda sleeper cells in Paraguay, he'd done a little mercenary work for Colombian cartels before the offer from the Cuban German who called himself Pogo came through. The albino had jumped at the opportunity to break free from lost causes, not to mention pursue personal enrichment, only to discover he was to be nothing more than a babysitter for the high-strung Mercedes Izquierdo on a scavenger hunt of a mission whose objective he still didn't understand.

Kidnap the Basque and his family, force him to plant a bomb in the Bolsa—that much was straightforward. There was a paying cli-ent somewhere who would profit from the chaos that ensued. Where things went sideways was in Paris. Beya had balked at carrying out the shawarma-café shooting, demanding to see his family, and they nearly got caught when their safe house was breached by police. The plastic IED that was surgically implanted in the unfortunate man in the wake of that seemed, to Yusupov, a reckless improvisation. But when the Basque was apprehended after his killing of the Russian target, it became clear that it was all of a larger piece: a bombing, a shooting, and then the deadly Trojan horse sent to whoever had taken Beya into custody. Mercedes had known the entire plot and withheld it from him. Why? And this part, the detour to the United States on Belarus passports, the stalking of the woman who had been with the shooting victim—even Mercedes seemed baffled by the purpose of it. They knew nothing about this American, Aubrey Sentro; the Canadian's threat, particularly when cornered, would be a given. Without support, with two unarmed women to worry about, his chances were slim.

Assuming the women were unarmed.

Yusupov knew better than to assume anything.

When a shadow suddenly separated from the shadows, he understood that it was a door opening and decided he wanted to keep the targets contained.

It was worth a chance; he opened fire. The flash of the AK momentarily blinded him. He heard his volley hit the motel and the sound of glass shattering.

There was no answer from the room. A shredded curtain fluttered and caught light. At the end of the breezeway he could see the turquoise glow of a courtyard swimming pool, which suggested his targets had a back way out of the room.

Yusupov took the gun from his shoulder and ran forward, into the light. For once, he thought, aware of the bitter irony, he wished the little Cuban bitch were with them.

———

Sentro had never much liked guns.

Watching your young, fragile mother put a .38 in her mouth and pull the trigger will do that.

Husband Dennis Troon used to say that her disdain was why she was so good with them. The hardware porn of make and model that many of her male colleagues enjoyed held no interest for her; a gun's sole purpose was to kill things, in her view, and she had learned in the field hard lessons of its empty promises and limitations. False sense of security. Illusion of power. Ignoring the obvious phallic associations—men and their tools—guns were necessary only because all the knuckleheads who kept her busy had them.

Like this one, who'd lobbed a long burst of bullets into the motel room, hoping to hit something and, no doubt, keep his targets contained.

Banks had tackled Jenny and covered her with his body. Sentro had stumbled backward in a storm of splintered wood and shredded drywall and landed on her already aching ass. Her ears were ringing. Something in her hip caught and stung. She scrambled to better cover, glancing back into the room to make sure Jenny was unhurt, keeping her gun aimed into the breach; saw the headlights again curling into the parking lot, disappearing behind Banks's rental, and tried to guess what the attackers were planning.

"Mom?" her daughter called out with a muffled shriek.

"I'm here. Stay down."

"They'll want to flank us," Banks said.

Sentro nodded. She felt him moving up behind her, his hand firm on her shoulder, and saw his SIG Sauer extended in his other hand, aimed at the open doorway just like hers.

"Now what?" His voice came at her muddled but close. His breath reeked sour of tequila and quinine.

She didn't hesitate. She felt the familiar composure come over her. Muscle memory doesn't forget. There was a threat to be managed, but making Jenny safe was her primary objective. "Guy with the AK will circle around back, as you say. Come at us from the courtyard, using the pool to his advantage. Driver will have been instructed to stay in the vehicle and cover any attempt to get away in your rental, but he won't want to miss the fun," Sentro mused. "I can tease him out. Deal with that if an opening presents. The essential thing is getting my daughter to your car.

"Pick me up under the office awning," was almost an afterthought.

She glanced back at the Canadian, saw a glimmer of the argument she expected, the reflexive, testosterone-fueled chivalry that made brave men so often cannon fodder for hopeless causes. But she watched Banks blink it away; in its place was respect, a deference to age and experience that the best field agents knew bettered their chances for long-term survival. He said, "Sounds like a plan." *Live and learn* wasn't just an empty meme, and the opposite was also true.

Finding Jenny in the darkness, Sentro told her, "Stay close to him. Do what he says."

Jenny had the thousand-yard stare of sustained shock. *Shit.*

"Jen."

Her daughter took a deep breath for courage, and her head bobbed twice. Their eyes met. There was a strength Sentro saw that her daughter didn't even know she had.

"It's going to be okay," Sentro added softly, and with one last hopeful look to the Canadian, she was up on her aching hip and darting out into the breezeway to bait her trap.

Chapter Seventeen

Struggling to unwrap the candy bar he'd been saving all day, Burdovsky just got a glimpse of the shadow that flickered out from the damaged door and darted low along the sidewalk to a breezeway before he fumbled the chocolate under the seat.

No sign of Yusupov, but that breezeway would lead to where the albino was planning to take his rearguard action. Uh-oh. Whoever the shadow was was flanking the flanking Chechen.

Something told Burdovsky it was their principal target, the American woman. A sixth sense; he'd grown up with sisters, the youngest of five children. Hide-and-seek with girls, he knew too well the way they moved. Or thought he did.

As he watched, the shadow hesitated and turned into the light where the breezeway split the motel units from the office. A woman's face, no question. Somebody's mom. Turquoise pool light danced on the wall behind her. Something pink in her hand.

Ambush, he told himself. A former soldier in the Russian army, Burdovsky considered himself a student of military strategy, although he hadn't scored high enough on the deployment exam to qualify for officer school; the fucking test was rigged.

The woman seemed to take a long, hard look at the car. He slumped down. She disappeared. If she'd seen him, she evidently didn't think he'd follow. She was wrong.

Burdovsky took the Kalashnikov off the seat beside him, made one last stab at the candy under the seat, and came up with nothing. In less than a moment he was out of the car, moving, sidestepping across the parking lot, eyes on the shattered motel room door in case someone came out that way, feeling the hot buzz that came from doing something, bringing mayhem instead of waiting for it to happen to you.

He was on a mission to save the albino and show the Cuban tart and the condescending Chechen motherfucker what was what.

———

The courtyard pool water heaved, clotted with a swirling mat of leaves. Light shone up through them, eerie, casting its rippling, lurid colors across the back of the motel, reflected off the sliding doors like they were mirrors, blank, harmless—except for the one that was dark and open.

Yusupov drew back into his cover and scanned the courtyard. Had they already come out this way?

After firing at the motel room, he'd not expected to see the Sentro woman run out. Because he was also on the move, she was down the breezeway and into a walkway before he could register it; all he could do was run parallel to the direction he'd seen her take. He stole under the big plaster driveway awning and slipped past the office with the motel check-in desk, behind which, through the big glass window facing the drive-through awning, he could see a night clerk cowering in the wake of the gunfire, pleading with someone on her phone. The albino's command of English was poor, but he guessed it would be the police she was calling, which meant he was on borrowed time to get his task completed.

There was a narrow service road that cut behind the motel and a line of small windows for the units with courtyard entries. The only access door was steel, reinforced and locked—perhaps the American had

Daniel Pyne

locked it after going through—and while he was momentarily tempted to just blast it open, he knew that would be stupid. He'd fucked up. He had to either retrace his steps or run to the end of the wing of units and hope he could access the courtyard on the far side.

Luckily, he could. There was a low fence and some drought-ravaged shrubbery that he was able to vault, enabling him to find temporary cover in a utility nook with coin laundry and an ancient, humming soda machine leaking wan light from its front panel.

He could hear a siren, faint but growing louder, whooping forlornly in the vast emptiness of the prairie. Time was compressing, and he needed to adjust again; satisfied there was no one in the courtyard, Yusupov began to creep along the concrete deck, around the pool, rifle barrel sweeping back and forth, his finger on the trigger, his eyes on the dark square where the sliding doors were open. The smell of chlorine stung his nose, the brackish water heaved, the pool's light rippled manic, despite the absence of a breeze—and before he could fit these odd puzzle pieces together, a shape was surging up out of the leaves and the water near the pool's coping and something sharp punched into the side of his head and then the world roared and a bright fire flashed twice and he was down on the deck, stunned, breathless, unable to move his arms or legs.

———

Three rounds were not enough, except in the movies. You were taught to aim center mass and double tap for a reason. But that left Sentro with only a single chambered round and at least one other shooter at large.

Pool water rivered from her as she stood over the pale albino man, whom she hadn't quite managed to kill. She had waited, waist deep in the shallow end, until she heard the distant siren and saw a ghostly face under a white halo of hair vault over the courtyard fence; then she'd slipped under the surface, knowing the leaves would help hide her,

116

holding her breath and watching the turbulent shadows at the far end of the pool, hoping he'd be impatient, hoping she could stay under long enough to give her a good, clear shot. Having the six-shooter was in this case an asset; less likely to misfire when wet.

Her lungs were burning when his rippling silhouette finally floated up to the edge of the decking; she rose and fired in one smooth motion, but the sign with the pool's liability disclaimer was in front of him; both shots were deflected, one sailing harmlessly wide, the other glancing up to strike his forehead as he limboed backward in self-defense.

He was breathing, his wild pink eyes open but unfocused. The head wound bled slowly, matting the colorless mop of hair, dripping to the concrete, where it swirled away in the puddled water from Sentro's clothes. A fleeting, fractured memory of a similar scene from her past or a dream teased Sentro but wouldn't settle. It skipped away, and she shivered, looking down at a man she couldn't bring herself to kill— didn't want to waste her last bullet, had no appetite for other options. If the man didn't die from his wound, it was likely she'd regret it. But the siren kept coming closer, and it might be better if they weren't on site when it arrived. She puzzled for a moment over where the woman she'd sensed in her house could be. Still back there? Why? She hoped Banks and Jenny were already in his rental.

She kicked the wounded man's Kalashnikov into the pool, then reached into his jacket for the pocket litter: Belarusian passport, money clip, some sugar-free gum, and an old, foxed ferryboat boarding pass, folded in half, with a fifteen-digit number and some Cyrillic writing on it. Eyes fluttering spastic, darting, watching her, helpless; the albino's bluish lips gaped as he struggled to draw breath.

There was a scuffling noise in the pass-through behind reception. She slipped the passport and boarding card into her pocket. Voices echoed into the courtyard: Banks, Jenny. Why weren't they in the car?

Metal on metal, a sliding door scraped open to the courtyard, and Sentro whirled toward it. Two children in pajamas stood in a darkened unit's back door, eyes wide, the smeared flicker of a television behind them. A boy and a girl. Sentro thought of her own children, wondered where the parents of these were, worried that they had seen her shoot a man in the head, and she didn't know what to do except put a finger to her lips, whisper, "Shhhhhh," and wave them back inside.

Scuffling footfalls erupted in the pass-through, along with Jenny's stubborn "No no no!"

Sentro was already heading toward the disturbance when she heard the frightened kids whisk their door shut again and lock it.

———

The driver didn't speak English, so there would be no talking him down. Banks was angry at himself for letting it come to this. He'd watched the man spill out of his car and stalk Sentro's movement, just as she'd intended. But Jenny Troon had followed Banks out the door when he made his move—he'd neglected to tell her where he was going, and she naturally assumed they were headed to his rental—so when he crept up behind the unsuspecting gunman and whispered for the man to stop, get on his knees, and lay his automatic slowly down to one side of him, Banks got confused by the flicker of menace in the man's backward glance. Then Banks looked and saw it too: Jenny, frozen in the breezeway, realizing her mistake.

That momentary disconnect, the incidental distraction of Banks having to account for her, enabled the gunman to make his move. He blocked Banks's gun upward with a forearm and launched himself backward into Banks with his shoulder and his head. They sprawled on the pavement, grappling for control of the SIG Sauer, and when the barrel swung toward Jenny and Banks felt the man's finger slip through the trigger guard, he made a calculated decision to let go of the gun rather than risk it going off and killing Sentro's daughter.

The man scrambled up and barked at them in a Russian dialect Banks had no hope of even slightly understanding. Jenny barked back at him, scared but defiant; Banks told her to stay quiet.

Gunshots erupted in the courtyard, and all three of them froze. Two rounds, a rush of water, the slapping of waves on the side of the pool.

Banks sized up the indecision that flickered on the gunman's face as he listened to the quiet that spread afterward. It looked like the Russian wanted to call out to his partner, but he checked himself.

They all heard the siren too. Wailing, growing louder, a lonely lament.

The gunman's attention drifted over Banks, to Jenny Troon. Perhaps assessing how he could leverage her in case the courtyard hadn't gone his way.

And then Banks watched a different idea click into place. The man's cold gray eyes clouded, glazed with indifference.

He was going to kill them, then get the fuck out.

Banks had seen the look before: on the *goz* lowlands of eastern Darfur, off an empty back street in Bangladesh, in a Syrian refugee camp near the Turkish border. But never directed at him.

His scalp tingled; his mouth was dry. The gunman got awkwardly to his feet, Banks's SIG aimed unwavering, running shoes scuffing the walkway.

Banks eased sideways, trying to get some distance from Jenny. "Me," he murmured to the man, buying time. "Me first."

He heard Sentro's daughter's brave, stubborn "No!"

He watched his own gun swing around and stared down the barrel, imagining he could dive into its cruel darkness and change what was going to happen.

Then the gunman's head snapped forward, like a puppet whose string got cut, and Banks was misted with sweat and blood and cranium gristle and the man just folded over and dropped, as if rendered boneless by the last bullet in Sentro's pink revolver, at the other end of the pass-through, more than forty feet away.

Nobody said anything while they ran to the rental car.

Sentro told Banks to drive, with Jenny riding shotgun; she slumped in the back and told her daughter to guide him to the fire road that snaked away from the motel in the opposite direction. The flashing bubble pack of the sheriff's Escalade was racing up the frontage road, headlights winking.

"Where are we going?" Jenny asked, her voice hollow and small. Her mother didn't answer. Banks guessed maybe she hadn't thought that far ahead yet.

For a while Sentro stared out the rear window into the darkness, unreadable, and nobody said anything. Jenny looked drained. The road they were on followed the sandy lows of an endless arroyo.

Vast above them, the star-washed sky was more amazing than anything Banks had ever seen, even in the remote northern reaches of Saskatchewan, where you could go a hundred miles without seeing another car on the highway.

"Banks?" Sentro broke the silence finally.

"Yeah."

"Kyiv," Sentro told him.

"Excuse me, what?"

"Take me to Otter," Sentro said, and Banks didn't even bother to ask how she knew.

———

Smoke and embers wheeled across the ceiling. The house was on fire as Mercedes walked through it one last time in a daze fueled by rage over what she'd heard from Fischer on the phone. Tears streamed down her face, perhaps from the smoke, but most likely from all the lies. Out the door, off the plank patio, across the stubbled yard, irritated that the albino hadn't come back yet and knowing she should get some distance from the flames before the propane tank exploded.

An agitating confusion rattled her; her world had been tipped on its side, and everything in it was heaped in an angry jumble. If what he'd said was true, she wanted the Sentro woman to have nothing to come back to. She wanted her running, cast out, the way Mercedes had felt most of her life.

Dawn leaked up the horizon, the blush of orange announcing another hot, rainless day. It reminded her a little of Spain, where Fischer had taken her twice as a child, to a little village in the Meseta Central where he would meet with a group of old German men who looked broken and bitter and argued and drank until they passed out, every night.

Dust on the road in told her someone was coming.

She drifted to a place where she couldn't easily be spotted, took from her bag the long rifle, and raised its scope to her eye.

If it was the gringa, she wouldn't kill her until she got more questions answered. This wasn't so much because Mercedes thought she'd been lied to as that she suspected she hadn't heard the whole truth.

She didn't want to think he would lie to her. Or what that would mean. A lie about a lie? She wished she could call her mother but wondered if even she would have told her the truth.

She wiped tears from her face with her sleeve.

Listen, friend,

don't stray from the path.

The approaching vehicle came into focus, dipping in and out of the crosshairs of her rifle's sight. Even in the morning's gloaming, even though the unfamiliar truck's interior was dark, she could make out the hazy pale of Yusupov's hair, the craggy shadows that were eyes, the outline of his knuckles on the steering wheel.

The propane caught, and a fiery explosion was unleashed behind her. She didn't flinch. She dropped the rifle and hunched her shoulders and covered her head with her arms, but no debris blew out to where she was. Glowing embers of the demolished half of the house were still floating down when the albino rolled up in an old, sun-bleached Ford pickup.

No Burdovsky. The news would be bad.

When a side window came down, she looked in at Yusupov and winced. Shocking, clotting blood had sheeted down the side of his head from a wound high on his temple. One of his half-mast pink eyes had flared a hellish red from broken vessels.

"The bullet did not go into my head," he explained slowly, as if struggling for each word, and unnecessarily—if it had, Mercedes thought, he wouldn't be here.

"And the target?"

A slight, painful shake of his head. She was strangely relieved.

"Where's our car?"

"This one will be less conspicuous."

Ah. It wasn't hard to read between his words. She didn't need to ask about his missing *jamonero* wingman. She didn't ask what fresh hell had gone down at the motel with Aubrey Sentro. She didn't get in the truck; still simmering in her silent fury, she considered for a moment just blowing a hole through the albino and dragging his body into the smoldering ruins of the adobe house to add another layer of useful confusion as to what might have happened there. And why.

But she knew she might still need him. Getting out of the country had become significantly more complicated.

No te rajes.

Sunlight creased the eastern plain, turning the ground smoke swirling from the house pink and gold. The acid smell of the cowboy's charred corpse stung. Mercedes left the sniper rifle and the Makarov and all the phony paperwork in the carryall and walked around the pickup to the other side.

"You look like you've been crying."

"The smoke," she snapped. "Shove over, you are not driving."

He did so, grunting, hurting, chastened, self-consciously wiping his blood from the headrest with the sleeve of his shirt. Looking back at it, much later, if she'd known right then about the passport he'd lost, she would have shot and killed him, for sure. And perhaps everything would have turned out differently.

Part Two:
IN WHICH SHE TRIES TO SAVE HERSELF FROM HERSELF

CHAPTER EIGHTEEN

She expected to be totally freaked out.

People had come to kill her mother. She'd watched a man die.

Like Alice, she'd tumbled down into her mother's fever dreams, one of the stories she'd promised to share with her children but that, when told, always felt tentative—heavily censored, stripped of emotion, distant and incomplete. Well, this was no story; this fucker was happening, immediate, hectic, visceral, and Jenny was part of it.

There would be no waking up.

She felt numb; she felt fear but somehow wasn't all that scared anymore. And she didn't want to look away.

"Jenny, I need you with me," her mother had said, and the words had thrilled her, even if, yeah, she was well aware that it was only because the two professional spies had decided there was nowhere to stow her that was safe.

I. Need. You.

Albuquerque to Los Angeles with a shopping spree in Duty Free; they'd left everything at the ranch when they fled it. LA to Frankfurt required passports Banks conjured through some kind of spook magic in less than two hours; from Frankfurt, a commuter flight to Boryspil International Airport, and a taxi took them to a fancy hotel in downtown Kyiv.

This, Jenny kept telling herself, was her mother's real life. Exhausting. Exhilarating. Every moment had a raw edge to it; she felt a strange electricity from merely being alive. It was like stepping into the batter's box, late innings of a tied game, runners on base, and a pitcher throwing wicked inside-out risers nobody was able to get a bat on.

A feeling Jenny hated but also missed.

No wonder, even with babies and a guy she'd been crazy in love with, Aubrey Sentro wouldn't give it up. In this fraught new setting, her mother wasn't so much changed as she was exposed.

Around Banks they talked practicalities: meals, travel, logistics, barely skimming the surface of the harrowing events they'd just survived. And Banks was always with them. A solid, reassuring presence; when he stood too close, Jenny felt a dizzy charge. She found herself doing that thing, that stupid thing, where she avoided eye contact and pretended he was nothing to get worked up over.

If her mother was aware, she made no comment. They danced their dance, avoiding sore subjects, like Clete and the horses, putting off discussion of what they both knew needed sorting out at some point; grudgingly gifting each other the space to get through whatever this transitioned to, without adding any extra family drama. There'd be tons of time for that. If they survived.

Time zones skipped, a lag set in. The fractured past loomed and cast long shadows; everything that was happening now looped back to it, but Jenny knew her mother well enough not to ask.

Wait. Wait.

The white rabbit raced ahead of her, all mysteries to be revealed.

———

"How long has it been?"

"Not long enough." She meant it. A reunion with Henry Otter was something Sentro had hoped she would never have.

"That's funny. You were always a hoot." Otter didn't smile when he said this.

"Was I?" Sentro had insisted on a neutral location. Otter for some perverse reason had chosen the Hydropark and the tourist attraction called Kyiv in Miniature on the banks of the Desenka River near where it merged with the mighty Dnieper. She stole a glance to the parking lot; she'd brought Jenny along because she didn't want her left alone at the hotel; Banks agreed to babysit and was no doubt hoping to eavesdrop on the two old American ops, but Sentro kept Otter moving, a tactical reflex because there were still no guarantees she hadn't been followed, wasn't being watched.

"Your kid is fairly easy on the eyes," Otter noted.

Sentro wasn't keen on small talk, especially about Jenny, specifically with Otter. Her personal life remained off limits. "What kind of spook fuckery have you dragged me into?" She couldn't help falling back into familiar locker-room talk, the inside baseball of espionage; she and Otter had such a long, troubled history, only part of which she remembered clearly. They made an odd couple, strolling among the tiny replicas of Kyiv's famous buildings like Gullivers in Lilliput. Otter was compact, his steel wool hair still thick and uncombable and his arms jacked and bowed out like pot handles from too much upper-body work. His stroll more waddle than walk.

"Me? Me? I'm not the one rubbing elbows with skeezy oligarchs in Paris," he said. "Or rabbiting after Five Eyes rendition units while claiming, *Ooo, I'm outa the business.*" He grinned, revealing a missing tooth that made him look even more disreputable.

"Oh, I'm out, all right. And for the record, I don't think I've ever said *ooo*. Wanting to stay out is why I'm here."

"That's bullshit. Hell, Aubrey, you're one of those . . . I dunno. I mean—like, they'll have to carry you off on your fucking shield."

"People change."

He studied her with empty, feral eyes, then seemed to try to dismiss the thought. "More bullshit." He faked outrage that she saw right through. "And anyway, you think I have some say in the matter? Any of us? Suicide bomber blew up my fucking facility."

"Your torture chamber? Your black-op prison?"

Otter ignored her. "Three good operatives dead. Another one missing some important pieces, prolly the end of a brilliant career."

"Why would *you* be a target?" she wondered. "I mean, other than the obvious: you're a mercenary piece of shit beholden to the highest bidder, a hired man who toils for so many different masters it must be impossible to keep track."

"Mostly on the right side," Otter said defensively.

"How can you tell?"

"At least I'm a team player."

"Well, what does your team think Witt is up to, blowing things up, shooting my clients?"

"You're veering into classified territory, Aubrey. Eyes only and whatnot."

This got under her skin. "You owe me this. I saved you, Hank. You and the others. Back in Berlin." She knew how much he resented it.

Otter went quiet. "Nobody asked you to," he muttered.

"Nobody had to," she pointed out.

They did half a circuit on the paths without saying anything. Otter took out a tin of dip and slipped some tobacco between his lip and teeth; as a seeming gesture of conciliation he offered the can to her, but she declined. "Banks seems to think the Basque was at the least an unwilling deliveryman," Sentro said, still hoping to get something useful.

"They all are, aren't they?" A cold wind was coming off both rivers, swirling around the island. He shifted gears, no subtlety to it. "Banks lost a friend in my shop. American. Another dark star for the wall at Langley."

Sentro wanted to know more but didn't want Otter to get derailed. "The Basque's family was the leverage?"

"Likely. Civil Guard found their car in a turnout, signs of a struggle. A man can be made to do the craziest things to save his wife and kids."

"You'd know." For a while in the late nineties, Otter became infamous for devising cruel, devious Manichean stratagems with which to compromise and coerce useful idiots. Then sold them to the highest bidder, friend or foe.

He barked an ugly laugh. His gaping teeth flashed brown. "You're not really making points with me here, girl."

"Any word? Have they been let go?"

Otter shook his head as if to signal that he didn't know, but in a way that told her he was holding something back again. Both of them stopped at the same time and stared at the gloomy replica Horodecki House, with its riot of architectural chimeras—mermaids, dolphins, falcons, frogs, and African trophy animals; sinking ships and gargoyle catfish ensnared by the stems of lotus flowers. The little art nouveau structure rose as if fleeing, panicked, from a thick flash flood of autumn leaves.

Sentro knew how it felt. "How can you be sure it's him?"

"The Basque's last words were like a riddle," he said.

"Pogo."

Otter nodded.

"Nobody ever told me that was his code name."

"No shit?"

"No shit."

"That sucks." But Otter didn't seem too upset by her complaint, and she knew that it wouldn't have been his decision, anyway, so she let it go.

"I guess he wants us to know he's behind this." It was a question that she'd framed as a statement. Otter shrugged his big shoulders again and looked away, evasive. Sentro shook her head. "Why?"

Silence from Otter. She traded unreadable looks with him; then he started walking again, and she had to follow.

"Why, Henry?"

"Did I say anything that would suggest I would know?"

"All these years he's stayed completely off the grid. Off your radar. Where do you and the Five think he's been hiding?"

"Wherever he wants," Otter pointed out. "Prolly in plain sight, is my guess. As you are the only one on our side who knows what he looks like."

Sentro resented the insinuation that she hadn't told the truth about her nightmare in Berlin. "Not counting all the East German state security brass and support staff who have, what, covered for him? Really? For thirty fucking years?"

"*Schild und Schwert der Partei*," Otter recited. *Sword and shield for the party* was the Stasi motto. "He had so much fucking kompromat, from all the agents and informants he ran. On both sides of the wall." He turned his head and spit.

Sentro knew he was right. Even after all this time, German reunification was imperfect. East resented west, trust was so fragile, and spymaster Günter Witt had become the stuff of myth for certain angry revanchist Ossi who yearned for their former communist Eden.

"Which is why," Otter continued, not even bothering to be coy about it, "it could prove helpful to have someone who knew him back in the day, even if she can't remember his face. Give us some insight as to what makes him tick. Where he might have landed. What he'd be up to." He held her with his guileful eyes, and she shuddered. Same old slippery Otter.

"I didn't remember him then; I don't remember him now," Sentro told him.

"So you say. So you've always said." Of course he didn't believe her; no one ever had. All these years later even she wondered why she drew a blank.

"Plus, I'm retired."

"He's afraid of you," Otter said, ignoring her.

"What?"

"Afraid. Yep. Of you."

"I seriously doubt that."

"For what other reason would he bother to send someone after you, Aubrey?"

Sentro decided it was best to say nothing and see where Otter went with it.

"It tracks, you gotta admit." He fashioned a cartoon frown and slid her a sidelong, melodramatic look. "You were a ferocious little brat."

"I didn't know what I was doing."

"Okay. And yet, for a crew of Agency assets and case officers you were barely aware of and had no operational responsibility for, you sacrificed yourself. Endured however many months of imprisonment and torture and God only knows what else at the hands of the most cruelly efficient state security service the world has ever known. And lived to walk out and tell about it."

Had she? That was more or less what had been written in the final white paper on her ordeal, and her signature was on the last page. But she was nineteen years old, posttrauma, desperate to get back to her new family and heal, and what loose fragments she remembered of that ordeal were, in fact, a disappointment for everyone. Otter and the others—older, worldly (or just more worn down)—never accepted the official story. They were sure she was hiding something. Covering up the terrible secret of how she'd survived. To think otherwise would be to admit they owed their lives to an inexpert errand girl sent in (they insisted) by the Defense Intelligence Agency and a cynical CIA Berlin COINTEL desk as an unwitting swallow to unmask Günter Witt.

"I'm having a real hard time believing," Sentro said, trying to take back control of the conversation, "that he just disappeared from the radar of every Western intelligence agency after the wall came down."

"Welp." Otter shrugged again. He spit into a drift of leaves and had to wipe his face because the breeze sent some spray of it back at him; Sentro sidestepped and felt a little queasy. "There were rumors the KGB had him killed so he couldn't sell what he knew to the West. There were rumors his own comrades killed him because of what he had on them." He waited, then obviously tried to hook her again: "Feel free to speculate. That's pretty much all we're doing."

She didn't take the bait. "We? Since when are you and the Eyes a 'we'?"

"Team player, Aubrey. Like I said. At the end of the day, I'm still a flag-loving Yank. Give me liberty or, you know, death, whatever. I still got a moral compass."

It was nice that he thought so. Over the years since Berlin she'd crossed paths with Henry Otter more than a couple of times, but the names of the places escaped her, and on the nature of those missions she drew a blank.

What she did remember was wondering each time if she could trust him. And knowing that she couldn't, not really.

"Sure you do," she lied, and he seemed pleased by her saying it. "I just wish I could be more helpful," she added, another lie. Like it or not, she needed to keep Otter close as a matter of survival.

She glanced absently to the entrance, where Banks and Jenny were waiting by the car that had brought them all here. They looked deep in conversation. She wondered which one of them she should be warning about the other.

"Good luck if you're planning to spend the rest of your life running away from him," Otter pointed out.

But that thought hadn't crossed her mind.

She breathed in the humid river air, felt the force of it flowing past the island, relentless. It was time to tell her daughter about what had happened in Berlin.

Or at least, a version of it she could remember.

December 3, 1990, 16:23 (Utc+01)

Smoke from destroying so many shredded documents had been shrouding Lichtenberg district streets and alleys for several days and nights. To the unwitting it was explained away as another sign of East German incompetence, coal and fuel oil shortages forcing citizens to burn whatever they had to stay warm.

But he knew otherwise. The Stasi was unraveling, purging its crimes, erasing its secrets. In many other GDR cities, state security buildings were already being stormed by protestors; it was only a matter of time for Berlin. And driving from Haus 1 to the special annex building near Hohenschönhausen, he couldn't help feeling he was in some kind of terrible dream, the gray slattern winter sun taunting him, the streets and sidewalks crowded with celebrating East Berliners, all traffic heading west to the wall at a standstill.

His plan was to have her released into his custody while he still had some official standing; the necessary paperwork was in his satchel, stamped and signed by Mielke—well, it had Mielke's seal and signature on it, anyway—and there was the little tenement safe flat he'd secured on the edge of the Volkspark in Prenzlauer Berg, where she could recuperate while he sorted out her future. He expected resistance, from all sides. But the moment he drove into the gated courtyard and saw the double front doors unlocked and open, he knew that all his plans were in tatters.

Files were scattered across the slate stones outside; a chair had come through an upper-floor window in a scatter of broken glass. Inside, a scruffy gang of scavenging children scattered at the sight of his uniform, shouting, visibly panicked, dragging and shouldering pillowcases filled with whatever they seemed to think they could sell.

A football magazine, cup of cold coffee, and half-eaten pastry on the security officer's desk indicated that the staff had left quickly, and suddenly, much earlier in the day. He should have come first thing. Slogans spray-painted on the corridor walls showed that protestors had been through the building. A trash can fire someone had tried to light had died out.

Power had been shut off. Gray light seeped through the windows, and the resulting hard shadows made the annex feel even more unforgiving. Secret dungeon of the legendary Stasi überspymaster they'd codenamed Pogo in Berlin Station, he thought bitterly, and could imagine the lurid tabloid headlines and photographs; the West would be thrilled to document its ruins. As the reality of "the Turning" settled on him, he had tried not to think about all the borderline acts of espionage and aggressive interrogations in which he'd participated that might, in a future unified Germany, be called crimes. He knew what they were doing was often illiberal, blunt, and even cruel, but the argument (or justification) was always, *This is temporary; terrible acts are committed by both sides in a cold war; we still cling to the ideals and values that will enable us to change the world.*

The cell rooms on the upper floors were empty. Her cell on the fourth was empty. Borrowed books and her meager belongings were all that remained; pictures of American prairie land had been cut from a magazine and taped to the wall above the sagging bed. Soap, towels, toothbrush and powder, a ration of generic Soviet-bloc cosmetics. Two blue plastic hair clips, lots of pills.

She was long gone. He felt a weight lift and a sadness spread.

A phone jangled somewhere below him, unanswered. Echoing like a tuneless requiem.

Then he saw it: faint, a dried, bloody footprint. Small, high arch, only the toes and outside edge articulated. Had she cut herself? There was a towel with some blood on it in the lidded slop bucket. He fought back a shiver and followed a trail back out into the hallway, where, now that he was aware of them, he could see on the glossy checkerboard tile that they led back to the stairwell he'd just climbed.

An open cell door revealed a young, listless prisoner still sitting on her cot, dazed, hair a tangle, eyes dulled by drugs. She called out something as he passed, and when he stopped to look, he remembered she was the infamous sports-federation physician, Liesl or Lina, one of Höopner's doping protégés, who'd tried to go over the wall with her husband not three months earlier.

The husband, Uli Grün—a minor apparatchik with the Ministry of Culture, wasn't he?—had regrettably been shot and killed. Afterward, the doctor's grief had taken her mind, and she was put in the annex on a hefty course of lithium and Thorazine because no one quite knew what else to do with her. You couldn't have her out in the population spreading doom and gloom right when everything was threatening to implode.

"When is supper?" the doctor asked him.

He hesitated. "Soon."

Nodding, the doctor looked at her hands. "No one brought lunch."

"I'm sorry," he said and hurried down the stairs.

Administration offices on the second floor had been routed and looted, the medication lockup breached and emptied. The diminishing trail of bloody footprints took him directly to the director's office suite.

A well-fed civilian psychologist lay dead on the thread-worn carpet of the reception office, facedown, his thick neck broken, the side of his head crushed by a paperweight on the floor near his feet. The shrink,

Janke, was a predatory weasel; it appeared that his serial abuse of the woman prisoners had been avenged during their escape.

But glancing reflexively into his own office, he saw the bare ivory legs of a woman on the polished hardwood floor in there, and his breath became shallow. He drew his gun and crept to the doorway. Oberleutnant Greta Kimmich was splayed on her side, the skirt of her uniform tugged indelicately high, revealing cheap polyester half stockings and a lattice of blue veins. The holster on her hip was empty, and the Makarov pistol that had been in it had been dropped near a third victim, half-hidden by the metal office desk. Several chest wounds had spilled a considerable crimson-black puddle that had spread and seeped into the cracks of the flooring and was thickening.

He blinked and stepped back.

The desk phone jangled shrill, and he flinched. How long before they sent someone to find out why the annex wasn't answering?

A million anxious worries and certainties tangled, then thinned into one clear, unshakable plan. It was so pure and simple it almost made him laugh. He counted as the phone rang twelve times before falling silent.

He stayed very still and listened for movement. He stared down the empty hallway. There was no prison staff in the buildings besides him; he was sure of it. No one from state security, but they would be coming soon.

Covering his tracks wouldn't take long.

CHAPTER NINETEEN

Deciding where to have the conversation became more stressful than the thought of having it. The hotel room wouldn't do; they were sharing a big suite at the InterContinental, compliments of the Five Eyes as part of their campaign to recruit her, but Sentro felt it necessary to go somewhere neutral so the toxic vapors of her confession wouldn't linger where they slept. She worried what Jenny might think of her when all was said and done.

"If you're gonna just weave another tapestry of lies, don't bother," Jenny said amiably. "I've come to terms with not knowing shit about you, Mom. Either fess up or fuck off."

That seemed fair.

A flock of thrushes kept circling the victory column like barnstormers, chirping and darting and occasionally settling for a moment in the alley of trees, beneath which Sentro sat with her daughter on the grass, struggling to find a start to her story. She wasn't sure she could make it through even what she remembered but was determined to try.

"I had volunteered and mustered in," she began, more abruptly than she had intended. "Your dad stayed in Dallas with your brother, who was . . . I don't know, eleven months, almost a year. I was midway through basic at Fort Bragg when they short-timed me out and put me on a plane to Germany. So this was about six months after I enlisted."

"Why?" Jenny interrupted, after having tacitly promised she wouldn't.

"Something about how I performed on these aptitude tests they gave us."

The wide, stately Independence Square was busy with Orange Revolution and Euromaidan sightseers along with the usual gathering of panhandlers, students, buskers, pensioners, and downtown Kyiv office workers having a smoke. Sun glinted off the golden-bronze statue of the river goddess Berehynia and scattered her light through the dancing fountains and over the domes of the Hlobus underground shopping mall.

"You always told us you were lousy at tests."

"A documented fact."

"I guess not. What'd you score so high on?"

"I don't remember." Sentro pressed forward. "I'd never been out of Texas, not even to Mexico, because my dad said it was way too sketchy down there for American girls."

"Grampy was so old school." Clearly, a forced breeziness was going to be Jenny's first line of defense against what she seemed to sense was coming. Sentro didn't blame her.

"I was flown alone in an empty troop carrier to Rammstein Air Base, southern Germany, where I was met by a bunch of intelligence officers, a jet-lagged blur of clean-cut men, almost all of them white; no women interfaced with me until much later. They sequestered me, no official record of my arrival, no opportunities for me to be seen by random surveillance and my cover blown later. I got a crash course in tradecraft, nothing like what I learned later at Camp Swampy."

"Wait, what. Where?"

"Covert training facilities at Camp Peary. I liked calling the place Swampy instead of the Farm. On account of the biting-bug life was unreal. Defense Intelligence runs their own base at Harvey Point, North Carolina."

Jenny nodded. "No nickname, like 'Swampy' or 'Farm'?"

"Insiders call it Harvey's Point."

"Okay. Harvey's instead of Harvey. Wow. That's . . ."

"High-level hilarity for the Pentagon, yes."

Jenny held her mother's eyes, then cracked a faint smile. *It's the small details like these she wants to share*, Sentro realized. The journey, not so much the destination.

"Looking back on it," Sentro continued, "the mission was meant to be so simple—I would play an innocent, and I *was* an innocent—low security risk because I didn't know anything about intelligence networks or agents in place—the only worry would be my getting caught, and they seemed confident that the East Germans would simply toss me back over the wall or, at worst, trade me for some other low-level spies that the West Germans were getting tired of taking care of. Remember, this was 1989. The Soviet Union under Gorbachev was in full perestroika, the Kremlin was cutting their Eastern Bloc loose, every comrade left to fend for themselves. Satellite countries were thrown into turmoil. It was just a matter of time before their governments collapsed."

"Well, why send you in at all?" Jenny asked.

"The CIA and BND wanted to put a face on a high-level Stasi officer named Günter Witt."

"The guy Ryan calls Pogo."

"Yeah, and note how they didn't bother to tell me his code name at the time," Sentro said, then admitted, "Or I forgot." *Ryan*, Sentro noted absently. First names. Uh-oh. Would she need to talk to Banks about setting some boundaries where her daughter was concerned?

"Mom, don't drift."

"Witt was the heir apparent to Markus Wolf, the legendary Stasi spymaster who had retired in . . . ," she said, then hit a blank, but best-guessed, "'87? Or wait, '86?"

"Legendary."

"Pretty much. Mastermind of what is still considered by those who consider these things the greatest spy network the modern world has ever seen."

"And nobody knew what this Pogo looked like." Jenny looked skeptical, much the way Sentro had when they first told her. "How is that even possible?"

"That was the world, before Facebook. Before widespread video surveillance. He had slipped in and out of the West for three Cold War decades, like a ghost or a rumor."

"Pretty hard to believe, though," Jenny pointed out.

"I guess." Sentro wondered if anyone who hadn't lived in it could understand what the world was like before the information overload. "Anyway. He worried them. The thought that he might disappear before they could get their hands on him. Through his Stasi roster of agents and informers on either side of the Iron Curtain, Witt was believed to have gathered a massive data bank of human intelligence—provocative, extremely sensitive, compromising dossiers and materials on both Western and Eastern Bloc spies and diplomats, of course, but also business leaders, party loyalists, scientists, journalists, bankers, judges, terrorists, revolutionaries, soldiers, and soldiers of fortune—life-altering blackmail that, in the wrong hands, it was argued, could be leveraged in any number of horrible ways."

"Okay, but if it was that big of a deal—and don't take this the wrong way, Mom—why send you?"

In the years since, Sentro had asked herself the same question. "I was young, I was female, I spoke competent high school German. A tabula rasa on which Berlin Station wrote a compelling fiction that suggested I might be useful to the Stasi leadership—and Günter Witt—as a sleeper agent when I returned West. In a future fast approaching, the Ossi bigwigs planned to settle into a supposedly democratic East Germany with their newly privatized businesses and pilfered fortunes, and they would still run things from the shadows.

"The West Germans had a deep-cover asset who worked as a secretary in Witt's office at Stasi headquarters and who was about to take a pregnancy leave. She presented me as her American cousin, a fervently socialist college girl who had come East to write my thesis on"—Sentro was amazed it came back to her—"'Alternative Political Theory and Economic Successes of the Soviet Communist State.'"

"Wait, seriously?"

"CIA invented this whole fake life for me, documented down to the tiniest details—but if you keep interrupting, we'll never get through this."

"Okay, okay." Jenny nodded, all the breeziness gone. "Sorry." Then she dug in her purse for a cigarette and fired up for the first time in the months they'd been together.

"Because she was vouching for me, it was just assumed I would get her job and direct access to Witt." This time she anticipated Jenny's next question: "Yes, they gave me a crash course in typing and dictation. I wasn't half-bad." Jenny threw her a did-I-say-anything? face and smoked.

"I crossed over through Checkpoint Charlie." Slipped from the glittery, vibrant, slightly manic chaos of West Berlin into a muted, shabby, demoralized East, where the people were like abused children, scared, paranoid, angry, and all the party bureaucrats were in denial or making their escape plans.

Did she remember that, or was it what she'd learned later?

"The line was long; I was wound tight. Guards checked my papers, rummaged through my purse, my backpack, my bags. Asked their endless questions. Even the air on the other side of the wall felt oppressive. I found out later the East Germans called it sticky, because it would cling to you, all the pollution from the coal and diesel and decay.

"I lived with the asset, who dabbled in Euro-goth when she wasn't working, had a soldier boyfriend stationed in Rostock, but wasn't married and had no plans to be. She'd been recruited by a small CIA cell that had been operating in the East for about six months, trying to keep tabs on all the Stasi brass and government ministers who were known to be already siphoning money into numbered bank accounts in Switzerland and South America. As the senior operative, she would be the one who'd pass back whatever I uncovered to the CIA." Memories were flooding back in a mad rush, and they overwhelmed Sentro; she nearly drowned in the roil of them.

"Very first night she took me to this underground dance club in an abandoned factory in Friedrichshain. I forget what it was called. Mosh pit. Dark and smoky and filled with skinhead undercover Volkspolizei in cheap leather jackets and black-market jeans. Or maybe I just imagined that part."

Jenny looked bemused. "Trying to imagine you at a punk rave, Mom."

"The drinks were Jägermeister and cola. Eight months pregnant, my deep-cover roomie danced like a whirling dervish, and I got so sick and hungover we both were afraid I might die and compromise the mission."

"What was her name?" Jenny asked, interrupting.

"Who?"

"The asset."

Sentro drew a blank and got rattled. A real blank, on a name she'd assumed had been there all along as she told the story. Right there.

Think.

Acne scars, dancer's body, unruly blonde curls; Sentro hadn't thought about her in years: the long, hard, sad face, violet lipstick, and raccoon mascara—a cartoon pregnancy that ballooned the oversize red turtleneck sweater she wore as a dress. Cheap inky tights on skinny legs, black lace-up jackboots; Sentro had promised her she'd send some better leggings when she got back to the States but never did.

But what was her name?

"Mom?"

144

Jenny touched her lightly; Sentro blinked back the drift. How long had she slipped off this time? "But I didn't get assigned to Witt," she continued, pretending her stumble hadn't happened. "They put me in a clerical pool, transcribing depositions and confessions." She felt light headed, recalling a fragment of that first day, walking into the ministry building, the laser looks from the other women, the raw fear of being found out.

"You sure you're okay?"

"Yes. It's just some of it's not as clear as—" *Helga.* Helga had been the asset's name, but now other parts of the story were skipping away; she took a breath, exhaled, and tried to hold on to it. "So I had to find another way. To get close to him. Because that was the mission."

Jenny frowned. "What does that mean?"

"Just what I said. We—they wanted—"

"No. Close to him?"

Another blank. Sentro shifted, feeling a gnawing discomfort, and Jenny's eyes narrowed, a thread of smoke trailing from her untouched cigarette like Sentro's memories, evanescing into nothing. She found herself drifting again, speculating that maybe Jenny had been smoking in secret all along, at the ranch, and wondered how in the world she'd missed it.

"Mom."

Again Sentro blinked and focused; Jenny stared at her with worried eyes.

"I'm fine. Really, I'm fine."

"You want to stop? We can—"

"No." Now that she'd started, Sentro was determined to finish telling it. She didn't know why, but of all the secrets she held, this was the one she wanted her daughter to know.

"Okay."

"Where was I?"

"They sent you to seduce him," Jenny said, a good guess, "didn't they?" She looked a little stunned as she said it.

All that it implied.

"Not exactly," Sentro lied.

For a moment, neither one of them said anything. Sentro's attention strayed across the vast square, corner to corner, by instinct, the way it always did in public. The way she'd been trained.

"I've read about this. A whatayacallit. Honeypot."

"Honey *trap*."

"Jesus, Mom." Jenny looked upset.

"But that's not how it played out—"

"And you fucking said okay to the mission?!" She stubbed out her cigarette so hard she broke it.

Sentro felt her face flush but didn't back down. "Jenny, I was a soldier. They didn't tell me the specifics until I got to Germany, and by that time I was in so far that—"

Again, Jenny cut her off. "Did Dad know?"

"It was a covert operation. Classified. I wasn't . . . I mean, I couldn't just—"

"He didn't," Jenny clearly decided.

Another awkward pause. "No," Sentro admitted, "he didn't," and it was as if she felt the shame of it all over again. "But I told him everything, afterward." *Or all that I could remember of it,* she added to herself.

"As if that made it okay."

"I was afraid you'd react like this."

"Like what?"

"This."

"Normal?"

Sentro didn't have a comeback.

"Nineteen-year-old American girl, creepy old Stasi spy. You'd just had a baby. Mom. What the fuck was the army thinking?"

Sentro frowned, confused. Wait: Jenny wasn't mad *at* her; Jenny was mad *for* her.

She found herself blinking back a tickle of inexplicable tears. "It was a CIA op. I was an army grunt loan-out; they needed an unknown girl. I wanted so badly to prove myself; I wanted to do something special, be something special." She hesitated. It was only afterward that she found out she'd matched a psych-unit profile of the kind of woman Witt might be attracted to. "Nineteen," she echoed and admitted to her daughter something she'd never said aloud before: "I wasn't ready for a baby when I had Jeremy. I just wanted your dad and an adventure . . ."

She couldn't finish the thought. But in gathering herself, she felt a hitch in her heart release, and the fog lifted a little. Inhale, exhale. "Judge me later, Jen. Can I just . . . tell it?"

"Can you?" Jenny seemed to wonder aloud, sounding more annoyed than she might have intended. She lit another cigarette and smoked it in silence as Sentro waited, letting her daughter decide whether it was worth lifting the veil and seeing her mother in the cold, harsh light of Sentro's defining winter.

Then, wiping away her own leaking tears, Jenny shook her head. "I don't know, Mommy. I don't know." Moody, she gazed out at the victory column, with its flock of gyring birds, then back at her mother for a long time, studying her.

"Fuck," she said sadly. "I *still* don't know you, do I?"

Chapter Twenty

Memories floated in on her pitching sea of consciousness like Arctic ice: brutish, heavy, only the suggestion of what danger lay below ever showing.

That was the metaphor she'd settled on; it felt right. Or was it a simile?

It seemed her daughter hung on every word.

Did it matter if she got the story exactly right? Broken, drifting puzzle pieces that would never quite connect again. All she could do was leap from one to the next and hope the gaps between them didn't grow impossible to span when she tried to get back.

———

Primitive Soviet word processors she wasn't trained for, so a black-market IBM Selectric became her accomplice and best friend. Her chair gave her back spasms; her Russian-made pens leaked and stained her fingers; the smell of copier chemicals followed her home.

They'd assigned her to a clerical pool because her shorthand skills were deemed "lacking." She felt like she'd failed before she even got started. Another woman was shifted into Helga's job in Witt's fourth-floor office, and the closest Sentro got to him during the first six weeks working at Stasi headquarters was typing his name on field reports, intelligence assessments, and interrogation transcripts.

In the hallways, in the elevators, she would play a game watching the Stasi senior staff, agents, and ministers come and go, trying to guess which one could be her target: this slender one, with the mustache? Or *that* one, with the papery skin, gelled-back Gestapo hair, and eyes like little briquettes?

She was always cold. She took to wearing two pairs of tights under her long dresses and the heavy Norwegian sweaters she bought from vendors at the Tempelhof black market, in Kreuzberg, across the river Spree.

None of the other typists responded to her attempts at friendship, because trust was in short supply. Everyone in East Berlin was a likely snitch: neighbors, friends, lovers, family. The Stasi had almost a hundred thousand employees and two hundred thousand informers. Files were kept on more than six million people; there were entire old tenement apartments that had been cleared out and kept simply for storing them.

And Günter Witt remained, for her, a rumor, a ghost.

———

Eight weeks in, Helga passed the word that the Pogo mission managers were threatening to pull the plug and bring her home. Failure was never going to be an option, though. Recalling it for Jenny, she couldn't remember why she was so stubborn. Ego? Arrogance? Desperation?

Or genetics. She was the willful widowed Texas Ranger's only child.

"Step by step. Trust your heart."

"Grampy used to say that," Jenny remembered.

Sentro smiled faintly and nodded. "When all else fails."

Contriving to stay later at Haus 1, Normannenstraße 20, Sentro took on extra work—internal reviews, reports, indictments. Invented reasons to go up to the fourth floor, but the dingy frosted glass suite doors were marked only with fading numbers, always kept closed, the voices inside rumbling and murmuring, and even the ringing phones sounded muffled as if by the cumulative totalitarian blanket of secrecy and paranoia.

The break for her came by chance. At lunch, a vulpine party girl in the translation department, the aptly named Ninki Wiesel (why did she remember that one?) told a raucous story Sentro couldn't help but overhear: there was this good-looking if painfully bashful young bachelor junior officer in Witt's elite COINTEL group whom Ninki had attempted to coerce into a carnal encounter. She'd stalked him to the staff athletic club, where he liked to swim laps late at night. In a racy red two-piece she sat waiting at the end of the pool, legs dangling in his lane so he'd find them when he reached for the wall; when he did, he got so flustered he almost drowned, she told her tablemates, followed, as he treaded water, by the usual provocative chitchat, blushing all around. Her plan was working to perfection until he came up out of the pool, weedier than she expected—rather underfed and, well, unimpressive—a raging but disappointing erection tenting his Speedo with an awkward, leftward banana curve that she couldn't help but laugh at. And she couldn't stop herself laughing, even when his face went red and warped with a scowl and he grabbed his towel and fled into the men's dressing area.

La-de-dah. Ninki's tablemates deemed it hilarious.

Sentro knew the young agent from his visits to her typing section. His shy, sidelong glances from across the room. His faint smile slightly less cruel than typical of his rank, but only when he was certain no one was looking. She plotted a campaign.

"You went to the pool," Jenny guessed.

"Yep. I borrowed Helga's swimsuit. It didn't exactly fit."

"Two-piece?"

Sentro's nonanswer was confirmation.

"Too big, or too small?"

"Both."

Jenny rolled her eyes. "We have the same body. I bet I can guess where."

The pool was overheated, Olympic size; steam rose from its surface and up the windowless walls to a high barrel vault ceiling, where drops of moisture rained back down. The decking was concrete, but every surface was covered with a mildewed teal tile in dire need of cleaning. The smell was overpowering.

His name, Sentro had discovered in the files, was Schmidt. Matthias Schmidt. Born in Dresden to chemical technicians, Prussian father, Spanish mother. Matthias was a former Volksmarine seaman recruited, much like Sentro, into the Stasi after a single tour on an intelligence ship in the Baltic.

He swam with long, easy strokes, breathing once every three. His faded blue eyes found her before he reached the end of the lane. Maybe he was still jumpy from the previous girl he'd found sitting there. With his wet hair flipped back, he looked like a seal.

"You fucked him," Jenny blurted out, jumping the punch line, but clearly hoping she might be wrong.

"Yes," Sentro lied. She met Jenny's piercing, disappointed stare. And approximated the embarrassment she thought would sell it.

Smitten, lovestruck, Schmidt pulled strings to have her transferred into Günter Witt's special counterintelligence unit, where she transcribed English-language radio intercepts into German and cleaned up the notes from interrogations that Witt, for unexplained reasons, siphoned away from Department 9. Sentro was so caught up in her newfound powers of deception she didn't think twice about how it might break her new admirer's heart when he found out she was playing him.

"His job was forcing people to spy on each other," Jenny pointed out. "He tortured you."

"Later," Sentro concurred absently, though she wasn't planning to share the scant memories she had of that part.

But Witt? Still a ghost. And hardly a target for seduction, as it turned out—the CIA had him profiled all wrong, no surprise. Unprepossessing, an average, clean-shaven white man of average height who favored budget suits she would sometimes see flash past a doorway, or briefly from the back, hurrying down the corridor to the stairs (he avoided elevators; claustrophobia, Schmidt claimed). Married to a fetching younger actress, the father of a new baby boy, Schmidt said, dedicated family man and Communist Party icon. Sentro thought it through a bit differently, trying to recalibrate, frustrated with her clueless handlers: bottom line, Witt could have any woman he wanted; he never took the liberty. Why, why would he ever be interested in an awkward teenage American defector?

Helga pressed her for details. Time was running out, and her pregnancy was at term. The mission had crept far beyond its initial timeline. Sentro tried conjuring a description from memory of a man she would have a hard time recognizing on the street if she ran into him; the boys in Berlin said that wasn't going to be enough. What they needed was a photograph, so they dead dropped her a cheap plastic cigarette lighter slash spy camera, something right out of James Bond.

"You don't smoke," Jenny noted.

"We had a work-around. Let me tell the story, huh?"

Christmas with communists.

Silver blown-glass Sputnik ornaments bedecked scraggly fir trees; there was grim cheer and only secular songs. From the top of Großer Bunkerberg in the Volkspark, she and Schmidt could see all the pretty colored lights of West Berlin, teasing them with their happy abandon.

Schmidt mocked the capitalist decadence but offered her a forbidden joke he'd heard from a bartender who'd been arrested for telling it: "What would happen if the desert became a socialist country? Nothing for a while. Then the sand becomes scarce."

He laughed like a schoolboy. She tried to like him but only felt sorry for him. He couldn't help what he was, growing up behind the wall. There weren't that many other roads he could have traveled.

Whatever Helga wanted to buy was either unavailable or much too expensive: she was constantly hurrying from store to store. "And if no one knows you, you get nothing at all." Sentro had no one to buy presents for. She tried not to think about Dennis and the baby and what they might be doing back in the States. She hadn't talked to him in three months. She gave her roommate the Timex watch she never wore. Schmidt asked her to the Stasi Christmas ball.

Günter Witt would be there.

And she might get home before New Year's.

———

A bone-rattling cold night gave way to the overcranked steam heat of the cavernous Palasthotel conference hall. It was a Stasi nest—off limits to East Berliners because it took only hard currency from the foreigners who visited. All the rooms, elevators, corridors, and public spaces were bugged, and there were special suites with multiple cameras and videotape recorders for "intriguing" guests. The Secret Service branch booking a party there was considered a riotous inside joke.

"Udo Lindenberg performed here for Ingrid Mielke's thirty-fifth," Schmidt bragged as they walked in. He looked overwhelmed, star-struck, and Sentro had no idea what he was talking about but smiled and nodded and shrugged off her coat into his hands.

A string band was playing lively traditional music.

Helga had given her a sleek little beaded black purse in which the spy camera could be fitted and concealed with the shutter remotely triggered. Her instructions were to take as many pictures as possible of the target, then go to the restroom to eject the microcanister, crush the lighter-cam, flush it down a toilet, and conceal the exposed film in the elastic of her pantyhose, in case her purse got searched on the way out.

The ballroom floor tilted and swirled with suited Stasi and their families, everyone manic with the rictus grins of paranoia and naked ambition. Sentro felt like she was back in the pool with Schmidt, the heat already starting to go to her head.

This was where her memories began to fray, beyond the decay afforded by time and distance and concussions. She remembered dancing. A brief, sloppy, clumsy, groping make-out with Schmidt behind a velvet curtain, and his anguished apologies afterward.

The smell of boiled cabbage and flop sweat and too much alcohol. The shimmering blizzard of glitter from the catwalks that crisscrossed the ceiling holding the lights. An impromptu sing-along to "Weiße Weihnacht" that would have made Bing Crosby cringe.

And finally, Günter Witt.

In a Santa suit.

Full white beard concealing half his face.

CHAPTER TWENTY-ONE

"*Weihnachtsmann! Weihnachtsmann! Weihnachtsmann!*"

The crowded hall surged toward Father Christmas, and she was carried on its current. Bag filled with colored-cellophane-wrapped truffles and sweets; Witt threw handfuls of them out over and into the outstretched arms, booming, "Ho ho ho." Saint Nick was the original socialist. Sharing the wealth.

Taking her hand, Schmidt swam upstream to show her off to the boss.

Fathomless black eyes drilled into her. He knew her name. Spoke Queen's English in a soft, unexpected tenor. Peppermint schnapps on his breath. "*Grüß Gott*. Pleasure to meet you. Our lovely new American friend." She was sweating, felt almost feverish, the little purse clutched in her hand like a talisman. *Where are you from, Fräulein? What does your family think of this adventure? How did you come to sympathize with our cause?*

Schmidt was beaming, high color, his trophy being admired. Witt was taller than she expected, not average at all. A wrestler's body, long waist, wide stance. "It's hot as hell in here, Matthias, is it not?"

Schmidt concurred.

Santa tugged down his beard to reveal a toothy smile, face flushed with perspiration, blunt-cut features, all angles and planes. Her finger found the shutter button, and her purse floated up to her temple as she brushed back a limp lock of hair with her wrist.

Clickety click, the snick of the shutter opening and closing startled her, but the Stasi men didn't seem to hear it over the din. They were talking shop, a minor bureaucrat in Bonn they'd recently compromised and turned. Her hand and the purse dropped gently back to her waist, where Schmidt was clutching her to him like a bag of groceries, and she gently twisted free, apologizing, "Will you excuse me, Matti? I need to freshen up."

———

"Crafty girl," Jenny said, and it didn't sound facetious. She'd shifted her legs and moved closer to Sentro the way she had when she was a little girl, their knees making contact.

"It was all I could think of. Last time I'd been on a date with someone other than your father, I was fourteen."

"Well, it's every girl's get-out-of-jail-free card. Guy can't say no."

The bathroom was even more crowded than the ballroom, everyone rationing the coarse paper towels and sharing a bar of soap one thrifty comrade had remembered to bring in her bag. Sentro waited for a stall at the end and, once inside, quickly dislodged the camera and removed the tiny film canister. The false lighter crushed easily underfoot, but it took what seemed like forever to scoop up all the remnants from the filthy floor, and someone kept banging on the door, urging her to hurry up.

"Psssst."

Sentro froze. A hand over the top of the stall wall dangled toilet paper; there wasn't any on the spindle.

"*Danke.*"

"*Bitte.*"

More banging on the door. Sentro flushed the toilet, lifted her hem, and tried to secure the film as instructed, but her pantyhose were damp with sweat and the tape wouldn't take.

More urgent banging and pleading at the door; she was trying to wedge the canister into her hose when she fumbled it and watched the film clatter away under the stall and out among the shuffling high heels and flats.

Fuck.

The latch slid; the door swung in. Ninki Wiesel was outside waiting, very drunk and bladder bursting, mumbling an apology as she pushed past and pulled down her skirt and dropped to the toilet to pee, eyes fluttering closed with relief: "Oh God oh God oh God." There was the sound of a torrent and Sentro stepped out, letting the door swing shut and discovering she couldn't find the film.

Fuck fuck fuck.

"Fucking fuck," Jenny agreed, blowing out a fretful cloud of smoke as if she were in the bathroom too.

A heavy hand came down on Sentro's shoulder. "Is this yours?"

She steeled herself and made a pivot; a sturdy Stasi Oberleutnant named Kimmich had the microcanister between two fingers with manicured nails that matched her scarlet lipstick. With a flawlessly creased formal dress uniform and a gun she always kept holstered on her hip, Kimmich was known to Sentro from her frequent visits to the typing pool. She worked in some defector detention annex nobody talked about and had a crush on one of the steno girls.

Sentro told Kimmich that it was hers, yes, without thinking it through.

Jenny lit another cigarette with the last of her previous one, looking stressed. Her hand trembled. "That was reckless."

"I had this dull ache in the pit of my stomach as she turned the canister over in her fingers, studying it. She had those eyebrows"—Sentro gestured—"the ones that almost touch here in the—"

"Unibrow," Jenny said, translating.

Kimmich asked if it was film. Sentro admitted it was. Kimmich was curious to see the camera. Sentro stammered that she didn't have it with her; she'd been looking in her purse for her lipstick, and the film fell out; she'd put it in there to get it developed and forgotten.

"And she bought that?" Jenny wondered.

Not exactly. Kimmich looked unconvinced. The bathroom had emptied out some. Ninki was still in her stall, throwing up.

"Everything's so small these days," Kimmich had said, still holding the canister up between them, and Sentro somehow clicked on what she was getting at.

"She was hitting on you!" Jenny said, realizing.

"Tell me about it," was all Sentro said to the Stasi officer, and she reached out to take the film from her but let her hand go soft against the woman's fingers and left them there for a little longer than she needed to.

"Yikes," Jenny marveled. "Go, Mom."

"I'm Greta," Kimmich had offered.

"I know," Sentro flirted inexpertly, but thrilling at how easily she'd made the shift, and tucked the film safely into her purse, then introduced herself: "Aubrey. I work in Department 10."

"The American."

"Yes, Oberleutnant."

"No need to be formal, girl. Here with . . . ?"

"Spezialagent Schmidt."

"Ah. *Ja gut.*" Worry flickered behind the Stasi officer's eyes, and she reflexively stepped back as another massive shift of women shuffled in, and jostled apart by them from Greta Kimmich, Sentro was able to flash a regretful smile and slip away.

"Awesome," was Jenny's verdict.

———

Things got ugly in the cab going home. Emboldened by liquor and his mentor's stamp of approval, Schmidt was determined to seal the deal with his little foreign trophy, and Sentro spent most of the ride fending off his hands and keeping him from consummating in the cab.

"I don't need to hear this next part," Jenny decided.

"I can skip ahead."

"Just . . . tell me there was no way out of it."

"There wasn't." Sentro was relieved that she wouldn't have to flesh out a fiction of how she'd slept with Matthias Schmidt.

In truth, back in his spacious apartment, she had to endure only a short scrimmage before the lovestruck suitor, his pants around his ankles, passed out on the persian carpet in front of the fireplace and started snoring.

"Afterward, I straightened my clothes and found a glass for water," was what Sentro told Jenny instead.

"I've known that feeling," Jenny said ruefully. "Afterward. You drink and you drink and you still feel thirsty. And no less shitty." For a moment they both fell quiet. It was one of the most intimate things Jenny had shared with Sentro in a very long time.

Schmidt's kitchen had been spotless, with all the modern free-world appliances a typical East Berliner couldn't have and couldn't afford. Tasteful furniture, a bookshelf filled with the correct socialist dogma along with Nietzsche, Engels, Camus, and Che Guevara. In the bedroom, the poems of Pablo Neruda on the side table, framed photos of Schmidt and his parents. An old Aeroflot travel poster for Cuba.

For the first time she felt the agent-voyeur's shiver-thrill, looking through his things, forbidden fruit. *So this is what spying is like*—it all came so naturally, so effortlessly for her, the way sports did for Dennis.

Her husband. Reckless on the adrenaline rush of having the photographic evidence Berlin Station wanted, she actually thought briefly about calling Dennis Troon from Schmidt's phone, figuring a Stasi special agent would have international calling privileges, but had to remind herself that even Schmidt's line would be tapped and recorded. A sober surge of guilt sent her out to the entry door; she looked back to make sure she hadn't left anything, feeling the film canister sharp against the small of her back. It was going to be a long, frigid walk back to her apartment, but she didn't want to risk taking a cab. One benefit of living in a communist country was that the streets would be empty and at least relatively safe.

Her eyes landed on the modest round dining table and mass of paperwork that Schmidt had brought home. A square black-and-white photo was clipped to a thick gray file on top. Even upside down she could recognize the headshot of Helga. Sentro picked up the file and saw that others were beneath it, identifying photographs and surveillance. One of them was an American, Henry Otter—she didn't know him yet—the rest of them were identified as German.

The clandestine, in-country CIA cell.

They were about to be rolled up.

———

The old Lada taxicab fishtailed down vacant black ice streets, snow tires spitting tiny blizzards.

Darkened buildings pressed in, lightless, like looming danger. The occasional streetlight that was working cast down murky, milky light quickly swallowed by the darkness.

Desperate to save time, she took a chance with the taxi; the other joke Schmidt loved to tell her was how East Berlin cabbies might all be undercover cops, but "at least you don't have to tell them where you live."

Across the frozen Spree, weaving down narrow alleys littered with discarded mattresses and overflowing bins: this Stasi snitch knew all the shortcuts, and she tipped him too much so he'd hold his tongue for at least a couple of hours.

She was back home in ten minutes. Through the carved wooden doors, up the worn stairs, into the apartment, where she discovered a hastily written note announcing that Helga had gone into labor and was headed to the maternity ward at the Friedrichshain Municipal Hospital.

Her heart was racing, her breathing shallow. There'd been a backup plan for her, a cutout to contact in case of emergency, the supersecret number to call. But she somehow knew what was needed. Like the soldier who'd been taught to fall on the grenade, it was on her to make things right.

She calmed. There was no hesitation, no fear, no second thoughts. Ten agents operating on foreign soil, caught by the Stasi—she knew what would happen to them; she'd typed the reports.

The second cab ride sealed her fate, put her on Stasi radar. She made sure the microcanister could be easily found in the crease of the back seat after she paid and got out.

She told Jenny about getting lost in long, typically Soviet hospital hallways with worn-down linoleum and sick green walls. Patients left lying randomly on gurneys outside examining rooms, anguished eyes following her. Helga was already in the delivery-prep room when Sentro finally got to the proper ward waiting area; the door was open, and there were half a dozen prospective mothers in various stages of labor and audible distress. Helga was on a bed in the corner, quiet, sweating, knees up, only four centimeters dilated and already looking wiped out. Epidurals were apparently not available except in emergencies.

Helga looked miserable. Sentro was reminded of her own easy delivery, not that long before. Then she pushed thoughts of her other life and family aside; they weren't helpful. She offered a word of encouragement before a nurse came in and shooed her away.

In the waiting room, a square-set young man with a thick hedge of hair was smoking and pacing, and she knew it was Otter from the picture on the file back at Schmidt's. Their eyes met; his flickered recognition. He smiled with a feigned relief and crossed and greeted her like an old friend, big hug, two Euro-kisses, saying, in perfect German, "She called me when her water broke. I got her here as soon as I could."

There was a doughy, uniformed policeman behind the reception booth window, talking on the phone. Sentro angled her face away from him and asked Otter casually if he'd alerted Helga's boyfriend or family, because Sentro didn't have their numbers.

He said he hadn't, no. But would soon.

"That was code," Jenny observed. Sentro could see she was struggling to process what Sentro was telling her. The choice she had made. "You were talking in code."

Sentro confirmed that she was, and that Otter understood then, without her saying anything more, that his cover had been compromised, that his team needed to scatter West, and that he needed to get Helga across the border before she gave birth.

"She was already in labor," Jenny said.

"My challenge was to buy them enough time."

Four centimeters, first birth. With any luck, Helga was in for a slow labor. Sentro asked Otter how long he thought it would take for the family to arrive.

"More code," Jenny interjected.

Otter said perhaps four hours. The cop had hung up the phone and was peering out at them, adjusting his thick glasses, a frown creasing his brow. Otter told Sentro that she should go get some sleep; he'd let her know when the baby was close.

"Sleep?" Jenny wondered, sounding fretful. "What about *your* family? *Your* baby?"

"Spy talk for *Get the fuck away from here, as fast as you can*," Sentro explained. "He assumed I'd try to find a way to get over the wall."

"No shit. Anyone would."

Sentro didn't know how to explain to Jenny what she'd done. It had felt right in the moment. That was all that could be said. By the time the corpulent cop managed to squeeze out of his booth and strolled into the hallway to look for her, she was gone.

———

The cold Berlin night hit her like a brick.

A service door out of the back of the hospital put her on an angling side street, dark and deserted, an urban canyon walled by featureless Stalinesque apartments channeling a bitter wind. She began to walk, staying in the shadows, ducking into doorways when the occasional car or delivery truck passed.

She didn't know how long she walked that night, but it was tedious and uneventful, even if her pulse was racing and her feet got so numb they felt like rubber stubs. Somehow she wound up back on the Großer Bunkerberg in the Volkspark, a high hill made from the rubble of bombed-out Berlin. Its frosted trees glistened as the moon came up, and the gay lights of West Berlin still beckoned, even as the city slept, reminding her of everything she had just sacrificed to save a clutch of agents she didn't know. For something she knew was right, it felt so wrong.

She chose not to think about what might happen to her. She'd made her decision; she hoped Dennis would understand. Speculation was pointless. But it was impossible not to be scared.

It took longer for them to find her than she thought it would. Not until the end of his shift did the cab driver find Sentro's film on the back seat, and he clearly didn't report it right away because light was bleeding up into the eastern darkness and she was shivering uncontrollably and no longer wondering about her family or her future, just desperate to get somewhere warm, when the blue flashing lights of three boxy Wartburg 353 patrol cars finally came snaking up the gravel service road to the overlook where she had been waiting for them.

Chapter Twenty-Two

"How did they know you'd be in that park?"

"The Stasi knew everything."

"Even *where?*"

"Eyes were on me. The city leaked. Nearly everyone in East Berlin was an informant—willingly or unwillingly." Sentro fell quiet, frowning, probably thinking. Then, with an almost apologetic smile, she added, "This is where my memory starts to get really sketchy. So. Bear with me."

Listening to her mother tell the story of Berlin was giving Jenny vertigo. And a wicked headache. The world had been upended in the motel breezeway in New Mexico where she'd watched the man with the gun flop to the ground, head haloed with pink, life gone from him, and now her whole body ached with a formless anxiety, and she couldn't seem to catch her breath.

She'd smoked her last cigarette, but what she really craved was some weed, to put a million miles between her and this parallel world her mother had lived in. All this time she had wanted to know everything. Now she wasn't so sure.

"I remember being taken directly to Hohenschönhausen," her mother continued, "which was the political prison for the Ministry of State Security. I think it was originally built for the manufacturing of soup kitchen supplies. Expanded into a Soviet detainment center for defeated Nazis briefly after World War Two. Eventually the Stasi took over and turned it into the place where they put political captives. Officially it didn't exist. Left off all the maps, it was in an exclusion zone where even East German citizens weren't permitted to go."

"You talk about it like it's a Wikipedia topic."

"I'm sorry. It was a long time ago, Jen. Maybe I worked through all the feelings, maybe I just set them aside, but . . ." She couldn't seem to find the words to finish the thought. "It's what I did. I can't change it. Do you want me to stop?"

"No."

Her mother's brow creased again as she seemed to struggle at mining the past. "They put me in solitary. A concrete box. I don't remember a window. Maybe four feet by eight feet. No sink, no toilet. A wooden pallet bed. Thin cotton blanket. After that night on the hill, I was always cold."

Jenny tried to imagine her mother in a prison cell; she'd seen pictures of her from when her parents were newlyweds, from when her mom enlisted and her dad would visit Fort Sill on weekends with baby Jemmy. Her mother seemed so insubstantial in them—small, sturdy but unimposing, a goofy smile.

"Did they torture you?"

"In the trade it's called elicitation. More psychological than physical. They shot me full of drugs the first day and kept me cooked like that pretty much nonstop, up and down and sideways, while they did their nasty business and asked questions I could barely form the words to answer—and most of which I couldn't answer because, as I've said, I really didn't know anything." Cheeks puffed, she blew out a gust of air but kept going in the same dispassionate tone. Her breath was sour, her fingers restless, intertwined; her eyes looked almost opaque, unfocused, as if casting backward for these memories took her out of body, to a place where part of her still lived. And suffered.

"Not that it mattered. The Stasi weren't interested in the truth; they'd already decided what it was. They just wanted me to confess to it."

Her mother was dissembling. Jenny could sense she was starting to choose her words more carefully. Hedging. Why? "What kind of drugs?"

"The kind you never want to have in you. It got to where I didn't know whether I was awake or just dreaming."

Jenny studied her, trying to discern the scars of what she'd gone through. All these years; they were so well hidden. From her family or from herself? Jenny thought it might be both. "Did Helga get away? And the others?"

"Yes." But her mother didn't seem to want to elaborate on that. "They moved me after a while. Smaller building, bigger cells. Disgusting mattress." She was skirting some painful truth, Jenny could tell, so she gently pressed for it.

"Why did they move you?"

Jenny waited, but her mother didn't say anything more.

"Mom?" She had a look in her eyes, what Jeremy called "the good-bye look." As in, Aubrey Sentro had left the building. Maybe it wasn't from the concussions; maybe it was just how she'd learned to cope with her past.

"Mom. *Mom.*"

She looked at Jenny blankly.

"You floated away there for a sec."

"Ah. I'm sorry."

Jenny asked again why they moved her to another jail.

"I don't remember," her mother said, and Jenny somehow knew this time she was lying. Then, as if she sensed Jenny's doubt, her mother said, "Günter Witt was in charge of the questioning; I think now that the prison annex was his private storage bin for special cases."

"Like you."

"Yes."

"So you must have seen him, then? In jail. Witt."

"I must have." Her mother's brief hesitation made Jenny suspect she was hedging her answer again. "But from the time I was moved from Hohenschönhausen to the annex until I walked out eleven months later? Has always been mostly a blank. What I began remembering recently—what I think are memories of it—after our friendly neighborhood shrink started me on the brain drugs for my concussions? I don't know. It comes back in noisy fragments, calving off this huge glacier of images frozen up in the back of my head."

"But not the Stasi spymaster guy's face."

"No."

"So. Like . . . what things *are* you remembering?"

Her mother looked unsettled, and what she said next seemed to startle her. "Being pregnant."

A jolt ran through Jenny. "What?"

"Yeah."

"*What?*"

"I mean, of course I know that I was pregnant, in jail; I couldn't forget that. But on account of the drugs and the psyops, I had no recollection, until recently, of the pregnancy itself." She smiled uneasily. "Weird, huh?"

A queasy silence, Jenny at a loss for words. She felt like she might be sick.

"I know," her mother said softly, sadly. "I know," and she looked away, out across the plaza again. Checking sight lines, Jenny guessed. And points of egress, her mother had explained once. It was automatic, how she kept assessing risk. But no wonder: always operational, even when she wasn't. Jenny watched it happen all the time when they were together in public, now that she was aware of it.

"Fuck," Jenny said, for no real reason except . . . *fuck*. The vanishing line between professional and personal must be making things infinitely more complicated.

Her mother didn't react.

"Schmidt? From that one time?"

"Just like they warn you in sex ed." Her mother's hands went up and down, a vague, inconclusive gesture. There was something missing, though, an important detail Jenny felt sure she was still holding back.

"What happened to the—"

"Stillborn," her mother answered, too quickly, and Jenny was ashamed to feel relief. "Of course I've never forgotten that either." There was ragged emotion in her voice for a moment. "I think they showed me the body, but I blanked it then, and it's still a blank now. If they did show me, I mean. Like Günter Witt's face: a blur of nothing. But." Jenny watched her gather and file the feelings away again. "All those pharmaceuticals for all that time, I guess that shouldn't be so unexpected. The Nazi buzz bomb scientists went West after World War Two. East Germany got the medical kooks who were doing those horrifying experiments at Auschwitz."

Jenny refused to let her mother stray off topic. "Boy? Girl?"

"I don't know, honey. I don't know."

Jenny shook her head, over and over, numb.

"Don't tell your brother."

"Oh, sure, that'll make it like it never happened," Jenny said, too sharply, before she could stop herself. Her mother let it pass. The rest of her Berlin story unspooled in a hum that Jenny had a hard time following, she was so shaken by the news of the stillborn child. Her half sibling. Everything she knew and thought about her mother was scrambled; everything she knew and thought about her father was fundamentally changed.

Or had it just been made clearer?

Useless for intel, her mother had suffered through a monotony of empty days, one just like the next, week after week, month after month. In her conscious moments, she said, she'd wonder why nobody had come for her, why her handlers hadn't traded a captive East German agent for her. Did they even know she was still alive?

"I had days where I wanted to die, but I wasn't worried about them killing me. They didn't normally execute foreign agents in those days, despite what we see in the movies or on TV." Captured spies were Cold War currency, especially that late in the game, her mother explained, commodities with ever-shifting valuations, depending on the day, the developments, the market for leverage. When she was jailed, in the winter of '89, no one in the West was thinking that the wall would come down anytime soon. But in the East they were making plans for a future without a Soviet safety net. A transition to a quasi-democratic socialist country run by the usual suspects, with a new bag of free-market tricks to draw from.

"News seeped in, from Leipzig, about the protests, the summer of dissent, the unraveling of the German Democratic Republic. Which seemed crazy to us until one day, like magic, a group of students and dissidents stormed the little jail where we were kept. The staff fled. We were free to go."

She'd sat in her open cell for a long time, her mother remembered with a faraway look, as if transported back there. She had struggled to shake off the morphine cloud, unable to trust what her senses were telling her because her senses were so inside out. She kept thinking this must be some new level of sadistic Stasi abuse. And waiting for the vicious punch line she was sure was coming. But it never did.

"And then I walked home," she said and seemed to be finished.

Jenny stared at her. "This is so fucked up. But you know that," she added softly. "You shouldn't have kept it a secret." Her mother avoided making eye contact.

In a voice that was uncharacteristically fragile, Sentro said, "It was a bad time, a horrible thing that happened during a war that I was a soldier in. I survived it; I put it away and locked the door on what I remembered of it. On the upside"—the tone changed, got stronger, defiant—"I lost some weight. On the downside . . . everything else."

"How can you joke about it?"

"How can I not? And what would have been the point of telling you, before now?" This was the mother Jenny knew.

"It made you who you are."

"Okay. So? How does it matter how I got here?"

"You're still lying to me."

"I'm not."

"Holding back, then," Jenny corrected herself, triggered by a helplessness she didn't even understand. Her anger flared. "And hey, if this is what you're willing to admit to me, what the holy fuck are you hiding?"

"I don't know," her mother said. Her rare moment of vulnerability seemed to have passed. "The point is I don't know."

"Yeah. What you keep saying."

The point? Late light slanted across Independence Square. The sky was filled with shredded, incandescent clouds promising rain. Her mother looked stymied by Jenny's accusations. Not wounded—conflicted.

Jenny wanted—needed—to get away to think. Her head was a muddle, her chest so tight she wanted to scream. She put her lighter in her bag, got up, and started walking.

"Jenny, wait—"

She didn't. She just kept walking, through the long shadows, away from the past, all these new revelations, this woman she had always loved and rebelled against and whom, once again, she didn't even recognize.

Thinking: *If this is my mother, who am I?*

Chapter Twenty-Three

After quickening her pace and slipping around the corner, Madsen folded herself back into the darkness of an unlit walkway between two apartment buildings and waited there, her hand on the tactical knife she kept secreted against the small of her back.

Curzon Street was crowded with pedestrians traversing the West End installations of this year's London arts light festival, which Arshavin had helped underwrite.

She couldn't see who was tailing her, but she'd felt it ever since she walked out of Arshavin's Campden Hill terraced house, heading for the first installation in Holland Park.

She was trying to distract herself from Ilya's murder for a few minutes. Having made it all the way to Mayfair and its spooky neon nightingale in Berkeley Square and the puzzled, pixelated moon that seemed to float above the trees, her shadow and its watchful, probing eyes proved too distracting for her to ignore any longer.

Who could be following her?

While, resonant from little speakers in the trees, Nat King Cole and Sinatra had crooned the famous song in a continuous loop, Madsen had done a quick circuit of the park, then doubled back, scanning the faces and figures she passed for a tell and discovering nothing. After another couple of sharp pivots, she'd darted through gridlocked traffic, disappeared into the shadows of Charles Street, and circled around on Hill, where she found her hiding niche.

Footsteps on the sidewalk, quick, tentative—a hesitant approach, then stopping altogether. Madsen's body grew tense; her pulse slowed. She imagined the shadow listening for her and held her breath. It had to be related to her continued pursuit of whoever was behind Arshavin's killing. Lenkov's unlocked cell phone had provided a rough sketch of his contacts before and directly after the shooting in Paris, including repeated calls to and from a satellite phone with a Cuban dialing code. One of his last calls was from a prepaid phone with a Cuban prefix. The former had been removed from service. The latter rang, no message, just the beep for voice mail; Madsen had left her name and number, claiming to be an attorney attempting to sort out Lenkov's affairs.

The footsteps resumed, and a small woman in wedge-heeled boots clicked past where the bodyguard was hiding. False alarm. Madsen relaxed. She waited until the footsteps became inaudible and then stepped back out onto the sidewalk, only to feel the cold O of a handgun kiss the nape of her neck.

"¿Qué vuelta?"

"There's money in my purse. Take it."

"You wished to speak with me."

"No."

"Left a message, in fact."

The burner phone's voice mail.

"And here I am." She spoke perfect German in a heavy Spanish accent. Faintly nasal, with an easy rhythm to it. Caribbean. Gentle hands located Madsen's knife, and she felt it tugged away from where she kept it sheathed in the small of her back.

"I got your number from Ludor Lenkov," Madsen said. It wasn't, technically, a lie.

"How is he?" the woman asked, and Madsen felt the gun lift away.

"Dead," Madsen said.

"*Que lo siento.*"

Madsen didn't know if she was supposed to turn around. She felt foolish and annoyed for having let someone get the drop on her. "And what is it you want from me?" The woman sounded young, the light tones of a girl.

"I worked for a man named Ilya Arshavin. He was shot and killed in Paris a little over a week ago."

"Death is chasing you," the girl said.

"Lenkov hired the man who shot my employer. But I'm of the opinion Lenkov arranged it through a third party, and I'd like to find them." Madsen didn't see the point in playing coy.

"Find them," the girl echoed. "Kill them? Avenge your Russian billionaire's murder?"

Madsen didn't answer. She stared without seeing the dreamy school of LED fish swim upstream beyond the next intersection, because she was trying to visualize the geography behind her: the girl with her gun, standing a little too close, maybe not so experienced at this kind of thing. With the proper timing and a little luck, Madsen—who had been in this very situation too many times before—probably couldn't avoid getting shot but might be able to elude a mortal wound.

"I'm hungry," the girl said too quickly and circled around Madsen, cautious, revealing herself. Not a girl but girlish—still young, maybe thirty, and breathtaking. Fair skin, black hair, long legs but not tall, she had a dancer's grace and the heavy-lidded gaze of an apex predator. "Have you eaten? We could go to that takeaway place, Pret A Manger. Do you love it as much as I do? So much variety. There's one right around the corner."

Madsen wanted her knife back. It was a gift from her father, and now that she'd sized up her opponent, she had no fear of saying yes.

In English, the girl said, "Sweet." Her teeth, when she smiled, were not quite perfect, and from the way the girl quickly put the smile to bed again, Madsen could tell how much it bothered her.

"Your boots. Are they Clergerie?"

"Yes."

"*Chévere*. They're adorable. Please, order whatever you want. I am buying. Expense account." She waved a credit card from a Swiss bank, and Madsen caught just the first name *Mercedes* before it fluttered back into the deep pocket of a thick cardigan sweater. Madsen wondered where the gun had gone. "The mac and cheese is to die for. I get it every time. You've been here?"

Madsen hadn't. The self-serve chain seemed to have a storefront on every street in London, but she'd never been interested in takeaway food. The front of the shop smelled of espresso and fresh bread, with bright displays filled with ready-made meals and snacks and healthy juice drinks. She had already decided she would just walk away if this got any weirder, but she reasoned that with all the people here seeking rest and refuge from the light show crowd and London chill, there were too many witnesses for the girl to cause her much trouble. Although not fond of improvisation, Charlotte would let events unfold and go from there.

"I'll just have some tea. Thank you."

"My pleasure."

Mercedes ordered and paid and found them a booth against the wall, where they sat opposite and studied each other as if playing chess. Tense, still irritated, Madsen didn't like dealing with women in her work. Men were generally predictable, if thorny, always overestimating their abilities no matter how able they were.

"You're thinking," the girl said, "that because of the calls I might have something to do with your employer's death."

"It was really more that you might know something that could be helpful."

Mercedes ignored this. "You suspect that I am the front man. Or facilitator. Or perhaps even that it was me who took on the contract myself."

Madsen decided not to dance. "Did you?"

Macaroni and cheese was pushed forward. "Are you sure you don't want to share this?"

"I'm certain, yes."

The crooked smile flashed again. There was sadness behind it, a menace in it, and a worrisome recklessness that Madsen needed to manage. "Tell me about your friend Aubrey Sentro."

Madsen was puzzled by this next sharp turn. "Arshavin's consultant? I only know her in passing." She wondered: *How does this girl know about Sentro?*

"I don't believe you."

"Believe what you want; the facts say otherwise."

"Facts. Ah." With her mouth full, Mercedes amiably mumbled something about lies and their consequences, then wiped her mouth with her napkin and said, both questions and statements, "So. Factually. She is some kind of secret agent?"

"Was." Madsen nodded.

"What are the facts about how does he know her, your boss?"

"I don't know," Madsen lied. "But Ilya was KGB, back in the day. Maybe from that. Why do you ask?"

"Idle curiosity." She sat, fork poised over her food, as if pensive. "Why would your employer need a spy if he has you?"

"Wealthy people like Ilya often call upon individuals who have special insight into the shadow world, especially before making big decisions about investments that could be affected by what happens there. It's called thin-slicing. Do you know this term?"

The girl admitted she didn't and resumed eating her meal.

"It's the ability to find patterns in the world, to look at events and understand situations and behavior based on narrow windows, or slices, of experience. A kind of intuition."

"Oh, I would be really good at that," the girl said without looking up.

"We all do it, but for some it's a gift," Madsen observed, staying with a neutral tone. "And lucrative if you can get connected with the right people." Her present narrow window was telling her this young woman was not just closely connected to Arshavin's death but responsible for managing it. Not the contractor, though. Who sent her?

"She has two grown children."

"Does she?"

"Her husband died of cancer." It was like she had a list.

"It would seem you know more about her than I do." Madsen had begun absently charting the best way out of the Pret A Manger.

"You haven't touched your tea."

"So I guess you can't help me?"

The girl's green eyes went dead. "No. I wish I could. I'm sorry."

Madsen knew she should leave then, but curiosity got the better of her. "What is it you want from Aubrey Sentro?"

"Nothing," the girl said, scraping the last of the macaroni out of the recyclable bowl and then washing it down with Pellegrino. "Nothing *from* her, I mean." She looked thoughtful. "It's complicated," she said with a melodramatic sigh.

Okay. Now it was just getting weird. Madsen nodded and drank tepid tea.

"But do you think," the young woman started up again, "she would want to know that the baby she hoped had died didn't?"

Unsure she'd heard this right, Madsen frowned. "I don't know . . . but—what?"

"I mean, *I* wouldn't," the girl insisted.

A hazy rain was falling on the street outside, smearing the shop lights, encouraging light show strollers to take refuge under the doorway overhang. Madsen's mind was spinning, half-stunned, half-confounded. Mercedes was pulling on her coat.

"How would you know?"

The girl gave her a strange, serene look as if that was her answer. Madsen felt a faint stir of untethered fear. "The neon wave installation on Grosvenor is well worth the walk, if you have time. It stretches the entire length of the diagonal and reminds me of the morning surf in Maro."

She slid out of the booth and stood, pulling her coat off the hook. "Shall we?"

———

Together they walked to the front door. Madsen kept her eyes on the girl's hands. The threat she'd felt hadn't passed, but maybe Mercedes was just what Madsen's mother would call *gestört*. A phone call to Sentro would be Madsen's next move.

They pushed through the glass door, into the awkward, idle crowd looking out at the rain. The street hissed as if with static, and the girl was jostled in front, giving Madsen all the tactical advantage. They broke through the gridlock, and the drizzle made their faces shine.

"Goodbye," the girl said, turning, with the crooked, closed-mouth smile.

"Can I have my knife back," Madsen asked, then regretted it.

"Of course," the girl said, and it was in her hand, and with the gentle motion of someone giving a fond farewell pat, she twice drove the blade deep into Madsen's midsection and walked off.

The pain was unbearable; her field of vision narrowed, and Madsen couldn't catch her breath. Dizzy, disappointed, she swayed and stepped backward and heard exclamations of annoyance, felt hands not quite catching her, and heard her father's voice, scolding her for being so careless, and she hoped later he would forgive her and let her ride pig-gyback up the stairs and read her a story, and she smelled her mother's strudel and felt the cold brush of her hand on her cheek as she fell to the sidewalk, where she could see her blood splattering down to mix with the rainwater and drain away from her, like everything else.

Chapter Twenty-Four

How long before you start to worry when your grown daughter doesn't return to the hotel room you're sharing?

Sentro would have waited until the next morning if Jeremy hadn't called and awakened her from an agitated dream that scattered like dust motes when she reached for the phone.

"You know how you said to be wary of weird calls?" He'd had one at work with someone he'd initially assumed was a prospective client. Spanish accent, perfect English. Sentro took a deep, worried breath. A hard rain drummed outside against the hotel window.

"She dialed my private extension, so I picked up. Hello, yada yada, she said we might be related."

"What?"

"Yeah, right?"

"Name?"

"Carmen . . . something."

"Jeremy—"

"She only said it once; I wasn't paying attention. It was all on account of how she'd gotten the results back from one of those DNA tests that everyone's doing. Or so she said. You know, whatsitcalled—23andMe?"

"Did you have your DNA done?"

"God, no. But I thought maybe you. Or more likely Jenny."

"I've spent my whole life trying to stay out of unsecured databases. You know that. And Jenny would never even get past all that spitting into a tube—"

"Right. You're right. I'm sorry. I wasn't thinking."

"Anyway, they don't give out names and phone numbers without permission."

Jeremy got defensive, and his voice went up an octave. "Yeah, well, how the fuck am I supposed to know that?"

Backing off, Sentro told him she wasn't blaming him for anything—but there would no doubt be a reckoning with him in the future—she was keen to know what the woman wanted. He admitted that he wasn't exactly sure. "She knew a lot about our family. How Dad's parents were both doctors, how Grandpa Rand was with the rangers. Said next time she was on the East Coast, she'd like to get together." *It's a threat,* Sentro thought, chilled. "It was super weird," Jeremy added. "Who is she?"

"I'm working on that. This is why I wanted you to go away with Beth-Ann."

"Bryce-Ann. Shit. Mom. Am I in danger?" Jeremy sounded scared. The last time he'd become tangled in her world, it had nearly killed him. "Where's Jenny?"

"With me." And that was when she noticed with unease that her daughter's bed was still empty. She hadn't come back from Independence Square.

"Are you guys still in New Mexico?"

Sentro didn't want to tell him about the ranch, about poor Clete and Ilya Arshavin, Banks and the Five Eyes. If only she could rewind time by two weeks; if only she'd declined going to see the Russian in Paris, maybe none of this would have happened.

She wanted to believe it. She wanted to think she had some choice in the matter.

"Mom?"

"We're in Europe. For the moment."

Jeremy stayed silent. This was why it had been so much easier when her kids didn't know who she was. All the explaining was exhausting her. When her husband, Dennis, was their anchor, she'd conjured a comforting fiction that they needed to stay safe and feel loved. She hadn't been wrong to hide her life from them.

She heard the familiar squawk of Jeremy shifting in his lucky chair, the hush of his investment firm in the background. She could imagine him: it was late afternoon there, autumn sun slanting through the windows off the bay. A normal life, with normal risks.

She wished she could put a force field around her children so that they would never be touched by who she was. Now Jenny was gone, and she had to remind herself that adult children couldn't be swaddled and controlled.

"I have a friend with a family condo in Virginia Beach," Jeremy said. "I could probably work from there remotely for a week or so. Bryce-Ann has some paid leave coming."

"Do it," Sentro said to him. "I'll feel better."

"*You'll* feel better?"

"Until I can clear this up."

"How?"

The question was reflexive; he didn't really want to know. They said their goodbyes, and Jeremy was about to hang up when Sentro remembered something: "One more thing, Jem. Get a prepaid cell phone. Dial my number and hang up. That's what I'll reach you on for the next couple of weeks. Okay? Just in case."

Because Jeremy sounded worried again as the call ended, while she stared bleakly at her daughter's untouched bed, Sentro felt overwhelmed by the exponential complications caused by her children. There was a bad dream she'd sometimes had when she was younger: trying to cross a busy highway—I-94, in fact—with both kids in separate strollers. Pushing one, pulling the other. Jeremy kept struggling to get out. She'd wake up sweating and let Dennis assume it was mission creep. Because of what it might say about her, she was afraid to tell him the truth.

She couldn't get used to it, didn't want to get used to it, and there was no sense of satisfaction for her in shielding them from a threat she still couldn't identify or anticipate. If it was Günter Witt coming after her, why? After all these years, why? What she hadn't told Jenny—what she hadn't ever told anyone—what she'd spent half her life trying to forget, was the only thing, besides the dead child, that she truly remembered from the time after she was arrested: he'd broken her. Whether it was the violation, the psychological torture, or the raging hormones and stress of being unwillingly pregnant and alone and frightened, in prison, in isolation, Witt had turned Sentro inside out, worn down whatever resistance she had tried to mount, and left her postpartum, grieving, stoned, and empty, stripped of all semblance of who she was before she walked into East Berlin with the naive assignment to take a picture of him for the spymasters back home.

A pawn in their game, removed from the board early.

That part she never told her handlers. The breaking was her secret. And Witt's. She was certain it was in his evil fucking Pandora's box of Stasi-built blackmail he took with him when he fled his crumbling kingdom.

He held all the cards on her.

Pattern recognition—the Madrid bombing, Arshavin, an attack on Otter's private prison—it occurred to her that all of it was part of a larger scheme. *But what peril*, she wondered, *could I possibly pose to him?*

Then a dime dropped; non sequitur; her subconscious, grinding away behind the scenes, made connections, surfaced, and solved her current crisis riddle: Banks.

She dialed his cell, somehow sure he'd be awake. "Jenny's with you?"

"How did you know?"

"She's my daughter, Banks."

"A point that she might argue, evidently." He sounded distracted, and she heard movement from what she assumed was her daughter, close by. "What did you two talk about today?"

"Berlin."

Banks was quiet, no doubt thinking about what that might have included. Sentro wondered how much of her file he'd read, and if some of it was still classified and redacted.

"Jenny okay?"

Any American she'd ever worked with would have toyed with her at that point, teased and made her squirm because they could, but Banks, the good-hearted Canadian, answered honestly: "Yeah. Good now. Just shaken. And stray-dog wet."

———

He'd spent most of the day in Otter's new crib, an abandoned boat-repair shop on the river that the old spook callously called "Rendition Redux." The Eyes had approved access to a digital intel group in Christchurch; Banks sent them scans of the albino killer's passport and boarding pass and was waiting to see if they led anywhere. There might be surveillance footage of him from the Albuquerque airport, and a picture of his as-yet-unknown female accomplice. The number could be anything, and neither of them could translate the Cyrillic scrawl.

At around four o'clock Banks went back to his long-term hotel suite because Otter said there was "new meat" coming in from Tunisia, a possible dangle (Otter's colorful shorthand was beginning to rub Banks raw), and since this had nothing to do with Operation Pogo, the Canadian was off the clock. Otter's new quartet of interrogators (*how easily replaceable we all are!*) was already strategizing in the break room; Banks recalled that Gillian hated prescripted cross-questioning because of how it locked you in. The secret of a good interview, she liked to say, was letting the subject think they had some control over what they were telling. The slow suffocation of their lies.

Poor Gilly.

He missed her, he mourned her, but not for the reasons she would have wanted.

It was after midnight when someone knocking on his door awakened him. He didn't bother to dress to answer it, sleepy and guessing room service had the wrong suite. Jenny Troon stood out in the hallway, soaked through, so pale from the rain's chill she might have been a zombie. Mascara a clown show, her hair a matted tangle, she looked hopelessly lost and fiercely recalcitrant.

It took his breath away.

"What the fuck, Banks," she said, shivering. "Can I please come in?"

He convinced her to take a hot shower and gave her the complimentary hotel robe and slippers from the closet. Cleaned up, she was unabashedly pretty and knew it.

Nothing like her mother in that regard.

"Don't get any wise ideas; this isn't a booty call," she warned him, but it was false bravado, masking real pain. "I just didn't know where else I could go." He hadn't really noticed her intricate sleeve tattoo before, a serpent that wound up around her arm and disappeared under the back of the robe. Was she flirting? He couldn't read her. Banks had grown up with three sisters, but this woman was a different species. American, for one thing, but Gillian was a Yank and nothing like Jenny Troon. She had all of her mother's wily impenetrability, plus her own unpredictably volatile emotions, which he'd never seen Sentro indulge. It occurred to him that he probably couldn't trust her daughter; it occurred to him that he might not care.

Told that it was too late to order from room service, she proceeded to loot the minibar and, between pretzels, cheese crackers, and little bottles of Baileys Irish Cream, whinged her litany of gripes and grievances about her mother and her mother's life of lies. All Banks could think about was his expense report. Everything in the minibar was super expensive, even the nuts. How would he characterize Sentro's daughter? Entertainment? Damage control?

"I was so hungry," Jenny said after a while. "Did you know she had a baby who died?"

Banks said he did. "There's a big fat file in CIA archives on her Berlin kerfuffle. Probably with duplicates at the DIA."

"So everybody knew but me. And my brother."

"Top secret. Not everybody."

Jenny made a dismissive noise and screwed open a bottle of Kahlúa, staying with the cocoa theme. "If we had ice cream, I could make Moose Milk," she said and took a sip. She was looking a little drunk, the bridge of her nose and tips of her ears blushed pink, and color was back in her cheeks. Her eyes danced. "You got any weed?"

No, Banks didn't. And he wouldn't let her light a cigarette either.

"I thought everybody smoked in the Great White North."

Banks's phone started ringing, and in the time it took him to find it and answer, Jenny was asking, "Is it my mom?" Banks said, "How did you know?" to both of them, but only Sentro responded.

"Tell her we just fucked. Or we're fucking like bunnies." Jenny drained the Kahlúa and held him with bleary eyes. "She won't care. She's into cowboys and Egyptians."

He was juggling two conversations, and either Sentro couldn't hear what Jenny was saying, or she was pretending she couldn't.

"Good now," Banks said when Sentro asked how her daughter was. "Just shaken. And stray-dog wet."

"I think it's for the best," Sentro said then.

"What is?"

"You looking after her for me while I sort this out."

"Wait wait wait," Banks stammered. "The Eyes think Arshavin was one part of a bigger move."

"I've been thinking the same thing."

"We're a team; we need to do this together. You can't just go off and—"

"Is she leaving us?" Jenny wondered, talking over him, the words tangling on her tongue. She toppled slowly over onto her side, looking on the verge of a blackout. "Oh no. Oh no. I'm getting the whirlies."

Sentro was explaining, "You're a team, Banks—you, Otter, the Eyes. Me, I have this problem: I don't care about the big picture, and I've never really played well with others."

"Where are you going?"

"I won't get in your way, don't worry. Save the world, if you can. I just want my kids to be safe. If Pogo has a beef with me, I need to find what it is and fix it."

"Aubrey—"

She said, "I'm counting on you to protect her, Banks. I can't do this while I'm worried about that."

Do what?

Lying on the carpet, Jenny was crooning new words to a familiar melody in a thick phony Texas accent:

As I wandered out in the desert of Egypt,
as I walked the desert of Egypt one day . . .

"Aubrey?"

The line went dead on Banks.

. . . I spied this hot cowboy, was ripped like Vin Diesel,
was ripped like Vin Diesel and ready to plaaaaay.

Jenny Troon gazed deadpan at Banks from sideways on the floor. "Don't be sad. She'll come back. She always comes back."

There was one big bed in Banks's suite; he needed to get her in it and call housekeeping for some blankets so he could try to sleep in the big armchair.

"What was your girlfriend like? The one who got killed?"

There was nothing Banks could think of to say. The question blind-sided him as he turned down the bed, and he didn't look at Sentro's daughter for a while. The room lights glared.

"She deserved better than me," Banks said.

Jenny made a huffing noise. "Yeah. Ain't that always the case?" She rolled onto her back. "Shit, I'm sorry. I'm sorry."

"No reason for you to be sorry about anything."

"You have . . . no idea."

Banks turned around to face her. "Can you sit up?"

"There's all kinds of sad in your eyes, Banks."

Banks nodded. "Okay."

"But not the kind that comes from losing somebody you were in love with."

Drunk off her ass, Banks had to remind himself. *Doesn't know what she's saying.*

"You know what's really fucked up, Banks?" Jenny rolled onto her side, curled up, and shut her eyes. "I'm not mad at my mom for lying to me. I'm mad for not knowing."

Banks knew the feeling. He hoped she wouldn't get sick. She didn't look like much of a drinker. He remembered a kegger in university where he had to hold his then-girlfriend's hair back while she threw up.

That's so me, Banks thought, a little demoralized. *Mr. Dependable.*

Tears were leaking out of Jenny's closed eyes. "If I had known, growing up, that this is who she was . . ." She let the thought hang.

"Can you keep a secret, Banks? My mom—I wanted to be like her. I pretended I didn't, but . . . you know—mothers and daughters." Banks did know. "More than anything, what I wanted," Jenny whispered. "But with all her secrets and lies, I didn't even know what the fuck that would be." More tears leaked. "And now it's too late."

CHAPTER TWENTY-FIVE

The rain falls in pleated silver curtains.

Steam from her labored breathing shrouds her like a veil.

She's back in the forest camp of empty Quonset huts and out-buildings: the fierce storm, the augered holes, the icy drowning water flooding in. How many times has she stumbled into the anxious swirl of her arboreal dream? But this time she's aware, as it unfolds, of what's coming but is unable to stop herself from suffering through it all again. Half-engaged and half-detached, she keeps thinking, in a crawling panic, *This isn't real, I'm dreaming, I can wake up, and I will.*

High-beam headlights pierce the downpour, a road-worn, misfiring UAZ-469 rolling in from behind the other trucks.

She wiggles pregnant from the overflowing hole and scutters across the mud and past the nearest hut as light sweeps past her. But this time she notices the tarnished, peeling sign on the door, German words she can't translate, a swastika on all four corners.

Orders shouted to the guards over the pounding rainfall send her scrambling into the shelter of the machine room, where she picks a hiding place against a half wall of cinder block and crouches down to look out through a gash in the steel siding at the commanding officer, backlit, purple collar on his uniform and explosion of angelic white-blond hair slowly darkening and slicked by the water; he's directing his men to round up the prisoners and put them back into the truck.

Show's over. Eyes lost in shadow, his face is made all angles and planes by the cruel light.

The sound of gunfire; dull flashes reflect off the curved wet cartoon fenders of the troop carrier.

A drowned body is hurried through the streaming lights.

A blur of sobbing, broken captives lines up against the truck, counting off.

Her panic peaks; they will know that she is missing.

Wake up.

Wake up.

But what follows is new: hiding, waiting, praying they won't find her.

Wake up.

A rumble of the trucks turning around, pulling away, rain drumming on the roof where she's hidden, the spatter of water on the flooded yard, the desperate pounding of her heart—it didn't feel like a dream anymore, and it wasn't.

Wake up.

She had; she was already awake, snarled in her hotel bedcovers, breathless, soaked with sweat and remembering the forest and the old Nazi work camp; no longer a bad dream her PTSD or her subconscious had concocted from this and that, but a real piece of Kabuki theater for newly drugged Stasi captives, an elaborate psyops-contrived hellscape designed to destabilize and soften prisoners for what came next.

A Günter Witt production.

But even dulled by pharmaceuticals she had managed to slip away. She sat up and blinked her eyes in the darkness, looked to the window and the soft glow of Kyiv to confirm she wasn't sleeping. She remembered hiding in the cold little cinder block outbuilding, knowing they'd discovered her escape, and her confusion and surprise that the trucks had driven out anyway.

Nineteen and out of her depth, she waited, listening, but wasn't even sure what she was listening for or why. She didn't know where she was, which way to go if she wanted to try to walk to freedom. The hopelessness of her situation overwhelmed her. What was she thinking in escaping? She'd had no training for this; wherever she went she'd be a stranger, and in a country of informants it would only be a matter of time before the security service recaptured her and some lucky citizen got some extra ration cards.

And then what? She closed her eyes, feeling faint from hunger and fatigue. She'd fucked this all up. Now they could tell the West she'd died trying to escape.

The sound of heavy boots outside pulled her out of one panic and into another. There was only one door in and out, and someone was tugging on the rusted metal door, with its faded Nazi markings. A man's shadow filled the opening. A flashlight found and blinded her. She raised her open hands, like she'd seen people do a million times in the movies.

"Don't shoot me."

She expected Witt.

It was Matthias Schmidt.

———

She remembered the coarse feel and stale smell of the UAZ's scratchy blanket, which he wrapped around her after handcuffing her to a bracket on the dashboard. She remembered the way he walked around to the driver's side of the Soviet-made Jeep and passed through the headlights, and how she thought she saw in his face a grim ambivalence about the task at hand.

And the lingering sting of her betrayal.

For a while, driving back, they had nothing to say to each other. They'd found the film; her guilt was clear. She was also pretty confident that the operatives she'd shielded had safely made their way over the wall. Tires whined on the worn asphalt two-lane, the engine labored, and everything rattled. Schmidt tried to find something on the radio but gave up.

"Let me go, Matthias," Sentro said finally, breaking the silence. Schmidt glanced at her with wounded, hooded eyes but had no response. She took that as a good omen and pressed her luck. She had nothing to lose.

"He's going to kill me," she said.

"No, he's not."

"I've typed other incident reports, Matti. I know the drill. Enemy agent trying to escape."

"You are mistaken. We're a country of laws. Of process and procedures. Maybe on your side that kind of thing is acceptable, but we don't do it," Schmidt insisted, stubborn, but didn't look at her because he knew it was a lie.

"I'm a soldier," she pleaded. "This was the mission."

"Fortunes of war, then." He shrugged.

"I thought you liked me." As the words came out, she shuddered at their banality.

"I was deceived," he said. "Part of your mission."

"At first," she admitted. "But things changed. You changed them."

"Fuck off," he told her in English, and it sounded like the first time he'd ever said it.

"They sent me to take a picture of him. That's all. They didn't tell me why. I'm a common soldier, the lowest rank. I follow my orders." Schmidt glanced at her; he looked wounded, his pride dented. "I'm not a spy, Matti; you know I'm not. How could I be?" She reached out with her free hand and put it on his leg. It all felt so contrived, but it was the best she could manage. "Let me go. Say you didn't find me."

"You'd never make it over the wall."

"Not without your help, no. Please."

The road curved through heavy forest, then broke over a rise, and she could see a scatter of farm lights in the darkness and the glowing arc of light thrown up by Berlin above the horizon ahead. Schmidt found a turnout and pulled over, braking gently until they were stopped. Killed the headlights but left the engine running and misfiring, the heater blowing hot on her legs.

"And why would I do this?" he asked her, eyes straight ahead, jaw set.

"Because you're a good man. A kind man." She waited for a reaction, got none. "Dare I say, fair."

"I would be risking my career for you."

"I know."

She remembered how she'd softened her voice. Left her hand on his thigh. Crazy, but she had found herself drifting, distracted, thinking about Dennis in that critical moment—about who had made the first move on whom. It was him, though; she felt sure of it. For all her confidence, she'd been scared of her feelings, afraid he didn't share the intensity of hers.

But she couldn't remember the moment then, and she couldn't thirty years later, lying in the darkness of her hotel room, listening to the wet night wind's harmonics on the big windowpanes, rainbow smear of Kyiv outside while inside she grew cold remembering her humiliating effort to seduce Schmidt.

He looked at her, and she leaned across and kissed him. Lightly at first, and then he responded. Their teeth clacked, his tongue like a tumor, tasting of tobacco and vinegar. His hand found its way under her blanket, under her soggy shirt.

She forced herself to move her hand up his leg. The erection she discovered seemed tentative, so she worked on it; there was nothing sexy about this. Felt all wrong. But Schmidt had tears running down his face; he wanted her, he would sell his soul, he was every trope of a man blinded by love.

She felt evil. And nauseated. But she was determined to play things out to the end if the trade-off would be her freedom.

It was Schmidt who broke it off.

"All right," he whispered. "All right."

He sounded resolute. Gently disengaging from her, he wiped his cheeks with his shirtsleeve, flicked the headlights back on, and dropped the UAZ into gear. They fishtailed back onto the two-lane and sped back into the city.

But not to the wall, or some secluded stretch of the boundary between East and West where she could just slip over. He drove her to the unmarked annex building that would become her home for the next eleven months.

And like the dutiful guardian of the revolution that he was, he delivered her to Günter Witt.

———

Oberleutnant Kimmich was waiting outside the entrance, smoking, wrapped in an overcoat too big for her; that was the last clear image Sentro remembered. Fear had overtaken her. Harsh downlight, silky swirling smoke, the crimson glow as Kimmich took her final drag before dropping the butt on the pavement and coming forward to open the door and unlock Sentro's handcuff. Schmidt didn't look at either one of them. He seemed anxious to drive away.

Sentro's memory of almost everything that followed became shredded like the Stasi files that got purged after the wall came down. Piecing the year back together from a distance of three decades resulted in shifting, unreliable mosaics, fleeting at best.

Stripped, shorn, deloused, that first night she might have been forced to shower in front of a leering, pudgy male civilian shrink, who gave her a thin smock and rubber slippers and then injected her with a cocktail of narcotics that rocked her so hard she threw up and couldn't walk. Or maybe that was a different time.

There was the cell you took three steps down into, and it was filled with frigid water at intervals, making it impossible to sit or sleep.

When had that been? How long did she stay?

And the questions.

Who sent you? What is the name of your case officer? Who does he answer to? What are the names of the agents in East Berlin who supported you? What are the names of the East Berlin citizens you enlisted as assets? Intelligence she knew, intelligence she didn't. Witt's imperious tenor *Hochdeutsch* was a drone in her head, constant, indefatigable, beehive, swarming, probing.

Heroin. Cocaine. Speedballs. Steroids. Hallucinogens. She was their private testing ground for cutting-edge pharmaceutical torture. One long, brutal party. She had murky memories of Schmidt visiting, sitting by her bunk, watching her nod off. The open sores on her arms and collapsed veins where repeated injections had caused purple bruises.

And the nights (how many?) she surfaced helpless to Greta Kimmich and the shrink holding her half-numbed arms while Witt, pants unbuckled, boxers pulled down, would rape her ("Women have the very unfortunate disadvantage in war," he would tell her like he was narrating a nature film; "so it has always been") while she thought of her husband and her baby and begged him to stop.

Fragment of a conversation, but from who knew when? The silky, sinister tenor: *You'll spy for me.*

No.

You're the discard, Soldier Sentro. Your country has no intention of rescuing you. Negotiate a swap? Dream on. You're meaningless. A throwaway.

I'm not.

The sacrificial lamb.

Stop.

Tot. Ganz tot—

Please.

—Mausetot. *Which is why you'll spy for me.*

If you stop.

Stop?

I have a baby. I have a life I will go back to, and you've destroyed it.

Me? You enjoy this. You do. You're an addict. You're a whore. Pleasure, pain, it's all of a piece. But if you spy for me, I will have Dr. Jurgen put you back together like new. We can do that. Or even better.

And you'll stop?

Yes. You think I like it? You think I enjoy doing this to you?

She believed that he did, yes. Never doubted it, even when she doubted her own will to stay alive.

And then one day, in the regular examinations that were done to ensure she could endure more of the same, they discovered she was pregnant, and the interrogations, the disruptions, the torture, the hard drugs, the violation, stopped. Simply stopped.

But the gaps remained. Days, weeks—gone. Never remembered, or erased?

She had soft-focus memories of Schmidt, visiting. Were they real? His grave, wounded expression? Familiar bits and scraps stitched together to fashion something resembling coherence. Or failing that, somewhat bearable. And Witt? His face was a blank, by accident or design. But his voice was seared into her.

The cell she walked out of in December of 1990 was the cell she gave birth in.

The baby died.

Her depression was so crushing during and after pregnancy they switched her to more, but different, drugs. This was revealed in some duplicate medical files that the CIA recovered from the abandoned annex some months after the wall came down. Antidepressants, antipsychotics, experimental hormone therapies; she floated through a summer and fall. She'd missed Jeremy's birthday; she probably didn't even know when it was. She remembered dreaming of her one love, Dennis Troon, and crying herself to sleep wondering what he'd think of what she'd become.

Or was it all of a dream she'd had, and the reality lay somewhere else?

Trembling, Sentro slid out of bed and walked to the hotel window and pulled aside the curtain. The rain had stopped. A startling crisp darkness yawned over the lights of the city, and she felt hollowed by her memories, as she always did.

She couldn't hide from them, couldn't run from them. What had happened in New Mexico, the phone call to Jeremy—she could no longer shield her children from her past. She had to find Witt, settle the score with him again, and trust that Banks could protect her daughter. There was no other choice she could make.

A different woman had returned from Berlin. Dennis noticed it right away. She told him the truth: all that she remembered, and all that she'd been given by the analysts and case officers whose job it was to armchair quarterback. Still, big parts of what had happened to her were missing. Gaps in the tape. White noise that sometimes surfaced and troubled her.

She'd been broken, but it hadn't broken her. *You've shed a skin.* That was Dennis Troon's assessment, as he held her and loved her and helped heal her, and with Jenny's birth she bolted the door on an unfortunate episode that she would refuse, as she walked back into the world, to let define her.

Now she planned to open it. And put the past to rest.

CHAPTER TWENTY-SIX

"They assure me that I died in the ambulance," Madsen said. Ashen skinned, listless, she looked shrunken in the angled ICU bed, and she sounded defeated. Her voice had been torn by the ventilator they'd had down her throat for almost a day. Wires and tubes snaked out from under the heated bedcover, and the wild array of monitors and screens was making Sentro a little woozy.

"I'm so fucking stupid," Madsen added.

The text had come out of nowhere in the sleepless hours after she awoke from her fretful dreams. Unknown sender—eight words and a long-distance number: Your friend is in hospital, please call back. Apparently, before she flatlined, Madsen had begged an EMT to phone Sentro; Charlotte didn't even remember doing it. They weren't exactly friends; they had only Arshavin in common. But Sentro had returned the call and gotten the outlines of the tragedy that might be unfolding—a street mugging, mortal knife wounds, the name of the hospital. Still wrung out from her confession to Jenny, she nevertheless hurried a bag together, took a taxi to Boryspil International, and booked the first flight out to London.

Was it recklessness born of desperation, or a calculated risk?

"What does she look like?"

"Breathtakingly beautiful."

"Okay, but that's not helpful, Lotte."

"Female Caucasian, five nine, oval face, black hair, green eyes flecked with yellow, or maybe that was just the light. Cuban accent, speaks flawless German." Madsen wiggled her fingers weakly in the direction of her sippy cup, and Sentro held the straw up to her lips so she could drink. "She knew her way around a gun but didn't seem to me to be ex-military. Inexpert with the knife, to my benefit."

"Name?"

"She said Carmen. But I caught the name Mercedes on a credit card she used."

"How did she find you?"

"I found her. Lenkov had called her burner phone the day he died. Along with a Cuban sat phone, before and after Paris."

"Sat phones are illegal in Cuba."

"They are, yes."

"You went to see Lenkov," Sentro realized.

"It went sideways," Madsen admitted. "I wasn't thinking straight. Anger and grief skewed my judgment."

Sentro waited, but that was all Madsen wanted to say on the subject. "You contacted her?"

"I left a message. She's resourceful."

"A hunter," Sentro said, remembering New Mexico.

"At the very least."

"Have the police been by?"

"A few times, yes."

Sentro waited. *And?*

"So dark, the crowds. Somehow, she has managed to avoid the legendary London surveillance grid. They have my description of her, but I imagine she's in the wind by now."

Sentro considered the phone call her son had received. Thought: *No, she's not.*

"What did she want from you?"

Madsen hesitated. Closed her eyes. Sentro thought maybe she'd faded, but it was just a gathering. "I believe I asked her that exact question, but I'm not sure now. It's weird what we remember, isn't it?"

"I have trouble with my memory," Sentro said.

Madsen nodded. "Ilya mentioned it. It doesn't show." She tried to shift her position, failed, and fell back against the pillows framing her head. "She wanted to know about you."

"Me?"

"I'm told my heart had stopped," Madsen said, staring vacantly into the middle distance of the room, "but I so clearly can recall them rushing me into the ER from the truck. Cutting my clothes off. Crushing my chest, pushing air into my lungs with a balloon. They used the paddles. I tasted copper and lemon. It felt like I levitated and hung there, halfway to the ceiling. No bright light at the end of a tunnel. No slideshow of my life flickering past. Just the noise of the ER, the coded language of doctors and nurses." She opened her eyes. "They say I was dead for four minutes." It was distressing for Sentro to see Lotte like this. Madsen lay motionless for a while, lost in thought. "I don't remember her stabbing me."

In the business of black ops, it was typical to be less afraid of death than dying. "Better," someone had said to Sentro once, "to just wink out." But what about when you've opened yourself up to the people who care about you? Is your life really your own?

"I won't be the same, after this, will I?" Madsen asked.

"Maybe not," Sentro admitted. "Maybe that's a good thing," she added. Madsen looked at her for a while and then smiled faintly. An easy silence followed, which Sentro broke, finally. "Lotte, what did you tell her? About me?"

"Nothing. She seemed to know so much already."

"Did she say why she wanted to know about me?"

Madsen gestured for the water again, and this time she took the cup from Sentro with both hands and held it against her chest after drinking. The effort exhausted her. But she seemed to be avoiding Sentro's question. "A millimeter this way or that way," she wheezed, "my father's knife would have nicked my heart, and there would be no Lazarus rising for Charlotte."

"She didn't tell you, or you don't want to tell me?" Sentro pressed her.

"Four minutes dead, though. You take stock of all the vital lies and bitter truths."

"I guess."

"I was a little bit in love with Ilya, you know."

You were probably the last person to realize it, Sentro thought, waited. She knew that Madsen would circle back around.

"She has your eyes," Madsen noted, weary, after the longest pause, studying Sentro like she was a stranger.

"What did she tell you?"

"Something about a stillborn child?"

The air went out of the ICU, and the space seemed to swell—curtain walls, ceiling lights, and floor moving away from her. Sentro felt gutted, took an uneasy breath. Her mind went blank. She said, "I don't know what you're talking about," even though she did.

Fading, her eyes fluttering closed again, Madsen shook her head and murmured, "She thinks she's your daughter."

———

The voice mail Mercedes left for him was unsettling. He hadn't heard from her since their fraught dead-of-night argument in New Mexico; she was supposed to come home to regroup, but there had been only radio silence broken by this short, cryptic phone message she had left the night before: "It's me. I've sent the Chechen ahead to Andalusia. I need some time alone to think. I'm not angry with you, but I am shattered by what you told me. My life is a lie."

And Aubrey Sentro was still alive.

Ha—ha—ha—

The albino had confirmed that Mercedes had ditched him at Heathrow, and with a head wound only stopgap triaged, Yusupov was in no condition to go chasing after her. She'd never acted out like this before.

His *café cubano* had gone tepid; nothing on the island got cold on its own. As he watched a distant group of tourists walk from the museum to the farthest of the five former cellblock cylinders, his stomach rumbled and twisted, and he stretched to ease the pain. It was so quiet he could hear laughing gulls (*ha—ha—*) mocking the ocean crashing on the low cliffs west of the city, and the hot Caribbean wind that funneled through the exposed arc of the concrete panopticon set the gaping cells softly mewling like a huge harmonica.

The gulls would be coming at dusk to pick through the garbage bins behind the museum, the ones that seemed never to get emptied. And then they'd flock to roost in the windowless cells, cackle, and shit on his home. He despised them. But he would have the last laugh.

He wheeled back across the courtyard, past the observation tower, up a long, gently inclined ramp, and into his spacious living quarters, where, for almost two decades, he'd plied his tradecraft for the private sector. A crass, born-again capitalist in the last outpost of true communism.

Except for those times when he'd moved money in or out of the original Swiss accounts, he hadn't used the name Günter Witt for a long, long time. There was too much baggage that came with it; he no longer needed it after the first few months of getting resettled. But the code name Western intelligence had chosen for their elusive Stasi spymaster—Pogo—*that* he still took perverse satisfaction in using whenever he wanted to troll them for their abject failure to find him.

Or rekindle the Cold War myth that he was untouchable, and formidable, because of the secrets he could wield.

Here on Isla de la Juventud he was Señor Tomas Fischer, refugee from the collapsed GDR, unlucky paraplegic, a respected "geopolitical-conflict consultant" supported by a generous stipend from a Moscow think tank. It was a workable NOC. The Castro government knew who he was, since he had been instrumental in fine-tuning their Intelligence Directorate when he first settled in Havana after leaving Berlin—not to mention he was in possession of hard intelligence that connected certain powerful Council of State ministers to a Colombian drug cartel, which had been quietly covered up by framing and arresting several unfortunate and less powerful assembly members. A peaceful détente was achieved, the Castro brothers at the time none the wiser. For its part, the G2 was more than happy to provide him cover and support, quid pro quo. Many of the veteran special agents had been trained by Stasi attachés, so the relationship was almost brotherly, and when he moved to Nueva Gerona and struck out as a private intelligence contractor after a few years of lying low, a blind eye was turned to Pogo's activities as long as they and he remained in the shadows.

But that was the problem, what was keeping Fischer up at night and causing his diverticulitis to flare: he'd stumbled into the light. Or the Five Eyes had lured him there. He'd already had the warning call from G2 diplomatically reminding him that they couldn't afford to be connected to him if it came down to that. Perhaps, they suggested, he would find another base of operation. Port-au-Prince or Grand Cayman.

His past would unravel his future if he didn't get the next few days exactly right.

My life is a lie.

And Aubrey Sentro was still alive.

"You look like dog shit." Wolfgang was waiting in the kitchen, watching until his bread burned almost black in the oven. They spoke German when they were alone.

"I look how I feel. Fucking gulls."

Wolfie was, what, just north of thirty? Short, geek sleek, with rimless glasses; earnest but incurious, and arrogant as hell. *Not quite his father's child, more a reflection from a fun house mirror,* Fischer mused. Bloodless, though. Cold and calculating in his own peculiar way. Cruel enough. Wolfie would have made an excellent young Stasi recruit.

"Any word?"

"She's taking some personal time." *Mercedes will be searching for Sentro,* he thought. Just as Sentro would be searching for him.

Wolfgang's doubtful nod felt judgmental. Everything Fischer did seemed to piss him off. Oedipal or alpha male? He was young and impatient, and luckily still ignorant of his birthright. The butter he slathered on his bread turned gray with burnt crumbs. Mouth full, he mumbled, "What about her target?"

"Stay in your lane," was what the former Stasi officer who called himself Fischer snapped at his protégé, and the wheelchair's subsequent pivot squawked, angry, as he rumbled toward his office.

"What should I tell the client?"

You'll say what most benefits you, he thought, but said, "Assure them we're into the final phase," and swung the double doors closed as he rolled through them.

Ha—ha—ha—

———

From a café across the street, she watched Aubrey Sentro walk out of Saint Thomas' Hospital and make the turn toward the bridge over the Thames, most likely destined for the Westminster tube station. The older woman's sensible shoes were disappointing.

Never inclined to gamble, Mercedes nevertheless had wagered that Sentro, having heard from her son about a stranger's call, would come to London and visit the bedside of the wounded German bodyguard, sensing there was a connection. That was the only reason she hadn't let the knife's blade do its worst. Her luck held: here was Sentro, everything falling into place. The best improvisations, Fischer would have told her, were the ones that emerged organically from a strong structural foundation.

She'd never stabbed anyone before; it felt incredibly intimate. Her fingertips still tingled, thinking about it. But because her inexperience *had* nearly killed Charlotte Madsen, it was a fair warning not to take a similar risk again with her birth mother.

Shadowing Sentro from the café, she dodged through a traffic snafu on the Westminster approach intersection, then skipped over to the far side of the bridge, while Sentro went briskly down the opposite sidewalk, toward Parliament.

She'd practiced this with her stepbrother Alonzo, in Havana, growing up. A game of moving hide-and-seek through the Paseo del Prado, the objective: getting to Fuente de la India without the other seeing you. Lonzo always won, but she suspected he cheated.

Where was he now? Miami? Tampa? After their mother died, he'd taken a runner across to Mexico and from there found his way into America.

And the other brothers, much older, grown and gone when she was little. Carmen had rarely spoken of them, and the one time she'd asked, her mother had walked out of the room.

No one stayed true to you. This was just how it was.

At the end of the bridge, she crossed to the same side, but Sentro stopped, and Mercedes had no choice but to keep walking. For a moment she thought about making her introduction here, but it was so public, and the Thames smelled of diesel, fish, and sewage; it was all wrong—she kept walking.

She passed within a meter of Aubrey Sentro, smelled the familiar perfume of the New Mexican adobe, avoided the casual glance, kept her head high, and wondered, almost giddy: *What does she think, seeing me, not knowing?*

But now Mercedes had a small problem—Sentro was behind her—how to double back without getting noticed? She resisted the urge to look, which could only give her away. Bridge Street was wide open and congested—London in a nutshell: palace, House of Commons, the grassy parkway. She felt confident that Sentro would be there when she turned. A Chinese tour group passed, heading for the bridge, affording sufficient cover for her to slow as if to check her phone and then cast eyes back for her target.

Her mouth went dry. Aubrey Sentro had disappeared.

Chapter Twenty-Seven

"Do you think my mom is lying about Berlin?"

"As a rule? No."

"She's not telling me everything."

"That's different from lying."

As Jenny Troon recovered from her minibar hangover ("the kraken of hang-fucking-overs," she'd claimed), Banks discovered that she couldn't, or wouldn't, stop talking. Maybe it was her version of hair of the dog, or maybe it was to cover for how shaken she must have been by her mother's harrowing stories and then discovering she'd hopped the first flight out to London and had turned off her phone so she couldn't be tracked.

"You're not even curious about where she's gone?"

He was but kept it simple. "That's how we roll. Need to know."

"Oh. Well, I'd fucking for sure *like* to know."

He had to keep her close. Over breakfast, Jenny recounted, in impressive detail, what her mother had said about the scrambled mission and Stasi imprisonment, much of which Banks already knew, but it was interesting to hear what details Sentro remembered and note what she didn't. Like Jenny, he sensed there was something Sentro was hiding. Not lying, though. More like redacting, for self-preservation.

Jenny admitted, on the brisk walk to Otter's new crib, "I wouldn't have survived what she went through." Banks thought few people could have.

He learned that Jenny's dad had raised her while Sentro did her thing and that her mother and father's relationship was fraught and complicated but held together by the fiercest love. "I have that to aspire to, anyway," she said. "Set a pretty high bar, though. A lot of my boyfriends have shipwrecked and drowned on those rocks."

She said she had never been abroad, except Mexico, and kept asking him questions about Canada, which, like all Americans, she just assumed was the fifty-first state. "Why would Canada even need a spy service? The US has got your back, right?" Her brow furrowed. "Or ass, I guess. Geographically speaking."

"We're not your helpless little brother," Banks said, irritated. "Not 'America with manners' or 'America Light' or all the other condescending shade we get. Our native history goes back as far as yours—and by the way, the Vikings landed in Newfoundland five hundred years before Columbus showed up and didn't discover the New World."

"Yeah, but you're the loyal ones. We're the rebels. Everybody loves the rebel."

"We invented fucking Wonderbras. And peanut butter. And instant replay."

Otter just watched them, eyes going back and forth, like at a tennis match.

She cracked gum at Banks, poker faced. "I will say your national anthem rocks. Always makes me want to cry during the Olympics," she added, then pretended to get lost in the screen of her smartphone but clearly stayed attentive to the two spies at work.

The Christchurch crew had sent the Albuquerque airport closed-circuit camera footage of the albino, Mikhail Yusupov, a Chechen national traveling on an Austrian passport and zombieing, head bandaged, through the TSA checkpoints on the arm of a young black-haired woman whom flight records identified as Carmen Fischer. A first-pass scan by Interpol facial-recognition software showed the same woman arriving in Barcelona two weeks before the Bolsa de Madrid bombing using a Swiss passport with the last name Hirsch, then leaving Leipzig by commuter train the morning after Lenkov dove off his penthouse balcony. The Five Eyes was negotiating to have the Interpol gearheads in Lyon, with their ninja-like search engines, do a second, more expensive global search for her.

"Girlfriend is fucking *hot*," Jenny observed, shedding her pretense of indifference. She'd been following their every word. "Can't you just type that in the search box and filter for influencers, supermodels, and Ana de Armas?" Otter wouldn't let her smoke in his building, so Banks had bought some chewing gum from a vending machine in the yet-unfinished break room, which, Otter boasted, was going to be bomb-proof when all was said and done.

All the CCTV footage was angled, looking down, and became pix-elated when it got zoomed. But even from that unflattering altitude the girl *was* strikingly attractive.

"Makes me not just a little bit self-conscious," Jenny admitted, and her eyes bored into Banks for a moment, as if waiting for a compliment, then returned to her phone screen when it didn't come. "But she sure doesn't look Spanish."

"Had no idea there was a Spanish 'look,'" Otter muttered. He was annoyed that Banks had brought a civilian into his inner sanctum. When Banks explained that Sentro had made him promise he wouldn't let her daughter out of his sight, Otter grunted and did the fake-cough thing, growling, "Babyshitter."

Banks ignored the dig. He tapped the boarding pass Sentro had kept from Yusupov's pocket litter. "Did we get the Cyrillic on this sorted out?"

"We? Yes. And no," Otter said. "I've had it transcribed into the Latin alphabet, but the language is Kumyk. So. Slight hiccup finding a native speaker, unless our special guest"—he shot a withering side-eye at Jenny—"has Turkic language skills."

"Lookit this," Jenny said, deflecting his shade and baiting him. "'LGBT-owned kilt company slams Proud Boys for appropriating their designs.'" She showed them a Twitter feed they didn't bother to read. "My country in a fucking nutshell. The owner of the company said he was 'appalled' to see the white supremacists wearing his products. Jesus H. Christ." Then she glanced at the boarding pass, which Banks had noticed she'd been eyeing for a while. "Whose number is that?" Jenny asked, as if innocently, pointing to the unbroken string of digits below the Cyrillic scrawl.

It was a ferry ticket to Majorca, weeks old, something the albino had probably just used to take notes. "Fourteen digits," Banks said. "Some kind of code. Or a password, or bank account."

"Onetime pad," Otter ventured.

Banks shrugged, frustrated.

"What's that?"

Banks read Jenny's guileful expression; she was playing them. "A string of random numbers you use once as a key in enciphering something; properly done, the pad makes the message mathematically unbreakable."

Jenny cracked her gum, shook her head. "Satellite phone number."

Otter groaned. "Bullshit."

"Backwards," Jenny clarified.

Banks frowned at the number, trying to see what she had seen.

Otter said, "Why don't you go fix us up some fresh coffee, little lady; I've heard that's your superpower."

"Oh, Mister Otter?" Jenny showed him two sideways middle fingers. "Can you hear these? Or should I turn 'em up?" She rotated both hands.

"Like her mother," Otter griped.

"Wait," Banks said, still lost. "Sat phone?"

209

"Yeah." Jenny pulled the boarding pass toward her. "I'm good at puzzles." She aimed a cool look at Otter, then swerved the card in front of Banks to show him. "See? In the middle here, this six one two eight eight? Turn it around, it's eight eight two one six—which is a Thuraya satellite phone prefix."

Banks frowned. "How the heck do you know that?"

"My brother has one. He's in high finance, thinks it makes him look like a heavy hitter. He could bore you for hours about it, how every company has a unique prefix, yada yada. Here, at the end? One one zero? Reversed, that's the international access code for the US."

Banks thought it tracked. "He must've called from New Mexico."

Otter was already unscrambling the rest of the number and dialing it, but all he got was an error message: *The number you have called is not in service.*

Jenny was doing a search on her own phone. "So thirty-five is fifty-three . . . that's the country code for Cuba. Area code is forty-six . . . some place called Isla de la Juventud."

Otter was shaking his head. "Misdirect. They're spoofing the number. Sat phones are illegal in Cuba. That USAID guy just got eighteen months in jail for trying to sneak one in."

"You can if it's approved by the Intelligence Directorate," Banks said. He traded an odd look with Otter.

Jenny asked, "What?"

"He's in Havana," Banks mused aloud.

"Could be."

Otter, Banks thought, *looks distracted. Preoccupied with something.* "You all right, Hank?"

"Who?" Jenny seemed keen to know. "Who's in Havana?"

"Pogo," Banks told her, adding, "Nice puzzling," and cracking a playful smile to make her blush.

"Get a room, why don'tcha," Otter growled, which made Banks blush. Head down, Jenny stared blankly at her phone, clearly mortified.

"And this fucking albino," Otter continued, picking up the Chechen's passport to examine it. "Not a lot of cobblers in the world can do British paper this pristine."

"How many?"

"Oh. Half a dozen, max."

"Call them all. Tell them you have a client with a keen interest in Mikhail Yusupov. Give them my number, but only after saying you can't a couple of times."

"He's not going to fall for that," Otter said.

"No. I'm sure he won't," Banks said. "But he might send friends." Otter seemed unconvinced. They both stared absently at Jenny, who appeared lost in social media, until she seemed to sense the quiet and looked up at them.

"You hungry?" Banks asked her.

Chapter Twenty-Eight

The Cuban girl came hurrying down the river walk from the palace, heels clicking lightly on the sidewalk, glancing to the street and back over her shoulder, looking not so much panicked as upset with herself.

Sentro understood the reaction. One minute you're tailing a target; the next thing you know, either you've become the target or you've lost your mark, and either way it sucks.

It had started nagging at her on the flight to Heathrow and resumed as soon as she left the ICU: a close-quarter knife wound that *hadn't* killed Madsen? Or sure, okay: inadvertently killed her for four minutes but was not so carelessly done as to ruin the resurrection that would draw Sentro to London.

So that must have been the plan all along.

This was the same woman who, with the Chechen, had dispensed with Clete so quickly and skillfully Sentro had only felt it, and Clete, not a warrior but a brawler, would have been a handful in any fair fight.

No, Sentro was almost across the Westminster Bridge when all these pieces came together and she confirmed the vague sensation she'd had, while walking, of being followed. A trap. Stopping short, she saw her shadow without looking: a striking, dark-haired young woman not much older than Jenny and much too pretty to be tailing anyone on her own.

Slowing as she walked along the stone wall, the girl did a complete turn, scanning the faces of pedestrians, the windows of storefronts. Looking for Sentro. Behind her, across the river, the London Eye made its lazy rotations, the shrouded sunlight sliding up and down the cross-sarms and arcing over the glass cars, making Sentro's vision shimmer, and she fought back the tingle of a migraine. *Not now.*

A very public setting like this would ordinarily have been a good place for a confrontation, but the brazen attack on Madsen made Sentro wary. Carmen or Mercedes? She watched the girl lean against the wall and pretend to stare up the Thames to the London Bridge, a useful technique to focus peripheral vision. *Look for what doesn't belong* was tradecraft 101. She was hoping to catch Sentro moving.

Nice try.

The key to any surveillance was invisibility, and Sentro, who was sometimes self-conscious about how ordinary she looked, was incredibly skilled at going gray—blending in—or so they'd told her at the Farm. Traps. Tradecraft. Shadowing. Disappearing. Settled into mission mode, she let the girl walk away from her, guessing there would be a doubling back, which, after a hundred yards, there was. Sentro watched the girl retracing her steps, passing unaware within a few yards of her; waited until it looked like the girl was confident she'd lost her mark, and then Sentro trailed her to Saint James's Park, across the lake, skirted Buckingham Palace, and went up Constitution Hill through the tree-lined meadows of Green Park, where the girl took a phone call and argued with someone almost all the way to Wellington Arch. She veered off then and disappeared into the matrix of underground passageways that led to the Hyde Park Corner tube. Sentro knew this corner, because it wasn't far from the old US Embassy, but couldn't recall why she'd spent time there.

Taking another gamble that the girl wasn't headed for public transportation, Sentro dashed across Piccadilly and entered the pedestrian tunnels from the opposite side. She'd guessed right, because as she came off the steps, there was the girl again, hurrying toward her. It was a wide, white-tiled passageway, often vacant save for the occasional homeless panhandler or busker posted at the intersection with the main walkway leading to the platforms. Commuters tended to access the tube on the Knightsbridge side, where all the surface bus queues were.

This time there was a man in a long coat and motorman's cap, standing by his opened case, paying homage to Ornette Coleman blowing "Misty" on a baritone sax.

The girl was so distracted by the booming acoustics she didn't see her mark until it was too late to prepare for it, which was Sentro's primary goal. Strategically foolhardy but tactically sound: only two points of egress, well lit, narrow enough to contain any surprises, private enough to allow for a close encounter, public enough that the girl couldn't just pull out the handgun Sentro suspected she might still be carrying and empty the clip.

But now what?

They both stopped at the same time, twenty feet between them. The girl kept her hands in the pockets of her jacket. Unarmed and improvising, Sentro knew that on some level she was taking this risk to try to see herself in this young woman. Smaller boned than Jenny but sturdier in bearing as well, she looked light on her feet, had strong shoulders, an obdurate cant to her head, and green eyes that, much as Madsen had described them, stared fiercely back at Sentro as if from a mirror.

She thought: *Oh fuck.* A gnawing disquiet was clutching at her heart.

"I guess we should talk." Sentro stated the obvious.

"Talk?" The girl spit something in Spanish too rapidly for Sentro to understand. Then, in English, she added, "Pointless."

"What's your name?"

"You threw me away like trash," the girl snapped with a heavy Cuban edge in it.

She thinks she's your daughter, Madsen had said; Sentro didn't want to believe it but decided to see where this led. "Is that what he told you?"

What the girl said next was unexpected. "Why does he want you dead?" It was the next question Sentro had wanted to ask.

"I don't know. I haven't thought about him in a long time. I couldn't even tell you what he looks like."

The girl studied Sentro and looked momentarily disarmed. "You're lying," she said.

"They told me my baby died."

"He said you'd say that."

"Who? Witt?"

The name provoked nothing, which proved nothing. The sax squalled high and flat, and the girl shifted her weight, her hidden right hand finding a grip on something in her pocket—Madsen's father's tactical knife, Sentro guessed. It would be nice to get it back for her.

"Where is he?" Sentro wondered aloud. "Cuba? Is that where you grew up?"

"You have another daughter," the girl countered, stubborn.

Another. A word that scraped like fingernails on the chalkboard of Sentro's fragile brain. "Yes." She felt her whole body go tense. "Do me a favor and stay away from her? And her brother."

A big smile. "You don't want them to know about me."

"What's there to know?" Intending to provoke her, Sentro had closed the distance between them, anticipating what could be coming, giving herself better odds, she thought, of surviving it unarmed. "You won't even tell me your name."

"Too late for that," the girl said and sprang forward, quick on her toes; both hands came out of her pockets, the tactical knife in one of them, blade flashing cold in the fluorescent light. Was she trying to do damage or just getting away? By instinct Sentro braced, twisted, and fell backward as the girl arrived, parrying the knife hand away with her forearm and grabbing the girl's coat with the other hand, tugging her off balance, using her momentum to bring her to the ground heels over ass in a clumsy and no doubt painful somersault, because Sentro banged her head on the concrete and saw stars. The violent pas de deux had happened so fast the sax man didn't miss a note, and it left Sentro straddling her attacker's chest, the knife in her own hand, prepared to complete a move she'd learned long ago—where? In basic? The Farm?

Single-edged knife gripped with the back of the blade parallel to the forearm, make a sweeping motion, down and across the jugular. Then just let momentum swing the arm up and off the victim so that the resulting arterial spray doesn't soak you.

No.

Sentro just sat there, arm poised, head throbbing, while the young woman stared up at her with disbelief and the frightened resignation of a predator turned prey. And Sentro wondered: *Have I ever done this?* She couldn't remember. But—*Why wouldn't I, here?* What did that say about her? This girl had orchestrated two bombings and an assassination, maimed Madsen, killed Clete, and sent her accomplices after Jenny and Banks. Sentro sat, stymied, and thought: *She could very well be my daughter. It could also all be a lie.*

"They like to tell stories," she said to the girl for some reason, and the lights in the tube passageway began to take on a shimmer and make her squint. "Lies and half truths." She smelled her own perfume on the heat rising off the girl's fearful body and wondered if she'd suffered a new concussion. Shit. Nausea rose and she swallowed bile. "Don't trust them."

The girl got a leg free and kicked out at Sentro, catching her with a glancing blow across the side of her face, sharp heel just missing the eye. She fell back, and the girl who might be her daughter got up and fled the way she came.

Now the saxophone stopped abruptly. Sentro sat up and felt her stinging face for blood. Nope. The corridor was spinning, the receding sound of running steps swirled. Sentro folded the knife and put it in her pocket and then realized that, in her other hand, she was holding the hotel room key card she'd taken from the girl's coat when they'd tangled. It was still in the paper sleeve; Sentro often did the same thing—carried the key card in its complimentary sleeve because the room number was helpfully written on it and she was prone to misremember, even before her damaged-brain issues had begun to surface.

Metropolitan Hotel. Right down the street, past the Four Seasons. Room 1017.

Sentro didn't remember walking there or even making the decision to go. It was careless, since there was no guarantee the girl wouldn't be circling right back, but Sentro's face was throbbing and her judgment impaired. Every new insult to her head was its own terrible adventure.

There was the familiar gap, like a skip in her timeline. Then she was in the room, staring out across Hyde Park, the kaleidoscopic scotoma of an aura already messing with the center of her field of vision. *Would I have killed her,* she wondered, *if she hadn't run away?*

And then she wondered if she'd ever asked that question before.

Forcing focus, she turned away from the window and made efficient use of the time she had left before the migraine took hold; there was a small suitcase of clothes Jenny might own, fancy fuck-me pumps she most definitely wouldn't, and a leather backpack with the usual collection of maps, pens, tissues, hard candy, old notes and errata, gloves, scarf, cosmetics, emergency tampons, and a few different passports but all in the name of Mercedes Izquierdo. A burner phone, recently purchased, cheap and disposable.

She almost didn't see it: a creased photograph that, unfolded, proved to be of her two children. Jeremy looked bored; Jenny had a catcher's glove tucked under her arm—some random travel ball tournament Sentro couldn't remember. Had she even been there?

Izquierdo had taken it from the New Mexico house.

My other daughter. Sentro tried it out, in her head, and then dismissed it and turned away.

Another gap yawned. How much time, this time?

In the bathroom, with only cold dying day's light cast through the doorway from the bedroom, Sentro stared back at herself from the mirror. *Is this who I am?* Her pulse throbbed in her temples; her mouth was dry. *I have to stop.* The side of her face where Mercedes's pump had struck was slightly swollen and pink. The green eyes they shared—or did they? Sentro's, hard, weary, and ingenuous, lacked the feral, bitter longing she'd seen looking up from the floor.

Green eyes weren't that uncommon.

The ringing in her ears slowly relocated to the backpack burner phone, which she retrieved and flipped open to answer.

A low, youthful voice, likely male, bitched, "I've been calling you for two days," in German.

Sentro reflexively asked, "*Wer ist das?*"—*Who's this?*—before she could stop herself, and evidently the caller made the same mistake responding.

"It's Wolfgang," he said. "What—" She heard his voice catch as he seemed to realize he wasn't talking to the woman he expected. A long pause. "Who's this?"

Sentro hung up. The caller didn't ring back.

Wolfgang.

She fumbled for her own phone to call Banks, or maybe Jenny, but a searing pain came crashing down on her and nearly took her to her knees. It felt like her eyes were bleeding. She made it back to the bathroom and threw up, but then she couldn't find her balance, needed to lie down, groped and crawled her way to the big bed, climbed up on it, and closed her eyes even though she knew that the girl might come back, and having possibly suffered another concussion, Sentro should try to stay awake.

She felt vulnerable and exposed.

She would just rest for a moment, gather her strength.

Rest. Gather. Those words were tumbling in her head as she slipped off the cliff and plunged into the void.

Chapter Twenty-Nine

"Do you mind if I make an observation?"

"Would it matter if I did?" Banks wondered.

"No. But. Manners. It's polite to ask."

"I guess."

"You guys . . ." Jenny Troon meant the espionage service in general, Banks knew, and not just him, her mother, and Otter, because suddenly the spy game was all she wanted to talk about. ". . . I mean—go ahead, call me out for oversimplification—but can I just say that I think you use yourselves as bait way too often, and I'm guessing it doesn't work so good anymore."

He didn't want to admit she was right. Over dinner in a walk-down street café—chicken and rice and a sickly-sweet Alsatian rosé because he pretty much sucked at ordering wine—Banks had tried to explain how that wasn't, in fact, the case; it was more that the economies of the spook life had changed, and a lot of times you had to make it up as you went along, and unfortunately, sometimes the cheapest, most efficient way to draw the enemy closer was offering yourself up as the sacrificial goat. But Jenny kept talking over him. "C'mon. It's stupid. Right? I mean, I get that they do it in the movies because it's funny or, ooo, tense and dramatic. But what person in their right mind would do it in real life? No.

"And anyway, seems like it's mostly either you're following somebody or being followed, so. And why not just . . . why not get one of those cheap drones you can buy online and, I dunno, link it up with your iPad and follow a suspect that way? Which is not to say I think I could do what you guys do, ever in a million years. Or even want to. But."

"Don't sell yourself short."

"Don't patronize me," she warned.

No chance of that. By now, having killed a whole day with her, he knew better than to give her home fires oxygen. *She is*, he decided, *her mother's child*. Stubborn, ferocious, relentless. And angry right now, at Sentro, at what the Stasi had put her through, at the indifferent world that allowed such things. Thank God she didn't know her way around a gun.

They stood in front of the door to the hotel room Jenny shared with Sentro, Banks waiting impatiently for her to just unlock it and go inside. He craved some time apart: to sleep, to think, to prepare for what might be coming once Otter put the word out that Banks was looking for the Chechen mercenary. But he'd promised Sentro he wouldn't leave Jenny alone.

"Can I trust you to stay in the room until your mom gets back?"

Jenny's look had a lot of attitude in it. "I'm not a child."

"That's why I'm asking."

"She's gonna be pissed at you for leaving me."

"I'm not a babysitter," Banks said. "And you're not a child."

"No. I'm a helpless mess. And you're a big bad spy man," Jenny said, giving it spin. She slid her card in the reader, and the door clicked open. She didn't go in. "Don't you have to clear the room for me?" she asked.

Banks rolled his eyes, but she was right. He brushed past her and into the suite, which smelled like his sisters' rooms, decidedly female, whatever that entailed—he didn't really want to spend a lot of time thinking about it. Checked the bathroom, made a visual sweep of the furniture and decor, admiring the midcentury Ukrainian vibe while reassuring himself that nobody had been in here except Otter's black-bag tech crew, during dinner, placing electronic surveillance.

Banks had no intention of leaving Jenny unwatched.

"Clear."

Jenny came in, let the door swing half-shut, and stood studying him in a way he wasn't sure he liked.

"Now what?"

"You're cute," she said, but he thought it was just to try to keep him off balance. There seemed to be something else she wanted from him; he disregarded the obvious flirtation.

"In the morning, order room service and tell them to leave it out-side the door. Use the eyepiece to make sure there's nobody out in the hallway before you unlock."

"If you came into the barista bar," Jenny pressed him, "my friend Shayda would melt on you like butter over a bagel. She's super cute; you'd be the cutest couple."

Banks watched her walk past him, leaving the door open, aware that he was watching her; taking her time, and kicking off her shoes before she sat on the edge of the big bed. Something had shifted; despite all her posturing she looked adrift.

"Mom's not really a spy, though, is she? I mean, in the strictest sense of the word. Maybe she was, once. Like, starting out. Berlin. For a while after. But."

"I'm not following you," Banks said.

"That guy she killed in New Mexico." Jenny's eyes met Banks's, and he saw in them a rattled bewilderment. And fundamental disquiet.

"What about him?"

"*That's* who she is," Jenny said. "Right? *That's* what she's best at."

Everyone had their natural talents, the old spooks told Banks, back when he started training. Not everyone was good at the puzzle; not every agent was a code breaker or a chameleon. Sentro's reputation was as the eye of the storm, the eerie, preternatural calm in the face of the most violent turbulence. *Ice in her veins* was how she'd been summed up when they'd sent him on his errand to engage her. *Cold blooded* was the subtext.

A cold-blooded woman with a family, kids. It had mythic qualities in the shadow world, not so useful in the real one. Having finally met her, now he wasn't so sure it was that simple. But yeah, she scared him plenty.

"Your mom has a rare gift and peerless reputation for solving difficult tactical challenges."

"Hostages. Security. Extreme rendition. An agent of chaos."

"Where'd you read that?"

"This hot Egyptian summed her up for me once." Jenny found his eyes and fiercely held them. "I only really met my mom a couple years ago, Banks," she said. "Turns out we're still getting acquainted."

"You might cut her some slack," Banks advised.

"I might not," Jenny countered. But all the edge was gone from her voice.

Banks said, "Everybody likes to think that the intelligence business is cool and calculating; they read books about it and see movies and think, *Yeah, there, that's what it is.* The truth is a few teenage hackers in Belarus can crash Medicare, steal guest lists from your White House, or dox a Korean boy band they don't like. Not a government, a group of geeks.

"The spy game? Hell, it's clumsy and bureaucratic, petty and pointless more than half the time. The rest is 'best effort.' Groping in the dark. Muddling through. We're a *Gong Show*, drowning in information; double all the material in the Library of Congress gets collected by every first-world intelligence agency every bloody day, and yet we're woefully understaffed to figure out what any of it really means. And mostly politicians ignore it when we do. Our ranks have been decimated, privatized, trivialized—"

"Then why do you do it?"

Banks, caught short, felt his face flush and decided not to answer the question. "Your mom takes care of messy things that can't be left unchecked."

"The cleaning woman," Jenny said with heavy sarcasm. "Fuck. New twist on the traditional woman's role, huh?"

"She figured out a way to simplify the mission," Banks said, defensive. "And have a family. That's pretty epic." He walked to the door. "I gotta go. Please stay put."

"You didn't answer my question, Banks."

"I didn't, no," he said, because he couldn't, and he went out into the hallway, pulling the door shut on her quietly, without looking back.

———

In roiling, rootless dreams a young woman who looked like Mercedes Izquierdo was peering down at her from a luminous darkness, gently tracing the injury she'd caused with exquisite black manicured nails. Sentro's own hands and feet were tingling, and there was the long, cool caress of silken ice soothing the ache of her face, and she was running from something and standing in frigid water and awakened midmorning by an irritated housekeeping maid.

The bed beside Sentro was soaked with water that had leaked from a plastic bag containing a residue of melted ice. A shiver ran through her; Sentro hadn't put it there. The surly maid warned she was past her checkout.

"I'm so sorry." Her tongue felt woolen.

The suitcase and backpack were gone. So was Sentro's smartphone and the simple, thin gold chain that was the only jewelry she'd been wearing.

She rode out a wave of queasiness after struggling to sit up, and she asked what day of the week it was, and after the maid told her, Sentro realized that she'd been asleep for almost twenty-four hours.

Her first thought was of Jenny.

There wasn't a second thought.

———

Before she got the call, Jenny had every intention of staying in her room per Banks's instructions. Not only was she determined to prove to him—and her mother—that she wasn't the contrarian fuckup they thought she was, there was the hard fact that despite the dauntless front she'd been putting up, all the shock waves of the harrowing events of New Mexico hadn't faded. She felt totally schizo: buzzed by the journey but shaken and worried and scared. Add to this her mom's harrowing confessions about her long nightmare in East Germany, and Jenny was about as unsettled as she'd ever been, including those long months after her father died. She took to the big hotel bed like it was a life raft; she turned on the television for company and drifted, flipping through magazines, browsing social media, stripping the chipped lacquer from her toenails, jonesing for a cigarette, trying not to think about everything she now knew. Part of her craved the blissful ignorance of her childhood and understood—if only begrudgingly—why her mother had kept her work life a discrete mystery. A little weed would have been helpful, but she didn't miss it, for once.

Her phone hummed with her mother's caller ID. She answered, "Where the fuck are you?" and heard a hesitation and the hiss of what sounded like traffic's susurration before a stranger's voice asked, "Yennifer?"

Female. Trace of a Hispanic accent, and then a deliberate correction: "Jennifer."

Jenny felt her pulse skip. Her scalp crawled. "That's me."

"Don't hang up. My name is Mercedes Izquierdo. I promise I am not a stalker or a crazy person, and I know this is probably presumptuous, but I hoped I could convince you to come meet me for coffee or a cocktail and talk about a terrible deception that concerns us both."

A slacker sun broke through the low popcorn clouds that strafed the city. The skyline gleamed, fresh scrubbed, like a dream.

"Deception."

"Yes."

"I know who you are."

"I do not think so."

Jenny snapped, "You're the little bitch who sent some meatheads to kill us at our house in New Mexico. You murdered our friend."

No audible reaction. "I heard there was an unfortunate house fire. Often it's the electrical wiring. Did they discover a body? I do not think so."

The conversation had already turned crazy. *No fucking way am I meeting with you,* Jenny thought. *If this is anything like what my mother's life has been since Berlin, no wonder she's got issues.*

"Naturally, I was misinformed," this Mercedes added quickly, sounding defensive. *Naturally.* Jenny glanced at the pad on the night table where Banks had written his cell number. He was probably with the little creepy spy man, Otter.

"Remove the battery from your phone when you're not using it," Otter had told her.

"They can trace you," Banks had explained.

And at the time she'd wondered: *Who?*

"I won't hurt you," the crazy killer with her mother's phone was saying, sounding a little like a couple of Jenny's old boyfriends.

"Where's my mom?"

"Safe, when I left her. Resting."

Resting? "That's reassuring," Jenny told her, but her head was screaming: *What the fuck does that mean?* "Listen, I'm hanging up now and calling my CIA friends, who have a tap on my phone and are tracking you down as we speak."

"No, they're not."

"Black helicopter's on its way. They'll want to have a word with you," Jenny vamped. But a strange, icy calm was settling on her, and she was bolstered by a sudden fierceness that surprised her. "Waterboarding may be involved, if I have anything to say about it."

Mercedes laughed and advised Jenny that she might want to think twice about doing anything that would jeopardize her mother's status quo. "The situation is fluid," she explained, clearly trying to give it an ominous air, but added that she had enjoyed meeting Aubrey Sentro, and Jenny thought, *I fucking bet.* "In London," the girl said. "It wasn't productive," she admitted, "but I'm more hopeful about you," and Jenny felt another chill go through her.

"Run," Jenny advised, stubborn. "You might get away."

"Sklad Bar," Mercedes replied, pleasant. "Do you know it? Safe. Public. Don't worry. Not far at all from your hotel."

"You're there now?"

"I'll wait for you. Yes."

And I'll send Banks, Jenny decided.

"Don't tell anybody; don't bring anybody," Mercedes warned. "I should think you would want to meet your sister alone," the girl added then, and Jenny's whole body went rigid.

"What?"

"Your mother didn't tell you?" The Cuban girl seemed to enjoy letting a stretch of silence work on Jenny's nerves. "She had a baby in Berlin. I just learned about it myself."

Jenny's mind blanked. The phone felt heavy in her hand.

"We're sisters."

And from the way this was said, simple, measured, yet tentative, it sounded to a stunned Jenny like Mercedes was still trying it on for size.

CHAPTER THIRTY

Despite his better judgment, now every decision and every choice Banks made came into question because of Jenny Troon; all his attitudes screamed conventional, all his habits felt like tropes. For example, licking a strand of his own hair and pasting it across the top threshold of his hotel suite's doorway to let him know if anyone had gone in. In training they'd called it "tater tech"—from the old-school practice of jamming a potato into a tailpipe to disable a vehicle.

He could hear Jenny's complaint about his hair trick: *Why not just buy a cheap wireless camera and motion detector and link it up to your phone?*

The answer was simple: anything can be disabled, and Wi-Fi is easily scrambled and blocked. Still, he felt a little foolish checking the doorframe when he arrived home, until he realized that the hair had indeed been dislodged.

And the door itself was unlocked.

He'd spent the bulk of another day with Henry Otter, reasonably productive but freezing in the new place because the boiler broke down, and trying not to look at the little plastic water bottle filled with the brown sludge of Otter's dip spit. While they waited for a repair crew and word from Sentro, they had scanned untold hours of local private and public CCTV surveillance the Spanish authorities had been able to aggregate, tracking the albino to and from Majorca. Five Eyes was chafing for a breakthrough.

Sure enough, Yusupov had gone across on the Barcelona ferry six weeks earlier, with the same raven-haired Carmen Fischer he'd traveled with in New Mexico and back to Europe. They were picked up by two white males in a beat-to-shit Mercedes sedan with no visible license plate. But later they left the island in some other way, because there was no record of a departure or sign of them after they disembarked, ferry or otherwise.

"Islands," Otter had grumbled. "Talk about a spy trope."

"Isolated, contained, difficult to breach. Maybe she's confusing trope with convention."

"Keep telling yourself that, man," Otter advised. The in-room surveillance of Jenny was in split windows on a monitor behind them, and Banks was beginning to regret getting Otter involved. He'd get an earful from Sentro, he knew. But she'd put him in a spot.

Nothing from the enigmatic American for almost two days. Banks wasn't worried, but he was surprised.

Meanwhile the Cyrillic Kumyk had been translated. "A Russian proverb," Otter explained. "*Beda ne prikhodit odna* is the original saying." Banks had only a passing knowledge of Russian and shook his head, needing a translation. "*Trouble never comes alone,*" Otter clarified. "Or maybe *misery loves company.* It loses some specificity when it's translated from a Slavic to a Turkic language."

Neither of them had a clue why Yusupov would write that on his ferry boarding pass.

"Secret code," Otter joked. "Another trope."

Banks glanced at the Jenny cam feed. She had propped herself up with all the pillows on the bed, reading one of the in-hotel magazines while a rerun of the Eurovision Song Contest blared on the flat-screen. An irritated Otter had muted the sound.

"How much did she tell her daughter about, you know, Berlin and all?" Otter kept wondering. He seemed oddly unsettled by Sentro and her daughter. Prickly and distracted.

Banks lied and said he wasn't sure, and he thought back to the chilling debriefing tapes he'd watched, unable to resist comparing twenty-year-old Aubrey Sentro with twenty-six-year-old Jenny Troon. Totally different, yet so much the same. *For all her resented absences and all their differences*, Banks thought, *Sentro has rendered a heavy influence on Jenny.* Nature or nurture?

Guilt sent Banks back early to rescue Jenny from her isolation, something he hadn't planned on doing until dinner.

Or maybe it was something else.

After a day with the slippery black-site operator, it felt like a reprieve. Also, a not-so-bittersweet betrayal of poor Gillian, but he buried that contradiction for future penance.

A quick stop at his apartment first was all he'd intended. Until he discovered the telltale hair missing from his door.

Now, unarmed, he stood in the corridor for a while, debating his next move. Had his ruse to draw out the albino worked? Seemed unlikely. A careful man would go back down to the front desk and get hotel security to check if anyone was still in his room. A reckless man would crash in and subdue the intruder and turn him over to Otter's people for proper rendering and, possibly, useful intel.

And a woman? What would Sentro do?

He didn't have to find an answer because the door whipped open and there she was, disheveled and exhausted, with his own SIG Sauer from the bedstand held a little unsteady in her two hands and pointed at his heart—the second time he'd been caught unawares by Sentro or her progeny. "Jesus Murphy," Banks said.

"Where's Jenny?"

"What?"

"My daughter," Sentro said, brittle, pulling him inside. After sliding the SIG Sauer's safety on, she spun the grip around and handed him the gun.

"She's at your hotel," Banks said, confused.

"No." Sentro looked haunted. "I was just there. She's not."

———

There wasn't any one thing that convinced her; Jenny kept looking for the tell.

Early times, the Sklad Bar dozed, almost empty, bartenders readying for a busy night, some ska band doing a sound check. She picked out the girl right away, in a corner booth, even prettier than in her passport pictures or the CCTV surveillance. *Almost tragically fragile*, Jenny thought. Nothing threatening about her. But the seared image of the goon with the gun in the motel breezeway as his head sprang a leak from her mother's single gunshot kept nibbling away at the edges of Jenny's judgment.

Plenty of people around. Plenty of room to run, if the need arose.

Wary of the girl, but empowered by being there on her own, she believed she could do this—whatever *this* was. Curiosity? Defiance? No. Reconnaissance. Information gathering.

Spook life. For her mom.

Was she nervous? Not really.

Scared? You bet.

Like when she was little, she had flung herself rolling down a steep grassy hill, and there would be no stopping until the ground leveled out.

"Yennifer." The girl purred the Spanish pronunciation, and Jenny wondered if she was mocking her. Their eyes met: green, like her mother's, but flecked with tiny constellations of black and absent any mischief or warmth. "*¿Oye qué bola?*" She stood up, politely—"Mercedes"—and held out a hand that was strong and warm. They sat, and the young woman waved away steam threads wisping up from her mug: "Ukrainian coffee? It has cognac and lemon."

Still sweating out the alcohol from her bender with Banks's hotel minibar, Jenny said, "I'm fine with water," and then regretted it. Her face flushed like she was fifteen again. *Lightweight. Excellent first impression, Jen. Fuck.*

"Can you please show me your phone?"

"What?"

The girl gestured. "Your phone. I'm sorry. I need to know you're not using it to broadcast somewhere."

She made it sound so logical, so sensible, that Jenny took her phone out and handed it across.

"Thank you." The girl promptly dunked it into the mug of spiked coffee and left it there. "I hope you have it backed up in the cloud."

Fuck. Jenny stared at her drowned phone and felt embarrassed that she was so out of her depth.

"You're a little too trusting," the girl offered. Jenny noticed she was wearing a gold chain that looked just like her mom's. "Not a criticism, an observation. But don't worry, I will buy you a new one. This was necessary, to ensure our privacy."

"What do you want from me?" Jenny asked.

The girl's expression stayed neutral. "Is it cigarettes I can smell on you?"

"I smoked. Walking over."

"I think I would like to try. Papa forbids it."

Papa. She thinks Günter Witt is her father. Not Schmidt. Jenny parted her lips to say something, then realized she had a secret that could be useful later.

"I make you nervous," Mercedes said.

Jenny thought about lying. "Yes."

This elicited a nod, and the girl looked away. "Everything is so messed up." Her eyes welled up as she pushed her ruined, phone-filled drink farther away. "All the fictions and lies people we trust conspire to tell."

"Sucks," Jenny agreed but was curious whom she was talking about. Her mother? Witt?

"I can trust you, though," the girl decided. Real sadness seemed baked into her behind the empty grins and grandstanding; Jenny couldn't decide if it was a by-product of real crazy or if Mercedes was just tragically miswired.

She felt sorry for her.

There was an uncomfortable moment as conversation stalled, and they measured each other, dead serious, searching, and then Mercedes burst out laughing, as if at some secret joke they shared, and the relief was contagious. Jenny couldn't help but smile, acknowledging an unspoken connection the way Jenny wanted to believe that even accidental sisters sometimes would.

But mostly she was feeling the giddy pull of danger, like a drug. *Defying your fears. Proving your mettle.* And realized that she wouldn't have wanted to be anywhere else in the world, then, despite all the risks.

———

From the time she'd learned to walk, Jenny was always taking runners. Dennis had thrilled in retelling the best ones: slipping away at the National Aquarium, chasing geese by the lake in the park and falling in.

Sentro had felt jealous. Her daughter growing, headstrong, without her. But one blustery Baltimore day—Jenny might have been five or six—Sentro, just back from a short stint in the Fertile Crescent and making another clumsy stab at mom duties, had taken a work phone call while watching Jenny scream into the wind (hair flung back wildly, little fists clenched, eyes closed, mouth as wide as it could go; screaming into a storm was one of her favorite rituals of spring). Sentro had to step inside to fetch the paperwork to read back some data, and she told her daughter to stay on the porch. Sentro thought she'd been in and out in less than five minutes and didn't register that the screaming had stopped sometime during the interval. Work did that to her. Jenny was gone when she returned to the porch.

The utterly helpless sensation, a crawling panic she'd never felt on the job, ever—with no tradecraft to fall back on, motherhood would always baffle her; she looked up and down the street, desperate, trying to stop her thoughts from spinning so she could formulate a plan.

Failing that, she had started walking. Into the wind, because she had guessed that was how Jenny would decide to go. Headstrong. Always against the flow. Two blocks, three, heart pounding, furious with herself for having let the girl out of her sight, worried what her husband would think.

Fractured music phase-shifted on the air currents and, fading in and out, pulled her around the next corner to a backyard where a tweenage birthday party was in full swing. A DJ spun Spice Girls and *NSYNC, and the girls danced and the boys watched, and there was Jenny in the middle of it, staring, tiny, fierce, swaying, holding the hand of a neighbor woman Sentro had seen walking a corgi but didn't know.

"I remember that," Reno said, on the phone from the offices of her old employer, Solomon Systems. On the way back from London she had bought a prepaid phone and left a message on his private line, seeking his off-book help tracing Wolfgang and the ping locations for the sat phone burner calls from Lenkov and Mercedes. But she was at Otter's when Reno called her back, and the first thing she said was that Jenny was missing. "I had to talk you off the fucking cliff."

He was exaggerating.

"None of us ever really grow up. She's probably not missing, just acting out," Reno added, but Sentro didn't feel reassured. So she downloaded everything that had happened.

The birthday-party neighbor—Sentro had either forgotten her name or never learned it—had explained how Jenny had earlier come running into the backyard and then stopped short, as if afraid to join the dancing. The woman knew who the little girl was; she'd met Dennis and the kids on her walks; they would pet her dog. And she'd been about to call Sentro's husband, in fact, but Jenny had wanted to listen to one more song.

Sentro had been rattled by it; Reno was right about that. She never again lost vigilance over her children when she was home with them, as they grew up.

Now Sentro was too preoccupied with her daughter's disappearance to sustain her fury at Otter and Banks for putting voyeurs' eyes in her hotel suite. But the two views of the vacant room that glowed on the monitors in Otter's control center were a grim reminder of Jenny's absence.

"We weren't peeping," Otter assured her, which assured her that he was.

A further reckoning with Banks for letting her daughter simply walk away from his protection she decided to save for later. Nothing productive would come from it in the short run. "She's twenty-six," Banks had said, feeling the need to defend his decision to leave Jenny alone. "She's stronger than you think. And adults get to make their own decisions."

"Did you guys even see her walk out?"

"She got a phone call, after Banks left here. I assumed it was you." Otter admitted, sheepishly, "Sound was muted." As if that explained anything.

Her repeated calls to her own phone and Jenny's all kept going to voice mail. Otter announced after checking that both had gone dark; no tracking them.

"Last location?"

"Yours? Airport road."

"What about Jenny's?"

"Working on it. We didn't have the number. Since you were, you know—unreachable."

She ignored the dig. Thought: *They're together. Mercedes and Jenny.*

Sentro took a deep breath and tried to calm herself. Panic was weakness, but she hated that there was nothing she could do now except wait. There followed a swift, mutual download of all their separate intel: Madsen, Mercedes, the travel trail leading to Majorca, the sat phone calls that pointed to Cuba. Sentro told them about intercepting a call from someone named Wolfgang at the hotel.

"Wolfgang Witt," Otter said.

Sentro's thoughts tangled; worry about Jenny was fogging her ability to compartmentalize. "Günter's son?"

"Raised by his mother in Moscow after Witt went off the grid," Banks said. "SVR took them both under its wing, sent the boy to the best schools, wagering that the apple wouldn't fall far."

"I guess they were right?"

"Inconclusive." Otter shrugged. "The Five kept him on a watch list, in the event the old man surfaced. Kid came of age. Never got a yield. Wolfie said *nyet* to the Kremlin spy game, and now he works for the Wagner Group."

Sentro knew the name. "Private wet-job contractors the FSB uses when they want deniability."

"Pretty sure he's in account management, though. Not operations."

Sentro did the math; Wolfgang would be Jeremy's age. "Not a kid anymore." She flashed on a photograph of Witt, with his elegant actress wife and their baby—faces elusive in her broken memory, blurred out or fluid and indistinct. A framed picture on a desk. But when?

"So he's in Moscow?"

Assumed to be—Otter said the Five Eyes couldn't be sure—but Reno had an answer right away. "Cuba," he told her. "Couple of shady individuals we crossed paths with recently were recruited by Wolfie Witt in Havana. Anything else you need?"

"An address would be helpful. Or an in-country asset."

"I thought you were retired."

"Not from Jenny. I just got her back," Sentro said. Reno and his wife were raising three boys. He didn't know what it meant to have a daughter.

Did she?

"Fuck. Cuba, Aubrey," Reno cautioned. "You'll be working without a net. Let the Eyes handle it. They've got bodies and the beaucoup resources."

"I'm bringing one of them with me," she said, meaning Banks. Not that she didn't trust the Eyes with this task, but her agenda and theirs were not necessarily in sync.

"Okay, okay, lemme see what I can find," her old colleague said. "Meanwhile, sit tight. Maybe your daughter will turn up."

Not a chance.

When she told Banks that she thought the girl would bring Jenny to Witt, in Cuba, he looked skeptical.

"You don't even know that Jenny is *with* the girl."

"Girl's got my phone, and my phone came here."

"Okay. Still. If Jenny's not missing at all? Just went out for a run or something?"

"Then I'll be extremely relieved. And we'll be on our way to Havana and a reckoning with Pogo." But Sentro was sure she was right. Mother's instinct.

"No such thing," Reno said, before he hung up. "Or so the wife tells me. For twenty-odd years you made it a point to be an afterthought for your daughter, and now all of a sudden you're glued to her like that squeezy cheese they ooze over Camden Yards nachos?"

"Jenny's lived her whole life in the light. She doesn't know what she's up against."

"Neither do you," he pointed out. "Not entirely. And for the record, if they're really sisters? Sharing *your* genes?" It was as if she could hear Reno shaking his head at the dark irony. "Neither does this Cuban girl."

Chapter Thirty-One

Twenty-one hours, Kyiv to Havana.

Plenty of time to second-guess herself, which, for Sentro, was new and annoying.

Before they left, Otter had tracked Jenny's phone to a bar downtown. A server there remembered both young women Sentro described to her; they'd left a phone in their coffee drink and walked out together at least two hours earlier.

Gone, then. Together. Banks conceded the point and expedited plans for their departure.

"They could be anywhere, though," he pointed out.

"I'm not built for waiting," Sentro told him. "If I don't keep moving, I'll drown." Even if Jenny wasn't in Cuba, Witt would know where she was.

The gaps she suffered were becoming more frequent—capricious slips in time and presence continued rippling out from the hard knock she'd suffered in her brief tangle with Mercedes Izquierdo.

She didn't tell Banks, for fear he'd scrub the trip.

Well aware of how it could compromise them, she endured a considerable disquiet.

She'd run out of GalantaMind pills, the cholinesterase inhibitor; made from the bulb of the Caucasian snowdrop flower—*Galanthus*—it might have been what Hermes offered Odysseus in the *Odyssey* to give him purchase over Circe's poisons. The Santa Fe headshrinker swore this was nature's remedy for the trauma of serial concussions.

But unlike Odysseus, it left Sentro at the mercy of her mind's stormy seas.

———

Her one consistent memory of Stasi prison was the cold. Relentless cold. A kind of cold that stayed with her long after she'd returned to the world. It was why she wore socks in bed. Dennis would often awaken to her shivering in her sleep and have to hold her until it stopped.

Sometimes, during a midwinter blizzard, ice crystals would spritz through the mullions of the windows, behind the frosted bars, and the panes of glass would shudder and hum with ghostly harmonics.

The smell of certain household disinfectants still sickened her.

Exhausted and skirting stressed edges of fitful sleep in the hushed twilight of an Airbus cabin, she kept laboring to dredge up memories of her confinement. Some clue as to why Witt would be afraid of her. But that past was like a story she'd written and erased, and now only the faintest tracings of her cramped cursive scrawl remained, loops and lines, a stray word or phrase without context.

The depression alone had crushed her. A pregnancy she didn't want, the helplessness of confinement, a future that looked only bleak.

Witt had held her life in his hands.

He knew her shameful secrets.

And she couldn't even remember his face.

———

Against the off chance that Pogo was tracking aircraft arrivals, Banks had the Five Eyes contrive to bring Sentro into José Martí International Airport on a Canadian passport under her married name, Troon. Since she'd left Solomon Systems, all her fake paper had lapsed. Banks had almost too many well-supported aliases to choose from; he arrived as Jacques Tobin, a French Canadian software salesman (and evidently his go-to NOC), but because of some recent government advisory nobody knew about, that meant they were both detained for almost three hours while immigration decided whether or not he was there to undermine the Cuban tech economy.

The terminal was hot and crowded; her wrinkled tourist's sundress stuck damp to her back, and her flight-swollen feet were thick in her sensible flats. It reminded Sentro of a seventies-vintage shopping mall in Lubbock, dingy tile and faded orange and yellow highlights. Another hour got wasted at baggage claim, where a free-for-all seemed to be the organizational model, a couple of men leaping up onto the wheezy rotating carousel and heaving bags off into the crowd.

Their luggage had been opened and searched, but whether by customs or just a random baggage handler looking for items to take was inconclusive. Banks lost a phone charger and a pair of Nikes. Sentro's cosmetics bag was spilled out into the tangle of her clothes, but nothing essential seemed to be missing.

Cuba was the last outpost of a failed communist world revolution. She knew she'd been on this defiant island once, a Guantánamo Bay rendition, but couldn't remember when or why. A quaint, crumbling anachronism, defiantly decaying, where Cold War dreams came to die.

We have met the enemy, and he is us. Witt wanted them here. He was waiting for her.

And here she was.

———

Still no word from Jenny explaining where she'd gone. Banks had received a cryptic, slightly worrisome text from an unknown number—Don't worry, I'm fine—that both of them doubted was her daughter, and

Sentro used his phone to touch base with Jeremy, who hadn't heard from his sister either. Her son seemed to buy into the fiction that his sister was just acting out. At least *he* was safe.

Elsayed had been unable to dig up for her any intel on Günter Witt, not even a tentative confirmation he was in the country, but she and Banks had the solid sat phone data that pointed to Isla de la Juventud, and there was an old, blown, and broken British double agent living in Havana exile with whom one of the senior partners at Solomon—Laura Bugliosi, of all people, one of Sentro's longtime private-sector nemeses—had kept a back channel open.

"I'm thinking the Bug hauled his ashes," Reno gossiped, "back in the day, when she was an ambitious junior embassy attaché and he was still something of a star in MI6."

The image of Bug, a veritable hydrant on heels, hauling anyone's ashes was something Sentro worried she couldn't unsee.

———

Former SIS case officer Duncan Cranmer-Philips lived in a big squalid neocolonial mansion that the Fidelistas had carved up into a warren of baroque one- and two-room apartments with hot plate kitchens and communal toilets.

He answered the door in a bathrobe, wet and steaming from a bath, smelling of perfumed salts and holding a black-market Beretta in his hand. The disgraced spy was ancient, his body corkscrewed, his bandy legs red and swollen with edema; Banks had no trouble disarming him, and Sentro closed the door quietly while Cranmer-Philips spit out a string of colorful obscenities before sagging into the single, sprung wingback chair and searching his pockets for a cigarillo. The claw-foot tub in the corner, a flat-screen TV, and an unmade Murphy bed were the only other furnishings. It smelled of tobacco and old man.

"I've heard all the bloody rumors," Cranmer-Philips said, after Sentro explained why they'd come. "Pogo and his kompromat. It's rubbish. Thirty years, I've yet to see the front or back of him." Sentro didn't even need to glance at Banks; they could both tell the old man was lying.

"Who's running these nasty dark ops, then, out of Cuba?" Banks asked anyway.

"Wagner Group, inn't it? Vlad's lads. Russian rent-a-goons."

"Wolfgang Witt?"

"Ah. There's a proper wanker."

"Why do you say that?" It was a sly work-around by Banks, and Sentro was impressed he had shifted gears so effortlessly.

"Well." The old spook flashed yellowing teeth. "Boy's a legacy, inn't he?" Cranmer-Philips struck a match and smoked. "Moscow Center gives him the tidy pension and a pass on being but a shadow of his famous father. Ship him here to keep him busy."

"Not to be with Dad?"

"Like I said. Not privy to the elder Witt's whereabouts, or even his existence. My understanding is that the boy is mostly window dressing."

"Yeah, you said that. Well. Wolfgang's phone, at a minimum, has been involved in this latest series of missions," Banks argued.

"Perhaps the boy's stepping up."

"Or he's the cutout to his father," Banks said, stubborn.

"Look . . ." Cranmer-Philips made an ambiguous circling gesture with his cigarillo. Smoke swirled blue and gave the big room a nostalgic cast. Mid-twentieth century, Batista days, tropical sex, sugarcane money, Charanga bands headlining the mob-run casinos, and shapeshifters like this Englishman living off the skim. "*If* the famous faceless spymaster somehow survived his escape from East Germany after the wall. And *if*, as everyone seems to believe, he somehow retained possession of his personal cache of Stasi files." The old spy fixed his rheumy eyes on Sentro and hacked up some tar from his wheezing lungs. "He'd have a master plan, wouldn't he? Bloke that reputedly clever. Not some scattershot mercenary-extortion work for whoever will pay his fee." Gasping, he folded forward and tapped ash onto the filthy, threadbare kilim under his chair. "That'd be the *cover*."

"You've clearly given this a lot of thought," Sentro said.

"Nothing more pathetic than a ratfucker deprived of his rats. Too much bloody idle time. Only so many whores and rum you can have congress with, right." He'd turned his gaze to Banks. Sentro tried to imagine Cranmer-Philips having sex with anything and decided it was probably just the rum keeping him busy.

"What's your theory, then?" Banks asked, too impatient, and Sentro watched the old man's eyes go dark again.

"In my time it was customary to pay for your chips before sampling them."

"You were usually selling the same chips twice," Sentro pointed out. "Well chewed."

"Witt is dead," Cranmer-Philips insisted, cigarillo clamped fiercely as he gripped the chair's armrests and struggled to rise. "And my feet are cramping. So unless you'd like to rub them up for a bit," he said, shooting a lewd leer at Sentro, "I imagine you'll be on your way. Or . . ." Standing there, swaying, he tried to summon defiance. "I could ring my local *la Guardia* and tell him how some capitalist spies have showed up to chafe my ass and subvert the revolution."

———

"This is pointless," Banks said.

"No, it's not." She kept wishing that Banks's phone would quake with a text from Jenny, safe, back in Kyiv. "This is what we do. Locate, provoke, wait, follow."

"I could have squeezed it out of him. Saved us a whole lot of time." Banks was still irritated that Sentro had cut short their interview with

Cranmer-Philips. They sat cramped in a rental Kia Picanto, windows open to the sultry heat, ignoring the bitter vendor coffee that had gone tepid in the cupholders, and watching the front steps of the old spy's derelict neocolonial rooming house as tawny twilight sifted down on Havana.

"Probably made our surveillance already. He's not going anywhere."

"He's nearsighted," Sentro said. "And too vain to wear glasses. And he'll worry that we can hack his phone."

"How do you know that?"

"Knowing we tracked Wolfgang, he won't risk making a call." She explained, "The man couldn't even see the ashtray five feet from the chair he was sitting in, and there weren't any eyeglasses visible, anywhere, not to mention no marks on his nose." What she didn't say was that the old spy would nevertheless likely assume they would be watching him. She wondered if Banks was thinking the same thing.

"And you said your tradecraft sucked," he said.

"Observant is different from operational. I was a lowly hard man most of my career, Banks. Dark ops. Cleanup, security, rendition, and exfiltration."

"Not in Berlin."

No, not in Berlin, Sentro admitted silently. And not for the first time, she wondered how her life might have gone if Berlin hadn't happened.

"You ever thought about bringing your daughter into the game?" Banks asked, and when Sentro looked at him, she realized the light was gone from the sky, and she'd suffered another gap in time.

How long? Had he noticed?

"She'd be good at it," Banks mused. "Maybe that's what she's doing. Freelancing. Keeping tabs on the Cuban girl for us. Chip off the block."

Sentro shook off the brain fog, her thoughts still scattered. "Did you sleep with her, Banks?"

Banks tilted his head, didn't look at her. "No."

"Would you tell me if you had?"

"Probably no."

At least he was honest. "She never showed any real interest in what I did for a living," Sentro said, leaving unsaid the thought: *And now she's neck deep in it.*

"Sounds like she didn't really know what you did."

Fair enough. But not something Sentro wanted to get into. "There he is." Perfect timing: down the street, a leaden figure eased out of the flophouse door and limped down the steps. By the time Cranmer-Philips made it through the rusted iron-filigree gate to the sidewalk, a big old purple *almendrón* taxi, Pontiac by way of Chevrolet, had swung around the corner and cruised to the curb.

"Sweet ride, eh?" Banks's flat Ontario accent slipped through. "American iron. What year is that?"

"No idea," Sentro said.

"I'd say midfifties. They combine cars here. Salvage parts from different makes and models. My dad was a car guy; he'd be over the moon seeing these babies." There was a sadness in the statement but no opening for Sentro to ask about it, because Banks pushed the ignition button and pulled the Kia out into traffic to follow Cranmer-Philips's cab down the streets of Havana into what, they had both already decided and discussed, could only be some kind of trap.

"Full clip in that Beretta?" Banks asked after a while, confirming for Sentro that he, too, knew what lay ahead.

"I'm afraid to check," she told him of the disgraced British spy's sidearm, now tucked in her bag. "But if we need a full clip, Banks—wherever we're going—it won't be enough."

CHAPTER THIRTY-TWO

Sometimes she looked at Jenny Troon and saw so many subtle connections and intersections, a happy web of shared DNA.

Sometimes she saw only a stranger.

Mercedes still didn't understand why she had agreed to come along so willingly. She'd been prepared to force her, but the suggestion made, Jenny had jumped on it, hadn't even asked to go back to her hotel room, possibly because she was afraid she'd run into her mother—their mother?—and complicate what she was calling their big adventure.

"I can buy whatever I need when we get there," Jenny had said, with a guilelessness Mercedes envied. "My passport's in my purse. Let's do it."

What if that was all an act?

The American girl fell quiet, though, and pensive on the bus to Boryspil International Airport, while Mercedes was wrestling with doubts and second thoughts. Was Jenny playing her? No real discussion about what had happened in New Mexico. Or the cowboy who'd died. Mercedes sensed Jenny Troon was scared, but not as much as she'd expected, and she doubted Jenny simply had such a wild determination to defy Aubrey Sentro that it would outweigh any concern that Mercedes might be dangerous.

Am I? she wondered, then answered directly, *Of course I am.*

Was Jenny?

She had Mercedes feeling mystified and uneasy.

Jenny dozed next to her, the budget flight seat reclined only slightly, but that was as far as it would go. Mercedes had paid for the flight with her "company" card; Wolfie could go fuck himself when he got the statement and realized what she'd done.

Does he *know?* she wondered. *Has he always known?*

Twenty-some thousand feet below her, the pin lights of eastern Europe crawled past the airline window, tossed and scattered as if accidentally across the vast darkness. She was glad they'd have a long layover in Istanbul; there were so many questions she wanted to ask Jenny, so many things from her own life she felt the need to reevaluate. Mercedes had never had anyone for whom she felt responsible, never had a best friend besides her stepbrother. She'd had lovers but not boyfriends, no one other than Carmen to share secrets with, and some secrets you didn't, couldn't, share with your mother.

Your real mother.

Aubrey Sentro had lied to Jenny Troon. Lied to everyone. Given her unwanted daughter away, then gone and had another. What kind of person did that? Bile rose in Mercedes's throat.

Loose strands of thought twined and knotted, and her mood swung wildly from black to bright. Bipolar, she'd been diagnosed once, by a doctor when Carmen had caught her cutting herself.

Her hands were cold, restless on the armrests. She tucked them under her legs and took some long, deep breaths and tried to stay focused on what she had left to do.

———

"He's taking us to Cienfuegos."

"That's a city?"

"Up ahead, another hour or so, yeah," Banks said. "I'm guessing, but—dollars to doughnuts."

"What? Doughnuts. Jesus. Canadians."

Banks found he didn't mind Sentro's gentle goading. "Hey now. I picked that idiom up from a Yank."

They'd been driving for what felt like forever, on the ruler-straight A1 that split fields and lowlands, linking Havana with the rugged southern lands. About a half klick ahead of them, diamond taillights of the purple Pontiac rocked and swayed as it sped along the A1 highway. No working AC in the Kia, so the windows were open, but the blasting hot night air provided slim relief.

Did they have a plan? Banks glanced at Sentro, shoes kicked off, sweating in the passenger seat, her hair blown back and her battlefield stare telling him she'd gone on another trip to the twilight zone. Banks had his Five Eyes directive: locate Witt, secure his data files, arrange exfiltration. The question of Pogo's decommission would be situational.

Sentro seemed unhelpfully torn between her grudge against Witt and her worries about Jenny.

A plan was something he and Sentro didn't have, no.

They had a stratagem. Or was it a calculation? Working on the shared assumption that Cranmer-Philips was leading them somewhere treacherous but useful—for example, an ambush the old spook would have prearranged in the event of something like what had happened with Sentro and Banks banging into his apartment—and further assuming that walking into said ambush or whatever would, at the very least, expose his support network and provide the proper catalyst to get them to Günter Witt (and Sentro's daughter), they had decided to go full-on *Art of War*.

More or less.

Sentro didn't seem to care about drawing a distinction.

All warfare is based on deception, Hsun Tzu wrote. *Hold out baits to entice the enemy. Pretend to be weak, that he may grow arrogant. Appear where you are not expected. Feign disorder and crush him.*

"'Hold out baits.' That would be us," Sentro had offered, somewhat cynically. *This is where Jenny gets her edge,* Banks thought. "Sounds like you've memorized the whole book," Sentro added.

Banks was a little embarrassed to admit that he had.

"No plan is the plan," she said.

Banks had nodded. "Pretty much. From your file, it seems like you tend to wing it anyway."

Sentro didn't deny it and didn't offer anything more for a while. She stared out ahead, watching the lane stripes disappear under the car. The more time he spent with her, the more of a puzzle she seemed. All spies kept secrets, but Sentro's seemed primal, fundamental to who she was, as if she'd built herself, brick by brick, on a foundation of blind hope and self-deception. And yet, he suspected that if you stripped the lies away, what remained would still be formidable, rock solid.

"'Place your army in deadly peril and it will survive,'" she recited suddenly.

He glanced over. "Are you okay?"

Sentro looked at him blankly. "'For it is precisely when a force has fallen into harm's way that it . . .'" Sentro hesitated as if she'd lost recall of the rest of it, then seemed to claw the words back from a miasma. "'That . . . it is capable of . . .'"

"'Striking a blow for victory.'" He finished it for her.

"Yeah."

Was she just quoting more Hsun Tzu for him or explaining how she'd managed to survive so long?

"How's your head?"

"Fine."

"Listen, if we get separated—"

"We find each other again," she said simply, cutting him off. "Neither one of us can do this on our own." And then with a small wry smile she wondered aloud, "How fucked are we"—she was back staring at the road—"that we're quoting a two-and-a-half-thousand-year-old Chinese general like he knew what the hell he was talking about?"

"Um." Banks didn't know how to answer that, so he offered a final thought from the master: "'By persistently hanging on the enemy's flank, we shall succeed, in the long run, in killing the commander in chief.'"

Sentro looked at him oddly and shook her head. "Let's talk about something else."

But they didn't; they just fell into their own quiet funks, and the throbbing turbulence from the open windows, the fetid rot of the Zapata Swamp, and the perilous whine of the Korean car's tires on the worn highway asphalt were all they shared for the next couple of hours.

———

"I will tell you this: I grew up poor."

They sat in a darkened, empty concourse corner of the Zurich Airport, near a Pret A Manger franchise Mercedes had for some reason been devastated to find shuttered. They'd gone outside for Jenny to smoke a cigarette, but the night was cold and windy, so they looked for a place to crash. Dinner was a medley of strange Swiss snacks that tumbled perfectly from gleaming, glass-front machines, and they drank cans of cold brew and tried to stretch out.

"Of course, I could not know that then, and we were better off than many in Havana, with an apartment with hot and cold water and no holes in the floor and extra money every month that I always believed was sent out of guilt by my supposed German father's people."

A robot floor-cleaning machine whirred back and forth down the corridor, leaving a shiny residue that reflected the light in mirrored ribbons.

"But everyone in Cuba is poor. This is the nature of communism, yes? We share the poverty equally, as comrades in the ongoing revolution against American imperialism. Every man as miserable as the next."

The layover would be nearly five hours. Jenny was beginning to worry that her Cuban companion was going to try to fill every second with rambling monologues.

She had nearly convinced herself that Mercedes wasn't going to kill her. Jenny was the link to a mother the Cuban girl thought she deserved. The question was, What would she do when that mother showed up? Or didn't? Jenny thought she might need a plan B.

Even though she didn't fully have a plan A.

"Was I happy? Of course I was. And loved. But it was secondhand love, wasn't it? Not that Mama wasn't devoted to my stepbrother and me. She had an analyst job with G2 that afforded her family flex time, so we never felt like—what do you say?—latchkey kids. She'd been trained by the KGB in Moscow, in fact. That's how she knew Witt. Am I repeating myself? She was friendly with Ana Montes, who you might remember made a fool of your DIA." Jenny had no idea what she was talking about. "No? It doesn't matter. Not a field operative, like Aubrey Sentro, but a practiced liar just the same, as it turns out, right?" With the dark turn, Mercedes approximated a wounded expression. Jenny wondered if it was real. "We are, both of us, victims of an immaculate deception, Yenny Troon."

What does she want from me? The cartoon Cuban English was beginning to work Jenny's nerves, and the intoxicating adrenaline rush of her amateur spook-life adventure was waning. Mercedes talked and Jenny drifted, pretending to listen but mostly trying to ignore the uneasiness that kept creeping up on her uninvited. She thought about how this was her mother's real life, moments like these: empty terminals, night flights to the unknowable, gnawing uncertainty, risky encounters, hard choices.

Mom got addicted to the buzz, Jenny mused. It was wild and disturbing how it crept up on you. She wondered what would happen if she tried to run. She was fast; she doubted Mercedes would catch her, and she could make a fuss, get attention.

But—and she knew it was probably foolish—Jenny didn't want to run. Yet.

After she'd taken on the sea pirates and saved Jeremy, Sentro had been forced to admit to her children the texture of the secrets she kept from them—*a practiced liar*—and how most of the time she was making it up as she went along because the job, she said, contrary to what everybody thought, was oftentimes chasing blindly after what you didn't know.

Which was why Jenny found herself, dead of night, eating Kägi with a probable killer who claimed to be her sister.

What does she want from my mom?

Mercedes was midstory, describing the sun-browned, *tremendo mangón* boys she would meet on the Playa Bacuranao when she was fourteen and how her mama, Carmen, found out and marched her to Catedral de San Cristóbal to recite the Humility Prayer at the feet of the statue of Apolinar Serrano. "Do you know it?" She recited: "'Please prevent me from trying to attract attention. Don't let me waste time weaving imaginary situations in which the most heroic, charming, witty person present is myself. Show me how to be humble of heart, like—'"

Jenny interrupted to ask, "Remind me where we're going in Spain? Exactly?"

In fact, Mercedes hadn't said. She'd prepurchased the tickets over the phone, speaking German; Jenny had thought she'd be able to guess from context or recognize a few proper nouns, but she couldn't make heads or tails of any of it.

"This is a question you should have asked me before we left the bar in Kyiv," Mercedes pointed out. "Always get the details."

Jenny knew she was right, but at the time she hadn't cared. "Okay."

"There are so many things I will need to teach you." Mercedes frowned like a diva. "Another example of how Aubrey Sentro has been neglectful, no?"

"No." Jenny felt defensive. "And look—I had a father at home with me, all the time. He raised us."

It was as if Mercedes hadn't thought of this before. Her eyes went dark. "Your father."

"Yeah. Mom had to work."

Mercedes nodded indifferently, as if taking this under consideration. "No one has to do anything." Her mood seemed to have soured. "We're going wherever we can better get to know each other," Mercedes explained.

"I get that. But." Jenny waited. It didn't sound too treacherous, the way it was said.

Mercedes rummaged through their snacks, looking dissatisfied. "But first there is some unfinished business," she said. "On Majorca."

"That's in Spain?"

"Off the coast, yes. Spain. Incredible beauty. Why?"

"I'm thinking I should probably call my mom."

"No."

"No?"

Mercedes stared hard at her, with no expression. Like you'd stare down a dog you were training. "It's not necessary," she said.

"Oh," Jenny said, backing off; she'd struck a nerve. "Okay." And for the first time, she thought it might be wise to figure out a way to get her hands on Mercedes's cell phone.

Soon.

———

He was at war with the laughing gulls.

Ha—ha—ha—

White check marks wheeled and soared in shifting flocks above the circled cellblocks, looking for somewhere to spend the night. Shiny tape and silver Mylar streamers winked moonlight, fluttering in the top-floor window openings and on the railings of the central guard tower in a futile effort to scare the birds off. Mechanical spiders and rotating blades; spikes, wires and netting, placed to prevent them from perching—every deterrent he'd tried so far had failed. The smell of the guano in his hot, humid courtyard was pervasive.

Unspooling wire across the desiccated roofing of the panopticon to attach to an assortment of flat strips of metal arranged to lure and then deliver the gulls not-quite-fatal shocks, Fischer's hired men stepped carefully, their flashlights darting back and forth, avoiding the gaping holes. He watched their dark shadows from below, in his chair, grateful for the distraction.

The client had communicated a growing unhappiness to Wolfgang. The final phase was proceeding too slowly; the client wanted to "send his own people" to Majorca to sort the delays out. Fischer said, "Tell him categorically no," but wasn't confident that this was the message Wolfgang delivered. Was it all unraveling?

A sharp cry, and a chunk of tar paper and termite-damaged rafter came crashing down. A sheepish face appeared, dimly pale, in the newest gap in the roof, then resumed working.

Ha—ha—ha—

A foul mood swamped him. Why had he agreed to take on this fussy assignment for the client? Money that he couldn't hope to spend in Cuba? Pride, because Wolfgang had intimated that he was losing his edge? Maybe he had gotten old and complacent. For over two decades, his business model had worked with no messy complications, operating out of a calculated darkness; intelligence agencies didn't even know for certain that he existed.

No, he'd been reckless, and now he was exposed. The son lacked the Teutonic restraint of his father, insisting that the client's layered scheme could piggyback on Lenkov's pipeline acquisition. Then again, Wolfgang couldn't have known about Aubrey Sentro; hers was a name—a face—from the old Stasi archives, ancient history that only Fischer could know would be problematic.

Sending Mercedes to deal with it had been a mistake for many reasons, he'd realized much too late. The half truths he'd told her more recently had similarly backfired. She was ignoring his calls, but Wolfgang had tracked her back to the continent and Spain. Two one-way flights from Boryspil. But who was with her?

Whistling echoed down from the roof—the hired men had the new traps rigged. Fischer waved and rumbled his chair over the cracked concrete to a switched outlet providing power to the gull-deterring system.

He flipped the switch. There was a crack and a shout and a puff of smoke, and then something blew in the guard tower's main fuse box—he saw the spark shimmer across the grimy, broken windows. Up on the roof, the hired men were shouting, bitching at each other. Down below, Fischer scowled at the melted insulation on the extension cords that snaked up the wall to the traps. Now all the power would be down until morning, at least, unless they could locate a spare fused disconnect breaker.

The men's voices quieted. The gulls had scattered. The night seemed to swell and fill the darkened center of the cellblock with a bitter gloom.

Fischer remembered the frigid night in Berlin when Sentro had been captured.

His phone glowed. A text from Wolfie:

She's here.

CHAPTER THIRTY-THREE

Thunderheads glowed ghostly, piled up above what Banks said were the Escambray Mountains.

The air smelled of rain and a fast-approaching storm.

A party was in full swing at the Gothic-Caribbean villa when they finally found a parking spot in the vast, weedy lawn that stretched from a windbreak of banyan trees to the massive front door. Cranmer-Philips had been let off by his taxi at the stately front steps, where a pair of unconvincing probably off-duty soldiers slouched and smoked on the gallery portico, evidently a gesture toward security, although this estate was so remote from Cienfuegos Sentro couldn't imagine anyone finding their way here without invitation.

American hip-hop boomed from somewhere inside. She and Banks cleaned themselves up as best they could and got dead-eyed stares from the sentries but nothing more walking in. The British agent's gun was back in the car, too risky for Banks to carry, and Sentro's purse would be the first thing they checked, if there was any checking being done in the foyer.

There wasn't. Just a tiny, toothy matron, designated greeter, saying hello, introducing herself and politely asking who they were, since she didn't recognize them.

"CDR," was all Sentro said, in Spanish, and the little woman's smile died, and she nodded and nervously waved them past while getting busy with some flowers on a table.

"I should probably mention that I don't speak Spanish," Banks said.

Sentro just looked at him, then away. Canadians. Why was she not surprised?

The grand house was a survivor of the Batista era, probably home to an American tobacco executive and his family during the midcentury boom years, when Americans had plundered the island's resources and acted like the imperialists Castro later castigated to foment revolution. A flock of teenage girls in billowing ballroom gowns swept giggling past Sentro from a curving stairway and danced out into a big central vaulted room where party guests mingled, some in tuxedos and formal wear lovingly put together from disparate parts, some just decked out as best they could manage, like the old classic cars that still filled the roads.

Banks said, "Uh-oh. We're massively underdressed."

"Not massively. Socialist country," Sentro murmured. She unfastened the top two buttons on her dress and took his arm, fashioning a smile. "Pretend you're wearing your best clothes."

"Wedding?"

"Quinceañera. Coming-of-age fiesta for a girl turning fifteen." It flashed on her that at fifteen she'd been only two years away from having her first child. And Jenny, at fifteen, hadn't been talking to her.

"Who invited us?"

"Nobody," Sentro said. "We're with the Comités de Defensa de la Revolución." Banks gave her a doubtful side-eye. "Thought police. Just checking in. I'm the senior officer, so you can let me talk. But nobody wants to talk to the CDR."

They spotted Cranmer-Philips in the corner, at a small makeshift bar, pouring himself a tall drink and talking to a young man in a hipster suit, white shirt buttoned all the way up, no tie. Banks slowed and tugged Sentro back behind a group of men arguing about whose mother made the best *masitas*.

"What?" She was confused by his hesitation.

Banks waited for the hipster to angle his face more toward them. "Wolfgang Witt," he said.

Small in stature, eyes a little too close together, the imperious Prussian nose. Sentro studied him, trying to see the father in him, trying to remember the one photo she'd seen of the toddler in his mother's arms so long ago, and came up blank. Still, clearly her ruse in Havana had worked—the old double agent had panicked after they'd left him and reached out, and here was their possible best bridge to the target. It would just be a matter of turning the tables.

"You or me?" Sentro said to Banks.

He considered it. "You're not really asking me, though, are you?"

"No."

"Gotta be me," he agreed. "Because if we are at all right about this being a trap, he knows you by sight."

"From my cameo in Paris."

Banks nodded, and she could see that he was already beginning to plot his approach. Young Witt and the British double agent laughed about something that neither looked like they thought was amusing. Banks and Sentro made as if they were talking to each other intimately, but like hers, his eyes kept straying across the big room, assessing the crowd, trolling for threat.

"I've got your back," Sentro promised.

"Okay. Even unarmed, there's actually some comfort in your saying that," Banks said, no spin on it. She was getting used to his candor. But it seemed like there was something else on his mind.

"Okay. Well. Assume *he's* armed. And brought friends."

"Yep." Banks had let his gaze come to rest back on Witt. Cranmer-Philips was telling a story that, from young Witt's body language, the German clearly didn't want to hear. The hip-hop coming through open french doors from the backyard ratcheted up a notch, and the wooden floors of the house began to throb when the bass line crawled lowest.

Banks tensed like he was going to start moving but hesitated, and evidently his distraction needed airing: "Hey. I am sorry I let your daughter get away from me."

"She's a handful." Sentro was always surprised by what people needed to get off their chests as they dove into danger.

"I just—"

"We'll find her," she assured him, trying to sound convinced of it. Witt's son was on the move. "Let's focus on surviving this first, yeah?" She gently pushed Banks in the direction of the bar. "Go."

———

A mystery.

A thriller.

A very late coming-of-age cautionary tale.

Jenny was living her own patchwork fiction. If only she could guess how this ended.

Fog hugged the coastline of Majorca and circled the island so only the high ground rose through it, like a floating green archipelago. They landed at dawn in a soup of gray: the bright sun just rising was extinguished, and Jenny felt a gloom settle that was more than just the weather.

At baggage claim were two thick-necked Spaniards who just needed tommy guns slung across their shoulders to complete the pulpy Mediterranean melodrama Jenny was beginning to imagine she was in. They all got in a Citroën wagon that reeked of fish, and after a couple of turns Jenny lost any sense of direction. Storefronts and villa walls emerged from the haze like video game obstacles and then drifted back into the haze. They zigzagged through rugged backcountry, the two-lane road rising and then descending, and the air felt heavier. Mercedes and the Spaniards engaged in a lengthy discussion; Jenny got a little carsick and opened her window and smelled the sea. The brume broke; the car traversed a high bluff, waves crashing below them, until up ahead was a lone villa jutting out from the cliffs, ultramodern, clean angles and curves, with a sloping, gated driveway that the Citroën coasted down.

She was anxious. One on one with Mercedes had seemed manageable; now she was flying blind into who the fuck knew, and with unexpected strangers. The somewhat defiant thirst for a quest had given way to a more measured calculus: survival while trying to gather something useful for her mom (the road still might lead to Witt, but yada yada yada), which sounded pretty stupid if she thought about it for too long; in fact, everything she'd experienced in the last week had its stupid side, depending upon how you viewed it.

Intelligence. Jenny wondered who had coined that phrase. Because as far as she could tell from her admittedly limited exposure, it was all lies and secrets that defined her mother's world. Nothing so smart about it. It was high school cafeteria drama, laced with an unhealthy measure of violence.

Crusted piles of sand and pallets of bricks were stacked in a cobblestone courtyard; the huge house, still under construction, looked like it hadn't been touched by workers in months.

Inside, the blank hand-plastered walls of largely empty rooms flowed from one to the next, and big smudged windows looked out over a stone deck that offered spectacular views of the sea. Jenny imagined Paz Vega out there, breaking Javier Bardem's heart, or maybe pushing him over a railing into the breakers below because he'd betrayed her. The floors were unfinished, and there was minimal furniture, mostly draped with dust covers, but a seating area facing a huge TV had been exposed, and three more meaty Spaniards were watching a Spanish morning talk show and smoking weed. Jenny had a moment of craving but was more keenly aware of the black automatic rifles leaning against the wall. She found that by fixing on details, she could keep her fear at bay.

Had her mom taught her that?

"We'll be staying here for a few days," Mercedes advised her breezily. "The beach is quite beautiful. I think I have a bikini for you that will fit."

Fat chance, Jenny thought, trying to imagine her body in one of the Cuban girl's swimsuits, and not able to summon anything remotely flattering. *Just like Mom with Helga,* she thought. Shit. Déjà vu all over again.

What are we doing here?

She heard children's voices come up a banister-free stairway from rooms down below; then she heard Mercedes greeting someone and got a brief glimpse of an impressive computer array when a white-haired man came out through frosted library doors. The flat-screens glowed with code; there was a woman in a swivel chair working the keyboard.

The doors closed, the man turned, and thinking back on it later, she felt chagrined that she'd been so shocked seeing the albino who had wanted to kill her and her mother in New Mexico. An angry crimson gash creased his head, still scabbing over.

Of course he'd be there. But in that moment, unprepared, Jenny's heart jumped up into her throat, and her hands went ice cold, and she gagged and threw up.

———

Now *his* attention was divided, which was never good—thinking about Jenny Troon for some reason while he followed onto the tiled veranda the split-tail sport coat of Wolfgang Witt through the pastel flurries and perfumes of dancing teenage girls and their monkey-suit escorts.

Lightning jittered through the storm clouds. The moon disappeared. Music hopped; colored strobes turned the world stop-motion. The high-haired DJ, behind his canopied, twinkle-lit console, rapped into an oversize mike, and there was a sudden parting in the dance floor, and through it, Banks was sure he saw the bright-red lips and haunted pale features of his late girlfriend, Gillian, just turning away from the light, in flickering fragments.

A jolt went through him.

As if blindsided, he stumbled over the cartoon swell of the birthday girl's spinning, billowing white mushroom of a quinceañera dress and mumbled what he hoped sounded like an apology in a Spanish accent as he slipped past her.

Witt had disappeared, but Banks had his fix on the Gilly ghost and swam upstream through the gyrating crowd. Her shoulders, the generous curve of one hip, the spill of her hair down her back—he asked the obvious questions (*Why, and how?*) and plunged forward, desperate for confirmation. Desperate to look in her eyes. He'd witnessed the explosion that killed her, but one of the consequences of living in lies was that even known facts began to unravel. All those times you'd made the eyes of others deceive them. It worked both ways.

Betrayal gathered weight absurdly as he hurried through—was she doubled up? Working for whoever sent Xavi Beya into the stock exchange? Or Pogo himself?

Fireworks exploded above the trees, and the dancing girls whooped. He found the ghost girl again, floating out across the lawn, where propane torches cast hellish light on older guests who'd fled the din. The dress he recognized, too; he could swear that Gillian had worn one just like it to a fancy Five Eyes dinner in Kyiv.

An unlit canopy greenhouse loomed on the other side of what was once a clay tennis court, now overgrown with weeds. The ghost of Gilly entered through a side door. The glass panes reflected party lights back at him; he couldn't see where she'd gone. He knew he shouldn't follow her, but the remote possibility of her duplicity rendered him thick witted. His head said: *Get back to Sentro*; his pride cried: *Confirm or deny*.

Dimly it occurred to him that this could be prelude to the ambush they'd been expecting. The thought saved his life.

Loose panes in the rusting door rattled as Banks entered. A cool night breeze had wheezed inland off the bay, but the greenhouse was hot and humid, its air thick with decay, and the elevated planting beds were either overgrown or dying—and in either case unattended.

"Gilly?"

Banks listened to the faint rustling of satin, smelled some sort of musky men's cologne, saw a woman's face—red lips, pallid cheeks, black eyes—lit lurid by a pyrotechnic flash from the yard—and something about it made him duck his head. Over the appreciative cheers of the party crowd, he heard the fizz of a silenced gun, and the glass pane behind him popped. As he flinched away for cover, a man's hand clamped his shoulder, and Banks spun, reflexive, throwing his elbow back and connecting where he correctly guessed the hand's owner might be.

An expletive from pain and surprise. The unfortunate recipient crashed over the raised bed and into the next aisle.

A muzzle flashed behind the dense growth ahead; another fizz, and the second silenced bullet tore across the top of Banks's shoulder, spinning him down on the gravel pathway and sending him scrambling under the raised bed for cover as a few fat raindrops began to strike the glass of the greenhouse roof.

CHAPTER THIRTY-FOUR

Laughing chamberlains—fifteen-year-old boys, some in ad-libbed tuxedos, some in fancy-ass shirts, tired of masquerading as elegant quinceañera escorts—had escaped their young ladies and were joyously letting loose an armory of fireworks.

The wind picked up pace.

The result was a spectacular chaos of windblown fiery pyrotechnics and a giddy fibrillating drumbeat of deafening concussions that began to drive all the adults back inside.

Sentro had watched Banks wade into the roiling teens, then tried to shadow him by angling along a stone balustrade that edged the open patio beyond the veranda; now she couldn't find him. She scanned the dance floor in frustration—the crowded bar, the empty back lawn—nagged by worry she was off her game, as fireworks whizzed overhead, leaving contrails of sparks that showered down through the trees.

Lightning splintered over the dark mountains.

A duller flash blinked in the greenhouse beyond the tennis court. She waited. No one went in or out. Another flash, and the sound of glass breaking. She felt a drop of rain.

"Frau Troon?"

Wolfgang Witt was beside her, genial, a faint smile punctuating his German. *Too easy; serious rust.* "I'm told you've come in the hope of speaking with my father." No sign of Cranmer-Philips. Did the younger Witt know who she really was?

"I can take you to him," he continued. "He lives off shore. I have a water taxi waiting."

"I should find my friend," Sentro said, in German, as more fireworks exploded around them, and the sky began to open up to a downpour. *The rain*, she thought, *could prove useful.*

"What?"

"My friend. I need to—"

Witt was talking over her—"Herr Banks is already at the dock"— and she didn't see how that was possible or how Wolfgang even knew Banks's name, but when she glanced back at the greenhouse, there was a warning shout, and something detonated unexpectedly close behind them—*just a powerful firecracker, probably*, she would realize in a moment, but the initial blast-wave pressure from the explosion did something disagreeable to her fragile brain. Her eyes lost focus; all she could hear was a piercing tone in her ears that kept rising in pitch until it was too high to perceive, and she saw young Witt rise from where he had reflexively dipped down to catch her when her balance failed. His mouth was moving; she wondered idly what he was saying. Feeling the rain, now, eyes watering, she tried to blink away the gnawing throb of pain that overtook her and found herself back in Texas, with a gaggle of girlfriends and the one skinny, helmet-haired boy who hung with them, Denny Troon, her best best friend, night having fallen, sparklers tracing the darkness and a big bonfire leaping in the vast stubble field; fairground fireworks bloomed and flittered on the horizon as Troon set off his meticulously curated series of ground items—cones, spinners, waterfalls, whistlers, roman candles, and crimson snakes—until the stray popper ricocheted back under his eye and left the scar that Sentro loved, the one she'd lost herself in the first few times they'd made love after Berlin when he had cautiously, patiently, somehow helped her heal.

The hull slap of the cigarette boat brought her back from Texas, midocean. No Banks. A distant string of lights floated, beckoning, in the darkness.

Her clothes were still damp from the downpour. Someone had put a cold cloth across her forehead; she was lying on a cushioned bench, with sea spray dusting her and a long-haired woman with a split lip and a massive purple shiner staring back at her with tiny raptor eyes. *Shit.* She made a quick situational assessment. A pair of surly Cubans with tatty Che facial hair and holstered military sidearms stood braced against the windscreen, up front next to the skinny water taxi driver. Down below them, in a cramped, dimly lit cabin beneath the bow, Wolfgang Witt was arguing with someone on his cell phone. It would have been useful to know what he was saying, but Sentro had surfaced to a silent movie of stuttering, unstable images, feeling in her heavy head the pushback of every sawtooth wave as the boat knifed through them, but hearing only the hush of her jumbled thoughts.

An ambush, for sure.

The face he'd seen through the inky greenhouse flora wasn't Gilly's. The shooters were, luckily, inexpert. But he had to assume that Sentro was similarly under siege. He didn't panic.

Focus on surviving this. Then find each other.

Keep it simple.

As thunder rumbled outside, he rolled under the raised bed and scrambled as far as he could until some stacked pallets cut him off. Banks drew back into the shadowed recess to regroup; he waved away a cloud of mosquitoes and heard more movement—three separate assailants changing positions: the woman and two heavier threats, probably both men. He had little interest in killing them. That wasn't what he was there for.

Stupid, stupid, stupid.

His coat was torn open above his collarbone, and his shirt was wet and warm with what he knew must be blood. He felt no pain. That would catch up later. The rattle-crack of firecrackers popped through the hip-hop groove that bumped outside, providing some possibility of cover should he decide to run.

But where? Back to the car and the British agent's Beretta? Banks considered and dismissed it.

He closed his eyes and listened, struggling to separate and pin down the subtle sounds around him. Fake Gilly was at two o'clock. Rubber soles at six. One more. Where?

Shit, right behind him—eleven o'clock—so close Banks could smell the cologne again and just make out the sharp outline of black chinos, knee to cuffs, when fireworks flared.

As he shifted and tilted and braced on his good arm, there was a louder firecracker boom outside—not thunder—and a startled reaction from the party, followed by a quickening of the rain on the glass that helped mask Banks's movement when he kicked out the heel of his shoe and crushed the kneecap of the eleven o'clock foe. Another silenced bullet whistled harmlessly across the greenhouse. Crying out, the man collapsed, and Banks was on top of him, stripping his gun away and crushing his windpipe with the knuckles of his free hand. Pain shot down his shoulder, and he lost his grip and rolled away.

The other two were moving, trading sharp warnings in Spanish. The man on the ground struggled to get a breath. Banks popped up over the planting bed and double tapped blindly in both directions, only to realize he had it all wrong. There were two additional assailants at either end of the greenhouse, guarding the only exits. Muffled gunfire chased him as he dove over the next bed, and even before he tumbled to the footpath, he'd decided that his only option was to move fast, laterally, over and under the remaining beds to throw himself through the glass on the back side and hope to hide in the tobacco fields beyond.

Easier said than done.

He checked his captured gun's clip by feel. Five rounds. Four shooters, five rounds? "Shit!" He had said it out loud, in frustration, and they closed on him so fast he barely got over the next bed before another fusillade ripped through the foliage and splintered the bed rails around him.

A silhouette backlit by a photo flash from the party; Banks fired at it and heard the ragged exhale and collapse of his target.

Three shooters, now.

The girl's sharp voice came from his right. Somehow she had flanked him, positioned herself in the last aisle, covering the back of the greenhouse, jeopardizing his escape. She was in motion; he listened for the whisper of her satin and wondered how she could have known to wear *that* dress; he guessed that the two men would stay where they were and wait for him to move again. Heels scraped on the pebble path. She overshot where he was hiding but turned more swiftly than he expected when he came up from under the planting bed behind her. Her gun swung around wildly, and he punched her with the flat side of his pilfered weapon, whirled and fired twice blindly at where he thought the other shooters had posted up, then kicked his way through the glass panes of the greenhouse and sprinted out into the storm-tossed field. Fake Gilly was screaming, and the shooters were emptying their clips after him. A round creased his thigh as he plunged into the first thicket of head-high tobacco, and he crashed zigzagging through and between plants and rows, running for his life because he could hear pounding footfalls of the two men behind him and still hot on his tail.

Sandy loam soil provided precarious footing, and the cloudburst was sweeping across the field. His leg burned and his shoulder ached, and his pursuers split up to contain him. Stumbling, wet, he fell, rolled, crab walked backward under a canopy of broad, dripping leaves, and came out sitting and facing an astonished, onrushing gunman, whom Banks dropped with two silenced shots, center mass.

The other man had stopped short. Reacting, Banks guessed, to the sound of snapping stalks as his partner crashed to the ground. Banks discarded his empty weapon and clawed away the one the dead man still held in one hand. He could just make out the other shooter's winded wheezing over the rumbling thunder and the hiss of the rain and the distant music, still playing for a party that had fled indoors.

A flash of lightning revealed two more figures jogging around the greenhouse with flashlight beams that punched through rainfall. His new weapon's clip was almost empty. In a war of attrition Banks knew he couldn't prevail; he needed to disengage, locate Sentro, and reassess.

The downpour helped. Crouching low, Banks began sprinting toward the thick woods that bordered the field. The closest shooter wasted a couple of rounds chasing the sound of him, then decided to hold his fire. Banks reached the trees and circled back, above and around the house on a steep upslope; he could see the back lawn and veranda, now empty, and headlights of cars out front beginning to drive away from the party. The rain was already easing by the time he came abreast of where their rental was parked, but looking down from the cover of the foliage, he could see it had already been staked out by a man framed in headlights, while a partner stayed dry in an idling car.

Banks backtracked. Nearer the house was where a beleaguered valet service had parked the cars of favored guests who were presently packed under the portico, while two men in soaked white shirts dashed out to find their vehicles. Having spent a first-year summer working valet in Guelph, he knew that keys were sometimes tucked on the tops of tires for convenience. The yard traffic was gridlocked, headlights bright in all directions, affording him the kind of dark-light chaos he would need. Banks put his ripped coat up over his head and slip-slid down the slope, out of the trees, and into the complimentary parking area and quickly found a Fiat with keys waiting under the right front fender.

He got behind the wheel, and the engine rumbled to life. Praying that a valet or the owner wouldn't come running up, he eased out from between two big mixed-breed American sedans and joined the crawling queue leaving. He scanned the front of the house for Aubrey Sentro and was alarmed to see her on the far side, being helped into the back of an old Toyota Land Cruiser by Wolfgang Witt and the faux Gilly. Sentro looked unsteady, and Banks could only watch, dismayed, as the vehicle fishtailed away with her, swerving off road, bumping through the low plantings and flower beds that edged the long driveway, bypassing the traffic jam, and disappearing into the darkness beyond.

———

The water taxi docked at a crumbling concrete quay on the edge of a sleepy coastal town. The woman with the black eye stayed with the boat, while Wolfgang took Sentro's arm and guided her off the pier to where another drab and rusty Land Cruiser was idling, two more scruffy comrades of the perpetual revolution in the front seat.

Her hearing was returning, and although her brain haze had lifted, she still felt slug witted, the world coming at her on a five-second delay. Rocky shores covered with roosting gulls, an empty, unlit two-lane, the night sky clear and awash with so many stars. One of the men up front smoked a cigar. Boyish face softly lit by its glow, young Witt fiddled with his phone, but Sentro couldn't seem to focus on what was on the screen. It didn't seem like they traveled far, but her sense of time was so turned around it could have been hours.

The Land Cruiser veered off onto a long, narrow access road that led ruler straight to a cluster of big, squat circular buildings.

A prison. Cosmic irony that Witt would wind up living in one. She began searching for signs of Jenny, but it was dangerous to speculate; Sentro forced herself not to think that far ahead. Four levels of empty cells, gaping like broken teeth, windowless, doorless, curved around central guard towers just visible through notched openings that all faced each other. Lights glowed in the lower level of the cellblock farthest back. They rolled through the gap and parked next to a two-tone Chevy Nomad. Was it Dennis who had always wanted one? Inky puddles glimmered in the courtyard in patches where the roof high above was broken.

"How are you feeling?" Wolfgang, brows furrowed with feigned concern, asked in German.

For some reason this irritated her; he was unimpressive, cloying, seemed more errand boy than heir to the throne. Were children always a disappointment? Were hers? "I'm fine."

"Shall we?" One of the front-seat Cubans had already opened the door for her.

She wasn't panicked but did feel anxious. All the gaping blanks in her memory, added to the way her thoughts kept dragging, elicited some worry that she would not be able to manage whatever it was Witt had in mind.

His agenda could include killing her. But not right away. Not his style.

Her agenda was, as usual, extremely fluid. And would depend entirely on his. *Assess and adapt.*

The persistent drone of a generator filled the central courtyard with something like dread; three workmen were fussing with a breaker box in a mechanical room at the base of a central guard tower.

She wanted to ask about Banks but knew whatever was said would be disinformation. Inside it, the round cellblock seemed bigger, more forlorn.

Across the courtyard a carved double door opened on the lowest walkway, and a man in a wheelchair rolled out from the warm light of an eccentric living space that had been fashioned out of one long arc of the first two levels. Backlit, he was a silhouette, face in shadow. She braced herself for a rush of emotion.

"Aubrey Sentro," he called out, "or should we say, Fräulein Troon," and the voice confused her, then discomposed her, as she dredged from her memories why. "*Willkommen.*" He wheeled himself to a ramp that curved down into the courtyard, and his smile, always easy, lit up, his narrow features coming into focus. Something was very wrong with the picture. "I have dreamed about this reunion for a long, long time."

A dam broke. She stared in some shock at the man in front of her, speechless, while a tsunami of sudden, ugly memories threatened to drown her in icy black currents of the past.

"Frau Sentro. I trust you know my father," Wolfgang prompted, as if trying to help. "The spymaster you call Pogo. Günter Witt."

No.

No no no. Not Pogo.

No, not Witt.

This was an older, corroded, hollowed-out version of her former lovestruck Stasi paramour, Matthias Schmidt.

And his dead blue eyes were warning her: *Lie.*

PART THREE:
BITTER TRUTHS

PART THREE
SPECIFICATIONS

December 3, 1990, 09:37 (Utc+01)

For more than an hour after the power went out and the cell doors were opened, and the marauding student interlopers shouted how they were liberating everyone, she had been too afraid to move.

As they had done for several days, protestors gathered outside the building in the early morning, chanting their slogans, shouting their defiant songs, but something had changed; she could feel it, rising through the familiar slurry of her daily dose of uppers and opioids. And when the rioters breached the building, what transpired was almost anticlimactic, noisy but bloodless, because the guards and orderlies, nurses and doctors, had hurried their boxes and possessions out the back door as the mob surged in the front.

The building sounded empty. All the angry energy that rushed through and sent the staff fleeing had leaked back out onto the street and evaporated, someone on a bullhorn singing Pink Floyd until a new kind of uneasy quiet settled in. She didn't trust it.

Ever since a half-assed attempt at suicide over a month ago, her sanity had begun to slip. Strange visions, whispering voices, troubling dreams, and runaway trains of crazy thought. Dr. Janke—*call me Jurgen*—had tweaked the cocktail. After the first rush, each new dose felt like someone had hit her with a cartoon hammer—or she'd walked into her own diabolical trap—Wile E. Coyote, flat as a pancake, with stars pinwheeling and a wah-wah trumpet score.

Baby Jeremy loved the Road Runner cartoons, Dennis wrote. Her sluggish gaze found, taped to the opposite wall over the desk, glossy magazine photos of West Texas she'd cut from the *National Geographic* her husband had sent in the care package. Felt next to nothing—it had been less and less every day—thought: *Maybe I should take them down.*

She no longer grieved for the baby who'd died. Was that wrong?

The lone elevator clicked and rumbled up its shaft, but only to the second floor.

Familiar voices barely carried down the stairwell. A high, ironic female laugh. Something about the voices and the gallows humor got her up on her feet. Her first step found a broken piece of glass that had skittered into the cell; it sliced the bottom of her foot and caused her to sit back down again, grabbing for a towel to stanch the blood.

Pain registered, but dull and distant; she'd endured so much worse. When the cut's weep slowed, she dropped the towel and started walking, telling herself that it was to find a bandage and a pair of shoes. Hers had been taken away because she kept throwing them when they came in the cell to refresh her medication.

Frequently her moods took terrifying swings, giddy to bleak. This day was no different; the walls were closing in on her, and she knew she should be running to freedom, but there was one more prison door that needed unlocking.

"Aubrey?"

Liesl Grün was still in her cell, too, remorseless eyes screwed deep beneath a tortured frown. Six months earlier, she had been some kind of rock star Stasi biochemist, but Liesl's husband had died while trying to defect and flipped her perfect Ossi apparatchik world upside down.

"Take me with you." The doctor's bare arms were scratched red; she rocked like a metronome, side to side, glaring out. Different reading, this time in English, a more plaintive refrain: "You will take me out of here, won't you?" Liesl made a guess at a grotesque smile.

The chemicals coursing through her own veins were probably from Liesl's special brew.

"No."

Down the stairwell, the second floor was administration; she'd only been here once, for processing, at the beginning. Was there a doctor's examining room? Supplies? Bandages? A door marked STAFF LOCKERS seemed promising, but then the voices distracted her and drew her attention to the offices at the far end of the long corridor littered with files, photographs, and paperwork.

The suite door opened and Oberleutnant Kimmich stepped out, laughing again, high pitched, rattling the corridor like a coyote on the Texas prairie, the way she had laughed at the captured American spy's humiliated tears while she held her down so that Witt and the others could go about their business. And soften her up for interrogation. Stiletto heels clicking, Kimmich breezed into the men's bathroom without even glancing down the hallway where the lone remaining political prisoner stood, stoned, spectral, bleeding barefoot in her thin gray smock.

She heard water running as she passed the frosted bathroom door, not quite sure what she was going to do when she walked into the director's suite, but compelled to go. Compelled to give them an answer to the one question they hadn't asked, the one they'd spent eleven months circling. *They should want to know*, she told herself.

They needed to know.

Reception was empty, the desks turned over, the file cabinets gutted. She sensed movement in Schmidt's office, then Dr. Janke came out, and for a moment she drew only a puzzled stare; then his eyes flicked back toward the inner office, and he started to say something, but it was really not difficult to keep him quiet, the paperweight in her hand providing more than enough mass when, combined with the momentum of her two-step forward followed by the rotation of her shoulder and hip, it struck the side of his head, and she felt the skull shatter and give, yielding soft like the shell of a fractured hard-boiled egg, and he sank to the carpet almost gracefully.

No Liesl cocktail would cure him.

"Jurgen?" It was the voice she couldn't even shake from her dreams, and it barked its question from the inner office, more irritated than curious, and for a harrowing moment she thought she had blown her one chance. But Kimmich came back in from the corridor, wiping damp hands on her uniform skirt, bitching about "no hand towels" as she noticed Janke down and crumpled up, and she seemed to be still trying to puzzle out why when her Makarov got taken, slipped out of her hip holster, and shoved up hard against the base of the Stasi officer's slender neck—

"Move."

Together they did a clumsy glissade through the inner office doorway to where he was standing, behind Schmidt's desk, shuffling through the in-box documents for something, looking up incurious into the eyes of his American captor only after she pulled the trigger and Kimmich jerked and sprawled forward onto the floor.

And little, young, drugged and defeated, thoroughly broken Aubrey Sentro took her own sweet time, eleven months' worth, letting the quiet between them stretch and stretch until the great Stasi spymaster must have thought she couldn't do it—until the smug smile, the callous contempt, the arrogant certainty, the utter indifference to everything he'd put her through expressed itself fully—and then she emptied the Makarov into the heart of Günter Witt, dropped the gun, and walked out of one life and into the next.

Tot. Ganz tot. Mausetot.

That was that.

CHAPTER THIRTY-FIVE

"Am I being held prisoner?" She'd been trying to stay casual, but it was taking its toll. Again, she marveled at how her mother had done this kind of thing for almost thirty years.

And thought: *Where is she?*

"Whyever would you say that? You are free to go whenever and wherever you want."

"Last night my door was locked."

"Perhaps," Mercedes said, "for your protection." She lit a cigarette, then handed it to Jenny. "You know."

"From the outside? Locking me in?"

Mercedes had taken to smoking with a startling ferocity; she lit another cancer stick for herself, and they said nothing for a while, and Mercedes took long dramatic drags, and Jenny knew that her question wasn't really going to get answered. She'd gone to bed early, feigning sickness that had really been just a sobering moment of abject terror. She should have known the albino would show up sooner or later. Her only consolation was imagining that he was the one who had to clean up after her.

Petty but gratifying.

What the fuck am I doing here?

The string bikini Mercedes had offered, with its puzzle of crisscross-ing ties, was so insubstantial it made Jenny blush, and now the elastic was cutting across her butt. She had found an oversize T-shirt someone had left behind in a bureau drawer and was using it for cover. But it was hard not to feel resentful of any woman who could wear it.

You came willingly, she reminded herself sourly. And again, she wondered (it had become her refrain): *What the fuck am I doing?*

Nothing. Waiting. *Pretending I'm Mom.*

And like her mother, she had already scoped out potential avenues for escape, in case that became necessary.

"She never told you what she did at her work?" Mercedes had asked, clearly incredulous, on the flight from Kyiv.

"No."

"And you never suspected?"

An overcast day, little chance that the sun would burn through, but holding a heavy, oppressive heat. They stood on one of the lower balconies, looking down on a pool in a stone patio carved out into the cliff. Iron stairs zigzagged down to a spit of beach, where two small children were splashing in the waves of a presently calm, shimmery sea. Their mother watched from a blanket on the sand—bottle blonde with dark roots. Even from far above Jenny could tell she was the woman she'd seen sitting at the helm of the back room computer array.

"Why are they here?" Jenny asked, changing subjects.

Mercedes offered a shrug; nothing Jenny should be concerned about. They were, she said, "special guests."

"Oh." Jenny had come too far, taken all that risk; she didn't see the point in playing coy. "Having something to do with why you wanted to kill us?"

The look this elicited was unnerving. Sometimes, with Mercedes, a window would open and give a view to a very dark place. *Have I pushed her too far?* Mercedes smoked, studying Jenny, eyes narrowing, defensive. And after a while, she swept her hair back, dramatic, with a trembling hand and exhaled, "No. That was personal.

"This—" Overcome by a fit of coughing, Mercedes gestured with her cigarette to the unfinished house, to the family on the beach, to the lifeless ocean under the mournful sky and, recovering, sounded tired. "This is just business."

———

It was the one secret she had kept to herself. Not even Dennis knew. She'd locked it away, refused to revisit it, and over time, having healed and become the young survivor who'd walked out of the East changed, tempered, defined, she had almost convinced herself it might not have happened.

This was why, in New Mexico, when Banks had told her that Witt might be alive—that Pogo was still operational—she wasn't shocked. She believed it was possible.

"You can imagine my astonishment to have found him shot dead in my office," Schmidt (she refused to call him Fischer) was explaining. "Along with Fräulein Kimmich and poor Janke."

With a glass of brandy and salted almonds in a little dish, she sat facing him in a worn leather club chair, in the study he told her Cuban craftsmen had fashioned from several first-level cells, with wainscoting and false beams and bookshelves Schmidt must have imported from Europe. A screen saver of idyllic Baltic Sea coastline lit a computer screen on the vintage partner's desk; there were Kazak rugs and Nachtmann crystal and Holtkoetter lamps. But for the heat and the bugs, they could have been back in Berlin. *What does he want from me?* kept running through Sentro's head. Because he did. Want something, clearly. Or he would have sent someone else to kill her after Mercedes declined, and before she ever walked across the courtyard.

"Right away I guessed that it was your doing, the murders, and I took the gun with me to be sure."

"Also his identity. Not to quibble."

Schmidt didn't seem fazed. "Your prints *are* on it. Kimmich's Makarov, I mean. I had it analyzed by forensics here in Cuba. There exists a ballistics report done at the time, by the murder desk at the *Kriminalpolizei*, that I'm sure someone could use for comparison if they were so inclined." He smiled. The threat was clumsy and rather pointless. She was where she wanted to be. The only question was what she would do.

"I don't know," Sentro said, switching to English because the cruel consonants of German were making her headache worse. "I think you're more vulnerable in this than I am, Matthias."

"You killed three people!"

"I was a damaged soul, in a cold war. Yours is a cynical, thirty-year con. Plus possible treason for stealing state secrets. But forget the criminal exposure; you lose everything if it's ever discovered you're not Witt." She'd never been confident in her spycraft, but it was her turn to go on offense. "Does he know? Wolfgang? Who you really are?"

She gauged Schmidt's discomfort and watched as he tried to shake it off. "Wolfie was just a toddler when the wall came down," Schmidt said. "By the time the kid found me, so many years later, well. We see what we want to see. He assumed my appearance had suffered the ravages of time."

"If he ever finds out that you took his father's—"

"He won't."

"And his rightful inheritance."

"To the victor go the spoils."

"But surely his mother—"

"Had passed. Cancer. They were estranged even before the boy was born, Günter and Ilsa. And in the confusion of collapse and reunification, it was easy for me to float the rumor that Witt had faked his own death. Five years after I fled Germany, I sent a cable to her, unsigned: 'Don't look for me. Make a new life.'"

"She must have seen him dead."

"Or saw another diabolical Stasi deception. Who can say? We believe what we want to believe. Plus, I set up a very comfortable trust she could draw on for the rest of her life. So."

"Generous."

"Practical."

"Money Generalleutnant Günter Witt had stolen from the GDR."

"They all did it: the central committee, the Stasi command. As Witt's attaché, I was keenly aware he'd been filling up blind accounts in Zurich. And jealous, frankly. I knew where he kept the numbers, all the paperwork. I did all my bank business by phone. Now online. Ilsa had no idea what he'd stashed away. Nor did I, as it happened."

"More than you thought?"

"Much, much more."

"Not to mention the files. His precious kompromat."

Schmidt seemed giddy to be talking to someone about it after all these years. His hands flew, gestured, as he explained how Witt had begun as early as 1987 having trusted underlings copy select materials under the guise of archival redundancy. "My Generalleutnant understood the disastrous consequences of Gorbachev well before many of the others. That it was only a matter of time before the grand Soviet adventure would come crashing to an inglorious end."

"Where?" He looked confused. She clarified, "Where did you—or Witt—store all those duplicate files? There must have been tens of thousands of—"

He nodded and cut her off. "The sharp decline of the sugarcane industry here in Cuba, due to sanctions, embargoes, and so forth, resulted in a ready supply of cheap, empty warehouse space around Havana Harbor as well as in some of the southern cities. The Castro brothers were happy to have our business."

"You fled here and set up shop."

"I sought asylum from my Cuban comrades. On Witt's 'Fischer' passport, but with my picture. He had it all worked out."

285

"I'm guessing the files have been digitized."

"It took years. Now they're searchable, fungible, and not subject to accidental loss from fire or deterioration,"

"Private-sector concierge espionage. Blackmailing former East German assets, selling their services to whoever might need them."

"Not just our assets. We had sensitive intelligence on all kinds of Western VIPs." Schmidt smiled, smug. "Eastern Bloc entrepreneurs have proved to be especially generous, loyal repeat customers. Especially the New Russian Rich."

"And you and they never have to get your hands dirty. Like with Beya. Blame it on the Basque." She'd found no indication that Jenny was there or had ever been there; a hint of her perfume, a locked room, a slip from Schmidt, traces of Mercedes—anomalies, some affirmation she hadn't just told herself that her daughter would be with Witt so as to give some direction to the disquiet that kept clawing at her heart.

Schmidt shrugged as if indifferent and sipped his drink. "You can see why I was so annoyed when I realized you had intersected with the Arshavin contract. I admit I panicked. Rashly assumed that you would be my downfall. Sent the girl and the Chechen to clean it up."

"You told her lies."

"Lies? Hmm. Where do they start, where do they end?" Schmidt taunted her.

Sentro let it pass. "Who was your client?"

"Lenkov. But you know that."

"No. The bigger client you piggybacked on Lenkov to go after the Five Eyes."

"I don't double up operations, Aubrey." Something in the bitter way he scoffed at this told her that she and Banks were wrong: the add-on hadn't been Schmidt's idea; there was someone else. Someone using him.

And Jenny wasn't here.

"It's bad form," Schmidt was grumbling, as if trying to convince himself. "And far too risky." He drained his drink.

Sentro hadn't touched hers. The game needed changing. She didn't really care about his evil master plan unless—as she was beginning to suspect—her daughter, with Mercedes, was caught up in that. Now she wanted him to show her Witt's kompromat database and figured the best angle in was personal. "Where's my daughter?"

"What makes you think I would know, and"—the smug smile flared again—"which one?"

"I only have one. The other died."

Schmidt shrugged it off, still smiling. *Who is pulling his strings?*

"Fuck you. More of your Stasi bullshit," Sentro said sharply. "Classic disinformation, Matti. Was spinning that lie how you got her riled up to kill me?"

"No," he insisted. She could see that she'd touched a nerve. "And I called it off."

"Did you? Mercedes claims it was her."

Schmidt looked rattled that she knew the truth. "You're wrong. Listen," he said, softer, intent, "all these years I have wondered. That night. If I had agreed to help you escape—"

"You wouldn't. You couldn't. You were the loyal *Ministerium* soldier, Matti." Putting an aggrieved fury behind the words, she wanted him to think she still felt betrayed. "You took me back to Hohenschönhausen and fed me to Witt and his wolves." She flashed on his anguished look in the car as the memory of it all crashed back to her; his self-serving pretense of regret: *I'm not like the rest of them; I have a good heart.* "And your spymaster tortured me and abused me, over and over, and I gave birth to a dead child, and yet you can't stop yanking my fucking chain, even now." Tears would have been overkill, but she turned her head away from his wounded, ashen expression, unable to bear to look at him. She even heaved a ragged sigh.

Wait.

Wait.

"No." His voice was a whisper, hoarse with emotion. The wheelchair squeaked as he shifted his weight. "No, Aubrey, this was another of his sadistic tricks that they played on you.

"The child survived. I can prove it."

———

Because she hadn't been told about Wolfie's big job until it was already in motion, there was no way now for Mercedes to opt out. Fischer had promised they would cut the German loose after this. She hoped it wasn't another lie.

She wanted her birth mother to come find her and Jennifer in Spain and make her choice.

She wanted Wolfie's mission to be over. What lay ahead was mostly the unpleasant part.

High tide was churning the Basque children's sandcastle lumpy, while Jenny played with them in the shallow water farther down the beach. Mercedes found children needy and tiresome; Jenny was good with them, despite her claims otherwise. The bikini didn't fit her, which ordinarily would have given Mercedes some measure of narcissistic satisfaction. It didn't. It just angered her how desperately she wanted Jenny's love.

She was nervous that Fischer would ruin everything. When, after arriving at the house, she finally called him to report in, he claimed he no longer wanted Aubrey Sentro dead, but his word was unreliable. So often he said what you wanted to hear.

But when he told Mercedes that her birth mother was in Cuba, that sounded true. They'd been on a collision course since Paris. Then London had just confused her. She tried not to speculate what could happen. The task at hand wasn't done.

The Basque woman was asleep on a blanket, obviously exhausted from working all night again. Did she know what storm was coming? Mercedes was sure that she must. After all, Paola Beya had been a soldier of sorts; she would understand the wages of war.

Her kids would be unfortunate fallout.

Always the children, Mercedes thought, spiteful.

The innocent. Like me.

CHAPTER THIRTY-SIX

"She's damaged."

Schmidt let Sentro navigate the fussy search engine for Günter Witt's massive database of kompromat, while he sat angled beside her at a desktop computer, getting drunk and talking shit about the Cuban girl who thought she was Sentro's daughter. Mercedes was legally his ward, he claimed, raised in Havana by a former G2 agent who had trained with the Stasi and who, Sentro suspected, might have been Schmidt's first lover.

"Dr. Jankenstein did a number on her. Remember him?" *Too well.* She had tried to watch Schmidt's hands as he logged in so that she could do it herself later, if required, but his fingers flew so fast there was little chance she would be able to remember the keystrokes and reverse engineer his passwords and commands.

"What does that mean?"

"The late, great Janke and his pharmacological tinkering?"

"With Mercedes?" She wanted him talking. On the virtual desktop was a stray folder labeled *Majorca* that she was dying to open, but Schmidt was watching every stroke and click; while, clearly, he wanted to keep her hands busy so she couldn't cause him any other trouble, he also seemed giddy with a malicious anticipation of what he knew she would find at the end of her search.

Shifting subjects: "Took two years to get all Witt's precious shit scanned and properly indexed," Schmidt said, gesturing to the screen and then pouring himself three more fingers of the brandy. "The gift that keeps on giving. I'm discovering more and more useful intel all the time. However, much of what we have is aging out. So. Subjects die. Politics evolve. I strive to supplement what we have with new compromising material leveraged from many of those old sources, whenever I can."

She typed *Sentro* and got nothing.

"Guess again," he teased, then went on another tangent. "Did you know that this was the prison where Castro and Che were held by Batista as political prisoners? This very room was fashioned from their cells."

She typed *Troon*, and a trove of folders filled the screen.

"There she goes."

Folders filled with files. Everything that had happened to her at Hohenschönhausen and the annex. Everything she'd confessed.

"You're a quick study," Schmidt noted.

"Some perverse inside joke, Matti?" Or had she used Troon as her cover name in East Berlin? She couldn't remember. But it seemed wrong; she would never risk that kind of family exposure, would never have agreed to . . . or, no . . . oh. *Fuck.*

No. Witt got it from her, when she broke.

Staring at nothing, Sentro was momentarily unsettled. *What else did I tell them?* The folders glowed, tempting her. All the insults, indignities, and transgressions she'd forgotten.

"Try 'Infirmary report. September tenth, 1990, Troon, Aubrey, corporal, US Army,'" Schmidt dictated, impatient, and when she typed this in and opened the resulting file, all the medical records of her delivery were in front of her: crudely scanned photocopies by modern standards, gray scale, with blackened edges. She studied them, numb, but thinking—huge files, no buffering, no lag time downloading them—either

Pogo had a fiber network the Cuban government was providing (highly unlikely), or the servers and storage were on site. Close by.

"*Da ist es.*" Schmidt leaned in, brandy on his breath, wafting a stale, sour odor of unwashed bachelor clothes. "Birth certificate, see? Baby girl. 04:08 a.m. Six pounds, ten ounces, three weeks premature."

"No one's disputing there was a birth." Stubborn, Sentro scrolled down and found the death certificate: *04:13 a.m., 10 September 1990.* "Five minutes later," she pointed out. But seeing the exact time left her hollow. She had no clear memory of it. "Stillborn."

"*Ja, ja.* Of course there would be one," Schmidt said. "The cover story. Please. Keep scrolling."

More medical charts and redundant documentation. There had been delivery complications requiring a unit of blood, AB positive. Then puerperal infection. A course of penicillin. She didn't remember any of that, either, but she'd had a similar problem giving birth to Jenny.

"Down down down," Schmidt urged her, impatient again. Clearly, he'd been through these files, knew what was coming. "Stop."

Sentro squinted at official paperwork for "surrender of offspring." Her nerves went cold. This text was smeared, blurred by sloppy duplication. The usual GDR boilerplate, an official stamp, the confirmation of voluntary release by birth mother.

Troon, Aubrey. And on it, her signature.

"Didn't I tell you?" Schmidt said with satisfaction and sat back. "You gave her away."

Sentro was knocked sideways for a moment. "I was told the baby died."

"Perhaps, yes. Or perhaps you convinced yourself this was true." The memory was empty; Sentro had nothing to refute his drunken slight. "Because of the guilt, you know. It would only be natural."

Was he fucking with her? Absolutely. There was no way to vet the document, or for that matter to gauge whether any of the paperwork was accurate, given the breathtaking levels of half truths and obfuscation that existed even in the official Stasi records. Such was the tapestry of lies they embraced—that she embraced—not unlike when, in a rush of adrenaline and love for country, you take the oath of secrecy in a Berlin Station secure room and then slip behind the Iron Curtain under a false name to expose a different lie so that your side can use it to nurture even more untruths.

And on, and on, and on.

"I'm not here to judge," Schmidt assured her, although clearly he was judging. "The child was placed in a state orphanage, where Dr. Janke enrolled her in a clinical trial involving drug and hormone therapies for human performance enhancement. Those records did not survive the purge."

"How did *you* wind up with her?"

"How else, in a paranoid communist autocracy? With the proper paperwork: I forged Janke's signature."

Sentro studied him curiously. "But why would you take the baby with you?"

For a moment his guard came down. "Because she was yours," he said, looking sheepish. It was the same last look she remembered from Berlin; tentative, vulnerable, yearning. Right before he'd turned her over to Witt.

"You sent her to kill me, Matti."

"I thought I had to. But when she couldn't . . ." He didn't finish the thought; he rolled back from the desk, pivoted, and put some distance between them. Facing the wrong way, pretending to go for another drink, but he never even opened the decanter. For a week, Christmas of '89, before Operation Pogo had imploded, Sentro had worried that Schmidt was going to ask her to marry him. There was something so old fashioned and regressive about the man. So no surprise for her, really, when he said, "I can't let you go," with real emotion. His Cold War had never ended. "Surely you understand why."

She did and thought maybe she could use it. "What do you want from me?"

Sentro really didn't know anymore; Schmidt went quiet, didn't say anything for a while, so she clocked the room a second time, scheming her departure. Two points of egress, not much cover. Armed men in the courtyard; she would need to acquire a weapon. Her eyes came to rest on the back of his wheelchair, and she wondered how Schmidt's limited mobility could be turned to her advantage, but she also began to understand how stubbornly foolish and overconfident she'd been coming here, with only Banks as her wingman.

Mistakes she wasn't used to making.

"Forgiveness," Schmidt said finally, surprising her.

"What?"

He turned the chair, faced her. "Forgiveness." His eyes were wet. All those visits to her cell, after Witt's questions and abuse had ended. The sorrowful face. *He knew what they'd done*, she realized. *He knew what he'd let them do.*

"Is that why you lured me here? To apologize?"

"You were already coming; I just sought to define the terms."

"Quote from the comic strip? No. You wanted them to know it was Pogo."

"I didn't."

"And it was guaran-fucking-teed the Eyes would reach out to have me come find you."

"I didn't do any of that."

"We have met the enemy, and he is us." Schmidt's refilled glass froze halfway to his mouth. "Beya shouted exactly those words after he shot Arshavin. And again, to his interrogators, before he blew up the black site in Kyiv." Watching Schmidt try to pretend he wasn't blindsided by this revelation, Sentro suddenly realized: *He didn't know about Beya's final epigram.*

Then who made him say it?

"What are we going to do about you, Aubrey?" Schmidt seemed to muse but mostly deflected. He looked distressed by the discovery that someone had deliberately exposed him. Mercedes? Wolfgang? When he put down his glass, it rattled unsteadily on the crystal coaster.

There was a soft click, and Sentro was suddenly aware that the dull drone of the generator had ceased, and the lights glowed a little dimmer. Evidently they were back on the feeble local power grid, and all the puzzle pieces that had been scattered around on the edge of Sentro's thinking came together: Schmidt would never risk storing his Stasi treasure trove in the cloud—the robust backup was for dedicated data banks on site, to keep them from crashing during one of Cuba's routine power failures, from tropical storms or incompetence.

"Aubrey?" Schmidt was waiting for his answer. It hadn't been a rhetorical question.

"You've got what you need to keep me quiet."

He shook his head. "I don't believe that's the case. You and your friend came to decommission me."

"Nobody sent me. I came on my own, to get answers. I think I got them. My beef is with Mercedes and her pale Chechen sidekick."

"What about your friend?"

Sentro vamped. "I can't answer for him. He's Canadian. They hardly count, in the big picture."

Schmidt nodded, as if it were some universal truth. "He's also as good as dead. In case you were wondering."

She recalled the two odd flashes in the quinceañera greenhouse, and while she'd known then that this was one possible outcome, she felt a regretful jolt hearing the words come out of Schmidt's mouth. But she hadn't been counting on Banks to save her, so it didn't impact her present situation; time to provoke, time to cause havoc and hope to survive it. The usual Sentro fallback position.

"You'll stay here, as my guest. And a guest of the Cuban government."

"No. Your secret is safe with me, Matthias." She stood. "Don't worry."

He ignored her. "I'll have your daughter brought here. By the other one. As you have correctly guessed, they're together."

"Where?"

"Safe," he teased. "Still in Europe." And Sentro was pretty sure that she knew where. "You came all this way for nothing."

"I'm walking out." Her back felt stiff, her legs were rubbery, but she began crossing to the door.

"I may or may not have it in me to stop you," Schmidt confessed, "but one of the men outside most certainly will."

"I'll be halfway across the courtyard before you even get that chair in gear." But Sentro stopped, heard a subtle movement on the other side of the study door; saw, through the window, a casual confab between the workers and the two armed men from the Land Cruiser. Laughter. The blue glow of a phone screen they were passing between them.

But no Wolfgang. Her thoughts raced ahead of her: Was it Wolfie at the door, eavesdropping?

"The chair is yet another useful artifice," Schmidt was saying, sounding pleased with himself, and when she looked back at him, he was standing. Nothing about Schmidt surprised her anymore. His entire existence was a fiction. "Shorthand for nonthreatening. Trustworthy. I used the conceit of a cripple to help get myself out of Europe when all the borders were alert to Stasi runners. Then discovered it elicited so much empathy and cooperation I decided to extend its run—all these years, do you know? I never have to explain how it happened: the well-timed martyr's sigh, a reluctance to talk about it, here and there suggesting it was a heavy price I paid in perilous defense of the workers' and peasants' state."

Making her voice carry, Sentro said, "Does Wolfgang know?"

"He's an idiot," Schmidt scoffed, "but dangerously ambitious," and the door swung open and (she'd guessed right) standing in it was Wolfgang Witt, face flushed from having heard enough—

"Know what?"

—and just beginning to contort with slow-dawning, betrayed fury at seeing Schmidt standing—and his intricate web of lies unraveling—

"He's not your father," Sentro told him.

"How do you know?"

"She's lying." Schmidt was reaching back to the pocket that hung from one arm of his chair.

"You think *I'm* the idiot?" Wolfgang cried out, like a boy.

Time ticked deliberately forward, every motion distinct but not slowed down. "She's telling lies," Schmidt insisted again, but the fact that he was standing wasn't helping him make a case.

Wolfgang had his handgun gripped white knuckled at his side, his gaze twitching back and forth between them but his frown aimed at Sentro, as if oblivious to what Schmidt might want in that wheelchair arm pocket. "How do you know this?"

"Because I killed him. Thirty years ago," Sentro said, and she ducked down and twisted away, just slipping through the doorway behind the outraged and torpified Wolfgang as Schmidt drew his Glock from the arm pocket. He swung the gun around too late, looking hurt and dismayed to discover that Witt's orphaned son had already begun firing, four times, to hit him twice.

CHAPTER THIRTY-SEVEN

Huge blond concrete panopticons, streaked damp by the rain and stained with rust, loomed dimly uplit like the curated ruins of some lost civilization. Tiny windows unglazed and black, myriad boxy demon eyes.

Banks felt like he'd stumbled onto the set of a Fellini film.

The only sign of life was in the circular cellblock farthest from the road in. He had parked out of view. Scattered voices drew him forward. The hum of a generator. Three vehicles parked along the access tunnel. Banks was at least armed again; damp and shivering even though the shadows he'd used on approach for cover held a sticky, stagnant heat; when he heard the muffled gunfire erupt inside, he worried he'd arrived too late.

That he'd gotten there at all had been a minor miracle; the Land Cruiser that hurried Sentro away from the party was long gone by the time he cleared the parking gridlock. In the rearview mirror he saw the owner of his borrowed car shouting and chasing him down the long estate driveway.

A lucky guess took him to the Cienfuegos harbor, where, driving past with a gnawing panic, he spotted the boxy Toyota still lingering near the water, but the dock beyond it was empty. He surprised the driver midpull on a bottle of Bacardi, took an old Colt .45 away from him, and confirmed through some Spanish-deficient charades that the female Yuma—slang for American, Banks guessed—had been taxied by her amigos across to Isla de la Juventud.

It took him another half hour to locate an old bootlegger cigarette boat that was willing to ferry him over.

The miracle was seeing faux Gillian on a remote pier as his boat approached the mouth of a river that led into a sleepy coastal city. She was sharing a rum bottle and flirting with a water taxi captain; Banks gave his bootlegger a hundred American dollars to drop him down shore, fifty or so meters from an empty beach, and then anchor and wait for his return. Banks swam in, fully clothed, waylaid his would-be assassin, flashed the .45, and motioned for the taxi driver to get in his boat and go. His shoulder wound was weeping again; he felt the tingle of infection.

At least ninety minutes tardy, at gunpoint Banks had the fake Gilly drive him in her rattletrap Lada to the treeless grounds of what she called the Presidio Modelo, where she seemed to insist Sentro was an honored guest. After parking, while she attempted to negotiate her freedom in Spanish he couldn't understand, he hit her—but not too hard—and then carried her, folded her, and locked her in the tiny trunk.

As he crept into the courtyard, he saw Sentro burst from carved double doors and veer hard right along an elevated walkway, sprinting away from a group of startled-looking men standing a good distance to her left. Two of them were armed with rifles; the other three looked like day laborers until they drew pistols from the waistbands of their pants.

His automatic instinct was to rescue her. There were five rounds left in the vintage Colt, another four in the clip of Not Gillian's 9 mm Bren. But Banks didn't trust the guns or his aim.

He watched Sentro ignore the ramp leading down and instead high-step, splashing, through a deep puddle along the concrete platform to a stairwell between cells, where, as a single bullet popped off the wall, she disappeared into shadows, and the footfall of her ascent echoed up to the higher levels. He understood then—true to the Sentro he'd been told about—that she wasn't running away. She was taking the high ground; offense, not defense. The best way he could help her was to find a closer position and provide cover fire.

A rifleman and one of the workers gave chase. The other three lagged but drifted behind their colleagues, moving farther away from Banks, their gun sights trained on the empty upper cell openings, oblivious to Banks hauling himself straight up onto the walkway, where he found an unlocked door leading into the near end of the odd residence that Sentro had just fled.

Total darkness swallowed him. A small room lit, when his eyes adjusted, only by pin-size LEDs and some low-glow LCD screens. Air-conditioning took the temperature down twenty degrees. The boxy objects on a grid rack bolted to the prison wall were computers.

Massive old hard drive servers.

Banks thought: *This is the vault where Witt's precious kompromat is kept.* And if he stayed true to strict Five Eyes protocol, his objectives had narrowed.

———

From the sound of their boots on the cement, they were coming up the stairwell in fits and starts, alternating single file.

Trained, then, Sentro thought. It complicated things but didn't change the endgame. Separate and neutralize. Keep the high ground. She felt loose but centered; looked up and, through a broken part of the ceiling, saw a framed, bright wash of stars where the Milky Way arced across the heavens. Took a deep breath. It was wild to think this was her bliss.

Her pursuers emerged cautious from the shadows and shuffled along the walkway, staying tight to the wall between each cell opening, changing positions, a halfway-decent rolling clear-and-cover.

Her flats were still on the floor where she'd left them, asking their empty question just beneath the roof's gaping hole. The men stopped, puzzled; the one with the rifle gestured the other into the cell that was otherwise unoccupied and stood outside, watching the landing for movement.

Sentro dropped down on the worker with the pistol as soon as he came into view, checked the shoes, and looked up. Bare feet struck his shoulders and knocked him flat. She heard his head bounce off the concrete, the gun in his hand skittering away. From the walkway his cohort came charging in, but it's not that easy to aim a rifle at a close-quarters moving target unless you've practiced it, and it's not something people practice because, rifle, you're mostly shooting it on a range.

She recovered the pistol and fired at him; the round went a bit high and right, through his shoulder. Not a fatal wound, but it rocked him. And in his rush to backpedal out and behind the wall for cover, the man lost his balance and—the handrails had rusted away on this level—stepped off the edge of the walkway and plummeted down to the courtyard, nearly landing on the other men waiting there.

———

Banks was doing his own puzzling over a facedown body in the study when he heard something dull-dropping to the ground outside, followed by a wild burst of gunfire, and then someone shouting for the shooters to stop.

He couldn't get a visual on what was happening from the single window, so he made a cautious move into the next room—a big empty kitchen with a long dining table and windows looking out across the dark prison grounds. A collection of comfortable chairs beyond the kitchen offered a casual sitting area; a hallway from there presumably led to bedrooms. Big carved wooden front doors cracked open to reveal the three remaining hired men moving away from a crumpled body on the courtyard bricks, and young Wolfgang Witt standing over it, holding a handgun loose at his side. When Witt raised his eyes, Banks could see how emotionally gutted he was and assumed that the dead man on the floor in the study was Witt's father, Günter.

Had Sentro killed him?

More gunfire rattled around the courtyard. The men shouted to each other; Banks heard them shuffling along the concrete and splashing through puddles. He knew he would be expected to stay with the data bank, figure out a way for Otter to hack it and initiate a remote download. And he didn't relish the prospect of fighting this skirmish without more backup.

In a perfect world, the Eyes would need Wolfgang alive to direct them to whatever final-act misbehavior Mercedes Izquierdo and Yusupov were cooking up back in Europe, but because Wolfgang Witt was thirty yards away, orchestrating the hunt to find and kill Aubrey Sentro, Banks felt he had no choice but to act and intervene.

She would do the same for him.

He slipped through the doors and started moving along the walkway to close the distance to Wolfgang, his gun held ready in the event that Witt's son glanced right and saw him. Unfortunately Banks was so focused on his target he'd neglected to check his six, and sure enough, a burst of bullets from a semiautomatic ripped the wall just above his head and sent him sprawling, exposed, barely shielded from direct fire by the extended lip of the concrete walkway.

He popped his head up for recon. The fake Gilly stood in the arched entrance to the courtyard. *How the hell did she get out of the trunk?* She took another shot at him, and now Wolfgang Witt opened fire from where he'd been standing, then darted out of sight as Banks flattened himself on the landing.

The three hired men had breached the upper levels; Banks could see two of them moving low on opposite sides of the fourth-floor walkway, looking to pin Sentro down and contain her, while their third cohort was probably going up the other stairwell to flank her. Which meant that she was more or less directly above Banks, and he would be useless to her if he stayed where he was. They just had to look down to see him and have a clear shot.

Move.

Banks wasted a bullet to drive faux Gilly back into the shadows of the entry tunnel, hoping it would buy him time to duck into one of the cells to either side of him. But then he spied a shiny tremor of metal catching light against the starry sky. It was high on the broken patchwork roof, all the way on the other side of the rotunda and directly above one of the shooters, who was making a cautious slosh through a gathering of rainwater in a concrete sag and aiming his shouldered rifle intently back where he thought Sentro had to be.

The reflecting metal seemed to float into the gaping hole and then shower down like shooting stars to tangle on the man's rifle in a shower of sparks. The man cried out, seized, and collapsed. Above him, for an instant, Banks saw Sentro's face lit by the short circuit of the metal gull repeller she'd gathered from the roof and tossed down through the hole in it.

He thought: *I'm glad she's on my side.*

The fuse box blew. The courtyard lights went out. A backup generator kicked on, and a couple of emergency spotlights glared from the top of the guard tower, throwing randomly moving beams and mad shadows across the courtyard.

The remaining gunmen opened futile fire at where Sentro had been, bullets skipping off the concrete walls and punching through the roof.

Banks had his distraction. He leaped up and ran at where he thought Wolfgang Witt was hiding.

Too late. He sensed movement on his six again, saw faux Gilly step into the light with her assault rifle aimed right at him. His momentum carried him fully exposed through one of the bright beams of the randomly rotating guard-tower spotlights.

I'm either about to be dead, he decided, *or waking up from a bad dream.*

———

The woman with the Kalashnikov surged out of the tunnel as soon as Banks made his move. Sentro had dropped from the roof to squat beside the unconscious shooter below her and recovered his scruffy American M16—a relic from the Cold War, the rifle she'd trained on in basic. Wasn't it?

That felt like another lifetime ago.

Light limned the edge of the woman stalking Banks, half a silhouette. Stretched out at the edge of the walkway, Sentro aimed down into the courtyard and tapped the trigger. It took her three rounds to find the target and drop her. Meanwhile, the woman's burst of gunfire chased Banks stumbling into the shadows of the stairwell leading up to the higher levels.

Wolfgang Witt had disappeared.

She shouted, "Banks?!" but got no answer. She couldn't see him. She hoped he was still alive.

More bullets came Sentro's way, from different angles across the cellblock. Gulls exploded outward and upward from where they'd been roosting, a blizzard of white, screaming and flying a panicked circle under the roof. Shielded by the shocked man's dead body, Sentro rolled back into the relative safety of a cell and swiftly clambered back up onto the roof through another opening.

The night sky truly was spectacular. Impossibly perfect, like an observatory light show.

Now she was armed *and* holding the high ground.

She could afford to be patient. But she was worried about Banks.

———

There were a couple of times in Banks's career where, looking back on them later, he would imagine that, in fact, he'd lost his life and what he was experiencing since was some kind of parallel existence or simulation where in one life he had perished but in another he'd survived. Afterlife VR.

This was one of those times. He was dizzy from his flesh wound and thought he might be running a fever. He crouched in the darkness of the stairwell, catching his breath, wondering how he'd cheated death, and listening to the clatter of footsteps on the concrete stairs, coming down to him. It was good-news-bad-news because, while it meant he wouldn't have to move and suffer the stabbing pain in his shoulder, there was no cover to be had in the stairwell, and if the approaching gunman decided to open fire as he lurched around the corner, all bets were off.

It was a laser-tag tactic Banks remembered from birthday parties as a kid in Guelph. You just keep moving and shooting until your vest lights up.

Pattern fire was exactly what the hired man came running down using, and to make matters worse, he was armed with some kind of machine pistol. The muzzle flash was blinding, the rate of fire ferocious.

Banks employed another countertactic he'd learned as a kid. He rolled to the bottom of the staircase, pressed horizontal hard up against the lower step, and waited until the gunman was almost stepping over him before he shot the man through the pelvis and watched him tumble over onto the ground. The sound of bare feet right behind on the stairs caused Banks's heart to skip because he'd stood up, still assessing the dead man, only to see faux Gillian stagger into the courtyard opening and take one last point-blank aim at him. For a moment he froze, stunned, marveling at the woman's resilience, and for a split second wondered if it might even be the real Gilly about to kill him. Then a bullet went past his ear from behind him and into the woman in front, dropping her.

Banks turned, but Sentro was already moving past him.

"Two more," she said simply and kept going.

His shoulder throbbing, fatigue starting to drag at him—they hadn't slept in thirty-six hours. Banks watched Sentro trade her rifle for the one fake Gilly had been holding. *The American only has one gear*, he thought: *forward*. Quick scan of the courtyard; then she timed the spotlights' sweeps, dashed through hard shadows back toward Witt's residence, and ducked inside.

Banks sagged, exhausted, but found his way to the mouth of the stairwell and, careful not to step on the dead woman, peered out.

And listened to the steady hum of the generator.

No movement on the upper walkways.

The mag of the M16 Sentro had left behind was empty. Banks checked his handgun's clip. Four rounds, two hostiles: Wolfgang and the remaining hired man. What did it say about him that he was always counting bullets?

Sound of a car engine catching. Banks saw the retreat of its lights as it reversed away from outside the cellblock building, tires slipping on loose gravel, high beams juddering over the tunnel's arched concrete; he listened to the car brodie, find traction, then drop into gear and roar away.

And as this faded, he heard the last hired man come running down the stairwell on the opposite side of the rotunda.

Banks made himself move out to the edge of the platform, where he dropped to the courtyard and crossed to the cover of the guard tower before sliding around one side and taking aim at the stairwell's arched opening.

The man came flying out; he had only a snub-nosed revolver, and he looked like all he wanted to do was get away from this place and this night, as fast as he could. Banks sighted on him. Their eyes met. The man kept moving.

Banks let him go. Down the access tunnel and out across the fields, as if chasing the dwindling red taillights of Wolfgang Witt's getaway vehicle, until they both just dissolved in the darkness.

A shattering burst of automatic gunfire brought Banks back on edge. It came from inside Witt's residence; had they miscounted? He ran. The shooting stopped. Banks had to take the ramp; he was too sore and tired to climb up directly to the walkway.

Rushed through the open carved doors—tactically rash and leaving himself open to anything—but the main room was empty, and one last short burst drew him through the study to the back room, the data bank server room, where Aubrey Sentro was staring at the smoldering, sparking, shattered, shot-to-pieces ruins of Günter Witt's once-vast and priceless Stasi kompromat. His first thought was: *Oh shit.* Then he met Sentro's gaze and held it and thought he understood.

"The Eyes were kinda hoping I could retrieve those."

"I bet. Yeah, well. *C'est la vie*, Banks." The assault rifle Sentro had used was so hot from firing that when she dropped it, thin tendrils of smoke came up from the carpet, along with the smell of burning plastic.

"Sorry if I fucked up your protocol," she added.

Banks shrugged and felt a searing pain. He thought of Gilly and Delia, Nula and the other interrogation teams at Otter's, of Xavi Beya and Ilya Arshavin, Lenkov, Sentro's cowboy, all the untold casualties of one corrupt master spy's secret cache of transgressions, confessions, and lies.

Part of him wished he'd been the one to do it.

"Some tech wizard told me once, I can't remember who, that you have to destroy the disks themselves," Sentro said to him evenly, as if she were explaining how to scramble eggs. "Drill a hole through them. Or send a bullet." There was no regret in her eyes, but they were sad for some reason. A lingering hurt.

"Good luck trying to get anything from the pieces. I'm sure your people have the resources to give it the old college try." Then she noticed his shoulder and winced. "We'd better get you patched up."

Banks nodded, starting to feel a wave of shock catch up with him. "There's a number we can call. Five Eyes will send an exfiltration crew." Neither of them moved. There was so much he didn't know, didn't understand, and she just kept looking at him, eyes clear but unreadable. He studied her, trying to decide if he should envy or feel sorry for her. *Have fun with that,* was what he guessed she was probably thinking.

"You were in those files," he said.

"The girl I was, once," she agreed and walked out.

CHAPTER THIRTY-EIGHT

"What we still don't understand," the Five Eyes case officer with the shoe-salesman mustache told her, "is why Pogo would destroy his own database." He'd probably introduced himself, but she hadn't been paying attention. All her thoughts now were of Jenny: finding her, getting her safe. No more cross-purposes; the mission was clear.

"Yeah. Weird," Sentro agreed. She was juggling so many fictions she was starting to have a hard time remembering how they all linked together.

Poor Schmidt. No one would ever know how he'd masterfully stolen Günter Witt's life and legacy. He was erased. A final fuck-you to the man who had delivered her to Hohenschönhausen.

"Is it possible there's a backup? Somewhere in the cloud?"

"Very possible." Sentro hoped they spent the next decade or more chasing that fantasy and left her alone.

From the mayhem on Isla de la Juventud they had taken Banks's hired boat, which had been dutifully waiting for him at the dock, east into international waters, where an amphibious helicopter from Guantánamo met them and brought them back to the base. Sentro had almost forgotten how much easier life had been when you had an entire government at your fingertips.

While a medic tended to Banks, she told him where they were going next.

"Majorca."

"How can you be sure she's there?"

"Mercedes has been point person on the big scheme in Europe from the get-go. They've got Beya's wife and kids locked up on the island, for some grand finale prodigal son Wolfgang contrived to piggyback on Lenkov's standard-issue hit job. Madrid, Paris, Kyiv—they were just a prelude."

"Did Witt know about it?"

Sentro took time to appreciate the irony in her truthful answer: "No."

"Why Beya's wife?"

Sentro admitted she didn't know.

"The Eyes can provide us with an assault team. Even call in the Spanish Army for support, if necessary."

"Jenny's there," Sentro reminded him. "I don't want them getting her killed."

An old, unmarked Learjet was waiting on the airstrip, with the two administrative Five Eyes suits inside, both Canadian, and Banks got really nervous because they were the guys above the guys he usually answered to at CSIS.

Their focus, however, was on Sentro. And they had a thirteen-hour flight to indulge it.

"What was he like?" the other asked. "Witt, I mean." Overweight, affable, and clean cut, probably former RCMP, he told her his name was Hedges, and she made a point to remember this one, but Banks admitted later that both men had used cover names.

She wanted to sleep, to get some relief from the helpless, grinding worry she couldn't shake, but they wanted to talk. And talk. Hedges knew a lot about her and wasn't shy sharing stories with his colleague. Much of what they talked about was history that had slipped away from her: Sarajevo, Tirana, Cairo, Koudougou, Rabat. Juicy war stories for the two desk jockeys; for her, nothing but white noise. She'd learned to do what she had started calling "the slide" to bluff her way through it. But it required concentration.

Banks, shot full of painkillers and penicillin, got a long, welcome rest.

"And what about Witt's son?"

"What about him?" She guessed that because he'd be flying commercial they were at least a few hours ahead of him, if his intention was to go to Majorca to see the completion of what must be his first big solo operation. Pogo 2.0.

"According to our intel, the wife, Paola, was some kind of teenage black hat hacker queen," Hedges explained. "She did time in youth detention, where she was recruited by ETA, but they never really got their virtual terrorism up and running before the stand-down in twenty-ten. Spain says she's been inactive for a decade."

"Best guess is Wolfgang stumbled on her when they did background on her husband," Sentro said. "Unless he had her already tagged and waited for the right job to come up, where her husband could be the decoy."

The Five Eyes men chewed on this for a while, and Sentro closed her eyes, hoping they were finished.

"We've got an advance team setting up a command center in Palma," Hedges said.

"It's a big island," the other noted. "Lots of coastline. Rugged terrain. Caves and shit."

Great, Sentro thought, bone tired but fretting about Jenny again. Her anxiety wouldn't stop cycling. She felt old, out of shape, out of practice. Something something assault team. Blah blah Spanish Army. She glanced at Banks through slit eyes; he was smiling, faintly. Pretending to sleep.

———

All those babysitting jobs during high school were finally paying off. Given little else to do, and to keep her mind occupied so that it didn't wander to darker speculation, Jenny had become the de facto playmate for the Beya children, while their mother was locked away with the keyboard and computer.

Thiago and Nina. Seven and four. They didn't speak English, but Jenny could understand them way better than some of the American kids she'd taken care of. And what they told her had broken her heart. Their mother was helping the grouchy men in the house so that their father would be able to come home.

They didn't know he was already dead.

But Paola Beya did. She had wandered down to the beach toward the end of the day and bummed a smoke from Jenny, and they sat on a rock and watched her kids try to find sand crabs, the way Jenny had taught them. Two of the creepier armed guards were squatting on the rocks high above the beach, bucket hats shading their faces and rifles across their knees, staring intently down. Paola had slashed on some lipstick and brushed her hair, but purplish half moons were swollen under her eyes, and her mouth was set hard as if to will herself not to cry. "They've killed my husband, haven't they?" she said, not really asking, huffing out a lungful of smoke that made her cough.

What, Jenny thought, *am I supposed to say?* She wiped the salt spray off her sunglasses, feeling foolish and depressed for thinking she could be of any help to anyone. Least of all her mother.

Paola nodded that Jenny's silence was enough confirmation, then considered the cigarette, as if wondering whether she should be smoking it, and tapped some ash into the sand. "Do you know this story of Ulises?"

Jenny frowned. "The one nobody really reads?" *Nobody,* she thought, *except Jeremy.* Twice. "James Joyce?"

"No no no. Homero. *La Odisea.*"

Another book Jenny had never read, but oh well. "Sort of," she lied.

312

"Penélope. She is the wife of Ulises. She waits for him to come home, although she is also fretful he is dead. There are many *pretendientes*. She says, 'I will marry again when I finish weaving this burial shroud'—it was for her husband or her father. I don't remember: it does not matter. So. Every night, she undoes almost all the work she did that day. In the hope that she will never finish." Paola put the cigarette in her mouth and mumbled, "This is me."

"What is it they want you to do?" Jenny asked.

"Code. I weave code. Then undo it. Soon they will find out, and . . ." The thought trailed off. She shouted at Thiago and gestured for him to bring Nina back from where waves were crashing against the rocks they were exploring now.

"You mean programming? Computer code? What for?"

"Do you have children?"

"No."

"Don't wait too long. I got so busy with my politics. It seemed so important." Ignoring the cold reality that if she didn't survive this, bearing children would be pretty much a moot point, Jenny waited, the way her mother would when she wanted Jenny or Jeremy to tell their secrets.

"They want me to write them a hack to get secret files of certain governments so they can steal information about important people. And then use it for—I don't know how to say in English—*perfidia*—*la traición*—however you can use such things."

Kompromat, Jenny's mother had called it. But on a scale the Stasi could never have dreamed of.

"What governments?"

"You know. United States, Great Britain, Australia . . . they have some kind of English-speaking club, like." *Yeah, Banks's club*, Jenny said to herself. The Five Eyes. "It's all connected, one big data bank. Stupid."

Jenny's mind raced: the murder of her mother's client, the attack in Madrid, the bomb that killed Banks's girlfriend—had it all been just a diversion? Maybe whoever was behind it all hadn't really wanted Paola's husband; they'd wanted Paola.

"Why do they have you here?" Passing the cigarette to Jenny, wave of the hand, Paola gestured that she didn't want it anymore.

Jenny didn't know the answer to her question.

"They will kill me when I have done what they want," Paola had decided. "Like my husband." She stared at Jenny, vexed and thoughtful. "I have a sister in Barcelona; I will give to you her information."

For the children, Jenny realized. Paola watched them poke a stick into the tidal pools, a fierce smile forcing its way through the grief. *This,* Jenny marveled, *was another reason my mother lied to us.*

And then, with an onrushing horror, it occurred to her that the Beya kids wouldn't be allowed to live either.

———

The call woke Yusupov up. He just listened as the voice on the other end unloaded.

Everything was unraveling, but he was not surprised. Things always unraveled, in the Chechen's experience. The trick was to not get tangled up. Earlier that night they'd discovered that the Beya woman had been erasing the code she'd been writing, slowing progress, delaying the launch. The de facto leader of the local crew, Alonso, had lobbied to kill one of the children in front of her, but he was the most fucking fascist of the fascists, and cooler heads prevailed. Paola had been given an ultimatum. So what the caller was telling him made the timing a little trickier, but without any more complications they would conclude their business and be gone before the gang of Five got their camo makeup on.

The wound on his head itched like hell, taking all his willpower not to scratch off the scab.

Their client called next, voice brittle, sounding pissed, looking for Mercedes or Wolfgang. Since almost dying on the edge of the New

Mexico motel swimming pool, the Chechen had begun resenting always being the fifth wheel.

Fuck these amateurs.

Mercedes was indisposed, he said; Wolfie was en route. "Anything I can help with, sir?"

Complications: the client was sending his own people to take custody of the Beya woman and her children. They'd be in Palma by noon. Translation: a cleanup crew was coming to make sure nobody would ever know what had happened here. So the Spanish mercenaries were expendable. Was Yusupov himself at risk? It was a gray area, he knew. He'd been hired only as a facilitator for Wolfgang and Mercedes, but shit went sideways sometimes—and Pogo remained aggravatingly unreachable.

He thought about the woman they'd been sent to kill, in New Mexico. She worried Yusupov more than all the others. Her daughter was like a homing beacon; Mercedes never should have brought her to Spain.

The daughter was a liability. If he killed her, he was sure the woman would be relentless in pursuing him, and he did not want a rematch.

But if he didn't? There might be other hell to pay.

———

The hand shot out and grabbed hers as soon as she put the phone back on the night table. "What are you doing?"

Jenny tried to step away, but Mercedes wouldn't let go. Had she seen what Jenny had done?

"I need your help."

Mercedes sat up. She looked past Jenny, at Paola and her two kids, who stood just inside the door, in the darkness, their eyes shining. Scared.

"How did you get out of your room?"

Paola had come to Jenny with her children moments earlier. They were bundled up, backpacks and jackets, sleepy and scared, and their mother wanted Jenny to take them away from the house. "They know I have been erasing code," Paola said. She couldn't tell Jenny more in front of Thiago and Nina, but Jenny could guess the rest. An ultimatum. An implicit threat to the kids.

"I'm going to try to take Thiago and Nina away from here," Jenny told Mercedes. "They're not safe anymore."

"Jennifer, this is crazy."

She tried to channel her mother. "They can't stay. I could use your help."

Jenny imagined the tortured calculations going on in Mercedes's brain; sharp, whispered words in Spanish were traded with Paola; then Mercedes shook her head. "No," she said.

"Please."

"No."

"I don't know what the fuck I'm doing."

"You do not," Mercedes agreed. "It's pointless."

Jenny's heart sank. The darkness swaddled her; the house was silent. For a moment—sure, maybe it was fucking naive—she had hoped that somehow the weird sister bond Mercedes thought they had would tilt her toward becoming an ally in what Jenny knew would be a betrayal of Pogo and the albino, at the very least. But Mercedes held stubbornly to her decision.

"Well, I have to try," Jenny said.

Mercedes's bewildered eyes shone in the faint light. Tears? "I won't stop you, but you will fail."

"You're not my sister," Jenny said sharply, and as she turned to go, she thought she saw a flicker of the hurt that crossed the Cuban girl's features.

CHAPTER THIRTY-NINE

Somehow the Five Eyes had cloned her phone—which was still with Mercedes, she imagined, a trophy, like her gold chain and Jenny, somewhere on the island of Majorca—and when they landed in Palma, a stream of missed messages began to load.

Four missed calls from Jeremy. Didn't leave a message. He wasn't in danger, just anxious and upset by the radio silence on her end.

A very long voice mail from Marta, a friend in Maryland. Sentro would listen to it later.

There was a text message from Reno Elsayed, asking simply, so?

Two hours earlier, from an unknown number, Banks had received a text they knew must be from her daughter. It read: majorca mercedes albino pls hurry.

Her hunch confirmed, Sentro had nevertheless felt short of breath. Time crawled, torturous. The Five Eyes tried to get Spanish intelligence to track the text transmission to a cell tower, but because of the island the simple request had devolved into a jurisdictional clusterfuck.

Across the street, a rising sun lit up the café called Codelincuente, which she'd first seen when they'd driven past with the Five Eyes senior men, on the way from the airport to their new mission command center at the Hotel Amic Horizonte.

Codilencuente meant "partner in crime."

Yusupov had written *Trouble never comes alone* in Cyrillic on his ferry boarding pass.

"Grasping at straws, much?" had been Banks's reaction, when she told him about it in the hotel lobby, out of earshot of the Five.

"Listen. Your people are going to be sitting around drinking *café con leche* and rolling calls until the rest of their team shows up. Meanwhile my daughter is with the contract killers. You got something better to do?"

He didn't. So they were staking out her long shot on a bench just down the waterfront from the ferry landing, which, Sentro had pointed out, would be a pretty convenient, neutral place to meet if you were concerned about someone locating your safe house. Banks had found a Starbucks, so he was reasonably content, indie rock leaking from his earbuds.

"Wolf Parade and Metric," Banks explained about his playlist, too loud.

Sentro didn't feel like making small talk.

Half past ten, a black SUV cruised past the café and found a parking spot on the street. A quartet of beefy white men got out and stretched, coming off so patently American ex-military that Banks just shook his head. Buzz cuts, wraparound sunglasses, cargo pants, and T-shirts over torsos that had seen a bit too much upper-body tuning. Private contractors were, in Sentro's experience, mostly military washouts who were way too impressed with themselves and overestimated their abilities no matter how well trained they might have been.

A bowlegged swagger took them into Codilencuente and a table at the window.

"Jesus Murphy," Banks said.

"Mercs?"

"No doubt. Look up hired guns in the dictionary, you'd probably see a picture of those kooks." But then he glanced side-eyed at Sentro, shaking his head. "No. No, Aubrey, too easy—they're here for something else. Either on their way or just back from some foolishness. Knucklehead holiday on Majorca."

Was it?

She settled back to wait. Her head was clear; her thoughts were crisp. No more texts came from Jenny.

Another agonizing hour ticked by; they were due back at the hotel around noon. Banks took a walk down to the pier, rotating his damaged shoulder as he went, trying to keep it limber. She watched the Americans wolf down breakfast, then linger at the table, no apparent rush; shooting the shit, checking phone screens, but every now and then casually glancing out the window at the ferry landing.

They were waiting as well.

"What are you doing?"

Sentro had risen, was stretching her creaky hips, gauging the flow of traffic before she crossed the street. "I'm gonna do some recon," she told Banks.

He looked skeptical. "Okay."

"Brb." A term she'd learned from Jenny.

The incurious eyes of one of the Americans inside found her and dismissed her when she reached the other side.

Not a threat, his look seemed to say.

Depends on you, Sentro thought. And went inside.

———

Leaving the house proved to be more complicated than she expected. Jenny intended to go just before dawn, when it would be light enough to find her way across the rugged terrain without stumbling off an escarpment in the moonless dark. But the house came awake earlier; for some reason the albino had become agitated, barking instructions and sending Spaniards out to the perimeter. There was no way to slip out. Paola was hustled back into the computer room after fraught, hasty hugs and kisses goodbye for her children. But her last pleading look was to Jenny. After breakfast Jenny took Nina and Thiago down to the beach, the usual routine, but with little backpacks Paola had stuffed with essentials, and a change of clothes for Jenny because she couldn't see herself fleeing very far in Mercedes's ill-fitting bikini.

Only a single armed man sat on the cliffs watching them. Jenny had the kids play on the rocks, poking in the tidal pools, all the while gradually edging toward an outcropping that would block them from the sentinel's view. There was a skiff anchored past the breakers in the cove, but she'd never get to it with the children in tow. Instead, once they were just out of sight, they bolted away. Down the narrow beach as far as they could go, then up into the crags and fissures of the cliffs, trying to cover as much distance as they could before their absence was noted. Run to the cliffs, Paola had instructed her, because they were hollowed with limestone caves they could hide in.

All she could find at first were shallow dents that couldn't conceal them from the men who would soon be searching.

Run. Run away.

It was Nina who heard the shouting first over the roar of the breakers; little kids and their freakish hearing. Jenny didn't understand what the men were saying but could guess the gist of it. They were above her on the bluffs, which were rocky and slow going. Thiago turned his ankle, and she had to piggyback him the final fifty yards to an iffy shelter they curled up in, hearing the voices grow quickly closer.

Lungs on fire, her heart pounding, Jenny felt the heat of the children hugging her hips as they listened for footfalls on the rocks above.

"*Ellos vienen,*" Thiago whispered. Uncomprehending, Jenny shook her head. The boy walked two fingers down the arm she had around him. "*Ellos vienen.*" She heard the clatter of rocks as someone began to come down the cliff, and understood.

Fuck.

Despairing suddenly that she had promised Paola something she wasn't equipped to do, Jenny willed away the panic and tried to concentrate on the task at hand: escape, evade. And what? What would her mother do?

Kill them, Jenny thought darkly and knew that was impossible for her, but then she had a better thought, all her own. More dislodged rockfall went tumbling down to stipple the indigo pools swirling where the tide met the cliff. There was a narrow crevice angling up on the other side of their carve-out. Perfect size for little bodies to navigate, a challenge for Jenny, but impossible for a grown-ass man like the one chasing them.

They won't be expecting us to go up, Jenny hoped. She labored to calm herself. Panic was pointless. Sea mist rose, dusting her face with a salty chill.

Getting the kids' attention by walking two fingers up her own arm, she gestured for them to climb into the crevice. Fashioned an easy smile and found her calm to be contagious. The kids smiled back. A game, hide-and-seek; they were up for it. Thiago pushed his sister ahead of him so that he could catch her if she slipped. Jenny waited until the descending man drew level with her hiding spot, then gave him a glimpse of her bare leg and bikini-creased butt before clambering into the crevice to follow the children out.

She heard his shout; she knew he'd try to follow and in so doing wind up trapped in the tiny shelter with no way up and a precarious path back the way he'd come.

They came out on a low bluff, wide and green and rolling to higher ground stubbled with trees. Jenny looked back toward where the big house was and didn't see anyone chasing them; at the opposite tree line, like some strange apparition, were two beautiful calico horses grazing in the tall grass, tails switching. Relief coursed through her; this next part she could handle.

She put Thiago on her back again and, holding Nina's hand, started to run toward the animals. There was a different shout behind her, and the head of the second pursuer started to rise up from the low swale that had hidden him. He swung the rifle off his shoulder, running. An icy fear crawled up Jenny's spine. Nina's little legs were tangling in the weeds. They weren't going to make it.

The man screamed at them and shook his rifle. Jenny glanced back, saw him slow, begin to bring the gun to his shoulder, but as her mouth went dry and she braced herself for whatever a gunshot might feel like, there was a crack-snapping sound—another one, three—the man jerked, his arms going wide, windmilling, as bright red bloomed on his T-shirt and his legs gave out and he tumbled forward to disappear in the grass.

High on the ridge that hid the house from view, a small, perfect figure lowered a long rifle, pushed the raven hair out of her eyes, and then hurried away, as if she were embarrassed. And disappeared.

Stunned, Jenny backed away and led the kids to the horses. *Step by step, Jen,* she heard her mother say. No shit. One of the horses was much calmer and more ridable. From Nina's backpack, Jenny pulled a borrowed sweatshirt and shrugged it on, then unhooked and fashioned the bikini top into a bizarre but surprisingly workable halter and reins. Wary, but not so scared anymore—keenly alert, constantly checking back to the ridge and the field behind her—Jenny rolled herself up onto the warm flanks of the horse the way Clete had taught her, then helped the Beya kids settle in front and behind her.

Now, she thought. Now they could put some real distance between themselves and the trouble at the big house and maybe even find those caves.

And then what?

Trust your heart.

A frightening awareness washed over Jenny. What if her mother wasn't coming? What if something had happened to her and Jenny was on her own?

What would her mother do?

Jenny didn't have to think about it. She spun the horse around and started back across the meadow toward the ridge to find her sister and try to save Paola for her children.

———

How could he have missed the albino driving up? *Has to be that jet lag's put me seriously off my game*, he decided. The pale, almost featureless face on which mirror sunglasses hung as if by magic, the messy shock of spectral hair was creased with a festering scab where Sentro's poolside bullet had grazed him. Yusupov stood out like a white plastic lane divider parting the slow-crawling gridlock of passengers disembarking the Barcelona ferry.

Banks saw the Chechen first, then watched him greet Wolfgang Witt and realized that Sentro had been right. They were crossing the street as Banks pulled out his phone and rushed a text, misspelling half of it, cursing autocorrect, hoping that the message would get through in time.

———

The bell on the door jingled when Sentro's phone hummed with a text. A lucky coincidence, because it meant her back was turned, checking the message she hoped was from Jenny, when two men came in and greeted the rowdy Americans at the window table.

She was at the barista bar, having ordered an espresso, keeping an eye and ear on the rent-a-guns, who gazed dully at ever-present smartphones while the conversation so far was mostly "best titty bars in Texas" and a pointless ramble about escorting "State Department fucks" to some backwater village in Pakistan, where "things got sorta gnarly" and the hilarity of shooting at civilians ensued.

And then sharing some stupid tweet they saw. Knucklehead holiday, indeed.

Then Sentro recognized Wolfgang's voice and froze. In reflection on the polished brass framing the big menu above the racked syrup pumps, she saw his rippling shape shaking hands and then, more unnerving, the colorless smear of the Chechen she'd nearly killed back in New Mexico.

Her drink delivered, she paid cash and braced for one of them to notice her.

But it was a bro fest, the men all too preoccupied with impressing each other to notice the middle-aged woman getting coffee at the bar.

The albino traded familiar pleasantries with the barista and knocked back an espresso. Taking shallow breaths, Sentro went gray—invisible; pretended to fuss with her phone and kept her back turned.

These Americans, she gleaned from their banter, worked for the client behind Wolfgang's big intel hack. Lurking just under the breezy bonhomie was a palpable tension; Wolfgang didn't want them here, and they wanted him to know their employer couldn't give a rat's ass what Wolfie wanted. After a shuffle of manly bluster, they all walked out, agreeing that the American crew would follow the albino to "the house."

Sentro waited as long as she could bear, then sprinted out the door to get Banks. But not before asking the barista in Spanish if he had any idea where the albino who'd just come in—he must be a regular, right?—was staying.

CHAPTER FORTY

She couldn't explain why she'd done it. So she didn't try.

Mercedes didn't like to overthink things. In her experience it only led to an unhelpful confusion born of complexities she preferred to pretend didn't exist.

She'd dozed fitfully after Jenny had left her room, and then all the unusual movement in the house had roused her to dress and discover Yusupov had gone to get Wolfgang and left the Spaniards in a state of high agitation.

The client was sending an advance team. Which implied a cleanup crew. Beya's wife refused to come out of her room. The American girl was down on the beach with the kids, and Alonso, of all people, had been sent to retrieve them.

Mercedes was surprised to discover that Jenny hadn't already made her escape. And annoyed that the albino hadn't checked in with her before he left. She'd slipped away, with a rifle from the small arsenal in one of the big empty bedrooms on the lowest level. She saw the beach empty below, and Alonso and another, younger Spaniard, trim beard—she didn't know his name—humping across the rocky bluff; *Jenny's running*, she thought, *and they're on to her*. She watched the men split up; Alonso sent the other down the face of the cliff, then continued along the bluff, evidently to try to outflank the fugitives.

Mercedes stepped off the lower patio and loped across the bluff, shadowing the big Spanish mercenary. Maybe the children were expendable, but she didn't want Jenny to get hurt.

From the high ridge, looking down, she saw Alonso running across a rolling meadow—if you could call what Alonso did running—and Jenny trying to make it to the distant tree line with the boy on her back and the little girl beside her.

Not a fair fight, was all Mercedes was thinking when she shouldered the rifle and aimed.

Now, coming back through the house, she heard the splintering of a doorframe and the screaming of Paola Beya.

What a fucking mess Wolfie has made, Mercedes said to herself, hurrying up the stairs, already beginning to compose what she would say about it to Fischer.

But as soon as Mercedes reached the first landing, she heard a car's horn chirp in the driveway and saw, through the tall windows on either side of the front door, the albino's car roll in, with a black SUV she didn't recognize close behind it.

Beefy Americans spilled out into the gold Mediterranean midday, with their empty grins, pocket pants, and sunglasses. She was embarrassed and disgusted by the banality of it.

Fucking Yumas. *They're here to kill us all.*

———

Their taxi found a spot on the serpentine coastal road's shoulder, about a hundred yards short of what looked to be a house still under construction. Banks got off his call as they parked. Sentro was watching the cluster of men from both cars taking selfies and going in the front door, where shadows suggested more men were waiting. Sentro had a set to her jaw that worried him.

"Our backup is half an hour out," Banks reported. The Five Eyes handlers were not happy that Sentro had grabbed Banks and a cab and tailed Wolfgang's caravan out here. But they'd scrambled and found support.

"Okay," she said and opened the door to get out of the cab.

Not again, Banks thought. "Wait wait wait wait wait." He had no choice but to follow her. "What's the plan?"

She turned but kept walking backward. "More recon," she told him, but he knew she was lying.

"They'll see us coming. We're not armed. Again," he added unnecessarily.

"I'm gonna play the little-woman card. Between those big strong American GI Joe wannabes and whatever hired-gun hostage crew Wolfie's got waiting in there, I'm thinking we can divide and conquer and get Jenny the fuck out during the resulting confusion."

"Oh shit. No. Okay," Banks waffled with stress. "Well, I don't want to get in another firefight."

"Good. We're in agreement." She turned around again, eyeing the house up ahead. "And anyway, I'm old and harmless."

Banks had a sinking feeling; Sentro looked radiant. "Is this how you rolled your entire career?"

"I forget," she said. He couldn't tell if she was kidding. The cab driver leaned out his window and shouted that they hadn't paid. "Get a receipt," Sentro told Banks, "so you can expense it."

She kept walking.

———

At first Jenny thought it was laughter coming from the house, but as soon as she realized it was Paola's manic vitriol—warning someone to stay away from her—she slid off the horse and helped the kids down. They looked confused more than anything. Who could blame them?

Nina kept asking something Jenny couldn't understand. Thiago handed Jenny the automatic rifle they'd taken from the man Mercedes had shot. She wasn't sure what to do with it. All she'd ever fired was her mother's pink revolver.

Step by step, she reminded herself.

Their approach was still relatively well concealed by the rocks at this edge of the field, and there was no sign of sentries on the bluff overlooking the beach or on the stepped patios behind the house. The sudden sound of gunfire startled them. Flashes inside the house. The children flinched. Jenny motioned for Thiago to get down and keep his sister safe with him. Then, crouching, feeling only a little stupid and a lot scared, she started up a gentle slope to the stone steps that ran along this side of the property and zigzagged down to the beach. The shuttered window of the computer room where Jenny assumed Paola was locked in again looked out in this direction.

In a perfect world, Paola would look out and see her. They would plot an escape; Jenny would meet her on the back steps she could see from where they were hiding and escort her to the horse and send her away with her children to try to find help while Jenny stayed for when her mother came.

In this flawed world, more gunfire popped inside the house, more flashes, men shouting; she couldn't hear Paola at all anymore, and the task she'd set for herself seemed impossible.

———

One of the Americans was swaggering from the house with what she assumed was one of Pogo's men as Sentro came ambling down the driveway like any neighbor out for a walk—except there didn't seem to be other neighbors within miles, and Sentro looked as if she'd been dressed by accident, in borrowed clothes, which was what had happened at Guantánamo less than twenty-four hours ago.

Sentro waved, friendly.

The American frowned but kept coming. The Spaniard hung back. With the chirp of a key fob, the SUV hatchback unlocked and rose, revealing a careful clutter of lumpy duffel bags Sentro was pretty sure contained mostly weapons.

Prattling in French, "Welcome to the neighborhood" plus a memorized fragment of *The Little Prince* that came to her out of nowhere—she was hoping neither of the mercenaries would understand her, and from the puzzled look on the American PC's face, it was obvious that he didn't, and the absurdity of the ruse had him distracted, which was the point of it, allowing her to stroll up right beside him, his guard down.

She made it so the American blocked the Spaniard's view of her; she smiled sweetly and kept talking nonsense and yanked from a short holster the gun he had concealed under his faded QAnon T-shirt. Jamming it into his groin, she said softly, "Think real hard about what you do next."

He didn't. Maybe reflex, maybe just stupidity, he tried something he'd probably picked up in a Brazilian jujitsu class, thinking he could take the gun away from this old lady like the instructor had promised, but—real life—her finger was on the trigger, the safety was off, and any wild grab at her hand was going to cause the gun to fire first and foremost.

They don't teach you that.

The gun roared, the muzzle flash caught his fly on fire, and the bullet probably castrated him.

Down, screaming. A horrible wound, no doubt, but usually, she knew, not fatal. Sentro took the philosophical view: she had warned him.

Meanwhile the Spaniard, completely confused, pulled his own sidearm and stepped back, alarmed; hearing the commotion from their compatriot, the other Americans were running out to see what had happened. Sentro dropped the gun and kicked it out of reach, trying to look frightened and dazed, repeating over and over in French that she had no idea what just happened.

The Americans mistakenly thought the Spaniard had shot their friend; Sentro had counted on things taking this turn. Two PCs grabbed him and slammed him against the side of the vehicle. Banks came sprinting down the driveway out of breath, repeating, "Oh my God, oh my God," in his best shocked-tourist Quebecois accent.

The third American knelt by his bleeding cohort to do triage. "Fuck."

The Americans struggled to hold the protesting Spaniard. They screamed at Sentro something along the lines of *What the fuck just happened?* and she forced out crocodile tears along with enough panicky French that, for the second time in less than two hours, they dismissed her as no threat and let her stumble into Banks's arms.

To Sentro, he hissed, "This is you not doing a firefight?"

Sentro looked past him, past the confusion of hard men, scanned the front of the house, and saw the albino step into the light of the open front doorway.

He locked eyes with her.

She murmured, "Here we go," to Banks and pulled him low behind the cover of the SUV. Yusupov shouted something Sentro didn't quite catch, and from behind him in the house, the shadows of his Spanish hired men began shooting out into the driveway.

The tall glass windows on either side of the entryway exploded. Bullets raked the SUV. The captured Spaniard got hit.

Caught in no-man's-land, the Americans assumed the Spaniards were shooting at them. They returned fire with their handguns and took cover while the third reached into the back of their SUV and ripped open the duffels in back to distribute—just as Sentro had expected—an assortment of military-grade weapons.

A lot of hand signals were thrown. Sentro couldn't remember what they meant and didn't care. Her next objective was seeing Jenny safe.

The Americans repositioned near them. The closest man, shaved head and scruffy facial hair, frowned at Banks while tugging on some expensive tactical gloves, then smirked patronizingly at Sentro and said, "You'll be safe here, ma'am. Don't worry. We've got this."

Wiping her phony tears away, she told him in tremulous Spanish that she seriously doubted it; he, of course, didn't understand. Just nodded and popped up to resume firing rounds over the top of the car and into the house.

"Technically this isn't our firefight," Sentro reminded Banks, keeping her voice a whisper. She'd never kept track of how many she'd lived through. A new wave of exhaustion overtook her, and she had to fight it and stay focused. *Jenny.*

"Sure. Now what?" Banks grumbled.

"Mansions have other doors, don't they?"

"I guess."

"Wait until they thin each other out a bit, then borrow a gun from your cousins and secure the front entry. I'm gonna find a side way in."

Using the cars and stacks of construction materials for cover, she started moving in that direction before he could argue with her.

———

A blue haze from discharged weapons.

The sour funk of jittery, unwashed men.

Mercedes felt oddly detached from all of it.

Between exchanges of gunfire there were testosterone-charged shouts and disagreements among the Spaniards, and the more measured but stressed-out voices of the mercenary Yankee knuckleheads struggling to mount some kind of counterassault.

All these *comemierdas* doing *Call of Duty* cosplay.

The television in the big room was on, chattering farcically, some midday telenovela out of Madrid.

She was disappointed with the albino, not so much for opening fire on the client's advance team but for doing it without even half a thought for the predictable consequences, and moreover for the crime of letting Wolfgang convince him to *bring* the contract Yumas here, to the house, in the first place, where any of the potential outcomes of this pointless violence would involve serious complications.

Maybe his head wound had damaged his judgment.

Hurrying up the stairwell and then down a vaulted hallway, she stayed low, because now and then a stray bullet would punch through the plaster walls, and went to the computer room to secure the Beya woman, whose skills were still required for them to finish Wolfie's fucking job and get paid.

She got worried when she saw the door open, and furious to find Wolfgang in there with Paola, berating her for compromising his mission, promising to kill one of her children when they got found and brought back. A gash over her eye was bleeding; two of her fingers were swollen and looked displaced. Paola was terrified yet resolute, resigned to her fate, but Mercedes doubted Wolfie was the one who'd hurt her, because she didn't think he had it in him.

She said, "Stop," and when he turned, she even pointed the rifle at him, but she could tell that he didn't believe she would shoot. And she wouldn't. Couldn't, really. He was Fischer's pet. Pogo's prodigal son.

"Go ahead," he taunted.

She spun the rifle backward and jammed the shoulder stock against his knee as hard as she could, bending it backward. They both heard something pop, and he staggered back, astonished. Hopping on one foot.

"Oh shit." The color drained from his face as the pain followed. "Oh shit, that hurt." He fell to one side, holding his leg. "Mother of God."

Mercedes took Paola's good hand and pulled. "C'mon. Let's get you out of here." The client would be pleased.

"My children—"

"We'll get them," she said but wasn't sure if they would.

As they ran back down the hallway, Mercedes heard him screaming: "Pogo's not in charge anymore! He's not even Pogo!"

She didn't believe him.

But she had decided that pretty much everything else she'd ever thought was true had been a lie.

CHAPTER FORTY-ONE

It was either a sign of how her skills had eroded or a consequence of fatigue and an incautious rush to find her daughter that, before rounding the house, Sentro forgot to stop and listen. It was such a basic blunder. Somehow she just assumed all the Spaniards would be engaged with the firefight in the driveway.

She was wrong.

Rounding the corner and starting down the stone stairs, she saw, coming up the switchback from the beach, an angry, bearded sentry with a rifle that he raised and brought to aim as soon as he saw Sentro.

And she was unarmed.

He stepped up onto a shallow stone landing where a side set of doors led into the house, and he shouted in Spanish, demanding to know who she was and what she was doing. Sweat stained his shirt; he looked like he'd been running. The frequent short bursts of gunfire from the front of the house would make any explanation suspect, but Sentro's mind chose that moment to blank. Words slid away from her grasp—Spanish, English, German—it was as if she couldn't even remember how to form them. She struggled to push through it. A dull disappointment bloomed. She watched him shrug the rifle into his hands, heard herself saying, "Wait, no no no no no"—and then from the thick brush on the upslope beside the steps, there was a smear of movement, and Jenny emerged gripping an automatic rifle by the barrel, setting her legs, hips rotating, the rocking pivot, all her weight behind the compact swing Dennis used to call her "Barry Bonds inside-out."

The Spaniard never even saw her coming. The rifle stock caught him under his arms and crushed his diaphragm, sending him backward off balance, crashing to the steps and thumping down a few with only a soft intake of breath, the hollow rhythm of his head on hard edges, and the squeal of his sneakers on the stone.

Jenny dropped the automatic, squeezing her hands in pain. Hurrying down to the landing, buoyed by unprofessional relief, Sentro had never felt more like hugging her daughter, but her daughter's wild look said: *Not now.*

"I've got little kids back in the rocks," she said, breathless, gesturing. "Their mother—"

"Okay. Okay," Sentro said. She could just make out the sun-pinked, anxious faces staring out from the craggy rocks on the ridge. After securing the Spaniard's rifle, she checked him; he was not getting up anytime soon.

She looked at Jenny, who seemed dazed and kept flexing her fingers gingerly as if still feeling aftershocks of the home run she'd just hit. "Go back with the children," Sentro told her softly.

"They'll be fine," Jenny whispered fiercely. "I know the house. You don't."

Worlds having collided, the last wall torn down, Sentro reached out and gently pushed her daughter's damp hair back out of her eyes. Jenny flinched but met her mother's gaze.

"Let's go get her," Sentro said.

———

So hot, with the sun beating down and no shade. Narrow scraps of cloud cover hurried across the pale-blue sky now and then, but the day was already a scorcher.

The Americans had actually given him a gun, in the hope that he'd help them. "You know how to use this?" It was the shiny Smith & Wesson 1911 that the unfortunate castrato had been carrying before Sentro had helped him self-destruct.

Grip still sticky with blood, at least the clip was full. Banks played dumb and let the American flip the safety off and advise him, "Point and shoot. Squeeze easy."

Sure thing, pal.

Banks had scuttled around to the front of the SUV, putting the engine block between him and harm's way, and giving him a better view of the battle. He didn't shoot. Now what?

Just when he began thinking that Sentro's plan was going to be way too slow in developing, a dull, low frequency rumble and change in air pressure announced the arrival of an unmarked Sikorsky with open doors and sharpshooters in battle rattle. It strafed low and dramatic over the unfinished mansion, banking hard out over the ocean, then circling, predatory, back around like a wingless raptor.

Five Eyes reinforcements, flexing a little muscle.

Early for once, Banks noted sardonically. And then he worried that he was starting to sound like Sentro.

There were cries of urgency in the house, and the Spanish defenders melted back into cool shadows to regroup. The Americans decided this was their window to hump out their wounded; they were loading him into the back of their vehicle when Banks darted out from the cars and into the mansion. Glancing back, he saw Spanish government-security vehicles come cruising down the driveway to block the Yanks' way out.

———

A rumble like a small earthquake, the reflection in the french doors trembled as Sentro reached for the handle. A helicopter banked low overhead. There was movement inside, she stepped back just in time, and three Spaniards banged out to dash past her, guns rattling, down the steps, ignoring even their prone compatriot. Fleeing.

She wasn't surprised by the retreat. Keeping Jenny behind her, she peered in through the open door to see if any more hired men were coming and then crossed the threshold into the house.

Mass retreat was rumbling somewhere inside, for sure, but not toward her and Jenny. She felt so unprepared: no sense of who or what was in the house, where, how many, or the level of threat they presented.

To her right was a hallway, to her left a partly drywalled room that looked out at the sea. Directly ahead was a staircase leading up half a flight to the next level. Prudence dictated a fallback: protect her daughter and the children, wait for Banks.

"She's upstairs," Jenny whispered, close. Sentro felt a strange reassurance from her daughter's breath on her neck. And as if on cue, an anguished woman with a gash on her forehead stepped into view at the top of the stairs and almost stumbled as she descended.

"Paola!" Jenny gasped.

Behind her, Mercedes Izquierdo provided a steadying hand, with a long rifle held in the other, pointed harmlessly down. *So many fucking guns*, Sentro found herself thinking. Wasn't that what Dennis used to say?

She didn't trust Mercedes. Sentro's finger curled around the trigger guard of the rifle she was holding.

Then the girl's green eyes found and locked on hers. Steady, clear, defiant.

Like mine.

Sentro watched the girl weigh her next move.

A double pop of gunfire echoed from the front of the house as they reached the bottom, and the anxious Beya woman shuddered. She saw Jenny with Sentro, and as she started to say something, a new movement stirred in the dim light at the top of the stairs. Mercedes's eyes went wide with betrayal when Sentro raised her weapon.

Wolfgang Witt limped out of hazy shadow. A handgun extended, he opened fire.

———

The foyer featured a body on the floor, facedown. One of the Spaniards, bullet through his neck, a dark pond of blood.

All the fancy hand-troweled cold plaster was shot up and fractured, and glass glittered everywhere. Banks found himself thinking of the TV home-improvement shows his mother liked to watch after work while sipping her Caesars, and he wondered how whoever was building this place would react when they saw what had been done to it.

The great room beyond the entryway gloamed thick with bluish afterburn from the firefight; it smelled of overheated metal and fear. Another man was on the floor here, wounded but not dead. Head propped up against the wall, cigarette in his mouth, a shirt jammed against the wound in his side. He stared listlessly as Banks, eyes sweeping the room for other threats, eased toward him. All the fight had bled out of the man. Banks was hoping he'd know where Jenny Troon was being kept.

It was raw instinct, really, that saved the Canadian.

The albino stood in an alcove, waiting for him to walk into range, screened by a stud wall tacked with translucent plastic; Banks saw the wounded man's eyes narrow in anticipation of what was coming, and as Banks lunged sideways, Yusupov opened fire.

The floorboards weren't nailed down. Banks's foot found a weak spot and broke through, and he was jerked down hard as bullets ripped the wall behind where he should have been.

Somehow he caught himself, landed painfully on one knee while his other leg got wedged between joists. He twisted around, located the

Chechen mostly from the afterglow of the muzzle flash. Double tapped the trigger of the Smith & Wesson, and both rounds tore through Yusupov's chest.

———

She was shocked to see the gun come up. Outraged and confused. Would Aubrey Sentro really shoot her?

Her mind reeled. She couldn't believe it.

But as she shoved Paola away to make room to defend herself, something punched Mercedes in the back so hard she couldn't catch her breath. There was a flash in front of her, from Sentro's gun. The wings of an angel brushed ice cold past her cheek.

Jenny had a look of horror. Then Mercedes heard the gunshots— because sound is so slow—deafening, first behind and then in front, one on top of the other, and the strength left her legs. It was Paola clutching at her, trying to keep her upright while the searing pain coursed through, from shoulder to hip, like she'd caught on fire.

She couldn't get a breath.

Paola was struggling to hold her.

Blood. Terror. Swoon.

The outside light glared.

She heard Jenny Troon's voice.

And felt her mother's arms.

———

Sentro would have bad dreams about it later. She would, while dreaming, know what was coming and feel determined to alter the course of events, but the moment would replay, relentless, and she could never contrive to change the outcome.

Reaching the bottom of the stairs, Mercedes had paused. Rifle still at her side. It seemed that she was bringing Beya's wife to Sentro, as a gift, a prize, an act of contrition.

Then again, Sentro might have read it wrong. She never got an answer.

At the top of the stairs, Wolfgang had braced awkwardly. All his weight rested on one leg because something was seriously messed up with the other. A study in fury, standing there, his face contorted with vengeance and desperation.

Sentro saw him raise the pistol, but her reaction was too slow, too late. Or maybe that was just how she would remember it. A bullet burst through Mercedes's left side. Sentro aimed and fired and brought Wolfgang down with a short burst from the automatic.

Jenny might have screamed. Or maybe it was the shrill noise cycling in Sentro's head.

Blood soaking the front of her blouse, the Beya woman struggled to bear Mercedes's weight. They lurched forward. Sentro rushed to catch the girl and ease her down, cushioning her head in her lap while Paola searched for the wound and said something to Jenny, who stripped off her sweatshirt and offered it to stanch the blood.

"She's gonna be okay," Jenny said, with a kind of certainty that by saying it she could make it true.

"Where are my children?" Paola asked, frantic.

They were banging on the outside door, crying for their mother, who burst into grateful tears and rose to go comfort them. Jenny knelt to take her place.

"Stay with us. You'll make it." Sentro had never heard her daughter sound so strong.

But what in the world was Jenny wearing? A bikini bottom that fit so badly Sentro had to stop herself from laughing, which she knew was a product of battle stress and relief. She'd seen it before but couldn't remember where or when. Whether it was her or someone else. For a moment she drifted, weariness overwhelming her. A tactical team in body armor was at the top of the stairs talking to Banks. The soft music of children and their mother whispered outside.

Looking down again, she was startled to discover Mercedes still staring up fiercely at her, only at her, as if it were all that tethered the lost girl to this world; hopeful, helpless, cradled in Sentro's embrace.

Chapter Forty-Two

"They just wanted me out of there. Like, boom. Soon as they could book me a flight."

"All those secrets they cling to. No surprise."

Cartoon thunderheads piled in the southern sky, triple stacked, a sharp smell of rain on the wind. A soft-boiled sun shimmered, stuck overhead.

"I worry about Mom. She looked defeated."

Jeremy said, "Yeah. That's when she's decidedly not." He shot her a sidelong smile. She had told her brother the whole story (or at least her version of it, leaving out the parts he didn't need to know and a lot of what had happened with Banks) on the long flight from Maryland to New Mexico. Jeremy seemed glad to be hearing it after the fact but was quick to remind her that *his* ordeal with the pirates had been more harrowing.

"They rigged me with explosives," he said, still sounding traumatized.

Jenny didn't want to get into a pissing contest. They'd tried that once when they were little; he had the totally unfair advantage.

"Guess who called me."

"I'm too tired to guess."

"Some dude who claimed to be CIA."

Now she and her brother and his putative fiancée (Jenny didn't see a ring) poked through the charred ruins of their mother's New Mexico adobe, looking for anything that had survived the fire. The old barn was still intact and the horses safely in it. A neighbor Jenny hadn't known existed had found them and brought them back and would feed them, according to the note he left nailed on the corral gate, *until whoever all lives here comes on back.*

If you'da just let me know, he'd added open endedly and had scrawled his cell number a digit short. Back in the USA.

"What about this?" Bryce-Ann called out, holding up the charred remains of a leather coat.

"That was Dad's," brother and sister said at the same time; Jenny felt a lump of loss catch in her chest.

Their hands and arms were ash gray to the elbow; Bryce-Ann had come prepared with throwaway hazmat pants she'd borrowed from her airline ground crew and the longest rubber gloves Jenny had ever seen. Like, senior-prom-wear long, in a shade of electric blue that matched the cloudless New Mexico sky.

Jenny was starting to warm to her.

"Mom won't return their calls," Jenny explained to her brother about the government spooks. "That must chap their ass."

"*Asses.* Plural."

"Jemmy, get to the point?"

"It's why he said he was contacting *me*. 'Cause he couldn't get to *her*." Jeremy frowned. "But wait a sec. I thought you couldn't tell anybody you were in the CIA."

"Guys, look!" Bryce-Ann was standing knee deep in rubble just beyond the fluttering yellow police tape where they'd collected Clete's remains. She was holding up something between a gloved thumb and finger that, when she blew the black off, caught the sun and gleamed. "Wedding rings?"

His and hers. The flight attendant trudged over to deliver them, and Jenny brushed away inexplicable tears, smearing something on her face that Bryce-Ann gently wiped off.

"Thanks." Jenny turned them over in her hand. Two perfect circles, matched but separate. "I so loved them together," she said to no one in particular. "They balanced each other out."

"That's so beautiful," Bryce-Ann said.

"Now it's just Mom."

"So assuming it was the CIA, they want to help her out somehow," Jeremy continued, picking up where he'd left off, oblivious to her emotions, or just ignoring them, as usual. "On account of how she did the country a great service. Direct quote."

Jenny put the rings in her pocket. "She told her friend Elsayed what to say to them."

"The Egyptian? Yeah, he called them," Jeremy said. "I guess there's some history there or something. They didn't exactly trust him. He told them Mom wants FEMA trailers."

"That's right. The ones they didn't use during Katrina."

"The hurricane?"

"Mom wants two if they'll give them to her; she's gonna put them over there so she has somewhere to live while she rebuilds." Jenny gestured to a shady spot of high ground, under a couple of obdurate, wizened Chinese elms.

Jeremy scanned the stark horizon, shook his head. "I don't understand why she wants to live all the way out here."

"I think it's amazing," Bryce-Ann said. "It's like being in one of those big cathedrals. Or a mosque. But no walls."

Jeremy looked irritated; Jenny was liking the girlfriend or whatever she was more and more. Maybe they'd even be friends.

The warm wind picked up and swirled the sand and ashes, and all three of them turned their backs to it. The sharp black origami shapes of two birds hovered high and motionless above them, and Jenny wondered what it would feel like to be up there, riding the currents, weightless, untroubled. But not alone.

"Were you scared?" Jeremy asked her out of nowhere.

She looked at him. He wanted to know. "Yeah," she said. "A lot. A lot of the time."

"Mom's kinda unbelievable."

Jenny nodded and didn't add anything. What she'd been through still overwhelmed her; processing everything would probably take a long time. Bryce-Ann squeezed Jeremy's arm and crunched away through the cinders, saying brightly, "Well, I can feel that there's more good stuff to be found here," but mostly, it was clear, to give the two Troons some space.

"There's still so much she's not telling us." Jenny knew that he was aware of it.

"Maybe we don't want to know," he said.

Maybe you don't, Jenny thought. And she didn't fault him for it.

"So." Jenny could feel her brother working up to it, the question she'd thought he'd ask her first thing. "Is she?"

Jenny tortured him. "Is who what?"

"Mercedes Izquierdo."

"What about her?"

"Is she? Related?"

"Mom says she had them do a DNA test at the hospital."

Jeremy waited and waited, and when Jenny didn't say anything more, he looked exasperated. "And?"

"Ask Mom," Jenny said, because she didn't have an answer for him, and then started to walk away. She wanted to see the horses. Maybe she could take a ride to the arroyo before it rained, clear her head.

"Two trailers," Jeremy said, following her. "One for Mom, one for you?"

"I don't know what the fuck I'm doing," Jenny confessed. "I don't know where I'll be when I get back."

"Back?"

She waited while her brother processed what she'd said. It felt scary in a different way, weird and new to her too.

"Back from where?"

———

Cleaning up the mess on Majorca involved a considerable amount of tap dancing by the Eyes: interagency horse-trading, embassy interventions, back channel mea culpas, and a few strategic calls from the West Wing, Downing Street, and the Centre Block. Word filtered out of Cuba that a Stasi fugitive had died a natural death in exile there.

Wolfgang Witt and Matthias Schmidt had simply been erased.

An extremist cell of ex-ETA irregulars was blamed for the bombing of the Bolsa in Madrid. The Russian oligarch's Paris murder was ascribed to organized crime. A faulty gas pressure regulator was found to be the cause of a fiery explosion that had destroyed a former factory building in Kyiv, killing three foreigners working for a start-up that had recently moved in. At a reading of his will, Charlotte Madsen was named sole beneficiary of Ilya Arshavin's estate; she cashed out, left London, and was rumored to have settled in a farmhouse near Lake Como.

Sentro always marveled at the intelligence world's fine art of revisionism and disinformation.

———

Paola Beya swore during extensive questioning that she'd never successfully installed any malware into the shared intelligence database of the FVEY treaty countries. A granular system audit found no signs of corruption. Still, out of an abundance of caution, the governing council announced that the entire network would be rebuilt from scratch.

"They're dissembling," was Elsayed's opinion about it when they spoke on the phone. Her old security firm was keeping close tabs on the breach, because so much sensitive intelligence, private and public sector, was at stake. It was a matter of self-preservation. "Of course they're dissembling. But are they lying? Is there a virus or worm in there they can't find?"

"I don't know, Reno. I'm out of the game. I'm strictly need to know now."

"And your daughter's good?"

Elsayed only knew about one. "The best."

Without prompting, Paola also insisted that she hadn't hacked her way into the Five Eyes network; she'd been given a back door that she assumed came from the client, whose identity was unknown to her. Sentro believed this. The Eyes had a leak. There was no other way to explain how Matthias Schmidt had been so ready when she and Banks arrived in Cuba.

At the end of a grueling week, Paola was deemed innocent of any involvement in her late husband's crime, reunited with her children, and driven back home.

"So was she the target all along?" Banks had asked Sentro. "Of the kidnapping and extortion, I mean."

"Separate agendas, but a two-for-one, I think," Sentro said. "Lenkov wanted his oil pipeline, so he contracted Pogo to make it happen. Wolfgang went into business for himself, saw an opportunity to double-dip—found a couple of ex-terrorists in the kompromat who could do both parts."

Banks still looked confused. "But why put a bomb in Beya and attack Otter's black site?"

Sentro had shrugged. "Misdirection?"

"From what?"

"Ask yourself, Banks: Who opened that back door Paola was using?"

He couldn't quite follow her reasoning, it seemed, but she could see he was too proud to admit it. And maybe unwilling to contemplate the threat it presented. As a consequence, she had no patience for spoon-feeding him. She and Banks were debriefed and released.

"When you get back," Elsayed flirted, "I'm gonna buy you an aged rib eye at Capital Grille. We'll have dirty martinis, and you can regale me with the whole heroic saga."

"Right. How's your wife?" Sentro asked pointedly.

"Pregnant again," Elsayed admitted. "Last one."

"You're a fertile pair."

"How's your head?" he countered.

"I can't remember," Sentro said, an old joke that she wasn't yet tired of.

Her knees and hips ached, her back was acting up, but her head was clear. A Spanish hospital checkup cast doubt that she'd suffered a full-on concussion in London, but there was no way to really know.

Go home, get healthy, and stay out of trouble was the unsurprising recommendation of the Andalusian brain doctor.

Soon, Sentro thought.

———

"Tea? Coffee? Anything?"

"No, thank you, sir."

Turning to the camera: "Are we recording?" The colors seemed washed out, like peering back through a thickened glaze of time.

"Where's Agent Otter?"

Turning back: "He won't be part of this."

The chyron burned in at the bottom of the 4:3 frame said: *January 14, 1991. 10:31 a.m. Berlin, Germany.* Exit interview with Aubrey Sentro following her traumatic ordeal in Stasi prison. They were sending her home.

"How are you feeling, Aubrey?"

She looked better, hair cut short, good posture. *Chain-smoking like her daughter does now*, Banks noted. A soldier reemerging from the wreckage. "I feel healthy, sir." Only her restless hands gave away the riot that must have been raging beneath the surface.

"We just want to—" This video was the worst of the batch, with the image breaking up and audio drifting. "—some closure on your—" Banks fast-forwarded through a badly damaged stretch.

"—leak that burned the cell you saved had to have come from inside."

Banks watched young Aubrey process this. The liquid room tone filled the quiet left in the absence of their talking. The questioner was older, wearing a uniform, salt-and-pepper hair cut high and tight. A full-bird colonel, if Banks wasn't mistaken. Shoes polished so perfectly they gleamed, even under the table.

"A mole?"

The colonel shifted in his chair.

Aubrey asked, carefully, "What are you telling me?"

They had flown to Kyiv together, Banks and Sentro. She said she needed to retrieve her things; he wondered why she didn't just have them sent to her. But he had lied to her about *his* reasons for coming—something about unfinished business with Otter—and didn't feel bad about it because he knew she was still holding on to so many secrets that even Jenny didn't know.

With no official standing, Sentro had been unable to visit patient Izquierdo, but she said she had heard from the hospital that the girl's wounds were grave. She was in the custody of the CNI. It would be touch and go for a while.

"Where are they sending you after this, Banks?" Sentro had asked him on the plane.

"I got some time off, actually. My family has a cottage on the bay; I'm going to go kick back, do some fishing, and chill."

Sentro had nodded, staring at him blankly. "Use condoms."

Banks felt his face flush hot. "I'm sorry, what?"

"I don't want to be a grandmother," Sentro said to him. "It's hard enough having grown children at my age."

Banks thought: *How did she know?* And then he reminded himself: *Spies, duh.* But no, he sensed this was something else, something deeper. It was like she could see right into his heart. "Listen, we're . . . no no no, we are nowhere *near* that point," he stammered. "I mean, we haven't even—"

She cut him off. "I don't want to know. I don't need to know."

"Fair enough."

"And don't let Jenny break your heart," she warned, before turning toward the window and—he could tell—pretending to sleep.

The hotel had packed her bags and Jenny's; claiming them was made complicated by their different last names. He left Sentro to sort it out, book another room, and try to get some sleep. Otter wasn't at his new facility, but Banks had a key card and let himself in.

"You saw files in Schmidt's apartment." The video flared out, but its audio soldiered on.

"I did."

"Photographs."

"Yes. Agent Otter, and the others. But, like, I didn't know them, then."

"Understood." The colonel hesitated, spoke precisely. "The cell you helped exfiltrate could only have been burned by an insider. There was no exposure. They hadn't started their mission."

Banks watched Sentro sit back and stare at the colonel, and for a moment he saw not Jenny in her—though Jenny was there—but the Izquierdo woman. And he was confounded.

"Who?" Sentro asked finally.

The colonel shrugged and shook his head.

"Member of the cell or someone supervisory? Like, in Berlin Station."

"We don't know. We do know that somewhere in the Stasi files," the colonel said, "is a name. But those files were systematically destroyed after the wall came down."

Neither of them said anything for a while. The colonel gestured to Sentro's pack of cigarettes; she slid it across to him, and he tapped one out and lit it.

Banks rewound the tape a bit and pushed play. "The cell you helped exfiltrate could only have been burned by an insider," the colonel said again. "There was no exposure. They hadn't started their mission."

Banks punched stop. He stared at the screen, time frozen: Sentro at eighteen, a bird colonel who was probably dead. A burned mission that led to a nightmare but that, in the big picture, like most of the Cold War, had amounted to nothing.

A game, Sentro called it. And what else had she said? *Ask yourself, Banks: Who opened that back door Paola was using?*

Suddenly he knew why Otter wasn't part of this last exit interview. And why Sentro had been so quick to send him away at the hotel.

Chapter Forty-Three

Is it a dream or a memory?

It's raining and sunny, and her cell window frames angry low clouds racing across a deep-blue sky; bright rays of light blink through the bars to fall in fiery ribbons across the concrete floor.

Schmidt is visiting. He's brought a letter from her father and three Cuban tangerines because she's been craving citrus. She's already too pregnant; her feet are swollen but cold, and she wears doubled-up Russian socks. Her bladder feels tender, the drugs they've got her on looping a tuneless song she can't shake.

My dear Aubrey.

Schmidt reads the letter because she can't keep the words in focus. His thick accent on her father's spare West Texas plain talk is almost comical. But she's crying.

They tell me that you can receive letters in jail, but they might be censored by your captors, so I won't talk about why you're there or what we're doing to try to get you back. Just trust that no one has forgotten you. You are loved. Your family misses you. I hope you are staying healthy, and I am confident that you will

endure and survive this, because you are the strongest
person I have ever known . . .

"Aubrey."
She loses the thread of what Schmidt is reading; his mouth moves,
but her mind has drifted off. She'll have to get one of the guards to try
to read it to her later.

—

The baby is dead. She can't feel it moving.
"Aubrey?"

—

She's in an augered hole in a forest, looking up through the bars at her
husband, Dennis. He's so young and handsome she can't stand it, and
she's trying to assure him that everything is going to be okay, the army
pays well, with super health benefits and the GI Bill, but her lips are
sewn shut so she can't tell any more of her lies.

—

. . . Well, I guess that's all for now. I apologize for not
being the best correspondent. Hang in there.
Love you. Dad.

"Aubrey."
Sentro surfaced to Otter's rabbit stare, dark rodent eyes shining in
the darkness like dying stars. His tobacco-stained teeth flashed grim
their missing incisor. He held the gun she'd found in his bedside-table

drawer after she broke into his house earlier. An hour ago? Two? She remembered not being able to decide whether she'd use it.

"Intruder in my space. This won't turn out well for you." He stood facing her. His flannel pajamas still had creases in them from professional laundering.

Modern architecture is so seductive, and Otter's place was all clean lines, glass, and plaster. Stealing her way through the dark rooms, she'd been struck by how sterile it felt, tidy and insensate, not unlike the man himself. She'd rested in the chair in his bedroom, listening to him snore, trying to work up the energy to straddle his chest the way she'd made Jenny brace Banks, and then maybe shove the gun in Otter's mouth.

Instead, she'd dozed off.

"You burned everybody working with you in Berlin," Sentro said, getting right to it. Her heart was pounding. She'd made such a stupid mistake. Or had she? Doubt tugged at her, something she'd done that she couldn't remember. "You were giving them up to the Stasi." She didn't see an upside in restraint.

"But only burned you, in the end, though," Otter said. "The noble sacrifice, yeah? Gotta say, I didn't see that coming. Sorry."

Her phone hummed. She reached into her pocket to check it; Otter's hand did some perilous twitching. He wasn't, Sentro remembered, very good with guns, but at such close range it wouldn't matter. Glowing SMS screen, message from Jeremy; she'd read it later. And put it away again. "Sorry." Otter just watched her with hooded eyes, as if predatory. But it was all an act. "Was it money or politics?"

"I don't pick sides," he claimed.

"Money, then."

"Does that offend you? Ms. Security Specialist? I'm sorry, I wasn't aware that you gave it away for free—"

"You've been his asset all these years."

"Nothing quite so black and white. You know how it is."

"I don't, no."

"Worlds within worlds. A wilderness of mirrors."

"And what went down in '89 gave Pogo the leverage over you to get him his back door into the Five Eyes database?"

Otter squirmed, tried to act delighted with his shabby transgressions, but his Faustian bargain was obviously gnawing away at his soul. Because of the interrogators who'd died? "Kompromat on steroids," Otter crowed. "I mean. Do you know what someone could do with the intel the signatory nations have gathered over the years? Private, public, world leaders, celebrities, Mafia dons, traitors, patriots, captains of industry . . ."

"Depends on the someone. Who is it?"

Otter wagged a finger: *No no no.* "Did you come here to kill me?" He waved the gun. "Was that the idea?"

"I paid a heavy price for your betrayal." Making it seem personal would, she hoped, buy her some time. What the fuck was the thing she couldn't recall?

"Is that my fault?" He sounded so aggrieved. "Nobody asked you to do it. Fuck me. Correction: fuck you, Aubrey. You were a day player, soldier girl with a simple mission. If you'da stuck to it."

"Nine people would have paid a heavy price because of what you did back in Berlin. Four people died here in Kyiv." She sat up, planted her feet. Assessed the distance between them. Plan B? "Five if you count the Basque."

"So?"

Sentro said nothing. There wasn't an argument you could make with someone as cynical as Otter. Everything was shit. The game was rigged. Why bother to play by any rules?

He bragged, "Do you even know what they were doing? The top-secret cell you saved? Their mission—our mission—straight from some genius at Langley, was to burrow inside the Ossi underground club scene and convince rebel musicians to play our subversive free-world music." His laugh was artificial; the Otter who had survived this long was joyless. "CIA power rock. What a joke. God only knows who wrote it. And the songs? They were so shitty even the shitty East Berliner metal bands wouldn't touch them.

"That's who you suffered for, Aubrey," he sneered. "And PS, they left you to rot because you didn't matter. In the big picture. Your government didn't give a fuck. You were a throwaway."

His words had no effect on her. She never expected anyone to save her. Daughter of a Texas Ranger, she just did what she thought was right. "Who's the client who wants to burn the world?" she asked again.

Otter's chin jutted, defiant. It was natural for him to assume she wasn't a threat. After all, he had the gun. She was damaged, past her sell-by date; a shell of what she once was. He jacked back the slide to chamber a bullet. He seemed disappointed that she wasn't panicked. She had no doubt that he would use it in the next sixty seconds.

"Oh, wait. You don't know."

His eyes flickered a disquiet, and she knew she had it right. "I don't care to know," he claimed. "Just another job."

"No?" She studied him and gathered herself. They were almost the same height, but Otter was bulky, top heavy, probably outweighed her by forty pounds. That would help. "Somebody's gotta pay for the failure to deliver, Hank. Pogo's dead. Wolfgang. The Cuban girl's locked away. That leaves you with the bull's-eye on your forehead, and you don't even fucking know who's gonna pull the trigger."

"I did my part," he said, defensive. "I'm not worried."

He was, though, and she gave a dismissive little shrug and powered up into him from the chair like she would with a kettlebell in the gym. Smacked his biceps with both palms, grabbed hold, and butterflied his arms apart so the handgun was momentarily useless. He tapped the trigger—CLICK CLICK CLICK—and she remembered then removing the bullets from the Glock's clip before she napped. She got him tilted; he tried backpedaling to get his footing, but she kept driving him across the carpet, across the room, using his weight and momentum and her acceleration to shoulder him hard up onto the balls of his feet and crashing into the closed bedroom door, where, as Otter began to muster his strength to overpower her, she let go of his arms, ducked under the gun as he swung it around on her, and came up holding Charlotte Madsen's father's razor-sharp tactical knife—which she jammed as hard as she could in under his clavicle, all the way through his shoulder, to pin him into the solid wooden doorframe.

His gun tumbled to the carpet.

His face drained of color, he gasped, and she saw the whites of his widening, agonized eyes.

"Oh fuck."

"You know, for a moment there I spaced it out? The bullet thing. Lame ploy. I should probably apologize," she said. "But. We do what we gotta do, right?"

"Fuck."

By design, she'd plunged the knife in with edges perpendicular, so as to slice up through the muscles of his shoulder should he try to come down off his tiptoes.

"Oh Jesus, Aubrey. What have you done?"

"Finished," Sentro said. Finishing, in her long experience, was essential.

"Don't . . . oh, don't, don't . . . oh man . . ."

She stepped back, flicked the blood off her hand, took her phone from her pocket, and showed him that she'd been recording their conversation. "Anything else you want to say before I tap send?"

———

An Uber car was waiting. *Like cheap magic*, she decided, when she walked out to the street. The app had been on her phone for a while, and Jenny had shown her how to use it, but this was the first time. Her bags and Jenny's had been sent ahead to the airport; she had a one-way flight booked to the States by way of Majorca.

Headlights flashed in the rearview as the driver pulled away. She twisted to the back window, feeling a disk complain in her back. It looked like Banks, hopping out of the rear door of a big black car that had just pulled up with a flashing police light on the dash, but her own ride was already too far away for her to be sure.

Two other figures joined him, and they ran into Otter's house.

CHAPTER FORTY-FOUR

Everything smelled uncertain.

There was the music you heard but didn't register.

Light cast like polite apologies.

The surreal terminal concourses. The empty rumbling people movers, the hushed tunnels, the strange malls of snack shops, juice bars, and duty-free shopping.

The dreamy landscape of impermanence. Of now, and then now, and then again now.

Sentro loved airports.

She'd spent enough time in them.

There was something comforting and romantic—even lyrical—about all the comings and goings. Anything was possible, all destinations reachable, escape a reality, reunion a certainty, the stasis just temporary. No one got grounded forever.

Airports were eternally between here and there.

She could see it in the eyes and faces of the people she passed: anticipation, trepidation, hope.

Memory was unimportant; the pressure was off. She sat on the threshold of ever new ones, studying the faces of her fellow passengers, wondering where they were headed, whom they were meeting, how it would turn out for them, and waiting for the cattle call, the shuffle through check-in, the walk down the Jetway to find a seat with not enough leg room in a flying tube to tomorrow.

Sentro had no argument with tomorrow. It was the past that tripped her up.

———

"Gone?"

Yes, the voice on the other end of the call said.

"Dead?"

No. Missing. Run away.

How was that possible? "She was in custody."

The hospital in Granada, it was readily admitted, had many security issues. The patient had improved enough to be transferred to another facility for rehabilitation, and somewhere in that process, well, she'd slipped away and disappeared.

"Where could she have gone?"

Recriminations would fly. Promise of an inquest, hell to pay, blah blah blah, the usual drill. Lots of finger-pointing. Review of protocols, personnel reassigned. A nationwide, then global search for the fugitive, Interpol advisories, border checks, but utter confidence that she'd be found.

She was not.

And perhaps not counterintuitively, Sentro found herself thinking, whenever she was reminded and thought about it in the weeks and months ahead: *Good girl.*

ACKNOWLEDGMENTS

Some books that were helpful: *The Year That Changed the World*, Michael Meyer; *Man without a Face*, Markus Wolf; *The Book of Honor*, Ted Gup; *The Comedians*, Graham Greene; *The Looking Glass War*, John le Carré; *Telex from Cuba*, Rachel Kushner. Plus the music of Mingus, Miles Davis, and the Buena Vista Social Club.

Some indispensable early readers: Erich Anderson, Scott Shepherd, Aaron Lipstadt, Stefanie Drummond, and Steve Cohen.

My brilliant editors: Benee Knauer, Tiffany Yates Martin, Liz Pearsons (and the whole crew at Thomas & Mercer). A special shout-out to the unsung heroes whose copyediting and proofreading repeatedly rescued me from my predilection for the mangled modifier: Riam Griswold and Sylvia McCluskey.

My extraordinary and supportive reps: Victoria Sanders and Bernadette Baker-Baughman.

My children. My geriatric dog.

In November of 1991 my wife, Joan, and I traveled to Moscow and Kyiv for a movie I was asked to write that never got off the ground. We felt the last stale gasping breaths of the Soviet Union in the icy streets and hard-cash Mafia restaurants and empty hotel lobbies with KGB kiosks manned by stone-faced officers who looked lost. But there was hope, too, everywhere; a palpable excitement that with the end of the Cold War a brighter world was dawning.

Instead, for better or worse, we got this one: overcast, overcooked, too often confounding, and forever haunted by the misremembered but immutable past.

About the Author

Photo © Katie Pyne

Daniel Pyne is the author of five novels: *Water Memory*, *Catalina Eddy*, *Fifty Mice*, *A Hole in the Ground Owned by a Liar*, and *Twentynine Palms*. Among his many screenplays are *Pacific Heights*, *Doc Hollywood*, *The Sum of All Fears*, Jonathan Demme's *Manchurian Candidate*, and *Backstabbing for Beginners*. He directed and cowrote the iconoclastic *Where's Marlowe?* His list of television credits (creating, writing, and show running) spans *Miami Vice* to *Bosch*. Pyne has worked as a screen printer, a sportswriter, an adman, and a cartoonist and taught screenwriting at the UCLA Graduate School of Film for more than two decades. He splits his time between California and New Mexico with his wife, their rescue dog, a stray kitten found hiding under the hood of their car, and a surly box turtle who will probably outlive them all.